The
Revelation
of Chester Fortunberry

don waitt

Two-Headed Calf Press
©2019

First English Paperback Edition: December 2019
ISBN: 978-0-9857817-1-2

Cover art by Amanda Lanzone.

Also by don waitt
leaving early.

To my offspring.

Nowhere Man, please listen
You don't know what you're missing
Nowhere Man, the world is at your command

— Lennon-McCartney

Chapter One

A short time ago, on a Monday morning at 8:15 to be precise, Chester Fortunberry, after a hot shower and a fulfilling bowel movement, in that exact order, had a sudden and startling revelation, which was that he was the only real living person, or real anything for that matter, on the planet.

Everything, he realized, including the aforementioned planet, were simply figments of his imagination.

That revelation shocked the hell out of Chester.

Then, at precisely 8:20 that same morning, Chester heard a knock at his front door. When he opened the door there was a smiling postman and in his hand was a certified letter.

"Please sign here," said the smiling postman.

Chester did as requested, then closed his front door and, while still standing in the foyer, he tore a little piece off the end of the envelope and slipped a finger into the tiny hole, ripping it down the top of the envelope. He pulled out a crisp sheet of twice-folded, cream-colored stationery, unfolded the paper, and read aloud what the letter said, which was:

"Dear Chester,
Stop it.
We know what you are thinking.
We are not happy.
There will be dire consequences if you continue."

The letter was signed, *"Sincerely, Ed and Edna Pringle."*

The letter also shocked the hell out of Chester. Which was two shock-the-hell-out-of-Chester shocks in a five-minute period.

The revelation, understandably, was a real shocker. But the letter was also a shocker, not only because of the content and tone of the letter, but also because Chester did not know anyone named Ed or Edna Pringle.

Sometime later, a man named Theodore would be able to verify how surprised Chester was by the events of that day. He would know this for a fact because Chester told him so.

While Chester was being held captive in Theodore's basement.

Chester had become quite talkative the longer he was in that basement. He wasn't curled up in a dirt pit under a metal grating or anything like that, but he wasn't going to be going anywhere soon.

Not until Theodore had decided what to do with him.

But that was later.

▼

The nothing-is-real-except-me revelation, coupled with the prompt arrival of the strange letter that morning, threw Chester off of his regular schedule.

And Chester, if nothing else, is always regular.

He is regular in how he looks and in how he acts and in how he slips almost unseen and unnoticed into the stream of everyday life. He is a nondescript man living in a nondescript house with a nondescript wife and a nondescript job. His only child is now married with a child of her own in a state far away, and when she lived at home, she too was nondescript, but she's been gone for so long that her status has changed from nondescript to nonexistent. Even his dog, an unattractive mutt of indistinguishable origin, is nondescript.

Chester lives in the same house he has been in since he was married at the age of thirty-two, which was twenty years ago. He knows the names of every couple that lives on his street, and even the names of most of their children, but few of them know Chester's name. They have all met and talked with him over the years, some more often than others, but he is the kind of nondescript person whose name you forget just seconds after hearing it.

Chester and his wife, Harriette, are never invited to parties at their neighbors' houses, and usually whoever is tasked with coordinating that year's annual neighborhood block party will forget, intentionally or unintentionally, to invite Chester and Harriette. On those occasions, Chester and Harriette will look out their bay window and see their street packed with kids riding bicycles and grown-ups sipping cocktails around smoky barbecue grills with sizzling hot dogs and hamburgers. They will hear the good time rock 'n' roll music playing, and as the evening darkness rolls in they will even see the fireworks shot off from a safe spot in the middle of the street by youngsters under the watchful eye of their parents. Chester and Harriette will watch all of the festivities and hear all of the laughter, but they will do it from behind the cold glass of their bay window because, yet again, somebody forgot to invite them. And they would never dare to impose by showing up uninvited.

The reason Chester is not part of his neighbors' lives or invited into their world is not because he is a peculiar or strange man who frightens or repulses them. It isn't about his race or his religion or his politics because no one has the slightest notion of what his interests might be in those areas. It isn't because he doesn't keep his house up, or has drunken parties, or lets his grass grow too high, or allows his mongrel dog to defecate in their yards. It isn't because he is a loud and gregarious and opinionated man or, on the flip side of the coin, because he is a quiet and sullen and secretive man. If he did any of those things, or if he was any of those things, then he would stand out and he would matter, in either a good way or a bad way, and his neighbors would have no choice but to pay attention to him.

He would be somebody.

But Chester does, and is, none of those things.

So he is a nobody to them.

To the parents on his street and to their children, and even to their pets, Chester just doesn't exist. He's in their world, and at the same time, he's not. They know he's there because they see him drive to and from work five days a week, and they see him walk to the curb to get his mail from the mailbox six days a week, and on Saturday they see him mow his lawn, and on Sunday they see him walk to the end of his driveway to pick up the Sunday newspaper.

They see all that.

They just don't see Chester.

▼

Later, in that sometime-later phase, Chester found out that Theodore's full name was Theodore Sanders. Theodore said he could tell

Chester his full name because it was not that unusual of a name. There were probably thousands of other Theodore Sanders across the country. Obviously, though, Theodore could not tell Chester where he lived, what city or state the basement he was being held in was located.

What Theodore had said was, "I can't tell you where I live because I would prefer if nobody knew how to find me. What with kidnapping you and all. I'm sure you understand. Actually, in my mind, I don't really consider it kidnapping. I just needed to get you out of circulation. You were jeopardizing everything. I really had no choice. I look at it more like an intervention, rather than a kidnapping."

After he said that, he had winked at Chester and added, "But then again, I'm pretty good at rationalizing things."

▼

After reading the letter that Monday morning at precisely 8:20, Chester folded it and placed it in his back pocket. Then he got into his car and drove to work.

Which was not his regular routine.

That's how flustered he was by the revelation and by the letter.

Normally, after his shower and his morning constitution, Chester will go to the kitchen and put a small pot of water on to boil. While he waits for the water to boil, he will pour a cup of coffee from the pot that Harriette made earlier before leaving for her job as a nurse at Aston Gardens, an assisted living facility on the other side of town. Into his coffee he will put one teaspoon of sugar and one medium-sized dollop of milk. When the water reaches boiling, Chester will place two eggs into the water and start the little egg timer on the kitchen counter, the one shaped like a chicken, and cook the eggs for exactly three and a half minutes. A perfect soft-boiled egg, one that has yolk you can still dip your toast into, is cooked for four minutes, and for a more runny soft-boiled egg the cooking time is three minutes.

Chester likes his eggs right in the middle.

While the eggs are cooking, Chester will place one slice of whole wheat bread into the toaster and take the tub of margarine out of the refrigerator. The toast will pop up, Chester will butter it, and then he will wait. At the three-and-a-half minute mark, he will pull the eggs from the boiling water, run cold water over them in the sink, peel them, put them in a small bowl, chop them up with a fork, sprinkle some salt and pepper on them, and then eat them, alternating a bite of egg with a bite of toast. He will do the entire process, from putting the water on to boil all the way to the last bite of egg, while standing up in the kitchen. And he will go through the exact same process every work day, five days a week, fifty-two weeks a year. Always one teaspoon of sugar, always one medium-sized dollop of milk, always one piece of toast, and always two eggs cooked for exactly three and a half minutes.

Most people would consider such a strict, unvarying routine to be odd.

To Chester it's just what he does. To him, the fact that everybody does not follow a similar routine would be odd.

Chester will swallow the last of his coffee, then wash the pot, the bowl, the fork, the butter knife and his coffee cup in the sink, dry each item off and place them back in the cupboard. Then he will get his briefcase and drive to work.

But on that Monday morning he had no soft-boiled eggs. So, in addition to being unnerved by the revelation and the letter, he was uncommonly hungry the rest of the morning.

On the drive to work that day he could hardly concentrate on the road. He even turned the radio off so he could focus better. His mind was in a whirl about the revelation and the letter. The more he drove, though, the more he concentrated on the revelation over the letter. Because Chester is a smart man. A regular and routine man, yes, but a smart man too.

His favorite joke of all time, told to him by his father in one of the few instances he could remember where his father paid any attention to him, was about a motorist who has a flat tire outside the fence to a mental health facility. Although when Chester's father told the joke, he referred to the facility as a funny farm.

The motorist jacks the back of his car up, unscrews the four wheel nuts and places them into the upside down tire hubcap. He gets the spare tire out of the trunk and puts it on. But when he reaches down for the wheel nuts, he accidentally kicks the hubcap, which flips over and all of the wheel nuts roll down the storm drain. Now he has no nuts to secure the spare tire.

"Gosh darnit," says the motorist, although when Chester's father told the joke, he said "Goddamnit." The man puts his hands on his hips and shakes his head.

He hears someone say "pssst" and he turns around to see a strange looking man on the other side of the tall chain link fence. The man has his fingers curled into the metal links of the fence and he is smiling a crazy smile. The motorist, knowing that the strange man is a patient from the mental facility, ignores him and looks back at his car, trying to figure out what to do.

"Hey mister, I have a suggestion," says the strange man.

The motorist reluctantly turns back around, and the man says, "Just take one wheel nut off from each of your other three wheels and use them to put the spare tire on. That'll get you to a service station nice and safe."

The motorist's eyes pop open as he realizes that it is the perfect solution, and that's when the strange man smiles and says, "Hey, I might be crazy, but I'm not stupid."

Chester could relate.

So Chester knew the revelation was more important than the letter. No matter how enticing the letter might be—like who were the people who sent it and why did they send it and what did it mean?—he knew it was just a symptom and not the cause. If he had not had the revelation, then he would not have received the letter. Even trying to determine how a letter about the revelation could arrive a mere five minutes after Chester had the revelation would have to wait.

Figuring out the revelation, Chester knew, was the most important thing.

▼

Theodore, Chester found out later, lived alone. There used to be a Mrs. Theodore Sanders but she died ten years ago. She was run over by a train. She wasn't in her car when it happened. You know, one of those cases where someone either tries to beat the train or doesn't see the train coming or gets stuck on the tracks when the train is coming. No, she was run over by a train while she was standing in the middle of the tracks holding a bag of groceries.

When Theodore told Chester the story, Chester immediately had one question, but he didn't want to be callous or disrespectful, so he didn't ask. He wasn't curious about whether or not Mrs. Theodore Sanders had intentionally stood in the middle of the tracks waiting for the train to hit her. No, what he was most curious about, the question he didn't ask, was, what groceries were in her shopping bag? For some reason, that seemed important to Chester.

Theodore and his wife never had children, so after the train incident, it was Theodore all alone in his house. He told Chester that after awhile he got used to it.

"It's just been me ever since. It's not that bad. Sometimes I have company."

After he said that, he did the winking at Chester thing again and added, "Like right now. You, in my basement."

▼

Chester was curious why the revelation had come to him that day, and not before that day and not after that day. Or, to be more specific, why had it come to him on a Monday morning, when he was fifty-two years old, while he was in his bathroom of all places?

Chester knew the answer to two of the three parts of the question, and had a suspicion about the third part.

First, the revelation came to him on Monday morning because it is the start of his week.

No matter what month it is or what year it is, Chester feels his life starts over every seven days, always on Monday. Chester could live to be a hundred years old, but what it would really mean is he had lived 5,200 weeks where he started his life over again on 5,200 Mondays. Wednesday is the middle of his week, and Saturday and Sunday are the end of his week. Nobody is going to have a monumental revelation in the middle of their week or at the end of their week. It just makes sense it would happen at the beginning of the new week. Which would be Monday.

So there was that.

Second, the revelation came to him in the bathroom because of the nature of the revelation.

If Chester were to have the revelation that driving his car into an oncoming tractor-trailer rig would kill him, he would expect to have that revelation while he was driving. Or if he were to have the revelation that only co-workers who sweet talk the boss get promoted, he would expect to have that revelation while he was at the office. But if Chester were to have the revelation that he was the only real thing on the planet—which is a very intimate and personal revelation, because nothing is more intimate and personal than coming to the realization that you are completely alone in the universe—then he would expect to have that revelation in his bathroom. In Chester's world, no place was more personal and intimate than his bathroom.

Chester could think of no other place where he was more intimate

7

with himself, where he more craved a private environment, than his own bathroom. In the shower, he was naked. On the toilet, he was half naked. It was the time and place each day when he was the most alone, when he felt the most vulnerable. He knew when he stood naked in front of his bathroom mirror, when his real eyes met the eyes in the mirror, that it was the one time of the day when he was literally and figuratively stripped to his core. And if he was going to realize something intimate and personal, that was the time for it to happen.

So there was that.

As for the third part of the question, the part about why he did not have the revelation until after he had spent more than five decades on the planet, Chester suspected it might possibly have to do with the radar.

In his head.

And so there was that.

▼

Theodore later told Chester the first thing Chester said to him when they met in the basement was, "I'm starving."

Theodore said he thought it was unusual Chester's first words to him weren't, "Where am I?" or "Why am I here?" or even "Who the hell are you?"

Chester's declaration that he was hungry had not given Theodore much advance notice, but he disappeared upstairs and reappeared fifteen minutes later with a tray of food for Chester. On the tray was a tuna fish sandwich, but not just any tuna fish sandwich. Chester saw the bread was lightly toasted with the crust trimmed off. One bite told him that mixed in with the tuna fish were diced up eggs, celery and olives. Between the two sandwich halves was a mound of crispy, kettle-cooked potato chips and a fat kosher pickle. As Chester chewed he had nodded approvingly at Theodore.

"Egg, celery and green olives, right?" Chester had asked.

"Yes."

"But I taste something else, a spice maybe. Basil?"

"No, cilantro."

"It tastes marvelous."

"Thank you."

When Chester finished the sandwich and licked the tip of his index finger to stab up the last crumbs of the crispy, kettle-cooked potato chips from his plate, he had looked up at Theodore and said, "Can I ask you a few questions?"

To which Theodore had replied, "later," and then walked up the basement stairs, locking behind him the door into the house, the sound of the heavy deadbolt sliding into the slot floating down to Chester.

▼

Chester is proud of his radar.

Some people might call it instinct or having a premonition or making a deduction, but Chester thinks it has more to do with his having a great memory. He has a knack for seeing and hearing everything and then remembering everything he has seen and heard. All those sights and sounds get sorted and organized and filed away in his brain, even things that initially don't seem to make any sense.

Harriette has lost track of how many times Chester, seemingly out of the blue, will connect a comment someone made or an event that happened months ago with something that was just said or just happened, and his observation will effectively solve what up to then had been a mystery.

"Now it all makes sense," is what Chester says to Harriette every time it happens, followed always by, "It's my radar, Harriette. It's my radar."

Though she has heard it many times before, Chester will again explain to Harriette it is a scientific fact that if some of your senses are seldom used, the senses you do use more often will become even stronger. And to prove his point, he always mentions Harriette's right arm.

Harriette's right arm is noticeably bigger than her left arm, the right arm muscles overdeveloped from her years as a grocery store cashier where she spent eight hours a day lifting and pulling a non-stop conveyor belt of food items through her checkout counter.

"Those gallon jugs of milk were the worst," Harriette told Chester when they first started dating.

When Chester laughed at her big right arm muscles, Harriette challenged him to arm wrestle her and Chester stopped laughing when she beat him three times in a row. Every few years since then, hoping Harriette's time away from the cashier counter and her getting older will give him the upper hand, Chester will re-challenge Harriette to arm wrestle, but she still beats him. Harriette is always pleased when she wins, but she never rubs it in, and she would never mention the arm wrestling to another living soul, which is just one of the reasons Chester likes Harriette so much.

Because Chester has always been in the background, to the point of being ignored most of his life, even by his own parents, things like acceptance and admiration and togetherness and being special and unique are things he sees around him as a spectator, never as a participant. From the observation deck of his life he has contented himself with fine tuning his ability to see and hear all the interesting and wonderful and nonsensical things that play out in front of him like a movie, filing each and every one of them away in his head. If he can't partake in those things, he can at least observe them and hide them away.

And that, Chester realized as he drove to work with the radio turned off, was most probably why on this particular day he had the revelation. There were fifty-two years worth of interesting and wonderful and nonsensical things stored up in his brain and all those little clues he had not recognized or understood when he initially filed them away had finally come together and crystallized for him into the revelation. Into an explanation of why Chester Fortunberry's life has been the way it is.

His life was the way it was before today, and his life will be the way it will be from today forward, Chester realized, for the simple reason that he is real and nothing else is.

"Now it all makes sense," Chester said to himself.

And even though she wasn't there, he also said out loud, "It's my radar, Harriette. It's my radar."

▼

As Chester drove to work that day, the pinkie finger on his left hand started to twitch. Then it started to tap against the steering wheel like the clapper on the outside of a boxing ring bell. It was a steady rhythmic tapping, the wayward pinkie finger on his left hand oblivious to the actions of the other nine digits on his hands.

Chester had both hands on the steering wheel because that's how he had learned to drive. He knew it did not look masculine, and that the guys in high school had driven with their right hand on top of the steering wheel and their left arm propped on the open window, a Marlboro cigarette in their hand. They would be slouched down in their car seats with a studied air of nonchalance, and their radios would be blasting.

That looked cool, but Chester knew driving a multi-ton automobile was a big responsibility, so whenever he drove his car, or anybody else's car, he sat up straight, put on his seat belt, made sure the side mirrors and rear view mirror were positioned properly, turned the volume of the radio down low, paid attention to the road in front of him and to the cars all around him, and always kept both hands on the steering wheel.

Even when the pinkie finger on his left hand went crazy.

The pinkie tapping only happened when Chester was nervous or stressed. If he concentrated hard enough he could get the pinkie to stop tapping and join the other fingers in steadily gripping the steering wheel, but as soon as he stopped concentrating, his pinkie would go all hyper again. Having it happen to him when he was alone in his car was one thing, but having it happen at a crowded staff meeting could be highly embarrassing. It was like having non-verbal Tourette syndrome. He had heard the words, "Chester, must you?" too many times from his boss when Chester's pinkie did a noisy Macarena dance on the boardroom table.

Once his pinkie starts dancing, Chester knows what will happen next. He will start thinking about Bora Bora. Because whenever he is nervous or stressed, he always thinks about moving to Bora Bora.

"That's it. I have had enough. I am moving to Bora Bora," Chester will say to Harriette.

"You mean 'we' don't you, dear?" Harriette will respond.

"Yes, I mean 'we,'" Chester will answer.

"That's nice," Harriette will say, and then pat Chester on his leg or arm or shoulder, whichever is closer. If she is standing and he is sitting, she will pat Chester's balding head when she says, "That's nice." She seems to like patting Chester's balding head the most.

Chester is an aficionado of Bora Bora because of an article and photo spread about the tiny French Polynesian island in an issue of *National Geographic* he read when he was a teenager. Like most red-blooded American boys, he looked through every monthly issue of the magazine that came to his house in hopes of seeing photos of native women from the Congo or the Amazon with exposed dangling breasts. For a boy entering puberty, a breast is a breast, regardless of whether those breasts look like sausages hanging in the local deli or if their owners have bleached white animal bones in their noses. This particular issue was woefully short on native breasts, but there was an article and photos about Bora Bora that caught Chester's interest. He read the

11

article and looked at the photos numerous times and decided that Bora Bora was the place he wanted to move to one day.

It wasn't because of the crystal-clear turquoise water in the lagoon that encircles the island or the majestic coral reef flush with manta rays and multi-colored fish. It wasn't because of the lush vegetation covering the two peaks of an extinct volcano or because of the thousands of exotic trees dotting the island. And it wasn't because it was predicted that in the future the island would play host to lavish resorts that could only be visited by the rich and the famous.

No, Chester was enamored of Bora Bora because it was isolated and nobody he knew had ever heard of it. There were less than four thousand people living on the island, and in every photo the people looked happy and friendly. Which, for the pimply-faced teenager who was Chester, made isolated and hidden-away Bora Bora look like a place where people would not make fun of him and might even accept him. It looked like a place where Chester could be somebody.

Which is why, over the next forty years, whenever the stress in his life got to be too much, Chester would say to anyone who would listen, "That's it. I have had enough. I am moving to Bora Bora."

And when Chester says that, most people, as they tend to do whenever Chester says something that has the appearance of being a pronouncement, will just ignore him. Even the people who do not know what Bora Bora is and who, under normal circumstances, would ask about Bora Bora just out of natural curiosity will pretend like they don't hear what Chester has said.

The only person on board with Chester and the whole Bora Bora thing is Harriette. And not just to humor him. Harriette has said many times she would be more than happy to go to Bora Bora with Chester. Deep down she knows they will never go, that they will never leave the house they live in. Still, it never stops Harriette from reminding Chester every time he mentions leaving, that it is "we" and not just "I" that will be going to Bora Bora.

That Monday morning Chester found his brain filled almost to capacity with a swirling tornado of thoughts about the revelation and the letter and Bora Bora and even about how he had missed breakfast, and it made him dizzy just trying to juggle everything in his head. And the whole time he was juggling everything in his tiny little head, the pinkie finger on his left hand just went tap, tap, tap.

▼

When Chester first awoke in Theodore's basement, he had surveyed his surroundings. He was on his back on a twin size bed with a fluffy and comfortable mattress. He was laying on top of a down comforter with a design of red and brown autumn leaves on it, fully dressed except for his shoes. He looked over the edge of the bed and saw his shoes neatly arranged on the floor. Next to the right side of the bed was a night stand with a light on it and across the room was a dresser and a small bookcase.

There were no windows in the room and that fact, combined with the exposed brick walls of the room and a set of stairs in the right corner that went up and around a small wall to the next level, led Chester to believe, correctly so, that he was in a basement. In the left corner of the room he saw an open door and behind it the edge of a toilet seat and part of a shower curtain.

Looking straight up at the ceiling he saw a large dome light which was on. Next to it was a metal grate about ten inches wide by a foot long. In the days to come, of all the things in the basement, the thing that would become the most important was the grate.

When Chester sat up and swung his legs over the side of the bed, he heard a door open and close above him. He heard loud footsteps on the landing behind the small wall that blocked the top of the stairs, he saw two feet on the stairs, and then two legs, and then the full body of a large man. The man was tanned and muscular, wearing black loafers, black chino pants and a crisp white short-sleeved cotton shirt, the sleeves rolled up exactly one inch, emphasizing his powerful arms. His hair was jet black, full and thick, combed straight back. He was clean shaven, but he had the type of heavy beard that no matter how recently he shaved, you would always see the faintest shadow under his skin. He wore glasses with thick black frames, like the glasses Buddy Holly wore. His eyelashes were long and dark, and behind them his eyes were a sparkling steel blue, which on any other man would have appeared effeminate, but instead made him look both mysterious and dangerous. He looked like he could have been thirty years old or fifty years old. And he looked like he could have been a college professor or a shop foreman. It was hard to tell. What Chester could tell, though, was that he looked like one of those guys you didn't want to accidentally bump up against in a crowded bar.

The man stopped on the second step from the bottom of the stairs, which made him look even bigger and more imposing from where

Chester sat on the edge of the bed. The man looked directly at him and said:

"Hello, Chester. My name is Theodore Sanders."

Chapter Two

Chester closed the door to his office, took a sip of his coffee, and unfolded the twice-folded, cream-colored letter and laid it flat on his desk. He read it again. And again. And a third again. It didn't make any more sense to him on the third read than it did on the first read. He was so focused on reading the letter again that he hadn't noticed that, like every other day, not a single person in the office, not even the receptionist, had said hello, much less good morning.

Who the heck, pardon his French, were Ed and Edna Pringle? Chester had an excellent memory and knew he would never forget anyone with a last name as strange as Pringle, much less a married couple named Ed and Edna. What were the chances a man named Ed would meet and marry a woman named Edna? Pretty slim, he thought. Perhaps they were Harriette's friends. But Harriette and Chester did not have exclusive friends. Neither of them knew many people at all, and the few people they did know, they both knew.

Chester pulled the envelope the letter had arrived in from his pocket and looked at the return address. Instead of a handwritten return address, it had one of those address stickers the Veterans Administration mails out with a donation card. The sticker has the outline of the map of the United States with the interior of the map colored in like the American flag.

Chester receives the same packet of VA stickers every year. He dutifully makes a donation each time he receives the packet, and it seems like just when he is on his last address sticker, another envelope will arrive from the VA with more free address stickers and a donation card. Chester wonders how the people at the VA always know when he is on his last sticker, and he also wonders how they got his name and address in the first place.

The VA sticker, the one with the map of the United States colored in like the American flag, read:

Ed and Edna Pringle
2649 Shady Grove Blvd.
Casper, WY 82601

Chester knew WY meant Wyoming, so he spent a few moments thinking about whether he knew anyone from Wyoming before realizing that not only did he not know anyone who lived in Wyoming, he did not even know anyone who had ever visited Wyoming. In fact, Chester knew if he looked at a map of the United States that showed just the outlines of the states and not their names, he couldn't even tell which outlined state was Wyoming. He was pretty sure it would be at the top of the map, somewhere near Montana and the two Dakotas, but that was about it. And he didn't know anyone who had ever been to those states either.

But apparently someone from WY knew him.

Chester picked up the phone on his desk and dialed information.

"City and state please?"

"Casper, Wyoming."

"Say the name of the business or say residence."

"Residence."

"Please say the first and last name of the person you are looking for."

"Ed, Pringle."

"We're sorry, that number is unpublished."

Chester scrunched his brow, hung up the phone and took another sip of his now lukewarm coffee. His stomach grumbled.

He logged onto his computer and did a city and state search using both Ed and Edna's names and their street address. Their names came up several times, but never with a phone number.

So Chester knew the Pringles existed.

He just couldn't get them on the phone.

To ask them about the letter.

Chester picked up his phone again, punched the inter-office button and buzzed Darlene Rogers in the personnel department.

Darlene and Chester were hired on the same day seventeen years ago. You would think that would make Darlene and Chester buddies, but that's not the case. It doesn't bother Chester, though, because he knows Darlene is not really friendly with anyone at the office. Some of the unkind people in the office say Darlene is irritable and miserable because of how she looks. One particularly unkind coworker said Darlene bore an uncanny resemblance to a spider monkey. Darlene did suffer from psoriasis, was substantially overweight, and had probably never been on a date in her life. Which Chester thought would, naturally, tend to make anyone a bit irritable and miserable.

Still, when Chester heard people in the office say mean things about Darlene, he would stick up for her and say, "That's just not true." It bothers him when other people are made fun of. He doesn't want any part of that, and he will even say something about it. It's one of the few times Chester will take a stand.

When Chester was first hired and people asked him what he did for a living, he would say, "I make ball bearings," which was the truth because that's precisely what the company he works for does. His answer always elicited the same response from people who inquired about his job, which was a short, clipped "Oh."

Not, "Oh, really, that's interesting," or even just an, "Oh, really."

No, all he ever got was, "Oh." One word. Short and clipped.

Chester presumed most people just weren't that interested in ball bearings. He thought it was somewhat short-sighted of them because the world runs on ball bearings. He would like to see them try to drive a car without ball bearings.

Still, after awhile, whenever he was asked what he did for a living, Chester would just say he was an accountant, which was also the truth because that's the job he did at the ball-bearing-manufacturing company. He juggled and organized and categorized and polished numbers for the company. And he did it in a small, windowless office at the end of a long corridor of offices in the three-story corporate headquarters building. His office was on the second floor, which was for the accounting department, with marketing and sales on the first floor, and management on the third floor. The company owned three ball-bearing-manufacturing plants, one in South Korea and two in Mexico. Chester had never been to those plants, but felt like he knew them intimately since he juggled and organized and categorized and polished their numbers every day.

The phone rang two times before it was picked up.

"This is Darlene Rogers," said Darlene Rogers.

"Hi Darlene, it's Chester in Accounting."

"Yes, Chester, what can I do for you?" Not friendly, not unfriendly.

"Can you please tell me how much vacation time I have accrued?"

"Hold, please."

Chester waited patiently.

"Chester?"

"Yes?"

"You have twelve weeks accumulated."

"Really. That much?"

"Yes, Chester."

"That's grand. I would like to use one week of vacation time."

"Starting when?"

"Tomorrow."

"Okay. I will fill out the paperwork. Clear it with Mr. Dundee, please."

Mr. Dundee was the head of the Accounting Department. Chester did not know how good of an accountant Mr. Dundee was, but he did know Mr. Dundee played a lot of golf. Usually with the president of the company. Which explained why he wasn't in his office very often. Like this week.

"I believe Mr. Dundee is out this week, Darlene."

"Okay. I'll make a note that your vacation request is approved."

"Darlene?"

"Yes, Chester?"

"Guess where I'm going?"

"I haven't a clue."

"To Casper, Wyoming."

"Good for you, Chester."

▼

Chester hung up the phone and folded his hands in his lap. Anyone looking in on him would have said he appeared to be lost in thought. Which he was. Now that he had a week of vacation time, he thought of what he would say when he flew to Casper, Wyoming the next day and showed up unannounced on Ed and Edna Pringle's front doorstep.

Because that was exactly what he was going to do.

▼

The first time Chester and Harriette flew on a plane together was on their honeymoon. They went to Hawaii, which was an amazingly long flight. Chester was surprised a place that was one of the fifty United States could be so far away from the other forty-nine states. Neither Chester or Harriette liked being cooped up in a coach seat for that long, particularly over water. They often recall how long the flight was, both the coming and the going, but they conveniently forget that fact whenever they talk about escaping to Bora Bora, which is also an amazingly long flight.

When they boarded the plane, Chester had whispered in Harriette's ear, "Whatever you do, do not look into the cockpit."

"Why?" asked Harriette, perplexed, and, understandably, a little worried.

"Trust me," said Chester. "I'll explain later."

Which Chester did once they were seated and buckled in.

Which took a little longer than it sounds.

Chester had Harriette sit in the middle seat. He positioned both of their carry-on bags in the overhead compartment so the zippered pockets were easily accessible, so they had breathing room and were not smashed together, and were far enough back that the overhead compartment door would not hit them when the stewardess walked down the aisle and closed the compartment. Chester sat down in the aisle seat, pulled a small, white, plastic trash bag from his pocket and reached into the pockets on the back of the seats in front of he and Harriette and collected empty peanut packets, crumpled napkins and other trash items that he placed in the bag. He lowered both of their table trays, pulled a moist towelette packet from his pocket, opened it, cleaned the tops of both trays, and raised the table trays back up. He opened a second towelette and cleaned his hands with it, then placed the used towelettes and empty packets into the trash bag, tied the bag up tightly, and handed it to one of the flight attendants, giving her a sheepish shrug of his shoulders as he did so. Chester put on his seat belt, cinching it nice and tight, and then checked to make sure Harriette had done the same. From a bag in his lap he took out two magazines, two bottled waters, and two bags of snack chips, *Cheetos* for Chester and *Fritos* for Harriette, that he had bought at the airport newsstand earlier. He placed one of each item into the now-clean pockets in front of he and Harriette.

Chester then let out a satisfied sigh and turned to look at Harriette, who was smiling at him and who had watched his every move. As had the young man in the window seat next to Harriette, who, instead of smiling, appeared to be looking around the plane for another open seat.

"Okay, here's how I see it," said Chester.

He explained to Harriette that the average passenger jet, say a Boeing 727, loaded with both fuel and passengers, could weigh as much as 180,000 pounds, which would be the same weight as forty-six Cadillac Eldorados strapped together with bungee cords and tossed off a high cliff.

"Something that heavy, made out of steel, just should not be up in the air," said Chester, leaning closer, whispering into Harriette's ear. "Birds fly, and birds are supposed to fly, but chunks of metal are not supposed to fly. The biggest flying bird in the world is the Koro Bustard of Africa which weighs forty pounds and can barely get off the ground for a very short flight. The plane we are on right now weighs almost 5,000 times that. Do the math, Harriette!"

Harriette had nodded her head and patted Chester on the knee because she could tell he was getting worked up. It was the start of their honeymoon and it wouldn't do for her newly betrothed to be a bundle of nerves. The patting seemed to settle Chester down.

Chester mulled over the information he had just passed on to Harriette, analyzing it piece by piece in his head. Chester did that a lot, going over in his head things he said out loud, just to double check what he said for accuracy. It was like adding up a column of numbers more than once to make sure the total was the same each time. While doing the mulling, he realized he had neglected to tell her why she should not look into the cockpit.

Chester waited to see if Harriette would bring up the cockpit. He realized this was a defining moment in their relationship. If she did not ask about the cockpit, it would mean she did not pay attention to things Chester said. It would mean she did not share Chester's natural curiosity about things. It would mean Chester, who had spent his whole life trying to find someone who was interested in him and interested in what he had to say, had married someone who was not that interested in him and not that interested in what he had to say.

"Chester, what about the cockpit?" asked Harriette.

▼

Chester went to the mail room and made a copy of the Pringle letter and the front of the Pringle envelope. Back at his desk he put the letter and the envelope into a file folder and put the folder into his briefcase. He put the copies of the letter and envelope into another file folder, labeled the folder Miscellaneous Expenses and stuck it in the middle of a stack of other folders in his bottom drawer. The originals would go with him to Casper, Wyoming, but not the copies. Chester was a strong believer in keeping back-up records.

As Chester did his secret agent stuff, which in his mind was how he was starting to think about the stuff he was doing, he realized one of the things responsible for the revelation coming to the forefront of his thought process had been right there in front of him for quite some time. In fact, he had encountered it every morning and every evening without realizing he was even encountering it. But one day, in the days just before the revelation, that thing—a phenomenon really—revealed itself to him, like a light being turned on to illuminate a dark room, which, it turns out, was an appropriate analogy.

Because the thing, the phenomenon, if you will, was the light in his closet.

And the fact he had never replaced it.

Not in twenty years.

▼

At the top of Chester's fairly good-sized walk-in closet in the master bedroom is a light fixture with one long fluorescent bulb. Every morning Chester turns that light on and goes into his fairly good-sized walk-in closet to select the day's clothes. And every night he turns that same light on and goes into the closet to place his clothes in the dirty clothes basket in the corner. So that's a minimum of twice a day that he turns the light on and off, or 730 times a year, or 14,600 times over the past twenty years. And during those fourteen-thousand-and-six-hundred times that he has flicked his closet light on and off, not once has that fluorescent bulb ever gone out and had to be replaced.

When this surprising fact dawned on Chester, the first thing he did was go into the kitchen and ask Harriette, "Dear, have you been replacing the light bulb in my closet?"

"Oh gosh, no," said Harriette. "That's much too high for me."

Which is true. The Fortunberry's house has ten-foot ceilings, so to change a fluorescent light in one of the two master bedroom closets would necessitate dragging the heavy aluminum folding ladder from the garage through the laundry room, the dining room, and the living room into a good-sized but still somewhat tight walk-in closet, a feat of strength and agility that, if someone had ever done it, they would surely remember.

Which didn't stop Chester from asking, "Are you sure?"

"Yes, dear," answered Harriette.

"Never?" asked Chester.

"Never," said Harriette, patiently.

Chester continued standing in the kitchen. Harriette knew he believed her, but she also knew he would stand there forever while he mulled over whatever was bothering him. Unless she broke his spell.

"Why do you ask?" asked Harriette.

"Because," said Chester, excitedly holding his right index finger up in the air for emphasis, "we have lived in this house for more than twenty years and we have never had to replace the fluorescent light in my closet."

"Really?" said Harriette in what Chester recognized was her polite but that's-not-really-very-interesting voice.

"Yes, really," said Chester.

"Well, that's not so strange," said Harriette.

"Why not?" asked Chester, looking up.

"Because we've never had to replace the light in my closet either," said Harriette, who regretted saying it even as the words were coming out of her mouth.

Chester wheeled around, walked into the living room and sat on the edge of the couch. Not on the couch, just on the edge of the couch, his shoulders slumped, his brow furrowed.

"Chester?"

No answer.

"Chester, dear, would you like a glass of tea?"

No answer.

Chester was not being rude. He didn't even hear Harriette. Because he was deep in thought. Curious thoughts. Disturbing thoughts. Thought-provoking thoughts.

Did the light never burn out because Chester was only in the closet for a brief amount of time each day, so even though the light was on and off thousands of times, it was never on long enough to burn out? Was that the answer? Maybe. But still, a light that worked for more than twenty years? It just didn't seem plausible.

Chester had no idea what happened in his closet when he was not in it. Which was stating the obvious. And if he had no idea what was happening when he wasn't in it, did that mean his closet only existed when he stepped into it once in the morning and once in the evening? Because if that was true, if the closet only existed when he was in it, then maybe each time he turned on the light, it was the first time the light had ever been turned on. Which made more sense to him than thinking a light could be turned on and off fourteen-thousand-and-six-hundred separate times over twenty years and never burn out.

Thinking about his closet light got Chester thinking about Tiananmen Square in Beijing, China.

Like most educated people he knew about Tiananmen Square. He could picture what it looked like because of the photos of that fearless young man standing in the middle of the square with two shopping bags, blocking the advance of a line of tanks during the Chinese government's crackdown on student protests years ago. When Chester saw those photos or newscasts he was sure Tiananmen Square existed, way over there on the other side of the world. And each time he saw an old news video, or an old photo of the heroic young man, he was again sure Tiananmen Square actually existed.

But that afternoon, as Chester sat on the edge of his couch thinking about his mysterious closet light, there were no pictures of Tiananmen Square in that day's newspaper and no videos of Tiananmen Square on the television. Which made Chester wonder if, since he wasn't seeing Tiananmen Square anywhere, it was possible that Tiananmen Square did not really exist. Did it only exist when he could see it, just like his closet and the light in it only existed when he could see it?

Chester was sure about one thing.

He knew if he went to the airport right then and got on a plane for the fourteen-hour flight to Beijing and took a taxi to Tiananmen Square, then Tiananmen Square would indeed be there.

He could stand right in the middle of the square. It would exist.

What Chester wasn't sure about was this.

If he did not get on that plane right now.

If he just sat on the edge of his couch.

If he did not move an inch.

Would Tiananmen Square actually exist?

Chester was beginning to wonder.

That day on the plane to Hawaii, Chester smiled nice and big when

Harriette remembered to ask about the cockpit. It was at that moment Chester realized he had made the right choice in marrying Harriette.

"Oh, right, sorry" said Chester, with a smile to let Harriette know he was happy she had reminded him he had not finished making his point. "Well, in my mind the only reason planes can fly is because every plane has a gigantic cockpit that looks like the mission control room on all those outer space movies and there are twenty people in the cockpit with loads of brand new equipment and radar screens and fancy computers. And everyone is working hand in hand to make sure I have a safe flight."

Chester cinched his seat belt tighter and looked left and right to make sure no one was eavesdropping before continuing.

"But that's not the case, Harriette!" he whispered urgently. "Not even close. If you look into the cockpit you will see a space smaller than our kitchen pantry, with just two guys crammed in there, fiddling around with a bunch of worn-out looking levers and dials. Good Lord, it's not a sight that instills confidence. That's why I never look into the cockpit."

"That makes sense," said Harriette.

"Did you look?" asked Chester.

"No, you told me not to."

"Good."

"Did you?"

"Of course not!"

"Double good," said Harriette.

When the plane began to taxi for take-off, Harriette reached over and took Chester's hand in hers.

"Chester?" said Harriette.

"Yes, dear."

"How did you know about that bird?"

"The Koro Bustard?"

"Yes."

"I'm just smart that way, Harriette."

Harriette smiled. And she thought back to their wedding day a week earlier and it dawned on her right then, just as the 180,000-pound plane's wheels lifted off the ground, that she had made the right choice in marrying Chester.

The unbreakable light in his closet and the questionable existence of Beijing, and how they might tie in with the revelation, had started Chester's brain churning. He recalled another recent incident that might have sped the process along. It was the big argument at his office a few weeks ago.

Chester never gets involved in arguments. A mild debate is the farthest he is prepared go. If it appears voices are going to be raised, or feelings hurt, or someone is going to hold a grudge against him for a stance he takes, Chester will vocally reverse his opinion in a split second. On the inside, he still agrees with the position he had during the discussion, but on the outside he will make sure the other person knows they are right and Chester can now see the light.

Chester feels like he is usually always right, so to argue with someone who is wrong has no upside for him. Winning the argument brings him no satisfaction because convincing someone else he is right when he already knows he is right is a waste of time and energy. And the downside is the person he is arguing with will feel like a dummy and be resentful if Chester proves them wrong.

Chester knew it was better to just stay out of arguments, especially arguments that could get you hurt. Hurt like a sock in the eye.

Chester was in line at a fast food restaurant last year, which was unusual because he always eats healthy and lectures Harriette on the evils of processed food. This particular day, some errands he had run on his lunch break had taken longer than expected, so, reluctantly, he stopped into a fast food restaurant. Even if he ate quickly, he knew he would be late getting back to the office, which made that day double-unusual because Chester is never late and prides himself on arriving ahead of schedule for everything. So what was a double-unusual day to begin with became a triple-unusual day when the two men standing in line in front of him to order their processed hamburgers began to beat on each other.

Chester had been in the line long enough to be privy to some of the conversation between the two men before they began pummeling each other. The man in front, who had a thick Southern accent, was wearing a large blue and white football jersey that had the words *Dallas Cowboys* on the back. The man behind him, who had a thick New England accent, had tapped him on the shoulder and said something. Chester did not hear every word the man in back said, but he did hear two of the words, which were "you suck." The man in the football jersey responded with some words of his own and, despite his thick Southern accent, Chester was able to make out each and every one of those words, which were, "Why don't you just blow me."

The man with the New England accent then socked the man with the Southern accent right in the eye and the man with the Southern accent then socked the man with the New England accent right back, also in the eye. They were soon rolling on the floor, yelling and hitting each other as the other customers, many of them children, watched, eyes wide in amazement, half-eaten french fries visible in their open mouths.

That two grown men could inflict bodily harm on each other over a sporting event amazed Chester. It wasn't an argument about abortion or gun control or the death penalty or affordable insurance. No, it was an argument about guys who get together on weekends to throw a leather ball around on a grass field. If people could blacken each other's eyes over a game, it was no wonder people kill each other over arguments about politics or religion. None of it made sense to Chester, being the practical man that he is.

That day, Chester did what he usually did in situations like that, not that he was in situations like that very often. He turned on his heel and quickly left the fast food restaurant. He drove back to the office, his stomach growling nice and loud.

Later, when the argument at his office broke out, the one he thought may have helped speed along the arrival of the revelation, Chester thought about the battling burger men and hoped the same thing would not happen at the office. Chester did not want to get a black eye almost as much as he did not want to test the waters to see if he had it in him to give one.

The discussion at his office, the one that evolved into an argument despite Chester's best efforts to not have that happen, had been about babies, but on a deeper level it had been about time.

That's what Phillip just didn't understand.

Phillip has the office next to Chester and he too is an accountant charged with juggling and organizing and categorizing and polishing numbers for the ball-bearing company. Chester knows he does a much better job in the juggling, organizing, categorizing and polishing numbers department than Phillip, but he also knows Phillip is much younger, much better looking, a much better dresser, a much better socializer, and has many more friends, both in and out of the office, than Chester. Knowing all that, Chester is still friendly with Phillip, even though he knows Phillip sometimes mimics the way he walks, counting each step out under his breath.

Chester feels accountants are not particularly high on the totem pole of office hierarchy, which should give he and Phillip something in common and they should band together a little more, but it is apparently not a feeling shared by Phillip. Still, Chester never stops trying to bond with the man who is younger, better looking, a better dresser and a better socializer than him, because when it's all said and done, Chester too would like to be accepted.

The day of the office argument, Phillip was in the hallway outside Chester's office, talking to two secretaries who were oohing and aahing over a photo on his phone.

"Yep, I'm an uncle now," said Phillip proudly.

"When was he born?" asked one of the secretaries.

"Last week on Halloween, just before midnight."

"And your sister is in California, right?"

"Yes."

"A Halloween baby. How cute."

Chester swiveled around in his chair. No one noticed until he spoke.

"Well, technically, he's not necessarily a Halloween baby."

Phillip looked at Chester, not happy. The two secretaries looked at Chester, a little surprised.

"What do you mean?" asked Phillip.

"The minute your nephew was born it was Halloween day out there in California, but it was the day after Halloween here."

"What do you mean?"

"You know, the time change."

"Yeah, so what?"

"California is three hours behind us."

"Again, so what?"

"So in your sister's world, her baby was born on one day, and in your world, he was born on a different day. Get it?"

"No, I don't. My nephew was born on Halloween day."

"There, yes, but here, no."

"Yes, there. That's what matters. Where he was born."

"So there matters, but here doesn't?"

"Chester, you're pissing me off. What's your point?"

"It's all about time."

"Yeah, it is. It's about time you shut up," said Phillip, making the women laugh.

"I'm not trying to make you angry. I'm just pointing out how time is relative. It's just a concept people came up with, and it's not really all that accurate. Not when you have things like 'here' and 'there' in the mix."

27

"Chester, can't you just be happy for Phillip," said one of the women.

"Oh, I'm sorry. I'm not trying to be argumentative. Phillip, congratulations on being an uncle. Can I see the picture?"

"No," said Phillip, sticking the cell phone into his pocket.

Chester's shoulders drooped.

He wanted to tell Phillip and the secretaries about a picture he had seen of graffiti spray painted on the wall of an old building. The graffiti said, "Time doesn't exist, clocks exist." He thought it would bring home his point that everything is not what it seems to be and that when we try to make everything be what we think it should be, we tend to make mistakes. He thought he could even find the graffiti photo on his computer to show them, but the secretaries had walked away and Phillip had gone into his office and shut the door.

Toward the end of the work day Chester's desk phone rang.

"Hello?"

"Chester, it's Julie." Julie was the receptionist for the second floor.

"Look," said Julie, in a rushed voice, "I'm sorry. I forgot to give you a message earlier. You had a call on the answering machine last night. Someone asking for you."

"That's okay, Julie. What was the message?"

"He didn't leave a message?"

"Did he leave a call back number?"

"No."

"Well, did he at least leave his name?"

"Yes.

"What was it?"

"Theodore."

▼

Chester was in the break room one day ago when he overheard two of the company's salesmen talking at the next table.

"Where are you off to tomorrow?"

"Going to Vegas for the tradeshow."

"Oh, lucky you."

Chester thought the man was indeed lucky. That weekend Chester would be at his house puttering around, which he did enjoy but which could get boring if it was something you did every weekend of the year, while his co-worker would be in a city of bright lights and nonstop action.

Chester had never been to Las Vegas but had seen enough movies and television shows to know the salesman was in store for a heck of a good time. Chester had always wanted to go to Las Vegas for the ball-bearing-manufacturing industry's big annual convention there, but his company only sent their top sales and management people. He knew there was no reason to send an accountant to a convention that was all about pumping hands and slapping backs, but it didn't stop him from wishing he could go just one time.

What caught Chester's attention when he heard the two salesmen talking, besides the enticing lure of a Las Vegas trip, was what the one salesman said when the other salesman asked him if he had packed for his trip yet. He had said, "Oh no, I never pack for myself. My wife always does it."

For Chester the thought of leaving the comfort and security of his home to go to either a known or unknown place and not have any idea what he had brought with him until he got to that known or unknown place and opened his suitcase was just unimaginable. That would be like going to the front lines of a battle and not knowing what weapons someone else had packed in your backpack until you were in the foxhole. Because for Chester, traveling was a bit like going to war.

Chester trusted Harriette implicitly and he knew she had even better taste than him when it came to clothes and decorating and things like that, but it didn't make him any more comfortable about letting her pack his suitcase. What if she packed a shirt or a pair of pants that no longer fit him? What if she packed an outfit the people he saw on his last trip had seen him wear, and here he was wearing the same outfit again? And Chester didn't even want to think about all the mistakes that could happen if someone else packed his toiletry kit.

He knew part of his reluctance to let someone else do something of a personal nature for him was due to how he had been conditioned over the years. He was used to doing everything for himself, because for most of his life it had just been he and himself. It's why he could boil a perfect egg and why he could go to the movie theater all alone and why if he wanted his back scratched he could find a way to do it himself.

Chester had started out wanting somebody, and eventually became accustomed to having nobody. He had even accepted that the nobody phase would go on until the day he died. So, he was pleasantly surprised when the somebody phase became a reality when he met Harriette.

Chester thought his chances of meeting someone like Harriette were slimmer than his chances of winning the Nobel Peace Prize, and he tells her that every year on their wedding anniversary. When Harriette tells him he is exaggerating, he always says the same thing to her, which is, "So do you run people over all the time?"

Chester has a point.

Chester and Harriette only met because Harriette was in a rush to get to the nursing college where she was to take a final exam before getting her registered nurse certification, and because Chester was in a rush to get to the hardware store before it closed to buy washers for a leaky faucet in his apartment. The difference was that Harriette was in a rush in her little compact car, a blue Gremlin with a white stripe down the side, and Chester was in a rush walking in the middle of a crosswalk. And that's how they first met, looking at each other through the windshield of Harriette's Gremlin, her with her face inches from the windshield on the inside, and Chester with his face flat against the windshield on the outside. When Harriette finally applied the brakes, Chester slid off her hood onto the pavement.

Chester was laying flat on his back when Harriette jumped out of her car and rushed over to him.

"Hi," he said, looking up at her. "My name is Chester. Chester Fortunberry."

"I am so sorry," she said to him. "Oh, and my name is Harriette Templeton."

Luckily, nothing was broken, not on Chester's body and not on Harriette's car. Harriette, who was one exam away from being a medical professional, warned Chester that sometimes the body's reaction to an injury would not manifest itself for hours or even days after an accident.

"I would hate for you to wake up paralyzed," said Harriette.

"I would hate that even more than you," said Chester.

Then Chester, who later wondered where he got the courage to say what he said, while still flat on his back looking up at Harriette, said, "You have pretty eyes."

Harriette blushed.

The next day Harriette called Chester to check on him, and they talked for a half hour, a little bit about the accident and a lot more about nothing in particular. Harriette called him each day for the next six days and they talked for more than an hour each time. She didn't call Chester on the eighth day at all, so on the ninth day Chester called her.

"You didn't call me yesterday," said Chester.

"No, I didn't," said Harriette, and then she was quiet.

"Because you wanted me to call you, right?"

"Yes, Chester."

"Does that mean we're dating now?"

Three months later they were married.

That night, after work, when Chester told Harriette he had to pack his suitcase because he was going to Casper, Wyoming the next day, she did not say much. Which at the time Chester did not think was strange. But later on he realized it was quite strange and later, much later, he realized it explained a lot of things.

What Harriette did say, she said after she kissed Chester on the cheek when she dropped him off at the airport the next morning.

"Chester," she said, "whatever you do, do not look into the cockpit."

Then she smiled and patted his arm.

Chester stood at the airport curb watching her drive away.

He stared at where her car had been for a long time after the car was no longer there.

Chapter Three

Chester's plane to Casper, Wyoming leveled off at 35,000 feet, according to the pilot, whose name was Ned and whose co-pilot was named Lewis.

Because Chester seldom had lengthy conversations with other people, particularly discourses on topics of intellectual weight or the dearth of common sense in the world, he had come up with a unique way to still engage in those conversations. He talked to himself, or, to be more specific, he daydreamed with himself. He would lean back, whether he was in his chair at the office or in a seat in a waiting room, close his eyes halfway and slip into a daydream state to analyze and dissect those topics.

It was not really a two-way conversation because it was just him in the daydream state. He knew he was making a presentation to only himself, but he still structured his thoughts in such a way that they could easily be turned into spoken words if the occasion ever arose where someone was willing to listen to his opinion on things, both intellectual things and non-common sense things. Harriette would listen, but Harriette wasn't always around, and sometimes Chester just wanted to talk.

Even if was only with himself.

If Chester heard two people discussing an intellectual topic, say race relations, or a nonsensical topic, say reality television, he would control the urge to interject with his opinions. Later, he would slip into the daydream state and pontificate at great length on the topic. And when he did, he felt like he could make his points in both a rational and humorous way. Chester rarely told jokes and rarely said anything that people might think was funny, but in his daydream state, he thought he was the funniest person in the world. The daydream state made Chester feel like he had been part of a discussion, but without having to get his hands dirty, figuratively speaking, by interacting with other people.

It was something he had done since he was a small child. Later he would realize the daydreaming was more proof his revelation was true, since he had always acted as if he was the only person he could really talk to in the external world.

While he thought of it as his daydream state, Harriette, whenever she caught him sitting comfortably with his eyes half-closed, called it the Earth-to-Chester state, because she could always snap him out of it by saying, "Earth to Chester."

"What does that mean?" he had asked the first time she said it.

"It means you are off another planet and it's time to come back to Earth."

"Oh, that's clever. But I was just daydreaming."

"Same thing."

It was uncomfortably warm in the plane cabin, which made Chester sleepy and he slipped into one of his Earth-to-Chester states, Ned the pilot's voice in the background. Why did pilots insist on telling everyone on the plane their name, he asked himself? Did it really matter? Was it so if the plane crashed into the ocean and the Coast Guard plucked Chester out of the water, he could say, "I'm not really sure what happened, but I do know a guy named Ned was flying the plane."

The leveling off of the plane was a signal to Chester that things would be relaxed for the next three hours and Chester decided he would take advantage of that time to give serious thought to his revelation. Not the basic who, what, when, where, and why of the revelation, but instead a more in-depth examination of what the revelation meant and how it impacted him. Having a revelation that you are real and everybody and everything else is not was something that certainly deserved some in-depth mental exploration.

Chester put his noise-canceling headphones on, selected a Golden Oldies play list, and turned the volume up until all the background noise of the plane, from the jabbering of the passengers to the roar of the jet engines, was gone and the music was just a warm backdrop for his thoughts. He loosened his seat an inch, crossed his arms over his chest, and slid down in his seat.

He was in his own little world.

And it was then that Chester Fortunberry started to really examine the revelation in the analytical way only a good accountant could.

He realized he needed to do Three Things:

1. Determine exactly what the revelation was.

2. Determine if the revelation was true.

That order made sense because he could not judge the validity of a thing without knowing what the thing was.

3. If the revelation was true, what he was going to do about it?

Regarding the Third Thing—what to do next if the revelation was true?—that would just have to wait. He couldn't tackle the Third Thing until the first Two Things were figured out. As for the First Thing—what was the gist of the revelation?—that one was easy. He was real; nobody else was. Couldn't get much more concise than that.

So that meant most of his analysis at this moment would focus on the Second Thing—was the revelation true? And even the Second Thing had its own sub group of three-things, because to determine the Second Thing Chester thought it would be important for him to explore three things:

1. Time.

2. The mind.

3. The universe.

Or another way of saying it would be time, consciousness and space. Chester found it interesting that when considering another way of saying it, he could come up with different words for mind and universe but not for time. The mind was known by lots of different names like consciousness, soul, spirit, being, self, and intellect. The universe was also known by other names like space, cosmos, nature, the world, and the great beyond.

Time, though, was time. Chester couldn't think of any other words to substitute for it.

That made Chester think if he did have to bet on which of the three-thing sub group—time, mind or universe—might hold the answer to whether the revelation was true, he would put his money on time. If for no other reason than the fact it only had one name which meant it would be open to less interpretation.

Chester was already fairly up to speed on the concept of time. Time was nowhere near what people thought time was.

And that's what he had told Phillip.

▼

A few days after the afternoon Chester told Phillip his nephew might not have been born on Halloween Day, Chester was sitting at his desk when he felt a presence behind him. He turned in his chair to see Phillip in the doorway. He tensed, waiting for an unkind comment.

"You're right, Chester," said Phillip.

"About what?" said Chester, surprised.

"About time. I thought about what you said and, from a practical standpoint, it makes sense."

Chester was happy to hear Phillip make that statement, not the part where he said Chester was right, but the part where he said Chester was right from a practical standpoint. That meant Chester had not been wrong in thinking that Phillip, despite his superiority complex and his taunting of Chester, was still an accountant at heart and their shared appreciation of rational reasoning and deduction would outweigh any petty social differences.

If Phillip telling Chester he was right surprised him, what Phillip said next surprised him even more.

"Would you like to grab a cup of coffee and tell me a little more about what you know about time?" asked Phillip.

"It would be my privilege," said Chester.

In the break room, a cup of steaming hot coffee in front of both of them, cream and sugar for Chester and black for Phillip, Chester started his presentation. "Well, Phillip, the first thing you should know is that time does not exist."

Phillip, scowling, pushed his chair back and crossed his arms over his chest.

"Chester, don't ruin this. I can't believe I'm even sitting here with you in the first place. The only reason is because I have always been interested in the concept of time and you're the first person I've heard talk about it in an intriguing way. Don't screw this up by playing mind tricks."

"Oh, I won't. Can I ask why time interests you?"

"Because it's a measuring stick and, as accountants, you and I are in the measuring stick business. What concerns me is that time may not be a consistent measuring stick."

"You're onto something there, Phillip. Now, don't get mad, but basically just about every scientist and philosopher says time does not exist, or at least it does not exist in the way we think it exists. There are two big debates when it comes to time. First, is time real? Do events really happen in sequence, going forward like a bullet from a gun, or do we as humans just imagine that they do? And second, within the concept of time, do the future, present and past exist, and, if they do, when do they exist?"

Phillip uncrossed his arms and leaned forward, which Chester knew was a good sign. It gave him the courage to dive a little deeper. "We measure time by the changing of events, as in today I am clean shaven and tomorrow beard stubble has arrived," said Chester. "That's easy to understand. The controversy arises when an event does not change in any way while it travels the arrow of time. If your birthday is on June 30 a month from now, then we say that the event, you blowing out candles at your birthday, is in the future. On June 30th we say that you blowing out those candles is in the present. And a month after June 30, we say that your blowing out those candles was in the past. Same exact birthday and same exact blowing out of candles, but we say there were three different events: candle blowing in the future, candle blowing in the present and candle blowing in the past. But we're wrong. You didn't blow out those candles three different times. You only blew them out once. Which means that time, or whatever you want to call it, did not change or move forward or backward at all."

Phillip gave a half-hearted nod. Chester had him for a little while longer.

"What's interesting about time versus space is that you can't occupy multiple places in space at the exact same instant. You can't be in Singapore, New Orleans and Berlin all in the same instant. But you are always in multiple places in time at the same instant. We want to chop that time up into the three segments of future, present and past, but there are no segments. It's all one thing. Get it?"

Phillip hesitated, said, "yes," hesitated again and said "no."

Chester continued. "We use time as a framework to structure our daily life experience, to sequence and compare events. But time is subjective, or to use your word, arbitrary, because it is measured differently by each individual person through their own perception of that short period of time when their consciousness is in the present."

Phillip interrupted him. "Their consciousness is in the present? What does that mean?"

"We are constantly doing time perception in our minds, using the past and the future as reference points to determine the present. We know it is now 5:15 pm because a minute ago it was 5:14 pm. Now, while the three-inch mark on your ruler is always exactly three inches whether you or I look at it, time measurement is not as concise. When I access my past for a reference point, I have to rely on my own memory, and some things I remember better than other things. Sometimes I even remember things incorrectly. So that reference point can be suspect. When I access the future for a reference point, things can change. We know a picnic is planned for next Saturday because we are told it will be then. But the picnic might not happen on Saturday because of bad weather. So that reference point can also be suspect."

"That's confusing," said Phillip.

Chester smiled. "How about this? Did you know that your body and your mind are never in the exact same time? There is a window of delay between when you see, hear, feel, taste or smell something and when that information then registers in your brain. That's where deja vu and my-life-flashed-before-my-eyes come from. You may think that when you taste a bitter lemon your mind registers that information immediately. But it doesn't. It may only take a millionth of a fraction of a second to register, but it is a delay nonetheless. Which means that while your body is in the now of the moment, your mind is not yet in that same now of the moment. Your body is always in the present, while your mind is always ever so slightly behind in the past."

Chester paused, then said, "Phillip, what day is this?"

"Tuesday."

"Are you positive?"

"Yes."

"And what time is it?"

Phillip looked at his watch and said, "2 pm."

"Are you positive?"

"Yes."

"So right now you are positive it is 2 pm Tuesday?"

"Yes, for God's sake," said Phillip, irritated.

"Now, if I was sitting in a break room with a co-worker in Australia and asked him the same question, you know what he would say?"

"No, what?"

"He would say it was 5 am Wednesday."

"So what."

"So how can it be two different times and two different days at the same instant?"

Phillip shrugged.

"Because it is the exact same instant here and in Australia. The only thing different is how we have chosen to describe it. What if you asked me the time and day question and I told you the day was *Ardvarp* and the time was *orange minus two*?"

"That's ridiculous."

"How is the word Ardvarp any weirder than the word Wednesday?"

"Chester, this is all semantics."

"Exactly," said Chester. "And that's my point."

Chester could see Phillip's eyes start to glaze over. It was time for some show and tell.

Chester slapped his hand hard on the table, making both of their coffee cups jump.

"Why did you do that?" asked Phillip, in the irritated voice again.

Chester didn't answer and instead asked, "Did you hear that loud sound?"

"Yes."

"Did you see the coffee cups jump?"

"Yes."

"Did you feel the table shake?"

"Yes."

"So that slap was real. It existed."

"Yes, Chester, what's your point?"

"Wait thirty seconds and I will tell you."

A half a minute passed, Phillip staring impatiently at Chester.

"Okay, Phillip. You said the slap was real and it existed. Where is it now?"

"Where is what now?"

"The slap."

"It's gone. It's in the past."

"Yes, it is in the past. But is it gone?"

"Yes."

"How can you say that? That slap was real. It existed. How can something that existed all of a sudden no longer cease to exist? How can something that you heard, felt and saw less than a minute ago just simply disappear?"

"Well ..."

"Let's say you traveled back in time to Ford's Theater and tapped President Lincoln on the shoulder and asked him if he exists. He would say yes. And if you asked him what time he is in, he would say the present. But you know that is wrong because you just came from the present. Vice versa, what if someone from the year 2084 showed up and tapped you on the shoulder and asked you the same questions? You too would say you exist and that you are in the present, even though the person who tapped you on the shoulder would disagree. How can we be so sure that now is now? Is it narcissism that makes us believe time only exists when we are alive in it?"

Phillip thought for a bit, took a sip of his coffee. Chester zeroed in for the kill.

"The Eiffel Tower is not in this break room, so if someone asks you about it, you say the Eiffel Tower is way over there. You know the Eifel Tower exists and you use a special language to describe where it is, and no one has a problem with that. Mr. Lincoln is also not in this break room with us, so if someone asks you about him, you say he was in the past. Is saying in the past really any different than saying way over there? If they are both merely phrases used to describe the location of a thing, shouldn't both of those things still exist?"

"Okay, I think I'm following you," said Phillip. He looked around the break room to make sure no one else was listening in. "And I have to admit, this is all pretty interesting."

"It is indeed!" said Chester. "No event is just one thing. Every event starts as a future event, becomes a present event, and then becomes a past event. So if an event, like you blowing out candles at your birthday, can have the properties of future, present and past in it, who's to say those three properties don't exist all at once. Of course, it would mean that a person could be unborn, alive and dead all at the same time."

Phillip raised his eyebrows.

"Some theorists believe all moments in time are taking place at once, but our human consciousness makes us perceive those moments at a fixed rate so we only see the part of time we are meant to look at."

"Can you say that again, in English this time? " asked Phillip, his irritated voice back in play.

"Certainly. What it means is that, whether time exists or not, we feel like it does, no matter how strong the proof is that it doesn't. We perceive time, through our mind's processing of external stimuli, as the unfolding of one event after the other, even if all the events are happening at once. We only see them one at a time because that is all our mind wants us to see. Let me give you an example. You can give an alcoholic suffering from delirium tremors irrefutable evidence that bugs are not crawling on his body, but if his mind tells him they are, then he's going to keep trying to brush imaginary bugs off his body. What something is and what our mind thinks something is can be two totally different things. So, it can appear to us that time exists even in a timeless universe. We watch the sun come up each day and say twenty-four hours have passed and we watch the leaves turn brown and say a year has passed, but hours and days and years are just human measurements that mean nothing when applied outside of our limited scope of vision.

"And time is tricky. It gives rise to false assumptions. Since we perceive time to always be going forward, never backward, never sideways, always steady and measured, we assume all things in the universe operate similarly. But that's not the case. Both speed and gravity can slow time down. Scientists say they will soon be able to send sub-atomic particles backward in time. And a single atom can actually be in two or more different places at the same time."

Chester stopped talking. "Sorry, I don't want to sound like I'm giving a lecture."

"You're not, I really do find time fascinating because I can't control it. Everything else in my life, I can control. But not time. It's going to happen without or without me," said Phillip, his irritated voice replaced by a voice of genuine interest.

"To me," said Chester, "time is interesting because I think it can solve the biggest mystery in the universe which is, why are we here? I think the clue to solving the puzzle of why are we here is to answer the question of when did we first get here? We know, or think we know, where we are in time right now and we can predict where we will be in time in the future but we need to know what the starting point was."

"What about the Big Bang?" asked Phillip. "Haven't scientists already established the time when that occurred."

"What about the time before the Big Bang?"

"There was nothing before the Big Bang."

"Nothing is still something. It's just the absence of something. So if time exists when there is something it most probably also existed when there was nothing."

"Wow, this is some deep shit," said Phillip. "And all I wanted was for you to explain why I'm always late for work."

Chester wondered if that's how Phillip really felt about time or whether he was just making a joke like he usually did.

"That's a joke, Chester."

"Oh, I get it."

"So Chester, bottom line, do you think time really exists?"

"I have my doubts."

▼

Chester ordered an apple juice from the stewardess. He didn't fly much, but when he did, he always ordered a glass of chilled apple juice. It was so sweet and refreshing. He made a mental note to ask Harriette to get apple juice the next time she went to the store.

He sipped the apple juice to make it last. The plastic cups they gave you on the plane were small and Chester would never be so presumptuous as to ask for a second glass of apple juice. Regardless of how sweet and refreshing it was.

Plastic cup in hand, Chester continued to examine the revelation. He felt he had a handle on the time thing, so he decided to think about his mind, or his consciousness, or whatever one wanted to call it. He knew his physical body didn't play much of a role in understanding the revelation because of a term paper he wrote in college. The headline on his report was, "The Father of Modern Philosophy," and it was all about Rene Descartes, the French philosopher and mathematician from the 1600s who came to the conclusion that, "I think, therefore I am."

In other words, wrote Descartes, if "I" can contemplate my own existence, then somewhere there exists an "I" to do the thinking. So, Chester knew that inside of him was an "I," and that inside thing was actually running the show, not the outside thing.

What impressed Chester the most about Descartes was he was a die hard pessimist. He refused to accept the theories of other philosophers. Chester could relate. He knew if you believed everything you heard or saw or read, particularly what the prevailing thought on a specific topic was, you could be in a for a rude surprise.

Like how philosophers said the Earth was flat. They guaranteed it. And everyone believed them. Eventually everybody realized the philosophers were wrong and the Earth was not flat.

Then the philosophers said the sun revolved around the Earth since our world and the special people on it just had to be the center of the universe. Eventually everybody realized the philosophers were wrong again and that the Earth revolves around the sun. In fact, our sun is just one of many suns floating out there in the dark.

But the know-it-alls kept guaranteeing even more things.

Man was created, not evolved. Wrong.

The Earth is only 6,000 years old. Wrong.

Heavier objects fall faster. Wrong.

The earth's continents are stable and don't move. Wrong.

The universe is static and does not expand or contract. Wrong.

Chester often thought about that list of guaranteed-then-disproved theories from his term paper, and he would add to the list as the years went by.

Atoms are the smallest particulars in existence. Wrong.

Okay, Quarks are the smallest particulars in existence. Still wrong.

Y2K will cause a worldwide crash of computers. Wrong.

It impressed Chester that Descartes' theory, unlike many other theories, had stood the test of time. And it stood the test of time because it was a theory based on doubt. By questioning all those other philosophers, Descartes realized that, "Since I doubt, I think; since I think, I exist."

While Descartes did deduce that the body and the mind were separate things, Chester was disappointed he did not go on to address the most obvious question which was, if the body and the mind are two separate things, what happens to the mind when the body dies?" Everyone knows bodies die. No debating that. But do minds die? Chester would liked to have known Descartes' answer to that.

As Chester thought about Descartes, he thought about something people seldom if ever discussed. When Descartes came to the conclusion that he existed, it was only his existence that he was sure of.

Not anyone else's.

Chester was such a fan of Descartes that Harriette bought him a T-shirt with a drawing of the philosopher on the front with his long hair, flared mustache, pointy beard and ruffled shirt. Chester wore it every weekend when he mowed his lawn. One afternoon while he was cutting the grass a teenager from the neighborhood approached him. Chester, ready for a comment, maybe even a compliment, from the younger generation on his knowing about a thought-provoking philosopher, stopped mowing and nodded at the teenager.

"Nice shirt," said the teen. "What band is he in?"

▼

With time and the mind analyzed, Chester started to think about the third thing in his three-thing sub group: space. Thinking about space he couldn't overlook the irony that he was in a metal tube flying through space, or at least the clouds, at 550 miles per hour, over a planet that was spinning at more than 1,000 miles per hour, in a universe that was expanding at more than 150,000 miles per hour. Were all of those miles per hours going in the same direction?

He was ready to delve deeper into the subject of space when Ned the pilot came on to say they were making their initial descent to the Casper, Wyoming airport. It always confused Chester when the pilot said "initial descent." Was there going to be more than one descent? Wouldn't it be better for Ned to say, "We are making our descent to the airport, but if I mess it up, we will then make a second descent, and we'll keep making descents until I get it right."

Chester prepared for the landing and realized he would have to shelve the space analysis for now. He didn't like leaving a task unfinished. Time and mind had been addressed, but space was left hanging. He made a mental note to finish the space analysis as soon as some more free time became available on his trip.

After the plane landed and Ned the pilot thanked everyone for flying with him, Chester walked to the Avis Car Rental counter at the airport. There was no one in line, but there were some stanchions and ropes showing where the line started and a sign that said *Please Wait*. Chester stood at the front of the nonexistent line of people and waited to be called. There was one rental agent behind the counter, and with just one look at the young man Chester knew there was going to be trouble.

The young man was on his cell phone. He looked up and saw Chester but kept talking on the phone while looking right at Chester. Chester could tell by the young man's body language and the expression on his face that he was on a personal call, not a business call. He held up one finger to Chester, indicating he would just be a minute. But he kept talking and as each second ticked by Chester found himself getting more and more aggravated. Finally the young man finished his call, put the cell phone in his pocket, looked down to shuffle a few papers on the counter, then looked back up and, with a fake smile, said, "Next."

Chester walked up to the counter. The rental agent's name tag said Darren Tucker.

"Do you have a reservation, sir?" asked Darren Tucker.

"Yes I do," answered Chester. He handed over his driver's license and credit card and waited for what he knew was about to come.

"What insurance would you like on this vehicle?" asked Darren.

"I don't need any insurance. I have insurance through my credit card," said Chester, knowing his answer would not stop a lengthy sales pitch from Darren Tucker about the perils of driving without additional insurance. Darren started into that speech and Chester interrupted him twenty seconds into it.

"How much a day is the insurance you are suggesting?" asked Chester.

"It would be $45 dollars a day," answered Darren.

"And what is my cost to rent the car each day?"

"It is $50 a day."

"And that doesn't seem odd to you?"

"What do you mean?"

"That it will cost me as much to insure the car as to rent the car."

"Not really" said Darren, and then he continued his previously interrupted sales pitch.

"No," said Chester twenty seconds into the speech continuation.

"No, what?"

"No, I don't want the insurance."

"But ..."

"No."

Darren looked miffed.

"Okay," he said in the tone you would use for a person you felt was being ridiculous for not taking your advice. Darren turned his back to Chester and worked on the rental agreement paperwork.

Chester did not believe in insurance and warranties and things like that. Just because he was a practical man did not mean he was overly cautious in a nonsensical way. On the surface, insurance and warranties appeared to be things sensible people would want, but to Chester they were just another form of gambling. Whether a person gambled at a casino or gambled on paying extra for a warranty on an item that might never need to be repaired, Chester knew the odds were always in the house's favor.

It bothered him for two reasons that a store would ask him to pay extra for a warranty in case the brand new item he was buying stopped working properly. First, if the store was aware the item had a history of malfunctioning, then why were they selling him an item they knew was faulty. That was cheating. Second, if the store was confident the item was not going to break, then why encourage him to pay extra for a warranty he would never have to use. That was also cheating. When he juggled and organized and categorized and polished numbers for financial reports that his bosses then gave to the IRS, Chester did not turn in those reports with a warning that the numbers might possibly not be correct. Chester stood behind his work, so why couldn't the people who made toaster ovens do the same?

Chester recently bought a television cable for $49 and the sales clerk had asked if he wanted to pay an extra $7 for an extended warranty.

"An extended warranty for a cable?" Chester had asked, incredulous.

"Yes, it's an expensive cable. You want to be protected, don't you?"

"For a cable?" Chester had asked again, still incredulous.

"Yes."

"Why would a cable made of metal and plastic with no moving parts need an extended warranty?"

"Well, you never know. It's better to be safe."

"Do your customers often buy extended warranties for items made out of metal and plastic with no moving parts?"

"All the time."

"That's silly."

Warranties sold by store clerks making a few dollars over minimum wage were proof to Chester that people were inherently greedy. He knew the only reason sales clerks pushed extended warranties on everything from toasters to big screen TVs was because they received a minuscule commission for each warranty sold. What was sad to Chester was that, no matter how small the commission was or how big the cost of the warranty was, the sales clerk would still push the warranty, knowing the buyer was just wasting money. It was more important for the sales clerk to make a few dollars than it was to not gouge a customer by convincing him to spend hundreds of dollars on a warranty. It was the scale of the thing that bothered him.

The rental agent handed Chester a set of keys and told him his car was parked just outside in spot B7.

"Thank you," said Chester, who stayed standing in front of the car rental counter.

"Is there anything else?" asked the agent.

"Yes there is, Darren. Can I ask you a question?"

Darren looked wary, but he said, "Of course."

"Do you get a commission whenever someone pays for the extra insurance?"

Darren appeared taken aback by the question. "Why do you ask that?"

"I'm just curious. It's a simple question."

"Well, I'd prefer to not answer that."

"You don't want to answer it or you're not allowed to?"

Darren looked down, shuffled a few papers, and then looked back up. "Mr. Fortunberry, will there be anything else?"

45

"No, I guess not, Darren," said Chester. He turned and headed for the door to the parking lot.

As Chester reached for the door handle, he heard the agent call his name. When he turned, Darren said, in a not-too-friendly voice, "Mr. Fortunberry your car is due back by 2 pm on Monday. That's 2 pm and not a minute later."

"Thank you, Darren" said Chester. He opened the door and walked out into the rental parking lot.

Where he saw two dark men.

Both of whom were staring at him.

▼

In his mind Chester referred to the men in the Avis car rental parking lot as two dark men because, well, they were dark. Not dark like in the color of their skin, but dark in a foreboding kind of way.

The men were sitting in a shiny black Cadillac about twenty yards from the B7 spot where Chester's rental car awaited him and there was no question they were both staring at Chester as he walked to his rental car. Chester stopped halfway to the rental and looked at the two dark men. They stared right back, unflinching. It gave Chester a chill.

Chester put his suitcase in the trunk of the rental car. He got into the car and, before inserting the key in the ignition, started his process. He pulled a moist towelette packet from his shirt pocket, took the towelette out and used it to wipe the steering wheel, the turn signal, the radio dials, the back of the rear view mirror, the latch to the glove compartment, the lever for the front seat adjustment, the two inside front door handles, and the two door lock knobs. He folded the used towelette neatly and slipped it under the front seat. He felt bad about discarding it that way, but he did not want to put a dirty towelette in his pocket and, unlike his personal car, there was not a small bag on the floor behind his seat in which to place trash. He adjusted the front seat, sliding it closer to the steering wheel to accommodate his small stature, and put on the seat belt. He started the car and turned the air conditioning down to its lowest fan speed. He turned the dial on the radio until he found a soft rock station. He was about to put the car into reverse when someone rapped their knuckles on his window. Chester, his heart suddenly pounding, swung his head to the left, expecting to see one or both of the dark men. Instead, he saw an elderly man wearing a bright yellow Avis work shirt.

Chester rolled down the window. "Yes?"

"Is everything okay?" asked the man in the bright yellow Avis work shirt.

"Yes. Why do you ask?"

"Well, you been sitting in the car forever."

"I haven't just been sitting. I've been setting things up."

"What things?"

"Everything. The mirrors, the radio, you know."

"For five minutes?"

"It hasn't been five minutes."

"Pretty close."

"Well, I've rented the car. I can sit in it or drive it. It's mine for now."

"Can't argue with that."

Chester hit the window button and started the window back up. The elderly man stepped back a foot or so and watched. When the window was all the way up, Chester rolled it back down halfway.

"Can I ask you a question?" said Chester.

"Don't see why not," said the elderly man.

"Do you have to wear that incredibly bright yellow shirt every day?"

"No," said the elderly man, "on the weekends we wear a red shirt."

"Is it bright?"

"Oh yeah."

Chester nodded at the elderly man and cautiously backed up. As he put the car into drive and headed toward the car rental exit, he looked in his rear view mirror at the Cadillac with the two dark men in it. Their car did not move. Chester kept looking in his rear view mirror as he slowly made a right turn out the exit. And as the Cadillac was just about to disappear from his rear view mirror, Chester saw exhaust smoke come out of the back and the car start to roll forward.

Chapter Four

After telling Chester his name, Theodore had stepped down the last two steps of the staircase and crossed the room to the bed in three long strides. He put out his hand and Chester, still sitting on the edge of the bed, reached to shake it. Chester's hand was lost in Theodore's giant hand like a baseball swallowed by a catcher's mitt. Chester winced, waiting for a bone-crushing squeeze, but Theodore just gripped Chester's hand firmly and held it for a few beats, making direct eye contact, before saying, "Chester, it is very nice to meet you."

Theodore reminded Chester of Lucas McCain from the TV show *The Rifleman*. Lucas was one of Chester's childhood heroes. He envied the special relationship the widowed father had with his son Mark, and he admired how tough and reliable Lucas was, dispensing verbal advice or hot lead from his Winchester rifle depending on what the occasion called for. Lucas was a big, strapping man who the adjective raw-boned had seemingly been made for, and at a time when every youngster wanted a father figure who was strong and perfect and attentive, which Chester's real father was not, Chester had Lucas McCain.

While Theodore reminded Chester of Lucas McCain, it was more because of his aura than his appearance. The more Chester looked at Theodore, the more he reminded Chester of someone else, someone famous. He just couldn't place the face right then.

Theodore released Chester's hand. It felt warm. He rubbed it with his other hand and smiled at Theodore.

"Theodore?"

"Yes."

"I'm starving."

"I can remedy that. Just give me a few minutes."

Later, after Chester had polished off the tuna fish sandwich, that incredible sandwich where the bread was lightly toasted with the crust trimmed off and mixed in with the tuna fish were diced up boiled eggs, celery and olives, he tried to ask Theodore a few questions.

"Later," said Theodore. "Why don't you check out your room, grab a shower and take a short nap."

"But I don't have any clothes to change into."

"Yes you do. Everything from your suitcase is in the dresser," said Theodore, nodding at the dresser next to the bookcase.

"Where's my suitcase?"

"I have it upstairs. You don't need it right now."

"Why not?"

"Because you are going to be staying with me for awhile."

"I am?"

"Yes, you are."

Chester looked at his left wrist where his watch usually was. He looked up at Theodore.

"Do you know where my watch is?"

"It's upstairs. And so is your phone. You don't need them right now. I want you to be able to relax and not worry about things, like what time it is."

Chester thought for a second about whether there were any more of his things he should ask about. His eyes flew open wide.

"Theodore, my rental car is upstairs too, right?"

"Your rental car?"

"Yes, the car I rented at the airport. Theodore, please tell me you have it and nothing has happened to it."

Theodore stalled. "Maybe. I'm not sure."

"Oh no, oh no, oh no."

"What's wrong?"

"I didn't buy the extra insurance. I knew it. I hate when I'm penny wise and pound foolish. This is catastrophic."

"Chester, I'm sure the car is upstairs. Let me go check on that for you."

Chester laid back on the bed, his arms crossed over his chest and full belly. He felt his eyelids start to close. He had no watch, there was

49

no clock in the basement, and there were no windows to let in light, so he had to rely on Theodore to tell him what time it was. But his body chemistry told him it was early to mid afternoon.

His body told him because it was at this precise time of the day on weekends when he takes a nap on his living room couch. After making a nice lunch for himself and Harriette—bacon, lettuce and tomato sandwiches on Saturday and egg salad sandwiches on Sunday—he will lay down on the couch, prop his head up with two couch pillows, cover his body with his favorite throw blanket, the soft one with the cactus pattern on it, and tune the television to an old black-and-white movie. His favorites are the *Road to* ... pictures with Bob Hope and Bing Crosby, and all of the Abbot and Costello movies. Chester isn't a fan of today's movies. Too much sex and violence for his taste. If he wants to watch ugliness all he has to do is tune to one of the news channels to see latest graphic images of terrorist bombings, school shootings, and political corruption. No thanks. Chester enjoys movies that make him feel good.

He will start one of those movies, all warm and cozy in his little nest on the couch, with the best intentions of watching the entire movie. But he seldom makes it to the halfway point before falling asleep, his loud snoring competing with the voices from the television. Harriette will never wake him when he starts snoring. She just keeps buzzing around the house like a busy bee doing the things she does on weekends.

▼

Regardless of what the circumstances are, Chester prides himself on always being a good guest. He will act the way he would expect other people to act if they were a guest staying at his house, even though he has never had a guest stay at his house.

He and Harriette travel twice a year, staying at Harriette's parents at their home in Paducah, Kentucky for an extended weekend and staying for another extended weekend at the Postcard Inn on St. Pete Beach in Florida. Harriette enjoys the beach, but Chester doesn't. There is way too much sand for him and he burns no matter how much sunblock he puts on. Still, he always puts on his happy face when Harriette packs up the beach towels and the romance novels she will read in the bright sunshine.

When Chester is a guest at Harriette's parents' house, he tries to be as unobtrusive as possible. He never takes anything out of the refrigerator without asking first, and he eats whatever Harriette's mother cooks, even though salt and pepper and other spices are missing from the food. He uses his bath towel to wipe down the shower stall and the sink after his shower, and he makes the bed every morning while Harriette is getting dressed. He folds up his dirty clothes each night before going to bed and places them in a green trash bag that he puts into his suitcase, which he zips up and stores out of the way in the bedroom closet. He makes one-sided small talk with Harriette's senile father and doesn't complain when they sit and watch reruns of *The Honeymooners* for hours on end.

One night during their annual visit they will offer to take Harriette's parents out for a nice dinner as their thanks for hosting them. But every time the bill comes, Harriette's father will snatch it away with a claw-like hand and pay it himself, despite Chester and Harriette's protests. The old man doesn't have credit cards so Chester will watch as he slowly and agonizingly counts out wrinkled bills to pay the check, always only leaving a five percent tip, no matter how good the service is. That dinner is the one time on the trip when Chester could feel like a person of importance by stepping up and treating his in-laws, but Harriette's father, intentionally Chester thinks, robs him of that chance every single time. He'll give Chester a false smile and say, "Next time, you can pay."

But that next time never comes.

Chester does the same good-guest type things when they stay at the Postcard Inn. He wipes down the shower and the sink, folds up the used towels, and even makes the bed.

"Chester, what in the world are you doing? The maid will make the bed."

"Oh, she has so many rooms to clean. We shouldn't be a burden."

"But she has to change the sheets."

"No, she doesn't. That's just a waste of water," Chester will say and launch into a discourse on the growing global water shortage. "Why Harriette, don't you realize more than one billion people in the world today don't have access to clean, safe drinking water, and every year 3.4 million people die from ...

"Chester, please stop. Let's go to the beach. It's beautiful outside."

Chester will stop talking, grab his suntan lotion, his sunblock cream, a big-brimmed hat, and dark wrap-around sunglasses as big as a motorcycle visor, and follow Harriette out the door. Behind her back he will slip the *Do Not Disturb* sign on the door handle.

At the beach, side by side in the hotel's beach chairs, Harriette will set her romance novel down after the first hour and always say the same thing to Chester.

"Chester, remember when I used to be able to wear a two-piece?"

"Yes, Harriette."

"I used to be an attractive woman."

"You still are, Harriette. You are the most beautiful woman in the world."

"Chester, you're a doll. Now put some more lotion on your toes. You know how they burn."

"Yes, dear."

Chester would never think of taking home the soap bars or shampoo bottles or other toiletry items provided by the hotel. The first time they stayed at the Postcard Inn, as they were packing up to leave, he saw Harriette putting all of those items into her suitcase. Aghast, he told her what she was doing was highly inappropriate.

"But we paid for it, Chester."

"Well, using that line of reasoning, we could also take the bedspread and the pillows and even the television set."

"The television set is bolted down."

"You know what I mean," said Chester, hands on his hips.

"You're right," said Harriette, putting the items back. And when Chester left the room to pay the bill at the front desk, Harriette put every single item back into her suitcase, and stuffed in two of the fluffy white hotel towels for good measure, which Chester found out about later when he saw the items arranged around Harriette's bathroom sink at home.

Now Chester knows that whenever he goes to pay the hotel bill, Harriette will get sticky fingers again, but he considers it a small price to pay to keep her happy. He knows she takes the hotel items every single time, and Harriette knows he knows she takes the hotel items every single time, but they both pretend like neither one of them knows. Because what they both have learned is, it's things like that, pretending that is, that can make for a good marriage.

So being a good guest, Chester did just as Theodore had advised. He walked around the room, looked through the books in the bookcase, selecting one and placing it on the night stand, then looked through the dresser drawers. All of his clothes were there. He laid out a pair of underwear, some pants, a shirt, and a pair of socks. In the small bathroom he found his empty shaving kit, all of his toiletries lined up across the back of the sink. He moved the items around so they were in the order he would have put them in if he had done it in the first place. He took a long hot shower, dressed and then laid down on the bed. He picked up the book he had selected and read a few pages.

And despite knowing he was being held captive in a stranger's basement, Chester easily drifted off to sleep.

▼

"How do you feel now, Chester."

Theodore's voice woke Chester up. Theodore was sitting in a large, comfortable-looking, leather armchair against the wall across from the bed. Chester sat up and swung his legs over the side of the bed so that he was sitting facing Theodore. He didn't know then that the two of them would be in these same positions for many hours over the coming days.

"I feel much better, thank you."

"That's good to hear."

"Theodore?"

"Yes."

"Can I call you Theo?"

"I would prefer you didn't."

"Okay." Chester looked at Theodore, fidgeted on the bed, working up his courage.

"Theodore, where am I?"

"You are a guest in my home."

"No, I meant where am I, like what city am I in?"

"That's not the most important thing right now."

"It is to me."

"Well, I think you're wrong. So let's move on."

"Okay then. So, who are you?"

"I told you, my name is Theodore Sanders."

"No, I mean who are you, like what are you, what do you do?"

"I fix things."

"Like a mechanic or a carpenter?"

"Kind of. But I fix people instead of machines or buildings."

"Oh, that sounds interesting."

"Sometimes it is, sometimes it isn't."

"Well, can you tell me why am I here, right now, in this place?"

"That should be evident. You're a smart man, Chester."

"Apparently not smart enough because I don't know what the

answer is."

"You are here so I can fix you."

"Am I broken?"

"More than you know, Chester."

"I appreciate your hospitality, Theodore, but I'm not sure if I really want to stay here. Would it be okay if I leave?"

"No."

"But I would like to go home."

"Not yet."

"Am I under, like, house arrest or something?"

"Kind of."

"By who?"

"By me."

"And again, you are?"

"The only person you need to worry about right now."

Chester stopped fidgeting. He looked down at the floor. His shoulders slumped.

"Chester, don't be upset. This will all be sorted out soon. Think of this like it's a mini vacation ..."

Chester interrupted him. "You know, I am on vacation! I have the whole week off. And I have eleven more vacation weeks coming."

Theodore nodded, then continued, "... with me here to cater to your every desire. We will have plenty of time to talk and I will be happy to answer all of your questions. But there's no rush. You just arrived here. Okay?"

"I guess."

Chester stared at Theodore, the he-sure-looks-like-someone-famous thought popping up in his head again. He scrunched his eyes, cocked his head to the right and looked intently at Theodore. But his radar just wasn't working. He could not think of who Theodore reminded him of. If he didn't figure it out soon, it would drive him crazy.

Theodore stood up and stretched his arms over his head, leaned left then right, his back making a cracking sound each time. He looked at Chester and said, "So, what would you like for dinner tonight?"

"Do I have a choice?"

"Cranberry-glazed, center-cut pork chops with Rosemary roasted red potatoes and fresh-cut green beans with almond slivers ..."

Chester's eyes lit up.

"... or Parmesan-crusted chicken breast, scalloped potatoes with chives and bacon bits, and honey-glazed carrots."

54

"They both sound wonderful. I can't decide."

"Go with the pork chops tonight. I'll do the chicken tomorrow night."

"That sounds good."

"Theodore?"

"Yes?"

"Would it be possible to get some garlic bread with the pork chops?"

"Of course, Chester."

Ninety minutes later Theodore was back downstairs sitting in the chair. His lap was empty, but in Chester's lap was a tray with two large pork chops, potatoes, green beans and two slices of garlic bread.

"You aren't eating?" asked Chester.

"I already ate. Upstairs."

"I feel bad eating in front of you. It's not very polite."

"Don't worry about it."

"But it's rude."

"No, it's not. Stop being so nice."

Chester cut one of the small red potatoes in half and put it in his mouth, chewing slowly and enjoying the texture and flavor of the crunchy outside skin and the soft potato inside.

"Let me guess," said Chester, "besides the Rosemary, there's virgin olive oil, fresh garlic, and kosher salt."

"Very good, Chester."

Chester speared the other half of the potato and popped it into his mouth.

"Theodore?"

"Yes."

"Are you a nice person?"

"Sometimes."

"But not all the time?"

"No, not all the time."

Chester, startled, looked up from his plate. Before he could say anything, Theodore spoke.

"Chester, I'm curious."

"About what?"

"About whether you have told anybody."

"Told anybody what?"

"You know what. Don't be coy."

Chester cut a piece off one of the pork chops, making sure the piece included a small section of the pork chop fat which would make the bite that much more juicy. He put the bite in his mouth and pulled the fork out making a slight clicking sound, the metal tongs of the fork scraping his front teeth. Chester never heard the sound, but Harriette did, at least when they were first married. After years of mentioning the sound to Chester and telling him it was rather irritating for anybody eating across from him and it was also not good for his teeth, Harriette eventually stopped mentioning the sound, and Chester was sure she no longer heard it.

Chester took another bite of pork chop.

"What's that clicking sound?" asked Theodore.

"Oh, I'm sorry. When I eat, my fork hits my teeth."

"That's rather irritating."

"I know."

"And bad for your teeth."

"I know."

Chester continued eating. Theodore put his hands on his knees and leaned forward.

"Chester," said Theodore, more forcefully, "who else have you told ..."

Chester stopped chewing, but he didn't look up. He waited.

"... about your revelation."

Chester looked up quickly from his half-eaten plate of pork chops, roasted red potatoes, green beans with almond slivers, and garlic bread. "How do you know about my revelation?" he asked, a tremor in his voice.

"I just know. Why else do you think you would be here?"

"I really don't know."

"It's because of your revelation."

"But why?"

"Because we are concerned you will tell other people about it."

"Why would that concern you?"

"Because people could get hurt."

"But why?"

"Chester, stop asking so many questions. Just answer my question. Have you told anybody, anybody at all?"

"No."

"Not Harriette?"

"No," said Chester, going from being just somewhat frightened to

56

being extremely frightened as he realized Theodore knew his wife's name.

"Not anybody at your work?"

"No."

"Not anybody on your recent trip."

"No."

"That's good, Chester. That's very good. We might be able to fix this situation after all. Finish your dinner. I'll be back in a little while."

▼

Chester picked at his food, his appetite suddenly gone. But he didn't want to hurt Theodore's feelings after he had cooked such a glorious meal, so he continued to eat. After a few bites he ate faster, the tastiness of the meal overriding his concern about Theodore's questions. Chester took his final bite, planned perfectly to contain the last bit of pork chop, the last bit of roasted red potato, and the last two green beans with one almond sliver.

The basement door opened and Theodore came down the stairs with two glasses of red wine. He handed Chester a glass, and with his free hand took the dinner tray from Chester's lap, setting it on the night stand. He sat in the chair across from Chester and took a sip of wine. Chester did the same, even though he hardly ever drank, except on special occasions, and this certainly felt like a special occasion. Theodore set his glass of wine on the floor next to his chair, leaned back, and took an exaggerated deep breath to emphasize the seriousness of his coming question.

"Chester, tell me in your own words what your revelation is."

"Well," said Chester, "it's simple. I exist and you don't."

"Are you sure?"

"Positive. Actually, I said that wrong. I exist and you also exist, but only in my mind."

Chester thought for a moment and then said, "What I am trying to say is I am real, and you are not real."

"How can you say that?"

"I just know it."

"Do you have any proof you are right?"

"No. Do you have any proof I am wrong?"

"I'm sitting right here. I just cooked you dinner."

"Yes, and the pork chops were exquisite. Thank you very much. But that does not mean you are real."

"What about other people, your family, your friends?"

"They are not real."

"What about Harriette?"

Chester looked at Theodore, concern on his face. "I meant to ask you this before, Theodore. How do you know about Harriette?"

"I know everything about you, Chester."

"Everything?"

"Pretty much. Now, what about Harriette? Is she real?"

Chester didn't answer right away. His lower lip began to tremble.

"No, Harriette is not real. And that's the hardest part for me to accept. I can live without anyone else being real. But Harriette not being real means I am truly alone."

Theodore scooted his chair a few inches closer to Chester.

"What about things that aren't people?" asked Theodore.

"Like what?"

"Like the bed you are sitting on, like the pork chops you just ate, like this basement."

"Not real."

"The sun, the moon, the universe?"

"Not real."

"So nothing is real?"

"Just me."

Theodore paused to let what had been said sink in for both of them. He took another sip of his wine, then crossed his arms and his legs. Chester knew from his body language Theodore had closed up tighter than a clam. Theodore pulled out a pack of cigarettes and lit one. He took a deep drag and blew out a plume of smoke, some of which drifted over to Chester. Chester made a sour face and used his hand to wave away the smoke.

"Phew," said Chester.

"Oh, I'm sorry."

"That's rather irritating."

"I know."

"And bad for your health."

"I know."

Chester smiled at Theodore, an I-gotcha-there smile.

Theodore studied Chester's face for a moment and then smiled back. "Chester, there's more to you than meets the eye."

"Is that a good thing?"

"Maybe, maybe not."

"Are you going to put that out?" asked Chester, looking around to see if there was an ashtray in the basement.

Theodore, without breaking eye contact with Chester, pinched the red coal at the tip of the cigarette between his thumb and forefinger until it went out and then placed the broken cigarette into his pants pocket.

"Ouch," said Chester. "Did that hurt?"

"Yes."

"So, why did you do it?

"For expediency."

Chester thought for a moment, then said, "I like that word."

"There's a reason I used it. Let's move this along. When did you have this revelation?"

"I'm not sure. It might have been a few days ago, it might have been a week ago. I know it was fairly recently."

"Did the revelation come to you because of something you saw?"

"No."

"Something you heard?"

"No."

"Something you read?"

"No."

"Then how?"

"It just happened. I was in the bathroom ..."

"The bathroom?"

"Yes."

"What were you doing in the bathroom?"

"That's a silly question. What do you do in the bathroom?"

"You're right. Sorry. So you were in the bathroom ..."

"And it just came to me."

"What came to you? Be specific, please."

"The realization that I was the only real living person, or real anything for that matter, on the planet."

"And that was a revelation to you?"

"Yes, why? What would you call it?"

Theodore ignored the question. "Then what happened?"

"I got the first letter."

"First letter? How many were there?" asked Theodore, worry in his voice.

"Two."

Theodore looked surprised, but Chester just yawned and rubbed his eyes with his balled up fists. The big dinner, the wine and all the questions had tired him.

"Theodore, would you be terribly upset if we talked about this more in the morning? I am very sleepy."

Theodore nodded and stood up quickly. "That's a good idea. Why don't you get a good night's sleep and we'll talk about this tomorrow. What would you like for breakfast?"

"Can we have pancakes?"

"Certainly."

"With blueberries and whipped cream on top."

"Consider it done."

"Not blueberries on top of the pancakes. Blueberries inside the pancakes."

"No problem."

Theodore started up the basement steps. He turned when he heard Chester clear his throat.

"Theodore?"

"Yes, Chester."

"Earlier you said, 'We are concerned.' Who exactly is 'we'?"

"That's not important right now."

"I don't want to be rude, Theodore, but if you aren't going to answer my questions, then I don't see why I should have to answer any more of yours."

"Chester, you are in no position to dictate terms."

Chester stared at Theodore for a good ten seconds, studying every inch of his face until he saw something, something that told him Theodore might be bluffing. And it gave him confidence, the first confidence he had since waking up in the basement.

"On the contrary," said Chester, "I think I am in a position to dictate terms. At least some of them."

Theodore sighed. "Okay, okay. 'We' are some people, some very important people."

"Do I know them?"

"No."

"Why do they care about me?"

"Because it's their job."

"And what about you?"

"Let's just say I work for them."

"In what capacity?'

60

"Every capacity."

"Are these people powerful?

"The most powerful."

"What are their names?"

"They don't have names."

Chester looked confused. Even anxious.

"Theodore?'"

"Yes, Chester."

"Are these people God?"

"Perhaps."

Chapter Five

A few years ago, Chester had gone with his boss, Mr. Dundee, to New York City for a week to help him audit the financial books of a steel-piston-manufacturing company that their ball-bearing-manufacturing company was considering acquiring. For someone who had grown up in a little town and now lived in a small city, New York was a shock to Chester. There were so many people and so many cars and so many buildings and so many noises. He felt like a June bug dropped into the middle of a teeming fire ant mound. There were ants everywhere, going in every direction, constantly moving, always in a hurry, mowing down everything in their path.

Mr. Dundee stayed at the Ritz-Carlton while the company put Chester up at a budget hotel called the Happy Manor a half mile away. Each day Chester walked nine blocks from the Happy Manor to the Ritz-Carlton where he would meet Mr. Dundee in the hotel restaurant for a late breakfast. Mr. Dundee was not an early riser. He never got to the office before 10 am and when they were in New York he was explicit in his instructions to Chester to not show up for breakfast until 10 am. Chester didn't mind the walk, although he was used to eating much earlier, so by the time 10 am rolled around he was famished. It was worth the wait, though, because the food at the Ritz-Carlton restaurant was incredible and Chester took the opportunity to sample all of their offerings, free of course, courtesy of Mr. Dundee's expense account. That's where he had his first omelette with smoked salmon, cream cheese, red onion and capers. He told Harriette how scrumptious that omelette was every time they ate breakfast over the next month.

"Salmon and eggs together, who would have ever thought of that combination?" Chester said. "I know it sounds horrible, but Harriette, I have to tell you, it was delicious."

Harriette just nodded each time Chester said it. She knew eventually he would stop mentioning the salmon and eggs every time they had breakfast.

Mr. Dundee always ordered the same thing for his breakfast, a half grapefruit, wheat toast with no butter, and two Belvedere Bloody Mary cocktails with blue cheese stuffed olives.

"Got to keep my girly figure," Mr. Dundee would say to Chester each morning after placing his order, and then he would pat his stomach. Mr. Dundee was quite fit, but Chester was sure it wasn't so much because of dieting but more so because he spent more of his office hours on the golf course than in the office.

After breakfast they would take a cab to the steel-piston-manufacturing company, even though the office was just four blocks away, and meet with the company's accountants to audit their books. At precisely 12:30 pm each day, a delivery man would arrive with a huge take-out order from a famous New York deli. The secretary for the accountants, whose name was Juanita and who had a large strawberry-colored birthmark covering most of her left cheek, would open the deli bags and set out on the boardroom table an incredible spread of corned beef, pastrami, beef tongue, chopped liver and chicken salad sandwiches with condiments, fat crunchy kosher pickles, and containers of potato salad, macaroni salad and coleslaw.

And as Juanita placed the last item on the boardroom table, it would happen.

Just like it did every single day.

That's when Mr. Dundee, trying to score points by impressing the steel-piston-manufacturing company accountants with what a focused hard worker he was, would say, "Chester and I already ate. You guys dig in. We'll just keep working."

Even though he had eaten just a few hours earlier, Chester would always be hungry again when the deli order arrived. He wanted so badly to grab one of those hot pastrami sandwiches with melted swiss cheese on toasted rye and lather it up with spicy brown deli mustard, but he knew Mr. Dundee would not approve. Instead he worked away, shoulder to shoulder with Mr. Dundee, smelling vodka and blue cheese on his breath every time he turned to speak to Chester. He would try to not watch the accountants wolfing down those gigantic sandwiches, but there were six of them seated around the boardroom table so it was hard to not catch glimpses of sandwiches disappearing into mouths. When one of the accountants would reach out and grab a napkin to wipe a glob of brown mustard or creamy mayonnaise from the corner of their mouth, Chester would just lower his head and sigh.

The worst part was when the accountants finished eating their sandwiches, because that's when Juanita would come back into the boardroom with the last deli take-out bag, and ask, "Who wants cheesecake?"

The accountants would then take their time as they chose between an array of different cheesecakes, from strawberry cheesecake to chocolate chip cheesecake to peanut butter cheesecake, and Chester would start to salivate like Pavlov's dog.

"Chester, would you like a slice?" Juanita would ask every day, and Chester would look at Mr. Dundee who would shake his head. So, Chester would say each day, "No. Thank you Juanita. I'm still full from breakfast."

Chester could tell by the way Juanita looked at him she knew he was not full at all and that he would love a slice of cheesecake. Which is why she kept trying to give him a slice. Chester could not remember the names, or even the faces, of the steel-piston-manufacturing company's six accountants, but he still remembered Juanita. The whole week they were in the boardroom, Juanita had fluttered around like a butterfly, getting coffee, making copies, commenting on the weather, always with a big smile on her face. In a room full of somber pencil-pushers, she was a ray of sunshine. It made a big impression on Chester that a person who had an imperfection, the large strawberry-colored birthmark, would not let that imperfection affect her life, even though she knew every person she met saw it and judged her because of it.

To those people she would always be the lady with the birthmark.

To Chester she was the lady with the big smile.

At about 3 pm each day, Mr. Dundee would stand up, tell the accountants everything was proceeding quite nicely, and say he had to leave for an important business meeting.

"Chester, you've got this, right?" he would say.

"Yes, Mr. Dundee," Chester would answer, and he would stay in the boardroom working with the accountants for another three hours until the office closed at 6 pm.

Chester was on his own after that. He had no idea what Mr. Dundee did from 3 pm until 10 am the next day. Chester would walk back to the Happy Manor which was now a half mile away. He didn't want to waste the small stipend of a per diem he had by taking a taxi. A penny saved and all that.

He knew the city was full of incredible restaurants and theaters and museums and tall buildings he should visit, but the city intimidated him, so he would have dinner at restaurants that were on the same block as the Happy Manor. He didn't want to venture any farther than that. He had Italian one night and Greek one night and Argentinian one night. He even tried the Ethiopian restaurant on the corner one night, but he couldn't say he would ever recommend that kind of food, where you used your fingers to roll up balls of meat and vegetables. Not because of the using your fingers to eat thing, but more because the food just didn't taste very good. He was impressed, though, that on one square block in New York City there was a broader spectrum of international restaurants than there were in the entire city where he lived.

On Chester's walks on the streets of New York City, whether short ones to find a restaurant or long ones to Mr. Dundee's hotel, the thing that impacted him the most was not the hustle and bustle of what was the most vibrant city on the planet.

It was the homeless people.

Just a few blocks from the Happy Manor, on the first day he walked from his hotel to the Ritz-Carlton, Chester saw a large bundle of rags on the sidewalk wedged against the granite wall of an office building. The office building was majestic and beautiful in its architecture. And there were handsome businessmen in suits and attractive businesswomen in dresses walking on the sidewalk. And there were expensive cars parked along the street. And the sun was shining warm and bright. All of that pretty perfection was right there in front of Chester, but glaringly out of place in that pleasant picture was a pile of soiled rags, blackish gray like the sidewalk. Chester stopped and stared at the pile of rags and he wondered why the people who owned the majestic buildings and the well-dressed people walking on the street and the people who owned the fancy cars would allow a pile of dirty rags to be there in the middle of their perfect world.

As Chester stared at the rags they became like one of those trick pictures that appear to be nothing but squiggly lines, although the longer you look at the picture and focus, you eventually see something else in the picture like a sailing ship or a tiger in the jungle. That's what happened as Chester stared at the pile of rags. Slowly, what he thought was a rag at the top of the pile turned into a face and it was the face of a man and his face was the same color and rough texture as the rags that were covering him.

"Of my goodness, that's a person," thought Chester.

He pointed at the pile of rags and said "excuse me, excuse me" to the well-dressed people walking past him but nobody stopped. Nobody looked at the pile of rags and nobody looked at Chester. They walked around him. The beautiful people walked right around him.

Chester thought the man might be dead and if he was, what should he do? The man's eyes were closed so Chester leaned down and looked closer at his face. He still looked dead. So Chester leaned down farther. When his face was just a few inches from the man's face, two things happened. First, Chester saw that the man's mouth was open and the collar on his shirt was fluttering from his exhaled breath. Second, the man's exhaled breath hit Chester's nose and he gagged. It was the most foul smell he had ever smelled.

Chester stepped back, thinking that while the man might not be dead, he was certainly in need of help. Hoping to find a policeman, Chester started walking briskly down the block. He didn't find a policeman, but he did find another pile of what looked like rags on the sidewalk against the side of another majestic and beautiful building. When he examined that pile of rags more closely he saw it was a woman, asleep in multiple layers of tattered and soiled clothing. He kept walking and from the Happy Manor to the Ritz-Carlton he passed no less than five piles of rags that were real people, both men and women, sleeping in clothes that looked like discarded rags.

"Oh my," said Chester to himself, over and over.

He went into the dining room at the Ritz-Carlton where Mr. Dundee already had a table.

"Chester, you don't look well. Are you okay?" asked Mr. Dundee.

"What?" said Chester.

"I said you don't look well. Order some breakfast. That'll make you feel better."

"Okay," said Chester, barely focusing on what Mr. Dundee had said. He looked at the menu and ordered eggs and bacon, and when it came, he sat in the opulent dining room and ate a $40 plate of eggs and bacon off of fine china with a sterling silver fork and knife and washed it down with a $12 bottle of carbonated water, thinking the whole time about those five piles of rags just outside the ornate, floor-to-ceiling, lead glass windows of the Ritz-Carlton. For one of the first times, possibly the very first time ever, Chester did not finish his meal. One over-easy egg and one strip of bacon were still on his plate when he put down the sterling silver fork. He had no appetite.

"Not hungry?" asked Mr. Dundee, draining his second Bloody Mary.

"No," said Chester.

He told Mr. Dundee about the homeless people.

"They're everywhere," said Mr. Dundee. "Welcome to New York."

Chester had nodded at Mr. Dundee's observation that New York was full of homeless people, although he didn't think it was an adequate answer. His comment had been too short and dismissive.

Seeing people in such dire straits that they were reduced to sleeping on the sidewalk in rags bothered Chester. But what bothered him even more was seeing other people walking by and ignoring them.

Chester was sure the beautiful people no longer even saw the people in rags. They were there, but they weren't. Like parallel universes. The homeless person laying in his own excrement and the businessman in his pin-striped suit standing five feet away were in the same space but the five feet that separated them was wider than the space between the sun and the moon.

That day in New York City was not the first time Chester had thought about space and position and distance and how where a thing was could be very important and how where a thing wasn't could be even more important. The homeless man in a crumpled heap on the sidewalk and the businessman waiting to cross the street both took up the same amount of space. They breathed the same air and felt the rays of the same sun and heard the same car horns honking, but the space the homeless man occupied was nowhere near as wonderful as the space the businessman occupied. The homeless man could only dream about the businessman's space, his fancy suit, the money in his wallet, his high-paying job, his luxury apartment and the loving family that came with that space. That marvelous space was right there, just a few feet away. He could see it and even touch it. But he couldn't be in it.

Chester thought the same thing whenever he walked by a bank. On the other side of the bank wall was a safe full of money. If Chester had that money, he would be rich. The money in that safe could change his whole life. That money was in a space and Chester was in a space and all that separated those two spaces was a concrete wall. It was right there. He could almost touch it. But it was not in Chester's space. Just like the homeless man was not in the businessman's space.

And the distance between spaces did not matter. A centimeter could be as great a distance as a million miles. Chester could look up at the moon and see it, but he could not reach up and grab it. Too much distance.

When Chester thought about space and position and distance, he always ended up thinking about the consciousness thing inside of him. He knew it was not around just to be around. If it didn't have a purpose, a job to do, then it wouldn't exist. His knew his consciousness was a workaholic, constantly moving like a shark that dies if it stops swimming. It monitored everything from a fire engine siren in the distance to an ache in his big toe to the flashing cursor on his computer screen. It's job was to observe things and let him know about them. In addition to being conscious of physical things, his consciousness was also aware of his own consciousness, so it was self-conscious. It allowed Chester to know everything in his consciousness. He could know all sides of it, inside and out, which is what made him a unique being, a being that exists for itself.

He knew his consciousness was not physical since his thoughts had no form or substance. He couldn't take them out of his body and look at them or touch them. And nobody else could see or touch them. Those thoughts, or his consciousness or his soul or whatever you wanted to call it, were his and his alone.

That's the part that confounded him.

They were only in his space. Never anywhere else. Not on the moon and not in a glass of water a centimeter from his lips. How was that possible? How could something that was not physical be constrained by something that was physical, his body? At Chester's ball-bearing-manufacturing company there was a young secretary who was flighty and easily distracted. Other staffers joked you could keep the young secretary's attention until she saw something shiny, and then she would wander off from the group to follow that shininess. Why wasn't a person's mind like that?

It was even more confusing because Chester knew everything physical, regardless of the space it occupies or its position or its distance from other things, is still connected. There really are no individual things or individual spaces since everything that is physical is bumping up against every other thing that is physical. Two people standing ten feet apart may think they are separated by nothingness, but they would be wrong. The molecules of air in the space between them are touching the skin of both of them. It's a chain of connectivity.

Chester watched a golfer on television once make an incredibly long put, only to have the ball stop at the edge of the cup. The golfer stood over the golf ball so his body blocked the sun's rays from hitting the ball. In a few seconds the blades of grass under the ball softened from being shaded and the ball dropped into the cup. The golfer knew everything physical is connected, the sun to his body to the shade to the blades of grass to the ball.

So it had to be one of two things.

If his consciousness was physical, say made up of spinning atoms and such, then it should be able to flow out of his body and into other physical things just like heat emanated from his body. It should be able to flow into Harriette's body and she should be able to read Chester's mind and know is every thought. But if his consciousness was not physical, then how could the physical layer of molecules making up his skin imprison something non-physical inside him.

Chester knew scientists believe the brain creates the mind, so when the brain dies, the mind also dies. That perplexed Chester. He didn't understand how something physical, his brain, could create something nonphysical, his mind. It was like saying his kidney created his dreams.

Scientists even had a name for when the mind dies and no longer has consciousness. They called it eternal oblivion, as in gone forever and ever. But it was those same scientists who just sixty years ago didn't know particles smaller than electrons existed, so how could they be so sure that something is gone forever and ever?

And where were those minds, or consciousnesses, or souls, before they had bodies to be trapped inside? What space did they occupy before they occupied the space of a particular person's body? They had to exist somewhere.

Occasionally when Chester went into one of his Earth-To-Chester states, he would daydream that when a baby was born, which is a physical thing, at that very moment, a soul, which is not a physical thing, would pop into the baby's body. He knew it was a crazy idea, but he imagined all the souls not yet popped into bodies sitting around in a waiting room in the sky, reading magazines, and waiting to be called up for duty. He imagined them talking to each other about what type of body they wanted to pop into, worried they might end up in a criminal's body or an unattractive person's body. The souls would just sit around until someone, maybe God or maybe the Soul Waiting Room nurse, opened the door, looked down at a clipboard and barked, "Jimmy, you're up next. Let's go!"

And the rest of the souls would watch Jimmy shoot down to earth and into the body of the very next person born on the planet, and they would comment on how well they thought that soul had done. "Hey, looks like Jimmy got somebody named Charles Manson." When Chester had this daydream he always laughed inside at the Manson part.

Chester would finish his daydream wondering what the souls in the waiting room had said when they saw a soul shoot down and pop into Chester Fortunberry's body.

Had they said nice things or mean things then?

And what would they say now?

▼

Toward the end of their first conversation about Chester's revelation, Theodore had asked Chester an obvious question, which was, "If I am only here because you think I am here, then what happens to me and everyone else when you die? Do we all just disappear? Are you saying nothing existed until the moment you were born? Wouldn't that mean the past did not come into existence until you were born? Dinosaurs, knights in shining armor, the Lindbergh kidnapping, Hiroshima? Did all of that just happen retroactively, once you came on the scene? If you weren't alive in that past, how would you know what to put in it?'"

As Theodore expanded his question on the subject, it became clear to Chester what the answer was, and it tied in to the whole body-mind thing.

"Theodore, here's what you are missing. I have always existed. I existed long before I occupied this physical body and I will exist long after I leave this physical body. So I may not have been alive as a physical person in the past you refer to, that past with Tyrannosaurus rex and kidnapped babies, but I still existed in that past so I knew what to put into it."

Chester was impressed by Theodore's question. "That is an interesting point you raise, addressing the past and not the future. I tip my hat to you. Usually when people talk about death, all they want to know is what happens to them after they die, if there is a heaven or some type of life after death. Nobody asks where their consciousness, or soul, was before they were born. Wouldn't knowing where your soul was before it was in your body help answer the question of where your soul will be after your body is gone?"

Chester then told Theodore his daydream about the Soul Waiting Room. When he finished, Theodore said, "Charles Manson. Now that's funny."

Chester beamed. He liked that Theodore liked a story he had told.

"Do you think that's how it really works?" asked Theodore.

"Probably not."

"Why?"

"Other people don't have souls."

"Just you, right?"

"Just me, sorry."

"Okay, back to my initial question. What happens to us when you die?"

"You disappear."

"Everybody disappears?"

"Everybody."

For a change, Theodore looked startled. "So, you are saying that when you die, your world dies and I no longer exist?"

"Yes, you no longer exist in my world," said Chester.

"But," said Theodore, "your father died and you still exist after he is gone. Doesn't that disprove your theory?"

"No. Because my father died in my world."

"He didn't die in his world?"

"That I don't know. Maybe he died in that world also. All I know is when he died, he died in my world, so after he was gone, I was still here. There is only one real person. Me. And only one real world. Mine. And when I die, everything dies. It's that simple."

"You think that's simple?"

"For me it is."

Theodore shook his head and sighed. He looked a bit exasperated.

"Chester, how do you know there isn't someone else out there who, just like you, is the only real person in a world they have created?"

"Define out there."

"In another universe. Or another dimension. Wherever," said Theodore, exasperated.

"Well, that person wouldn't be here in my world."

"Of course not. They would be in the world they created."

"A different world?"

"Yes."

"Well, I guess that's possible."

"And what if you were an unreal person in their world?"

"That's not possible."

"Why not? It's their world."

Chester started to answer, then stopped. He thought about it and realized what Theodore was saying was possible.

"That would be very weird," said Chester.

"Tell me about it," said Theodore.

On their last day in the boardroom in New York, Mr. Dundee stayed until 6 pm so he could thank the steel-piston-manufacturing company accountants and their boss who dropped by at the end of the day. Hands were shaken all around.

As Chester and Mr. Dundee were leaving, Juanita said, "Wait Chester, you forgot your bag."

Mr. Dundee kept walking toward the elevator, but Chester stopped.

"What bag?" he asked, surprised.

"This bag," said Juanita, handing him a large brown paper bag.

"But I don't think ..."

"Yes, this is your bag. Just take it. And Chester ..."

"Yes?"

"It was a pleasure meeting you."

"It was very nice to meet you too, Juanita."

When Chester got back to his room at the Happy Manor, he opened the bag Juanita had given him. Inside were three packages wrapped in white butcher paper.

In the first package was a pastrami and swiss sandwich on rye bread.

In the second package were four fat crunchy kosher pickles.

And in the third package was a slice of blueberry cheesecake.

The accounting books of the steel-piston-manufacturing company all balanced out and it looked like Chester's company was going to make the purchase. But then word came down that the acquisition was not going to happen. The official reason given was the steel-piston-manufacturing company's purchase price was too high. Chester knew that wasn't the reason at all. While everyone had been waiting for the sale to be finalized, a young graphics designer at the steel-piston-manufacturing company, as a joke, had designed a new company logo that incorporated two ball bearings from the ball bearing company's logo with the standing-straight-up steel piston from the steel piston company's logo. He showed it to one person who promised not to show it to anyone else, but of course they did and before long everyone at both companies had seen the new logo.

And everyone could tell exactly what the new logo looked like.

So the sale was called off.

And the young graphics designer was fired.

In his room that last night at the Happy Manor, Chester slowly and lovingly opened the butcher paper on each of the three packages. He spread the contents out on the little table in his room and looked for a long time at the moist pastrami sandwich with swiss cheese that had melted a little bit from the afternoon heat and at the pickles that were so fat and glistening and at the cheesecake covered in a thick sauce with whole blueberries in it. He picked up one of the pickles and smelled the tangy aroma of garlic and vinegar brine. But he just looked at the pickle and did not bite into it. He put the pickle down and lifted up one half of the pastrami and swiss cheese sandwich, breathing in the wonderful aroma of the spiced beef and rich cheese. But he just looked at the sandwich and did not bite into it. He put the sandwich down and used the tip of his finger to touch a few of the crust crumbs that had fallen off the slice of cheesecake and put them into his mouth. But he just looked at the rest of the pie and did not bite into it. He looked again at all three items, and then he carefully re-wrapped the pickles and sandwich and the cheesecake in the butcher paper and put them back into the brown paper bag.

He left his hotel room and walked outside into the night, the bag in his left hand.

He walked for two blocks until he came upon a pile of rags.

He set the bag down next to the pile of rags.

And then he walked back to his hotel room.

The next morning Chester and Mr. Dundee had coffee at the airport while waiting for their departure flight. Actually, Chester had one cup of coffee while Mr. Dundee had two Bloody Mary's. Chester was quiet, lost in thought.

"Are you still thinking about those homeless people?" asked Mr. Dundee.

"It's hard not to. I can't believe no one helps them."

"Chester, I have a friend who never fails to give money to any homeless person who comes up to him on the street. And he is very generous. He never gives less than five dollars, sometimes he even gives ten or twenty dollars."

"That's admirable. He must be a good person."

"You think so?"

"Yes. He is very kind to help those less fortunate than him."

"Do you know what my friend says to me each time he gives away that money?"

"No, what?"

"He says he has just gone up one more rung on the ladder to heaven."

"I don't get it."

"He thinks he is buying his way into heaven. He doesn't give the money to help the homeless person. He gives the money to help himself."

"Oh," said Chester.

"Chester, it's the way of the world. It's always going to be about me first and everyone else second. It's all about, I got mine. Listen, if every single person on this planet lived in the same nice house, with unlimited food in the refrigerator, with two new cars in the garage, with closets full of nice clothes, with a fat bank account, and with college funds for their children, would it be a perfect world? Would we all live in peace and harmony and posterity?"

"Yes, Mr. Dundee. That would be wonderful."

"Well Chester, that would be wonderful until."

"Until what?"

"Until some of those people wanted a bigger house."

Chapter Six

After Chester left the Avis car rental lot he pulled into the first convenience store he saw. He parked the car, took the envelope with the cream-colored letter from Ed and Edna out of his pocket, looked at the return address and keyed it into the rental car's navigation system. It indicated he was just thirteen miles from the Pringle's house. He would have done the navigation-input thing at the Avis car lot but he had felt under pressure, sure that Darren Tucker was watching him. And the thought of entering in the Pringle's address information while he was driving, an unsafe thing to do, never even entered Chester's mind.

Chester started the car and put it into reverse. He was about to check the rear-view mirror when something behind the large plate glass window of the convenience store caught his eye.

It was an Icee machine.

"No way," said Chester to himself. He turned the car off and hurried into the store.

"Is that an Icee machine?" he asked the young girl behind the counter in a loud and excited voice.

They both looked at the Icee machine, the one with the word *Icee* in huge red, white and blue letters on it.

"What gave it away?" asked the girl.

"Does it have the Coke flavor?"

"Yes."

Chester hurried over to the machine and filled the largest cup they had with the frozen drink, put the plastic dome-shaped top on it, and stabbed a long straw through the hole in the top. He took a deep slurp and winced as the ice-cold liquid gave him a momentary brain freeze. He picked a bag of sour cream potato chips from a nearby rack and carried the chips and the Icee to the front counter, taking another big slurp from the drink before setting it on the counter.

"So, where are you from?" asked the girl as she rang up the sale.

"Not here."

"Shocker."

The girl's blonde hair was streaked with jet blue strands, but was buzzed to her scalp on both sides of her head. Chester counted the rings that pierced her head and face. Three in her left ear, two in her right ear, two in her left eyebrow, one in her right nostril, and two through her lip, one on each side.

"That's a lot of rings," said Chester, quickly counting all the piercings a second time and then a third time.

"I used to have a lot more," said the girl. As she talked, Chester saw her tongue was also pierced.

"Do they hurt?"

"Not any more."

The girl rang up Chester's two items. As she did, Chester said, "The store near my house where I grew up had Icees. I used to buy a large Coke Icee every time I got my allowance. I haven't seen an Icee machine in over thirty years. I've seen Slurpees and Squishees and Slush Puppies, but they're not Icees. Icees are the best."

"You don't say."

"Yes, I do say," said Chester, firmly but friendly.

"No, that's just an expression. I believe you."

"Oh."

The girl handed Chester his change. "Well, you're the first person to buy an Icee here. We just got the machine today. Seemed to show up out of the blue."

"How fortuitous for me."

"How what?"

"Fortuitous."

"What does that mean?"

"Lucky."

"Why didn't you just say lucky?"

"Fortuitous sounds better."

"I'm gonna remember that," said the girl. "Kind of a red letter day for you, then?"

"Oh yes indeed," said Chester pocketing his change and taking another swig of the Icee. "Have a great day."

Chester started to leave, then stopped and turned.

"You said red letter day. What does that mean?"

"I don't know. It's something my mother used to say. Don't you know?"

"Why would I know?"

The young girl smiled. "Cause you're old, like my mom."

Chester thought for a moment, took another swig of his Icee. "Yes, I am old. But no, I don't know what red letter day refers to. I could guess, but it would only be a guess."

"I like it better not knowing," said the girl.

"Me too," said Chester.

In the car Chester followed the arrow on the car's navigation system as he drove to the Pringle's house. He opened the bag of chips. He ate several of the tangy chips and washed them down with the Icee. He was in his own private heaven. On the way to a stranger's house to solve a mystery while enjoying a snack and a long missed beverage.

"Fortuitous me," said Chester. "Fortuitous me."

When Chester awoke in Theodore's basement that first day, before he actually met Theodore, before he told Theodore he was starving, the first thing he did was count the ceiling tiles.

He didn't wonder where he was. That could wait.

He didn't wonder how he had gotten there. That could wait.

He didn't wonder if he was in danger. That too could wait.

The first thing he had to do was count the ceiling tiles.

He had to. No choice. Because, well, they were there.

And there were more than five of them.

Chester has always been a counter.

When Chester was a child and first started counting things, no one knew to call it obsessive-compulsive disorder. His mother just called it Chester being a pain in the ass. It seemed natural to Chester to count things he saw that were similar to each other if there were five or more of them. Five was the magic number. Four marbles on the floor or four roses on a bush only got a cursory glance. But if there were five cat's eyes marbles on the floor or five pink moss roses on a bush, Chester would count them out loud, one marble, two marbles, three marbles, four marbles, five marbles.

Since Chester saw similar things every day that came in groups of five or more, it was understandable why Chester's mother, not to mention his father and his sister and his classmates and any other person within earshot, was less than enchanted with his counting out loud. It didn't take too many years of his mother telling him he was being a pain in the ass and his sister covering her ears with her hands and his classmates telling him to shut the hell up before Chester started counting things he saw in his head and not out loud.

Even then his mother would catch him.

"You're doing it again," she'd yell if she saw Chester focusing on a group of similar things, five or more, for too long. "Quit being such a pain in the ass!"

Chester couldn't win. His mother would yell at him if he counted out loud and she would yell at him if he counted to himself.

By the time Chester was a teenager he had perfected the art of pretending to pay attention to something else, a single thing like a conversation or a television show, while still counting in his head multiple things he could see out of the corner of his eye. Every now and then, but not as often as in the past, Chester's mother would catch him doing the inside-his-head counting thing. Chester learned you can fool all the people all of the time, but you can only fool your mother some of the time.

The counting thing never bothered Chester. It was just something he did as part of his daily life. Some people looked at clouds a lot, some people brushed their hair a lot, and some people tapped their feet a lot. Chester never asked those people why they always looked at clouds or repeatedly brushed their hair or continually tapped their feet.

Chester knew there were eighteen stairs from the bottom floor of his house to the second floor of his house, and there were thirteen stoplights on the road he drove from his house to his office, and there were thirty-four ceramic tiles across the wall in the bathroom stall he used in the office restroom. Always the second stall from the end. He knew exactly how many stairs were in his house and exactly how many stoplights there were on his drive to work and exactly how many ceramic tiles there were in the office restroom, but that didn't mean he still did not count them every time he saw them. Chester got as much enjoyment, or maybe it was peace of mind, out of counting things he had counted before as he got from counting new things. The only difference was, if it was a new group of things, he would count things in that group three times. Things he had counted before he only counted once when he saw them again.

Made sense to him.

▼

There were sixty-one tiles in the basement ceiling. And a domed light. The reason it was an odd number of ceiling tiles was because where one of the ceiling tiles should have been there was a metal grate instead.

After counting the sixty-one ceiling tiles three times, Chester could then concentrate on his situation. He was not scared or confused, because he knew it was just part of his journey. When he had made the decision to fly to Casper, Wyoming, while he was on hold with the airline company, he realized that for the very first time in his life he was about to do something unplanned, unstructured and unscripted. It was unfamiliar territory for Chester, but it filled him with a sense of wonder and excitement he had never felt before. Waking up in a stranger's basement, possibly as a captive of that stranger, was just the kind of unplanned and unstructured and unscripted thing he would expect to happen on his journey. Truth be told, if nothing unusual had happened, he would have been disappointed.

But that was the first day. On the second day when he woke up in the basement, after he counted all of the ceiling tiles just one time, he did have some concerns. Four of them, to be exact, which, in order of importance, were:

1. He was concerned Harriette would be worried about him since he had not spoken to her since she dropped him off at the airport and told him not to look in the cockpit.

2. He was concerned Darlene had only approved a one-week vacation for him and he was fairly sure he would not be able to get back to work by Monday.

3. He was concerned about where the Avis rental car was and, if it was missing or damaged, how much of the replacement or repair cost would he be personally responsible for since he hadn't bought the extra insurance?

4. He was concerned Theodore might have forgotten he had promised Chester blueberry pancakes with whipped cream for breakfast.

On a scale of importance, blueberry pancakes did not register as high as his other three concerns, but they made the list. Chester believed no matter what was happening in your life, be it good or bad, you still had to eat.

As he lay on the bed thinking about those four concerns, his eyes drifted to the metal grate in the ceiling above him, the one that was twelve by twelve inches square, and he noticed for the first time he could see light through the grate. He smelled the enticing aroma of cooking bacon wafting down. He saw a shadow pass over the grate, accompanied by the sound of footsteps. He realized he was looking up into the kitchen, and that Theodore was making his breakfast.

And that made him happy for four different reasons which, in order of importance, were:

1. He was happy pancakes were on their way

2. He was happy he would know in advance what his meals would be and could track the progress of their preparation.

3. He was happy he knew something Theodore didn't know he knew.

4. He was happy that, since he heard no other voices and only one set of footsteps, it was only Theodore, and not a group of people, keeping him captive in the basement.

Not that he could overpower Theodore and get away.

But it was possible he could out-think Theodore and get away.

Chester was waiting patiently for the pancakes when he heard a phone ring. It was the ring of a cell phone, and it was ringing in the kitchen above him. He stood up on the bed so he was closer to the grate.

"He sure likes to eat," he heard Theodore say.

Pause.

"It's no problem. You know I love to cook. Gives me something to do."

Pause.

"We might have another problem. He got two letters."

Pause.

"I know. I have no idea what the second one was. I'll try to find out."

Pause.

"Also, did you find the rental car?"

Pause.

"Okay, have them bring it here. I'll put it in the garage."

Pause.

"Are you sure? He seems harmless."

A longer pause.

"That won't be necessary. No need to get heavy-handed. Leave it to me. This is what I do."

Pause.

"I said I'll handle it."

▼

"Thank you," said Chester as Theodore handed him the breakfast tray. On the plate were three fat blueberry pancakes, each one as perfectly round as the next with a giant dollop of whipped cream on top of the stack, three strips of bacon, not too crisp and not too soft, a small fruit bowl with slices of banana, cantaloupe and apple, and a tiny glass pitcher filled with maple syrup. Chester held the tray in his lap as he sat on the bed, which he had made up earlier, after he had showered and folded up the clothes he had worn yesterday. He looked admiringly at the pancakes.

"My, those are some fluffy pancakes, Theodore. Let me guess. You whipped the egg whites didn't you?"

"Yes, I did."

Chester took a bite of the pancakes, chewing slowly. "And you added a little bit of vanilla extract and some ground nutmeg."

"Chester, are you sure you're not really a Master Chef?"

"I just like to eat, Theodore. No, let me rephrase that. I love to eat."

"That you do," said Theodore.

"So, is today the day I leave?" asked Chester, the third bite of blueberry pancakes on the way from the plate to his mouth.

"Why? Are you not happy, Chester?"

"Oh, everything is fine. The food is incredible. It is very peaceful down here. And I'm reading a great book right now, *Flowers for Algernon*. Have you read it?"

"No."

"But I found it in the bookcase."

"I got those books for you to read."

Chester stopped chewing and looked at Theodore.

"Theodore, there are quite a few books in that bookcase. Exactly how long am I going to be here?"

"That's really up to you, Chester. Why are you so skittish this morning?"

"That's a funny word."

"What word?"

"Skittish. You know how some words sound just like what they are? Skittish is one of them. So is delicious. And angry."

"You mentioned the word *angry*. Are you angry right now?"

"A little bit."

"Why?"

"Because I don't know what's happening. And I miss Harriette."

"I understand, Chester."

"I'm sure Harriette's worried about me. How long have I been here?"

"Two days, that's it. And I have good news. Your rental car is safe and sound."

Chester nodded and kept eating. He alternated a bite of pancake with a bite of bacon with a bite of one of the slices from the fruit bowl. He thought of how Harriette eats all of one item on her plate before going on to the next.

"That's so strange," Chester said the first time he saw her eat like that.

"Why's that?"

"Well, first off there's no variety from one bite to the next."

"But it all ends up in the same place doesn't it?"

"Yes, but before it gets there, don't you want to mix it up a little bit?"

"It gets mixed up when it gets there."

"Very odd."

"No Chester, to me it's odd you can't focus on one thing at a time. Your fork is jumping all over the place on your plate."

"But how do you decide what to eat first?"

"I work my way up. I start with the lightest item which is usually the vegetable, then I go to the medium item which is the potatoes or rice or noodles, and then I finish with the heavy item which is the meat or chicken."

That seemed to have resolved the matter, but when Harriette moved on to her mashed potatoes that day, she stopped before taking a bite and looked at Chester.

"Chester, is there any other observation you would like to make about how I eat?" Harriette asked with an edge to her voice, or not really an edge but more like whatever the word might be if it was halfway between not an edge and an edge.

Chester, aware Harriette's question had been asked in a voice with somewhat of an edge to it, resolved to never again criticize anything Harriette did in relation to eating. He also promptly said, in an attempt to change the subject, "Harriette, the meatloaf is exceptionally delicious tonight."

▼

When Chester arrived at the Pringle's house at 2649 Shady Grove Boulevard in his Avis rental car, he drove around the block a few times to work up his courage. He finally parked in the street in front of the house and walked to the front door. He saw a doorbell, but knocked instead.

Chester never knew if a person's doorbell was working or not and he didn't want to embarrass himself by ringing their doorbell a few times and not have them come to the door, and then knock on the door, only to find out the doorbell worked and the person was now angry he had both rang the doorbell and knocked. As if he was saying the person was too lazy to answer their door in a timely manner. It was safer, Chester thought, to just assume the doorbell didn't work and knock on the door. Which is what Chester did, three polite knocks, and in a very short amount of time the door opened. Holding the door open was a small man who didn't look too happy about having to answer the door.

"Why didn't you just ring the doorbell?" asked the small man.

"Oh, sorry," said Chester.

The man waited. Chester waited. They looked at each other. The man shook his head and sighed.

"Can I help you with something?" asked the small man.

"I came about the letter," said Chester.

"What letter?"

"The one you sent me."

"And you are who?"

"Chester Fortunberry."

"That's really your name?"

"Yes, it is?"

"That's unfortunate."

"Be that as it may, you sent me a letter."

"I don't think so."

"Is your name Ed Pringle?"

"Yes."

"Do you have a wife named Edna?"

"Yes, and how do you know that?"

"Because you both sent me a letter."

"What letter?"

"This letter," said Chester, reaching into his pocket.

Chester finished his last bite of the pancakes. He used the napkin on the tray to wipe away some maple syrup he could feel on his upper lip.

"Thank you, Theodore. That was a real treat. Can I ask you a question?"

"Of course. That's why we're here."

"Why are you so concerned about me talking to other people about my revelation? Nobody ever listens to me anyway."

"They might. And what would happen if those people believed they weren't real and whatever they did was not real. They would no longer have any accountability. They would stop working, they would stop eating, they would commit crimes. It would be chaos. Telling people about your revelation is like standing up in a crowded theater and yelling 'fire'. Do you want to be responsible for the repercussions that come from that?"

Chester nodded his head like he agreed, even though he wasn't sure if he did agree.

"Theodore, do you know what police tell women to yell if they are being attacked?"

"Help?"

"No. They tell them to yell 'fire' as loud as they can."

"Why would a woman yell 'fire' if she is being attacked."

"Because people won't go outside to help if they hear a woman screaming, but everyone will go outside if someone yells there is a fire. Another person in jeopardy doesn't affect them. But a fire does."

"That's a sad commentary on humanity."

"Isn't it?" said Chester.

When Chester and Harriette were first married and had just moved into their house, the girl with diamonds in her hair visited Chester.

It was almost midnight and Chester, uncharacteristically, was still up. He was watching an old black and white movie. Harriette had the flu and had gone to bed earlier. Chester, snug as a bug in his pajamas under a quilt on the recliner, had just finished the last of the popcorn from the bowl in his lap when there was a loud knocking at his front door. Thinking it might just be his imagination, since it did not make sense for someone to be loudly knocking on his door at midnight, Chester kept watching the movie.

And heard the loud knocking again.

Chester realized the knocking was real and it frightened him. He had lived long enough to know that phone calls or knocks at your door after midnight meant something bad had happened. He set the empty popcorn bowl down and cautiously walked to the front door. He turned on the porch light and moved the curtain on the window next to the door to peer out. What he saw was a pretty young woman with dark blonde hair.

And lots of blood.

The young woman turned her head slowly to look at Chester's face in the window. Chester made eye contact with her briefly but he couldn't stop looking at her hair. It was matted with blood and sprinkled throughout with little diamonds that reflected the light from the overhead porch light. The blood in her hair was dark while the two tiny rivulets of blood that ran from the top of her head down the sides of her face and onto her pink halter top were a fresher, lighter color. The girl mouthed the word *help* and Chester quickly opened the door.

"Are you all right?" asked Chester, realizing as he asked the question what a ridiculous question it was.

"Nobody would open their door," said the young woman.

Chester reached out and took the young woman by the arm and brought her into the house, walking her over to his recliner.

"Sit here," said Chester, wrapping the quilt around her shoulders. He went to the kitchen, got two clean dish towels and placed them on each side of the young woman's head. "Hold these tight," said Chester, "I'm going to call the police."

Chester called 911 on the kitchen phone. He told the operator he needed the police and an ambulance immediately because there was a young woman bleeding in his living room with diamonds in her hair.

"Sir, have you been drinking?" asked the operator.

"No, I have not. Please send help right now."

Chester brought the young woman a glass of water and held it to her lips for her to drink since her hands were occupied with the dish towels.

"What happened?" asked Chester.

"My boyfriend wrecked his car."

"Where is he?"

"I don't know," said the woman, looking furtively at the open front door.

Chester felt a chill run down his spine.

"Should I lock the door?" asked Chester.

"Yes, please," said the young woman, her voice fearful.

Chester locked the front door and then came back and crouched in front of the young woman.

"Don't worry. Help is on the way," said Chester, and as he said that he could hear the first sirens.

Chester looked at the young woman, who was crying softly, and then he looked at her matted hair and realized that what he thought were diamonds were slivers of glass. When he saw police lights bouncing off the window curtains, followed by the sound of heavy footsteps on his porch, he went to open the front door. The living room was soon filled with police officers and EMS personnel. And then it seemed that just as quickly as the room had been filled, it was empty, and Chester was again alone, sitting on the edge of his recliner with two bloody dish towels in his hands.

Harriette, heavily medicated because of her flu, did not wake up despite the sirens and flashing lights, and the next morning when Chester told her about his nighttime visitor and the blood on her face and the diamonds in her hair and the policemen and the ambulance, Harriette did not believe him. She told him he was probably dreaming because he had stayed up so late. She kept insisting he had been dreaming until Chester walked her into the laundry room and showed her the two bloody dish towels.

"Oh Chester, you weren't dreaming," said Harriette with a gasp. "How is the young lady?"

"I don't really know. The ambulance took her away. She seemed okay."

"Chester, that was so thoughtful of you to let her in and help her."

Harriette's comment surprised Chester.

It meant she thought he had had a choice.

▼

"I know how we can solve this predicament," said Theodore, taking the breakfast tray with its plate polished clean from Chester and placing it on the night stand.

"How?" asked Chester.

86

"If I can convince you that you are not the only real person on the planet, then your revelation would be incorrect. Right?"

"I guess so."

"You don't seem too sure."

"Well, convincing me that the revelation is wrong does not erase the fact that I had the revelation."

"I understand. But if your revelation was that there is life on Mars and I was able to convince you that there is no life on Mars, then you would certainly never tell anyone that you thought there is life on Mars. That would make you look stupid. Right?

"I suppose."

"Okay, so let me ask you a few questions."

Chester was happy to have Theodore, who knew about the revelation, ask him questions that might shed more light on what the revelation meant. Two heads are better than one, he thought. Chester knew all truths were linked with one another, and that finding a fundamental truth and proceeding with logic would open the way to all discovery. If he could find that one loose string on the sweater and give it a hard tug, he might unravel the secret of the revelation. But he had to find the sweater first.

"Yes, please. Ask me some questions. That's a great idea. I don't like thinking I am the only real person on the planet. That seems very lonely. I've been lonely my whole life. I don't want to be even more lonely."

Theodore pulled a small steno pad from his back pocket and flipped it open. He took a black felt-tip pen from the pocket of his crisp white shirt.

"Are you comfortable?" asked Theodore.

"Very much so."

"Don't be nervous. This isn't a test. I'm not trying to trick you. Just tell me the first thing that comes to your mind."

"Okay."

"Let's talk about cats."

"Cats?"

"Yes cats," Theodore nodded.

"But I don't really like cats. I like dogs. Dogs are friendly. Cats are aloof. I don't much care for aloofness. When I was young I had this dog named Duchess and ..."

"Chester, can I please ask my question?"

"Oh, sorry."

"Okay, if I brought you a cat and put him in this room and ..."

"What's the cat's name?"

"It doesn't matter. I'm just posing a hypothetical question."

"It doesn't matter what the cat's name is?"

"No it does not. Just listen and stop interrupting me. If I brought you a cat and you didn't feed him for three days, the cat would be hungry. You could tell he was hungry by how skinny he was getting, by his searching the house for food. You might even hear the growling of his stomach. That makes sense, right?"

"Yes. The cat would be very hungry."

"Now, instead, let's say I put that same cat in a cottage in Peru for three days. And I did not tell you about the cat, so you had no idea there was a cat stuck in a cottage in Peru without anyone there to feed him. At the end of the three days would that cat be hungry?"

"Yes."

"But why? If you don't know about the cat, then you couldn't have created him. Which means he doesn't exist, and if he doesn't exist, he can't be hungry. You're suggesting a thing in the external world can change even when you don't know about the thing or about the change."

"Trust me, the cat in Peru will be hungry."

"Why?"

"Because he's a cat. And cats get hungry."

"Even if you don't know about him."

"Just because I don't know about the cat does not mean I did not create the cat."

Theodore looked flustered. "Let me try this again. Let's say I bring two people into this room, Ralph and Alice. You can hear them talking and see their lips moving. Now I fly Ralph and Alice to that same cottage in Peru and ..."

"Theodore, is the cat still in the cottage?"

"No, he's not," said Theodore, starting to get aggravated.

"Why not?"

"Because he fucking died, Chester! You didn't feed him."

Chester jumped, Theodore's harsh words startling him.

"I don't believe that. And you don't have to swear."

"No, no, no, he didn't die, Chester, and he's not in the cottage. This is a different hypothetical situation."

Chester nodded his head, so Theodore continued.

"Okay, so you see these two people ..."

"Ralph and Alice?"

"... yes, and they are talking in this room in front of you. Now, instead, let's say I flew them to that cottage in Peru ..."

Theodore stared menacingly at Chester to stop him from interrupting again.

"... and they start talking. You have no idea they are in that cottage in Peru. You can't see or hear them. You can't even imagine them in that particular setting because you don't know they exist. So in Peru are they talking, are they making sounds, are their lips moving?"

"Yes."

"But how? How can people who you don't know about, who you maintain are not even real, do physical things like making sounds and moving lips?"

"Theodore, you have asked me the exact same question just using two different scenarios. Like with the cat, just because I don't know about the existence of Ralph and Alice does not mean I did not create them. They can exist whether I know about them or not, but they exist only for me."

Theodore looked painfully confused. Chester tried another explanation.

"You are suggesting things I create should only exist when they are where I can see them. And if I cannot see them, like a pecan tree a hundred miles from here, they either do not exist or they freeze in time like statues and only come to life when I move to a spot where I can see them. That makes no sense. If that was how it was, then nobody would age and leaves would not change color unless they were within my eyesight. That's not how it works."

Chester stopped to take a deep breath. "Theodore, have you ever had a dream where you are being chased by a bad guy?"

"Of course. Everybody has."

"In that dream do you know the bad guy?"

"No."

"As far as you know, that person does not even exist?"

"Correct."

"But you can see the bad guy running, see his legs and arms pumping up and down, and you can hear him yelling at you?"

"Yes."

"So you can see physical movement and you can hear physical sounds from an entity that is not real?"

"Well, of course he's not real," said Theodore. "It's a dream, a figment of my imagination."

"Yes, but you saw the bad guy and heard the bad guy. Are you saying his pumping arms and legs were real and his loud yelling was real, but he himself was not real. How can that be?"

Theodore didn't answer, so Chester kept talking.

"That dream was so real that you woke up in a cold sweat with your heart pounding. Your body had a physical reaction to something that you say is not physical. Your mind says the bad guy was not real, but your body is still sweating and shaking like he was. So, you see, the not-real is linked to the real, just like the doesn't-exist is linked to the does-exist."

Theodore nodded several times, but Chester could not tell if Theodore was nodding because he understood or if he was nodding just to be nodding. He felt like it was probably the latter.

"Well," said Theodore, "how do you know you're not just dreaming all this?"

"Because there's a difference. In my reality, things make sense and follow consistent rules and progress along a constant time line. In my reality, one plus one equals two, zebras are black and white and run on the ground, and rain drops fall from gray storm clouds. That's the reality I have designed and I don't deviate from it. But in my dreams one plus one can equal an apple, zebras can be orange and purple and fly, and lizards could fall from chartreuse storm clouds. So yes, there's a big difference."

"If you created it, why couldn't it be the other way around?"

"What do you mean?"

"Why can't zebras be orange and purple in reality and black and white in your dreams?"

"Because that's not how I arranged everything. And if I had done it that way, you would still be asking me why I didn't do it the other way."

Theodore looked at his notes on the first page of the steno pad and then flipped the page to look at the notes on the next page. He studied the page for awhile. Chester's eyes drifted over to the small bookcase on the other side of the room. Starting with the top shelf, going from left to right, Chester began to count the books. The books were all different sizes and colors, some hardback and some softback, some tall and thick and some short and thin, but they were all books so they fit Chester's group-of-five-similar-things criteria. There were knickknacks on the shelf as well, but those weren't books, so Chester didn't count them. Halfway through counting the books on the top shelf he could sense Theodore had finished reading his notes, so Chester starting counting the remaining books as fast as he could. That was one of the problems of counting things. It seemed like something always cropped up that made it hard to get to the end of the counting. Counting things in a moving car was the hardest.

"Chester?"

"... 22, 23, 24, 25, 26 27 ..."

"Chester?!"

Chester counted even faster. "... 28, 29, 30, 31, 32 ..."

"Chester, I'm talking to you," said Theodore, his voice sterner.

Almost there, Chester thought to himself. "... 33, 34, 35 and 36."
Done.

"Yes, Theodore. I'm sorry. You were saying?"

Theodore looked back down at his notes, a scowl on his face. Chester stole a sideways glance at the bookcase and saw there were two more shelves of books. The urge to start counting the books on the other two shelves was almost uncontrollable. The only thing worse for Chester than seeing a group of things he did not have time to count was starting to count a group of things and then not having time to finish counting all the things in that group. When that happened, Chester told himself he had just suffered *countus interruptus*, which he thought was a really clever turn of a phrase.

"Chester, doesn't the fact we are talking prove you are wrong?"

Chester forced himself to stop thinking about the books in the bookcase and focus on Theodore.

"How so?" asked Chester, his heart only half in the question.

"If you are the only real thing in the world, then you only have one entity to talk to, which is yourself. Why would you need language and the spoken word at all? Can't you talk to yourself without even speaking?"

"I could have created a world where there were no people. It could have been just me and the birds and the bees. But I didn't go the solo route. I created people. And if I decided to create people, why wouldn't I give them the ability to communicate with me and with each other? That would be like creating vanilla ice cream and making it smooth and creamy, but forgetting to also make it taste delicious. I didn't want to create a world full of mimes."

Theodore took the pen from his pocket and scribbled something on the legal pad.

"What are you writing?"

"Just some notes."

"Can I see?"

"No. What else, Chester. You seem to be on a roll. I'm here to listen."

"Well, as an accountant, I look not only at what is on the page, but also at what isn't on the page to get the true picture. Things that are missing are just as important as things staring you in the face. Take the Bible, for example. If you believe in God and believe he made everything in the universe and that the Bible accurately chronicles that ambitious endeavor, then what is missing from the Bible?"

"I don't know, what?"

"Cell phones."

"Cell phones?"

"The Bible says God made light and water and dry land and the sun and the moon and fish and birds and trees and Man himself. But nowhere does the Bible mention cell phones. Or space shuttles. Or strawberry popsicles."

"What's your point?"

"I did start the ball rolling on a lot of what you see around us, from the earth below your feet to the stars above your head. You know, the big things. But those basic building blocks went on to make all the other things you see. The more specific things. Like strawberry popsicles. Since I didn't create every single specific thing, I don't necessarily remember every single specific thing. Ask me how many legs a centipede has?"

Theodore frowned.

"Go ahead. Humor me."

"Okay, how many legs does a centipede have?"

"I don't have a clue."

Theodore frowned again.

"What I did is called the butterfly effect," said Chester. "The butterfly effect is when ..."

"I know what it is. I'm not a moron. So, you just flapped your wings and that lead to everything being here."

"Kind of." Chester thought for a minute, then added, "That's why I always flush the urinal in public restrooms."

"Because of butterflies?"

"No, because if the next person has a nice clean urinal to use, then perhaps it will improve their mood and they will pass it on, intentionally or not, by doing something nice for another person. Eventually that good deed could come back around to benefit me in some way. The last thing I want to do is touch the handle of a public urinal, but the reward is worth the risk. Everything that happens in the world has an impact on everything else in the world, no matter how small."

Theodore clapped his hands together loudly. "Chester, stop right there. Think about what you just said."

"What did I say?"

"You just said, and I quote, 'Everything that happens in the world has an impact on everything else in the world, no matter how small.'"

"And?"

"Well, if a butterfly's tiny wings can cause a devastating tornado, think about the damage revealing your revelation can cause."

Chester thought about that.

And he had to admit it made sense.

"Would you like some tea?" Edna Pringle asked Chester.

"Yes, that would be very nice. Thank you."

"I'll be right back," said Edna.

Edna was gracious. Ed seemed perturbed.

Ed and Chester stared at each other awkwardly, Chester at the right end of the living room couch and Ed in a well-worn but cozy-looking recliner, while Edna fixed their tea in the kitchen. Chester crossed his legs and folded his hands in his lap. After a few seconds, Ed did the same. They both continued staring at each other until Edna came back with the tea and a plate of pecan sandie cookies.

"They're Ed's favorites," she said.

Chester added one lump of sugar to his tea, took a sip, and then picked up a cookie and slowly nibbled at its edge. Ed ignored the tea, and even the cookies that Edna said were his favorites.

"You seem perturbed," said Chester to Ed.

"I am."

"About the letter?"

"Yes."

"Well, I didn't mean to perturb you."

"Not that letter."

"Not that letter?"

"No, not that letter."

"Then what letter?"

"This letter," said Ed, pulling a sheet of folded paper from his back pocket. He unfolded the letter and reached over the coffee table to hand it to Chester who, before taking the letter, placed his half-eaten cookie on the edge of his teacup saucer and wiped his cookie-holding hand on the napkin in his lap.

Chester read the letter and said, "Wow."

"No shit," said Ed.

Chapter Seven

"Theodore?"

"Yes."

"Just out of curiosity, if it had been important for the cat, you know the one who came here first and then flew to Peru, to have a name, what would his name have been?"

The slightest smile tugged at Theodore's mouth. He rubbed his left eye with the ball of his left hand and then his right eye, again with his left hand because he still had the pen in his right hand.

"Chester, why do I feel like I am George to your Lennie?"

"So we can live off the fatta the lan' an' have rabbits!"

"See, that's my point, Chester. One second you come off like you're half retarded and the next second you're a scholar. You are a lot like Lennie. On one hand you are simple and sincere and innocent, but on the other hand you have a brute strength you don't know how to control, and that brute strength is you spreading your ridiculous revelation around and getting people all worked up."

"Sorry, George."

"Stop that."

Theodore closed his note. He nodded his head and took a deep sigh.

"We're both a little winded right now. What do you say we break for a lunch?"

Chester started to answer Theodore, but then a light bulb flashed on over his head. A long simmering thought, courtesy of his radar, had come to the surface of his brain. The black hair, the thick glasses, the chiseled jaw, the muscular physique.

"Clark Kent!" said Chester in a loud, ah-hah voice.

"Excuse me?"

"Clark Kent! I figured it out. You look just like Clark Kent!"

"Superman Clark Kent?"

"Yes, that Clark Kent."

"Really? You think so."

"Absolutely. Do you dye your hair?"

"Uh, no."

Chester knew Theodore had just lied. It might have been a little thing, a vain thing like not admitting you dyed your hair, but it was a lie nonetheless and Chester filed that knowledge away for later use. Someone who will lie about a little thing is more likely to lie about a big thing than a person who doesn't lie at all.

"So is there a Lois Lane?" asked Chester.

Theodore didn't answer at first. He looked down at his hands for what seemed like a long time, and then said, "There was, but she's gone now."

Theodore told Chester the story about his wife being hit by the train, and he went into enough detail that Chester was pretty sure it had not been an accident at all.

"I'd rather not talk about," said Theodore, after he already talked about it.

"I understand," said Chester.

Theodore and Chester both looked around the room, everywhere but at each other. It was the first, and only, time Chester would see Theodore not in control of the situation. He felt bad for making the Lois Lane comment, thought about apologizing for it, and then thought it would be better to just be quiet.

Theodore's face slowly changed from sad to pleasant, and the in-control Theodore was soon back.

"How about that lunch suggestion, Chester?"

"Great idea. What were you thinking?"

"Well," said Theodore, the peppiness in his voice indicating he was happy to be back in the driver's seat, "I was thinking grilled cheese sandwiches with thin-sliced Black Forest ham and tomato soup with fresh basil and garlic croutons."

"Yummy."

Theodore stood and walked up the basement stairs. When he got to the top of the landing, which Chester could not see from where he sat on the bed, he stopped, which Chester knew he did because he did not hear the door open to the house. A second or two went by, and then he heard Theodore's voice.

"And Chester?"

"Yes, Theodore?"

"The cat's name would have been Coco."

Chester looked at the letter Ed Pringle handed to him. It was very messy. The paper was a sheet ripped out of a spiral pad, so it had those tiny torn tags on the left side. The text of the letter was handwritten in block letters with a pencil. Some of the words were smudged from where a sweaty palm had brushed across them. And there were quite a few misspellings.

Chester had to read the letter twice to be sure he had read everything correctly. What the letter said was this:

Dear Ed:

Inside this letter is a seeled envolope. Hide the envolope away. You will know when it is time to give it to someone.

Do not open the envolope. I will kick your butt if you do.

Do not throw the envolope away. I will kick your butt if you do.

Do not tell anyone about the envolope (except Edna). I will kick your butt if you do.

Sorry for being so bluntt.

It's just my nature.

p.s. Don't forget about the kicking your butt part.

As soon as Theodore went upstairs to make lunch, even before Chester heard the door to the house open and close, Chester started counting the books on the other two shelves of the bookcase.

There were thirty-four on the middle bookshelf, and twenty-nine on the bottom bookshelf. He counted the books on all three bookshelves two more times each, and then said the totals—thirty-six on the top shelf, thirty-four on the middle shelf and twenty-nine on the bottom shelf—in his head three times. He knew that tomorrow, if he was still in the basement, he would count the books again, but for now he was positive that the count was thirty-six, thirty-four and twenty-nine.

▼

Chester did not think it was possible for Theodore to make a grilled cheese and ham sandwich tastier than the tuna fish sandwich he had made the day before. Chester was wrong. He took a second bite of the sandwich.

"Good"? asked Theodore.

"Better than excellent," said Chester.

"Do you mind if we continue our discussion while you eat?"

"Yes, but it's not polite for me to talk with my mouth full."

"I'll pretend like I don't notice."

"Okay, then."

"Chester, can you move things with your mind? Without touching the candlestick on the dresser over there, can you make it move from left to right using just your mind?"

Chester looked at the candlestick for a few seconds. Nothing happened.

"No, I guess not," said Chester.

"So the physical world can't be manipulated by your mind?"

"Apparently not."

"Now, if you walked over to the dresser and grabbed the candlestick with your hand, would you be able to move it from left to right?"

"Of course."

"So the external world can be manipulated using your physical body but not your mental energies?"

"It appears so."

"Well, if the external world is something you constructed in your consciousness, doesn't it make sense that since you built it with your mind, you should be able to change anything in it using only your mind? Are you telling me you can build an entire universe with your mind, but you can't move a candlestick a few inches with that same mind?"

Chester pondered the question, popped the last bite of grilled cheese and ham sandwich into his mouth, chewed it thoroughly, and then spoke.

"I am a very organized and deliberate person. I don't like change or surprises. I am not going to recreate my external world every time I have a whim. My external world was built from a Master Plan put into place long ago. I can't be moving stuff around whenever I please."

"Why not?"

"Because that's not the external world I created. That would be like me creating an external world of breast milk and warm blankets when I was an infant. Then re-creating an external world of Playboy magazines and Chevy Camaros when I was a teenager. And then re-creating a world of beach front mansions and Nobel Peace Prizes when I was an adult. That's silly. Also, and this is important, while I may have created everything, that doesn't necessarily mean I control everything."

Chester savored the moment. People hardly ever asked him questions, much less listened to his responses. He was enjoying having another person be truly interested in what his thoughts were.

Just then, just when Chester was feeling pleased at being the center of somebody's attention, Theodore stood up.

And took one long stride to the bed where Chester was sitting.

And slapped Chester hard across the face, the sound of the slap reverberating off the basement walls.

"Did that hurt?" asked Theodore, sitting back down.

"Heck, yes! Very much so," said Chester, his eyes wide in shock. He held his hand to his cheek. It felt hot. "Why did you hit me?"

"To prove a point. If you created the external world, then part of that external world just bitch-slapped you. Why would you allow that?"

" I ..."

"You talk about how lonely you are and how nobody appreciates you. Why would you create an external world where you could feel any type of pain, physical or emotional?"

"Couldn't you have asked me that without hitting me?" said Chester, the pinkie finger on his left hand tapping away furiously on top of his thigh.

"Yes, but I didn't."

"Why not?" asked Chester, his pinkie finger still going crazy.

"Oh, I don't know," said Theodore sarcastically. "Maybe I thought since I'm in a world you created, you would be able to predict the slap coming and duck."

"Did you really think that."

"No."

Theodore smiled challengingly at Chester.

Chester, his cheek still stinging, found that the slap had stirred up a ball of anger deep inside him. His pinkie finger stopped tapping. He was surprised by the curtness in his voice when he spoke.

99

"Listen here, Theodore. Constructing an external world is not like ordering off a Chinese menu. You don't just cherry-pick all the good things. I signed up for the package deal because I want to experience everything. I want the pluses and the minuses. What if I created an external world where I was never hungry? Then I would never know the joy of waking up with an empty stomach and smelling bacon cooking in the kitchen."

Theodore still had a challenging smile on his face, egging Chester on.

"The world I built is the best world I could think of building at the time, the one that over the long run will give me the most perfect life. And maybe what makes it perfect in a way I can truly appreciate is that along the journey there will be imperfect moments that make the perfect ones that much more perfect."

Theodore's challenging smile started to wane.

"Look at me now. I'm chained up in a basement. Isn't it possible I'm not here because you want me here, but instead I am here because it's part of my Master Plan, a way for me to break out of an uneventful life? You ask me why, if I can create my own world would I have pain or fear in that world? I ask you the same question. If your dreams are thoughts that only you can have with your mind, why do you have nightmares? Why do you have that dream about a bad guy chasing you? Why wouldn't every one of your dreams be warm and fuzzy?"

Theodore didn't answer. Chester felt like a prizefighter who has his opponent on the ropes. He wasn't going to let up.

"Theodore, what if my mind is not actually inside the body that you see? What if I am something separate from this body? What if I am only peripherally inhabiting this body because to exist in the external world and play in the game I designed, I had to choose a chess piece so I could participate in the game? What if I chose not to be all of the chess pieces at once, all consciousness, because then the game conclusion would be forgone. I would be the entire game. Instead, I wanted to be *in* the game. I wanted to play.

"And what if I chose this particular chess piece, the Chester Fortunberry piece, which came with a specific set of marching orders that I have chosen to follow and not change. Because if I change the marching orders for Chester Fortunberry, then I can change the marching orders of all the chess pieces and I would be the entire game again. This chess piece, my body, is my peephole for observing the external world.

"That's why I am not the greatest painter who ever lived, why I can't play the guitar, why I don't know how to strip down and re-build a '57 Chevy car engine. If I knew everything, I would be everything, and then what's the point of being in the game? If a quarterback was also every other player on his team and every player on the opposing team, would he have any interest in playing the game? I think not."

Chester stopped. His face was flushed. He pointed his finger at Theodore and said it again.

"I think not."

▼

"I'll tell you one thing," Ed said after Chester finished reading the letter. "Whatever son-of-a-bitch wrote that letter better not show up here. I'll shoot his ass. I'm a Korean War vet. I don't mess around."

"No, Ed you don't," said Edna, "but there's no reason to get all worked up. We have company."

"To hell with that," said Ed, staring hard at Chester. "I think our company is the reason I got that damn letter."

Chester ducked his eyes behind the rim of his tea cup.

"I suppose you want to see the envelope," Ed said brusquely, standing up and disappearing to the back of the house.

"I'm sorry about Ed's temper," said Edna. "He's been testy ever since the war."

"Well, you know, Edna, technically there was no Korean War. Congress never declared war on Korea, so it was just known as the Korean Conflict."

"Good Lord, do not say that to Ed. I beg you!"

"Oh, okay, mum's the word."

Ed walked back into the room. "What are you two talking about?"

"The cookies," said Chester. Edna nodded in agreement and shot Chester a thank-you smile.

Ed handed Chester a sealed envelope. He used his finger to open it. Inside was another sheet of folded white paper torn out of a spiral binder. The letter inside was very short, more of a note. Like the letter to the Pringles, it was handwritten in block letters with a pencil. It read:

Chester:
We need to talk.
Bring Scotch.
Uncle Frank

Chapter Eight

Chester was still angry about the slap, while Theodore seemed pleased Chester was speaking up. "Don't stop now."

"Theodore, I'm just as confused as you are. I didn't ask for this to happen. It just did. And I'm trying to deal with it the best I can. My life up to now has been blessedly absent of questions. It's been a steady and comforting black and white world for me, with no room for gray."

"I know, Chester. That's why I'm here to help, so you can get back to that black and white world."

Chester nodded his head.

"Theodore, maybe you are real. I can't vouch for that, though, because the only thing I am one hundred percent sure of is that I am real. I know just three things for sure. One, the only thing I have access to is my own mind, my thoughts and experiences. Two, just because I see you sitting there does not mean you really exist because there is no physical link between mental thought and the external world. And three, since I can not get outside of my own mind to verify the existence of other minds, it could very well mean only my mind exists."

Chester paused, then said, "Can I answer your question with an analogy?"

"Must you?'

"It's like Thanksgiving dinner," said Chester and then he stopped, a satisfied look on his face.

Theodore sighed. "I knew it. This is going to make no sense at all."

"Well, I'm not done yet" said Chester, grinning.

Theodore didn't answer so Chester continued.

"You don't sit down at the dining room table and in a flash the entire table is covered with Thanksgiving dinner. You know, the turkey, the stuffing, the cranberry sauce …

"Chester, I know what is served on Thanksgiving. Get to the point."

"… the mashed potatoes, the green beans, the apple salad …"

"Chester!"

"Okay, okay. So that Thanksgiving feast doesn't just appear in a split second. It takes hours of preparation with many different ingredients. During the preparation everything looks disorganized. But once the dinner is placed on the table, then it's easy to see the meal in its entirety and understand each of the components that went into making it. That's how it was with my revelation. There were years of preparation, with many different thoughts percolating in my head. If I had looked at all those components then, they would have appeared disorganized and not linked in any manner whatsoever. But once dinner was ready—once my revelation finally came out of the oven—then, not only could I explain the revelation, I could also explain all the components that came together to make it."

"Your revelation is like a turkey leg?"

"That's funny."

"Okay, I get the analogy."

"Well, that's the long answer."

"And the short answer?"

"Since I made everything, it means I've always known everything. I just now got around to saying it."

"The turkey leg makes more sense."

"I told you it would!"

"Chester, you said you've always known everything."

"I'm assuming I have."

Theodore looked at Chester, pursed his lips and slowly said, "Quel est votre plat italien préféré?"

To which Chester responded, "Spaghetti et boulettes de viande."

Theodore looked shocked. "Chester, I didn't know you spoke French?"

"I don't."

"You just did."

"I did?"

"I asked you what your favorite Italian dish is and you said spaghetti and meatballs."

"That is my favorite Italian food."

"That's not the point. I spoke to you in French and you answered in French."

"But I don't speak French."

Theodore scowled.

"Is that what we're having for dinner tonight?" joked Chester.

Theodore looked hard at Chester. "Just continue."

Chester took a deep breath. "You're not going to slap me again are you?"

"No, I already made that point."

"Good."

Chester thought about asking Theodore if he knew where the slap he had given him had gone. It was the perfect opening for him to talk about time with Theodore. But he didn't ask because he was still angry about being slapped.

"Chester I am going to think of something right now. See if you can tell me what I am thinking."

Chester waited.

"Well?" said Theodore.

"Not a clue," said Chester.

"That's my point. If I can think of something in my own head and only I know what I am thinking, that means I have a conscious mind. I'm not a philosophical zombie."

"Yes but, and I really hate to say this because I know it will make you mad, you only have a conscious mind because my unconscious mind created it. Don't feel bad, though. My unconscious mind is what created my conscious mind. That might be why I don't know everything. If this world was built by my unconscious mind, a scheming Wizard of Oz behind the curtain, then that means I, consciously, had no involvement in the process and have no idea what is coming down the road."

"Chester, what's your point here?"

"My point is, why are you asking me all these questions? You should ask my unconscious mind."

"And how the hell am I supposed to do that?"

"I wish I knew. I have a few questions for him myself."

Chester waited for Theodore to laugh at his last comment, but he didn't. Instead, Theodore said, "Like what?"

"Well, to be aware of our surroundings we have to be conscious, obviously. But I don't think we are conscious in a straight line."

"A straight line? What do you mean?"

"I think we are conscious in spurts, from one second to the next. It's like a heartbeat. You heart doesn't beat nonstop in a straight line. It beats one beat after the other. So, like a heartbeat, I think we are conscious for a second and then conscious in the next second and then the next second, and on and on."

"So, what's your question?"

"What happens between the seconds?"

"Theodore, you think my revelation will frighten people by showing them their reality is not real at all, but people already choose not to live in reality. They don't even get to the point where they question whether it is real or not. They just don't want to be part of it, period."

"Go on," said Theodore.

"Whether reality was made by me or not, many people choose to escape it. Some do it with alcohol, some with drugs, some with television, some with organized religion, some with therapists."

Theodore didn't say anything, so Chester continued.

"When Harriette and I first moved into our house, we were invited to a neighborhood party. I watched a stream of adults go to the wetbar to mix their own cocktails. After watching the same people go back again and again to that bar, I realized they weren't just being sociable and making another drink. They were self-medicating. If that had been the counter at a pharmacy and they had gone up repeatedly to get pain killers or anxiety pills, everyone would have been appalled. But since it was a bar at a neighbor's home, nobody blinked an eye. Those people were plying themselves with liquor to take them to a different level, to put them into a different reality. It made me uncomfortable."

"That they were getting drunk?"

"No, that they could not just be themselves and feel the same reality the non-drinking people were feeling."

"Are you sure you weren't just jealous?"

"Jealous of what?"

"Of not being able to escape yourself."

Chester paused. "Maybe you're right. Maybe I wasn't upset they were escaping reality. Maybe I was upset I didn't have enough courage to do it myself."

"Something to think about," said Theodore.

Chester liked it when occasionally a conversation with Theodore was about something other than the revelation.

"Theodore, how do you feel about drugs?"

"They're bad."

"Why?"

"They kill people."

"Peanut butter and bee stings also kill people."

"Drugs are illegal."

"Says who?"

"The police."

"No, police just enforce the laws. It's society that outlaws the drugs."

"Okay. Where are you going with this?"

Chester held up his hand. "You'll see. Why do people take drugs?"

"To get high."

"Which means?"

"Feeling different."

"Do they also feel better?"

"I guess so. Otherwise they wouldn't take the drugs."

"So society outlaws things that make us feel different and better, things that change our reality?"

"If you want to look at it that way."

"Why do you think society is frightened of someone changing their reality?"

"I don't know."

"If a person, let's say a man named Arnold, moved to the Amazon jungle to live by himself, never seeing another person for the rest of his life, would that be against the law? Would society have a problem with that?"

"No."

"So, if Arnold decided to change his current reality of suburbia and minivans and fast food restaurants and replace it with a new reality of palm fronds and monkeys and rain forests, that would be okay?"

"Sure."

"Now, if Arnold stayed in the world of suburbia and minivans and fast food restaurants but chose to change his reality by taking heroin and LSD every day, would that be okay?"

"No. That would be illegal."

"But why? In each case Arnold has chosen to alter his own reality. Not anyone else's reality. Just his. Why would society have a problem with that?"

Theodore frowned. "Because it's against the law."

"But why are there laws that dictate what reality you can or cannot be in? Makes no sense to me."

The overbearing Theodore surfaced. "Listen Chester," said Theodore sternly, as if lecturing a child. "Everyone needs to be on the same playing field. We can't have some people living with their own set of rules. It would be mayhem. That's what I've been trying to explain to you about your revelation. Telling everyone about your revelation is like giving them all heroin and LSD and watching them spin off into their own individual realities."

"And what would be wrong with that?"

"Well, first off, nothing would get done."

"I agree with you there."

"And second, we wouldn't be able to control everyone."

"And that," said Chester, "is the real reason."

Theodore shook his head. "You're reaching."

"What about schizophrenics?" asked Chester.

"What about them?"

"They live in different realities than us."

"Yes, but they're sick."

"Not illegal?"

"No, just sick."

"What about people with Alzheimer's?"

"Again, sick."

"What about people who commit suicide?"

"They're sick, too. And I think it might be illegal."

"So people who alter their own personal reality are either criminals or are sick?"

"Pretty much."

"And that doesn't seem strange to you?"

Theodore didn't answer. He seemed sad. He spoke in a voice so soft that Chester could barely hear him.

"My father had Alzheimer's."

Chester's shoulders dropped. "I'm sorry to hear that. And I'm sorry I used that as an example."

Theodore didn't answer him.

Chester studied his fingernails in his lap, his shoulders still stooped. He didn't want to look at Theodore, but he looked up when he heard Theodore shift in the chair, crossing his legs.

"So, do you and Harriette go to a lot of neighborhood parties?" asked Theodore.

"No, just the one I mentioned."

"There haven't been other neighborhood parties?"

"Oh, yes. Lots of them. We just haven't been invited."

"Why do you think that is?"

Chester paused. It depressed him that he and Harriette hadn't been invited to any more neighborhood parties and it embarrassed him to have to think of the reason why and share it with Theodore.

"I guess it's because we don't drink."

Chester paused again.

"And because we're boring."

Theodore didn't say anything for a few moments. Then he shook his head and said, "I don't find you boring at all, Chester. On the contrary, I have found our conversations to be quite stimulating."

"I'm a different person now," said Chester. "Before I was boring. I realize that now."

Theodore sighed loudly. "Will you be sending out invitations?"

"Invitations to what?"

"Your pity party," said Theodore, then he stood up and stretched. He stuck his arms straight up in the air, clasped his hands together and then leaned to the left and to the right. He bent over at the waist and put his palms flat on the floor and bounced on his legs a few times. Chester looked at the muscles and tendons in Theodore's arms. They looked like steel cables.

Theodore, still bent over, looked up at Chester.

"Stand up," he said.

Chester stood up.

"Now, do what I do," said Theodore, walking Chester through several stretching exercises. When Chester bent at the waist to put his hands flat on the floor, his hands only got as far as he knees.

"That's okay," said Theodore. "Now bounce up and down a few times."

Chester bounced. His face was flushed and he was breathing heavily.

"That's enough," said Theodore. "Have a seat."

Chester took a few deep breaths.

"Good job," said Theodore. "Don't you feel better? It's good to get that circulation going. Clears your head, too. Now, tell me more about why I'm not real."

Chester's breathing slowly returned to normal.

"It's like that overweight woman in tight stretch pants you see at the discount store, the woman with six kids trailing behind her while she loads her cart with giant packages of toilet paper. Do you really think she has the same level of consciousness as you, that she thinks just as deeply as you, that she, from the perspective of mind and self, is every bit the same as you? I don't think so. Deep down you think she is less than you, that she is not on the same level of reality as you. And if you are honest, you will admit you feel that way about most people. And you would be right, except for one thing. You are also in that group. Because when the music stops, there is only one musical chair open, and it's just for me."

Theodore scowled. "Chester I'm looking for answers and you're talking about fat women and toilet paper."

"I didn't say fat. I would never say a woman was fat. I said overweight."

"Whatever. I just don't know why you even bring things like that up."

Chester scratched his head. He didn't have an itch, but it seemed like the right thing to do at that moment, a way to signal to Theodore he was taking the discussion seriously and giving each answer deep thought.

"Theodore, this is just how I put my Master Plan together, or, rather, how my unconscious mind put it together. You asking me 'Why didn't I do this?' and 'Why didn't I do that?' about every little thing makes no sense. Next, you're going to ask me why I made the moon out of rock, but if I had made the moon out of swiss cheese, you would ask me why did I make it out of swiss cheese? There are a billion different ways I could have made this universe and there are a billion different things I could have put in it. This is what I chose. I chose koala bears and meteor showers and pina coladas and the color red. I was the interior decorator of this universe, not you or anybody else. So why do you keep asking me why I put the couch where I put it?"

"If you don't mind me asking, what did that letter say?" asked Ed, after Chester had read the note from Uncle Frank and then placed it back in the envelope.

"It was more of a note actually," said Chester.

"Okay, but what did it say?"

"It was just a warning, telling me to be careful."

"That's all it said?"

"Yes, it was quite short."

"Was it signed?"

Chester knew why Ed was asking that question. He wanted to know the name of the person who sent the I-will-kick-your-ass letter to him that had accompanied the envelope with the note. Chester did not want an irate Korean Conflict vet tracking Uncle Frank down for an ass-kicking showdown. So, this being one of those seldom times when he lied, he lied.

"It wasn't signed."

"Are you sure?"

"I'm positive."

"Can I look at it?"

"No, I'd prefer you didn't. It was personal to me."

"But you said it didn't say much."

"Still, it was meant just for me. I'm sure you can understand."

Chester put the note back into the envelope and slipped it into his back pocket. Ed didn't look too happy, but he didn't press the issue.

Ed, Edna and Chester sat around the coffee table in quiet.

"Well ..." said Ed.

Chester looked at Ed and then Edna.

"Are there any more pecan sandies cookies?"

Edna started to answer, but Ed cut her off.

"No, we are all out of cookies. I guess you'll be leaving now."

Ed stood up, then gave Edna a look, so she also stood up. Chester saw them both standing and stood up himself.

"Yes, I guess I should be going. I really appreciate you taking time to talk to me and I appreciate you saving the envelope for me."

Ed walked Chester to the door, motioning behind his back for Edna to stay in the living room.

At the door, Ed and Chester shook hands.

"Chester, listen ..."

"Yes."

"Do you mind if I keep the letter? Not the note in your pocket, the letter that was sent to Edna and I."

Chester could think of no reason why Ed needed the I-will-kick-your-ass letter, and he knew there was nothing in it that would lead to

Uncle Frank, so he was naturally curious about why Ed would request the letter. He asked Ed him why he wanted it.

"What can I say? I don't get a lot of letters. No one ever writes to me."

Chester could relate to that.

So what he said was, "It's all yours, Ed."

Chapter Nine

"I like your 'where I put the couch comment," said Theodore. "That was clever."

"Thank you."

"What about God?"

"Good question. He probably doesn't exist either."

"Probably?"

"I'm hedging my bets."

"Well, if God doesn't exist, which means you have no one to account to for your sins, and if people don't exist, why do you need to be a good person, Chester? Why aren't you out there robbing banks or committing adultery or coveting thy neighbor's ox?"

"That's not the world I chose"

"So why be nice?"

"It's easier."

"How?"

"Not being nice takes a lot of work. I can maximize my positive experiences and minimize my negative experiences if I treat everyone as I would have them treat me. It's just common sense."

"But how can you love something that does not exist? Like Harriette?"

"Because some people are more of me than others, and of all the people in the world, Harriette is more of me than all of them combined."

Theodore nodded his head slowly. Chester, remembering the

emotion Theodore had shown when talking about his wife's passing, realized that when he mentioned Harriette, Theodore tended to be more sympathetic to what he was saying.

But thinking Theodore might have a tiny soft part inside him didn't stop Chester from saying, "By the way, I'm still not happy that you hit me. That was wrong."

"I didn't hit you. I gave a you a slap. A little love tap. If I had hit you, you would still be out cold."

Chester didn't doubt that.

"Chester, in life, sometimes you have to use violence if the only way you can accomplish your objective is with violence. Remember that."

"Theodore, have you ever used violence to accomplish your objective?"

Theodore looked at Chester with a coldness in his eyes that answered Chester's question better than anything Theodore could have said.

"Well," said Chester, "what if one of these days I hide under the stairs. Then when you come down, I jump out and hit you over the head with a table lamp and knock you out. Then I take the keys out of your pocket and I leave."

"Chester, you've been watching too many movies."

"It could happen."

"Not a chance."

"You're saying I couldn't attack you?"

"That kind of stuff doesn't happen to people like me. That kind of stuff happens to people like you."

"Why's that?"

"Look at me. Look at you."

Chester frowned. "Yeah, I know."

▼

Chester left the Pringle's house more confused than when he had arrived.

Neither Ed or Edna had mentioned his revelation. Chester had enjoyed the hot tea and pecan sandies cookies so much that he had forgotten to ask how they knew where to mail him the first letter. And he had forgotten to ask them why their letter said they knew what he was thinking and that there would be dire consequences if he continued. If nothing else, he would have wanted them to explain what they meant by dire. Was it dire as in something painful, or dire as in something fatal? Now he would never know. Chester banged his hand on the steering wheel and admonished himself for not asking the most obvious questions. It was not the first time a tasty food item had gotten him off track.

And why had Uncle Frank sent the kick-your-butt letter to the Pringles with the we-need-to-talk-Chester note in it? They apparently had no idea who he was. And if Uncle Frank needed to talk to him, why didn't he just call him? Why was everything so secretive?

The more Chester thought about the unanswered questions, the more intrigued and excited he became. He was having fun and he wanted the fun to continue. Easy answers to his questions would mean an end to his adventure.

Uncle Frank lived in Santa Fe, New Mexico, which was much too far of a drive from Casper, Wyoming, so Chester headed back to the airport. It was too late to get a flight out so he kept his eyes open for a hotel along the way. He would fly to Santa Fe in the morning. As he drove, Chester thought about calling Uncle Frank to let him know he was coming, but then he thought, if Uncle Frank was going to be secretive, Chester would follow suit and just show up on his doorstep.

Chester saw a Holiday Inn near the airport and pulled into the parking lot. As he took his small suitcase out of the trunk, he saw a shiny black Cadillac with two dark men pull into the lot, drive past him and then around to the back of the hotel. The men, and the car, looked very familiar.

Chester's antenna went up.

His radar tickled.

▼

Seeing the two dark men at the Avis rental car place, and then when he checked into the hotel, did not frighten Chester because there were only two of them. Had there been three of them, well, that would have been a different story.

When Chester was in his early twenties, before he met Harriette and before he got the job at the ball-bearing-manufacturing company, he worked as an accountant at a discount furniture store. He left after a few years when he realized the store owner was not declaring all of the cash receipts. By the time he left he had become a bit of an expert on couches and ottomans and bedroom sets. "There's a huge difference between cheap furniture and good furniture," he would tell Harriette later. "You really get what you pay for. It's all about the wood used."

On his drive to and from work, Chester passed a strip shopping center that had a small business in the far corner of the center, and the sign over the business read, *Esmerelda's Palm Reading*. It was not like Chester to suffer such foolishness as fortune telling, but every time he saw the sign, the thought of one day stopping in and seeing what Esmerelda could tell him about his future did cross his mind.

Chester did not have a girlfriend at the time. In fact, he had never had a girlfriend, so his love life, other than daydreaming about the occasional pretty woman who came in to buy discount furniture, was nonexistent. He was still paying off his student loans and his salary from the discount furniture store was embarrassingly low, so on top of not having a girlfriend, he was also broke. He had only a few friends, or, to be more precise, some neighbors in his apartment complex who occasionally said hello to him when he took his clothes to the communal laundry room.

He was pretty much a guy short on love, money and friends.

All in all, his future looked bleak, which is why he thought about Esmerelda's Palm Reading whenever he drove by her business, wondering if she could read the lines on his palm and tell him what was in store for him. The way he looked at it, no matter what Esmerelda told him, he had nothing to lose.

Little did he know.

One Wednesday, on the way home from work, Chester stopped at Esmerelda's business. He didn't know why he stopped on that particular day. He just did. It was like his car had a mind of its own.

When he opened the door to the business, it hit a small dangling bell that announced a customer had entered the store. Chester found it odd Esmerelda would have such a bell, considering she was a psychic.

The business was dark inside, the walls covered in thick drapes, a square table in the middle of the room with two facing chairs. In the corner was a doorway to a room in the back, covered with a row of hanging beads.

"Hello?" said Chester tentatively.

The beads parted and an attractive woman in her forties stepped into the room. She was wearing a blue-green muu muu and a thick jade necklace. Her makeup was heavy in an exotic way, dark blue eyeshadow, long black eyelashes, blood red lipstick. She looked just like what Chester thought a palm reader would look like.

"Hello, Chester," she said.

Chester was stunned.

"How do you know my name?"

"It's on your name tag."

Chester looked down and saw he was still wearing his name tag from the discount furniture store.

The woman smiled and said, "What do you think I am, psychic?"

Chester just stared at her.

"That's a joke, Chester. Have a seat."

They sat at the square table.

"So you're Esmerelda," said Chester.

"No, I'm Mildred."

"Oh, where's Esmerelda?"

"There is no Esmerelda."

"Did there used to be an Esmerelda?"

"Nope, never was. Just me."

"But your store sign says Esmerelda."

"Chester, nobody wants to have their fortune told by someone named Mildred."

"But, you know, what you should have done ..."

"Chester, are you here to tell me my fortune or to have me tell you yours?"

Chester just stared at Mildred

"Chester, lighten up. Put your hands out, face down on the table."

Mildred took his right hand in both of her hands and looked at the back of it and then the palm, and then she did the same thing with his left hand. She studied both hands for a long time, using her right index finger to trace lines on his hands that he could see and lines that he could not see. Mildred's hands were both soft and strong, the warmth of them traveling into Chester until his whole body felt flushed and tingly. After a few minutes of examination, Mildred placed both of Chester's hands palm down on the table and leaned back, interlacing the fingers of her own hands in front of her as is if she were praying.

She looked down at her clasped hands, being both quiet and still, and though Chester could not see her face because it was tilted down, he knew her eyes were closed. Eventually, she looked up, unclasped her hands and set them face down on the table directly across from Chester's hands, their fingertips almost touching. She looked at Chester for an uncomfortably long time and then spoke.

"Chester, you are a very unique person."

I'll bet she says that to everybody, thought Chester.

"You think I say that to everyone, don't you?"

"Yes," said Chester.

"Well, trust me, I don't. I mean it. I see a lot of people and I've never seen anyone like you."

"Why do you say that?"

"I can't read you."

"You mean, my palm?"

"No, you. I don't read palms, Chester. I read people, and you I can't read. This is a first."

"What does it mean?"

"I'm not sure. Yes, I can tell you a few things, a few surface things. But I can't go any deeper. Something is blocking me."

"Like what?"

"I haven't a clue."

"Well, tell me what you can. Will I ever get married?"

"Yes."

"When?"

"Not for awhile, but it will happen."

"Who will I marry?"

"The most wonderful person in the world for you."

"Are you sure?"

"Positive."

"What about my job?"

"Leave where you are now. And soon."

"Why?"

"Just do it. You'll find something much better."

"Like what?"

"Balls."

"Balls?"

"That's all I see. Balls."

"Okay."

"Chester, we're done now," said Mildred abruptly.

Chester was surprised the palm reading had gone so fast and Mildred had not told him more, but it was not in his nature to complain about things, so he stood up and pulled out his wallet.

"Well, thank you for your time, Mildred. What do I owe you?"

Mildred looked up at Chester.

"Put your money away. I'm not charging you."

"Why not? You told my fortune."

Mildred just shook her head. She stood up, put her hand on Chester's arm and walked him to the door. Chester opened the door and the little bell clanged.

"Chester?"

Chester turned around.

"Do you travel very much?"

"No, not much. Every now and then."

"When you travel, be very careful. Be wary of three dark men."

Chester, startled, started to speak.

"That's all I can tell you. Three dark men. Don't ask me any questions."

Chester, still startled, stepped outside. Mildred stepped into the doorway and caught the door as it started to close.

"Chester?"

"Yes."

"One last thing."

"Yes."

"Don't take this wrong but ..."

"Yes."

"... please don't ever come back here again."

"Theodore, are you sure you exist?"

"Of course."

"And you want to keep living and not die?"

"Obviously."

"So if I told you that if you answer the following question wrong, you will die immediately, how would you answer?"

"Depends on the question."

"Does Tiananmen Square exist?"

Theodore started to answer, but Chester interrupted him.

"Remember, you will die immediately if you answer incorrectly. So, does Tiananmen Square exist?"

Theodore started to answer, then.

"Well?" asked Chester.

Finally, Theodore answered.

He said just one word: "Maybe"

Chester was pleased with Theodore's unsure answer. Score one for Team Chester, he thought. He kept going.

"Theodore, you are familiar with DNA aren't you?"

"Of course."

"That every person has their own unique DNA?"

"Right."

"Which means even though there are more than seven billion people on the planet, every one of those people is different as far as their DNA is concerned?"

"Yes," said Theodore, irritated. "What's your point?"

"What color is the rug in this room?"

"Chester, why do you always answer a question with a question? It's very irritating."

"That's what Harriette says all the time."

"She's right. What the hell does DNA have to do with the color of my carpet?"

"You'll see. What color is it?"

Theodore looked down at the carpet and said, "Brown."

"What kind of brown? Can you be more specific?"

"Chestnut brown," said Theodore.

"It looks hazelnut brown to me."

"Well, that's your opinion."

"It's not my opinion. It's what I see. I see the color hazelnut brown and you see the color chestnut brown."

"So what? The carpet is brown. What's the big deal?"

"Theodore, can you hear the drip in the bathroom?"

"What drip?"

"The faucet in the bathroom sink has a small drip. I can hear it; can you?"

"No."

"It's there."

"Maybe it is, but I don't hear it."

"One more question, Theodore. Are you comfortable?"

"What do you mean?"

"How's the temperature in this room?"

Theodore thought for a second, looked around the room and said, "I'm a little warm."

"Not me," said Chester. "It feels perfect to me."

Theodore sighed. He stared at Chester and waited. By now he knew how the game was played.

Chester liked that. It meant he had Theodore's full attention and could make his point.

"Don't you see? Just like every person's DNA is different, every person's world is different. If we walked everybody on the planet through this basement to look at your rug, they would all see a different shade of brown. In your world the carpet is chestnut brown and there is no faucet drip and the room temperature is a bit warm. But in my world the carpet is hazelnut brown and I can hear a faucet drip and the room temperature is perfect. You can't see the carpet color the exact same way I do or hear a faucet drip the exact same way I do or feel the room temperature the exact same way I do. It's impossible.

"You believe you are in this basement, on this planet, and in this universe because of how your senses perceive those three places. That's your world. But I perceive them differently. That's my world. And billions of other people perceive them differently. And those are their worlds. When you look around and see your world and see me, you think of me as being in your world. I see it differently. I see you as being in my world. So who's world is it? Since I trust my own senses more than I trust yours, since I know exactly what shade of hazelnut brown the carpet is, I would have to say that this is my world. Which means your world, at least the world you sense, doesn't exist to me."

Theodore looked at a loss for words. Finally, he said, "Looks can be deceiving. You're splitting hairs."

"I disagree," said Chester. "What if we were both born in a coma and could not see, hear, taste, feel or smell. Our brains were alive but all we knew was darkness. We wouldn't know about the carpet or the drip or the room temperature or about anything else that makes up the external world. But our minds would still come up with a concept of what must be out there. That concept would be our individual attempts to describe the world beyond our mind. And there's no way that your concept would be the same as mine."

"Why not?"

"Because you and I can't even agree on the color of your carpet."

"Theodore, I feel bad."

"Why?"

"Because I misled you."

"How so?"

"Remember the test with the candlestick?"

"Yes."

"I didn't move it because I didn't want to move it. I know you wanted me to, but I didn't want to. So I didn't move it."

"Are you saying you could move it if you wanted to?"

"Of course."

"Chester, that's ridiculous."

"Theodore, you should really be nicer to me."

"Why is that?"

"Because if I wanted to, and I am not saying I want to at this particular moment, but if I really wanted to, I could think you out of existence."

"That's also ridiculous."

"Is it? What makes you so sure when you go to sleep tonight you will wake up in the morning? I might not want that."

"That's bullshit."

"Theodore, do you see that pencil on the night stand?"

Theodore looked over at the night stand. "Yes."

"You only see that pencil because I imagine that pencil. I want it to exist, and so it exists."

"And if you didn't want it to exist?"

"It would no longer be there."

"I still say bullshit."

"Really? Look again."

Theodore looked again, then smiled and, in a sarcastic voice, slowly drawing out each word, said, "Well, surprise, surprise, the pencil is still there. It still exists."

"Theodore?"

"Yes."

"What color was the pencil?"

"Yellow."

"Really? Look again."

Theodore looked at the night stand. The pencil on it was red.

"I'm wrong. The pencil was red."

"Are you sure?"

"I'm positive."

"Really? Do you want to look again?"

"No," said Theodore loudly, turning his head so he could no longer see the night stand. He stood, then hurried up the basement stairs.

"Well, I'll be," said Chester under his breath, allowing himself the tiniest of a smile, and wondering how in the world he had done what he had just done.

Chapter Ten

An hour later they were both back in their usual positions, Theodore in the chair across from the bed and Chester sitting on the edge of the bed.

But Chester wasn't looking at Theodore. He was looking at the tray on the floor next to Theodore's chair. On the tray was a plate with a five-inch-high slice of lemon meringue pie and a glass of milk so cold the outside of the glass had frosted. Chester licked his lips, looked down at the pie, then up at Theodore, then down at the pie again.

Theodore pretended he didn't notice Chester eyeing the pie.

"Chester, tell me where you were before you arrived here. What's the last thing you remember?"

Chester couldn't concentrate. He could see little beads of crystallized meringue sugar on top of the pie and smell the tart lemon in the air.

"My, that pie looks quite tasty. Lemon meringue is my favorite."

"It is quite tasty. It's so good that I had two slices upstairs."

Chester looked up at Theodore. He felt cheated. Theodore had enjoyed two, not just one, slices of the pie. And now there was a giant slice next to his chair, not in Chester's lap.

Chester licked his lips. "Is it homemade?"

"No, I bought it at the bakery. But I've made lemon meringue pie before, and this one is pretty near perfect."

Chester looked down again at the tray with the pie and the milk.

"Is that for me?"

"Maybe. Depends."

"Depends on what?"

"On whether you are going to stop playing games and get serious about answering my questions."

"I have been serious, Theodore."

"All right, so let me ask you again, where you were before you arrived here and what's the last thing you remember?"

Knowing the sooner he summarized his activities from the past few days, the sooner Theodore would slide the tray with the lemon meringue pie and ice cold milk over to him, Chester launched into a rapid-fire recap. He talked so fast that Theodore had to ask him several times to slow down.

"So that's where you got the second letter. At the Pringles?"

"Yes, but it was more of a note."

"Okay, and who was that note from?"

Chester didn't answer right away. Something told him he should not divulge the author or the content of the note to Theodore. But, on the other hand, there was that slice of lemon meringue pie.

"It was from Uncle Frank."

"Who's Uncle Frank?"

"He's my uncle. And his name is Frank," said Chester, thinking Theodore had just asked a very silly question.

Theodore frowned. "No, what I meant was, why did this Uncle Frank send the Pringles a note that was meant for you?"

"Good question. I have no idea why he did that."

"What did the note say?"

"He said he wanted me to come visit."

"Anything else?"

"Bring Scotch."

"Scotch?"

"Uncle Frank likes to drink."

Chester looked down at the pie. Theodore saw him looking.

"It's almost pie time, Chester. What happened after you left the Pringles and went to the hotel?"

"I saw two dark men in the parking lot."

"The same two men you saw when you got your rental car?"

"Yes, how did you know?"

Theodore ignored his question. "What were the two men doing?"

"I only saw them for a few seconds."

"Then what happened."

"A few minutes after I checked into my room, there was a knock at the door. But when I looked out the peephole, I didn't see anybody. Then there was another knock, so I opened the door just a little bit and peeked my head out."

"And then ..."

"The next I remember was waking up in your basement."

"I see."

"Theodore?"

"Yes."

"Do the two dark men work for you?"

"Chester, are you ready for some tasty pie?"

Chester ate the pie, timing it perfectly so there was one last swallow of the ice cold milk left when he got to the last bite of the pie. He wiped his mouth with the napkin on the tray and then placed the tray on the floor.

"Guess what, Theodore?"

"What?"

"I kind of knew about the two dark men way before I ever saw them."

"Oh, really," said Theodore, skepticism in his voice. "How's that?"

"A palm reader warned me about the dark men many years ago."

"She warned you about two dark men?"

"No, she warned me about three dark men, not two. So she was kind of right and kind of wrong at the same time."

"What else did she tell you? Anything that might have to do with your revelation?"

"Not really."

"Did she mention me?"

"It was almost thirty years ago, Theodore. How could she have known about you?"

"She knew about the dark men."

"Good point," said Chester, then out loud he said, "Thirty-six, thirty-four and twenty nine."

"What?" said Theodore.

"Thirty-six, thirty-four and twenty-nine," repeated Chester.

"Okay, I'll bite," said Theodore. "What are those numbers?"

"That's how many books are on each shelf of the bookcase," said

Chester, pointing at the bookcase. I always count things."

"Why?"

"Just because."

"That's a weak answer. Why do you always count things?"

"Well, actually I always count things three times."

"Why three times?"

"To be sure I counted them right. But after I count them three times, when I see them again, I only count them once."

Theodore nodded his head, and pointed his finger at Chester. "That counting thing helps to explain your revelation."

"Really? How so?"

"You count things because you need every question in your world to have a concrete answer. By adding things up you get a total, and that total is the concrete answer to your question. But you count things three times and you count them again every time you see them because you have no confidence in the answer. You're just never one hundred percent sure. Which means your revelation is just an answer you have come up with to solve a question, yet you have no confidence in the answer you have come up with."

"You got all that from me counting books?"

"Yes."

Chester thought about what Theodore had just said, and he had to admit, it made a lot of sense.

▼

"Theodore, I'm worn out. We can play these Q&A games all day and we're not going to get anywhere. Theoretically, since you are just part of my imagined world, you can't ever prove me wrong, because you don't exist. Even then, for every question you have, I have an answer. So I'm not convincing you of anything, and you're not convincing me of anything. You're looking for that one clue that will prove to me I am wrong. But I already have the one clue that proves I am not wrong."

"And that clue is?"

"I wouldn't be here, trapped in your basement, if I was wrong."

Chester shrugged his shoulders for emphasis as he said that last line, and then leaned forward and looked Theodore square in the eye as he said his next line.

"Theodore, you are not trying to convince me that my revelation is wrong. You are trying to convince me to believe that my revelation is wrong. And that's just not going to happen."

Theodore did not look happy. He stood up quickly and walked up the basement stairs, shutting the door behind him, much louder than he had done in the past.

"Uh-oh," said Chester. Out loud.

Within seconds Chester heard Theodore talking on his phone upstairs.

"It's me."

Pause.

"No."

Pause.

"I've tried everything."

Pause.

"That might work. It's worth a try."

Pause.

"Okay, see you tonight."

Later, when Theodore came down the stairs with a dinner tray, he seemed to be in a better mood.

"Remember the chicken I mentioned yesterday," said Theodore.

"I certainly do," said Chester.

Theodore put the tray in Chester's lap. Chester looked down lovingly at the Parmesan-crusted chicken breast, scalloped potatoes with chives and bacon bits, and ... sauteed sugar snap peas.

"Peas? I thought you said honey-glazed carrots."

"I didn't have fresh carrots, so I went with fresh snap peas."

"That was a good swap," said Chester.

Chester sliced off a piece of the Parmesan-crusted chicken. "Do you want to talk some more about my revelation?" he asked.

"No, let's just relax tonight. No more questions."

It felt rude to Chester to just eat in silence while Theodore watched him, so, for the sake of conversation, Chester asked Theodore what his hobbies were. Theodore said he enjoyed bowling and Chester knew enough about the sport to keep the conversation going while he ate his dinner. Chester wasn't surprised to hear that Theodore liked to bowl. As far as individual sports went, it was one of the most physical and Theodore seemed to be very physical. Bowling involved throwing heavy stone balls with aggression and precision and knocking down defenseless wooden pins with a loud explosion. Both of those things seemed to be right up Theodore's alley. Flying balls and exploding pins aside, it was a safe topic and Chester felt like Theodore was relaxed and happy as they discussed it. When both the dinner and the bowling conversation came to an end, Theodore did not stand up.

"Chester, I know I said no questions, but I do have one. Just one, I promise."

"Okay."

"How did you do that trick with the pencil?"

Chester started to tell Theodore it was not a trick at all, but he thought it might be better to let Theodore think the disappearing then reappearing pencil was just a trick.

"I can't tell you that. It wouldn't be a trick any more if I did."

"So, it was a trick?"

"Of course, it was. I got you!"

"Yes you did, Chester. Very clever."

Theodore laughed. He took the dinner tray from Chester and headed for the stairs.

"Good night, Chester."

Theodore turned off the overhead light at the same time that Chester turned on the night stand light.

"Good night to you too, Theodore. I'm just going to read for a little bit before I go to sleep."

Chester only made it through two pages before falling into a deep sleep.

"Chester," said a loud, booming voice.

Chester's eyes popped open, but he continued laying flat on his back, his arms crossed over his chest. His pinkie finger started a slow tapping on top of the bedspread.

"Yes?" he said, looking left then right.

"This is God."

The voice paused for emphasis. Chester's pinkie finger tapping sped up. It wasn't a frantic, tapping, though. More of a let's-wait-and-see-what-happens tapping.

"How are you doing down there?"

"I'm doing fine, God. Thank you for asking."

"Don't mention it. Listen, it's very nice to meet you."

"Really? That's interesting."

"Right. Now Chester, I'd like to talk to you about a few things. Do you have some time?"

"Well, as I'm sure you are aware, I'm not going anywhere at this particular moment."

"Good. Now, here's the deal. I am a very busy man and ..."

"Man?"

"Yes, man. Did you think God was a woman?"

"It was possible."

"No, forget that. Women may run the world, but they don't run heaven."

"That's amusing."

"Nothing wrong with a little humor now and then."

"I agree."

"Chester, I'm concerned. You can't go around telling people they don't exist. I know you haven't done it yet, but I want to make sure you aren't planning to do it in the future."

"Why would that be a problem?"

"If you tell people they don't exist, if they stop believing there is a heaven and life after death, they will have no constraints. They will run wild in the streets. There will be anarchy."

"Just from me telling a few people?"

"It will spread like wildfire, Chester."

Chester raised his head and looked around the room. There was no one there.

"God, where are you? I can't see you."

"Chester, I am everywhere."

Chester did not believe that. He was pretty sure God's voice was coming from the grate in the ceiling above him. But he kept that thought to himself. His pinkie finger tapping, which had already slowed down considerably, stopped completely.

"I have two questions," said Chester.

"Go ahead, my son."

It bothered Chester that the God-voice called him "my son" but he pressed on. "One, how do I know that God exists? And two, if he does exist, how do I know that you are God?"

"Two very good questions, Chester. Let me start with the first one.

If you open the back of a computer and look inside at all of the chips and circuits in that computer, and you look at how it is all tied together so perfectly, you know that only a computer expert could design such an intricate piece of machinery. Now if you look at the design of the universe and all the things in it, at their beauty and order and complexity, from the tiniest atom to the biggest planet, you know that only a super being could design it."

"You mean you, right?"

"Yes, me."

Chester sat up in bed, propped the pillows up behind him, and leaned back.

"Well, God, there are a few errors in what you just said."

"A few errors?"

"Four to be exact."

"You're saying God is wrong? Really, now."

"No disrespect, but let me explain. First, you just used an analogy, and the strength of an analogy is dependent on the similarities between the things being compared. And there is not a lot of similarity between a computer and the rings of Saturn. You can't compare designing a universe with billions of planets in it with designing a laptop."

"Yes, but ..."

"Second, if everything in the universe is part of a grand design at the hand of a master designer, there would be an order and purpose for everything. Nothing would be willy-nilly, if you will. This world is far from perfect. If we can expect a perfect watch from a master watch-maker, shouldn't we be able to expect a perfect world from a master world-maker?"

"Yes, but ..."

"Third, most people agree the world evolved through natural selection over billions of years to get us to where we are today. Nature did it, not a guy with a beard. So I ask you what makes more sense? Believing the universe was created by a self-ordered divine entity that we have no proof exists, or believing that the universe was created and continues to change because of a self-ordered thing called Mother Nature, which we do have proof exists?"

"Yes, but ..."

"And lastly, if only a master designer like God had the wherewithal to design the universe, then who designed God? Imagine how much more talented that designer was than God."

"Chester, I'm not sure if you are saying God does not exist, or if you are saying God does exist but he doesn't matter. Either way, I'm not happy."

The God-voice went quiet. Chester could hear faint wisps of conversation through the grate. He recognized Theodore's voice saying, "I told you so," followed by the God-voice saying "aggravating little shit." A moment went by and Chester heard the God-voice clear his throat. Which was strange. How could God have anything stuck in his throat?

"Chester, you are an accountant which makes you a practical man. Still, even being practical, can't you, like millions and millions of other people, just have enough faith to believe God exists? Why should faith be any less valid an answer than reason?"

"Faith can land you in jail, while reason won't. I once did the company books for a man who was cheating on his taxes. I could have had faith he would stop doing it, but if he didn't, then he and I were both going to jail. Instead, I used reason to determine he was not going to stop cheating, so I resigned before I was implicated in his fraud.'"

"That's a good answer, Chester, because you chose the path most likely to guarantee your well being, the option with the least amount of risk. Using that thought process, why not believe in God because that is the option with the least risk? If there is a God, then you win everything, and if there is not a God, then you lose nothing."

Chester had to think about that one. He mulled it over frontwards and backwards and then said, "You do have a point there."

"Chester, you said you had two questions. The second one was, how do you know that I am God, correct?"

"Yes. I'm sure you can see why I might be a bit skeptical. What proof can you give me that you are God?"

"Because I say I am."

"That's it?"

"What more do you need?"

"Can you show me a sign?"

"Like what? You want me to turn water into wine? That's silly."

"No. How about making that candlestick on the bookcase move from left to right."

"Chester, I'm not going to play games. I am who I say I am. You're just going to have to take my word on it."

"The word of God?"

"Yes."

Both Chester and the God-voice were quiet, each waiting for the other to speak next.

"God?"

"Yes?"

"I know Theodore thinks I am gullible, but I'm really not. And I have to tell you, I don't think you are God. I appreciate you taking time to talk to me, but you're not God."

"What makes you so sure?"

"Well, when we first started this conversation, you said, 'It's very nice to meet you.'"

"Yes, I was being polite."

"But if you created me, wouldn't you have already met me?"

The room got very quiet.

"Uh, well ..."

"When you said that, I did not answer back that it was nice for me to meet you. Do you know why I didn't say that?"

"No, why?"

"Because I had already met you."

"When was that?"

"When I created you."

▼

Now I've gone and done it, Chester thought. I've made God mad. Which he thought was kind of funny. His whole life Chester had gone to great lengths to not get into arguments with people and to not have anyone ever be mad at him, and tonight he had skipped right to the very top and made God angry. Well, the God-voice at least.

Chester couldn't help feeling just a little proud. He had stood his ground, which was something he hardly ever did.

I'm starting to like this new Chester, thought Chester.

He stood up on the bed so that he was closer to the ceiling grate. He heard muddled voices, but could not make out what was being said. He heard footsteps, so he waited, and eventually the voices became clearer as the footsteps got closer to the grate.

"Wanna beer?" he heard Theodore ask.

"I need one," said the God-voice.

Chester heard the refrigerator door open and close, then the sound of two bottle tops being popped off, followed by the sound of two bottle caps skittering across a counter.

"Oh, that's good," said the God-voice, which Chester thought would be quite hilarious if it really was God responding to that first swallow of cold beer.

"You're going to have to call them," said Theodore.

"I know," said the God-voice, nervous. "It's not going to be pretty."

"What else can we do? We tried our best."

"They don't want excuses. They want results."

"How much trouble are we in?"

"We'll find out soon enough."

Chester heard a bottle being placed on the counter and it sounded like the bottle was empty.

"Here goes nothing," said the God-voice.

A moment of silence.

"It's me," said the God-voice.

Pause.

"No. No luck."

Pause.

"We've both tried. He's not budging."

Pause.

"Now? Both of us?"

Pause.

"Okay."

There was a brief silence and then Chester heard Theodore say, "Well?"

"They want to see us."

"Now?"

"Right now. I'll drive."

Chester heard a second bottle, also empty, placed on the counter.

"Is it safe to leave him here alone?" asked the God-voice.

"He's not going anywhere. The door has two dead-bolts."

"Okay, let's go."

Chester heard footsteps leave the kitchen. He waited, still standing on the bed, for five minutes but heard no more sounds, and while he waited, he said to himself over and over again, I need to get out of here and fast.

He stepped off the bed and, for the first time ever, walked up the basement stairs and turned the knob on the door that led into the main house, hoping Theodore might have forgotten to lock it. But no matter which way he turned the knob, the door stayed locked tight. Chester stood at the top of the stairs feeling defeated. He knew it would not be in his best interest to still be locked in the basement when Theodore and the God-voice returned.

He had no idea what to do next.

And at the very moment that he thought he had no idea what to do next, it became clear to him exactly what he had to do next.

Chester walked down the stairs and sat on the edge of the bed. He closed his eyes and imagined that the basement door was unlocked. He pictured in his mind the two deadbolts sliding out of the door frame and into the door, hearing the click each one made as it snapped back. Then he walked back up the basement stairs, and put his hand on the doorknob. He turned the doorknob to the right.

And the door opened.

Chester stepped into the kitchen and stood still for a full minute, listening for any sound that would indicate someone was still in the house. Slowly he walked through the rest of the house. The house was sparsely furnished, but the furnishings it did have were very nice, particularly the living room furniture which Chester knew from his time at the furniture store was very expensive.

On the living room sofa was a folded newspaper. Chester picked it up and looked at the masthead which said Salt Lake Tribune. Somehow he had gotten from his hotel in Casper, Wyoming to Theodore's house in Salt Lake City, Utah, a six-hour drive away.

In one of the three bedrooms, the smallest one, he saw his empty suitcase on the bed and next to it his watch, his cell phone and a set of keys with an Avis tab on the ring. He put the watch on, put the cell phone and keys in his pocket, and then carried the empty suitcase back down into the basement where he quickly filled it with his clothes and toiletry items. He zipped the suitcase shut and started for the stairs, saw the copy of *Flowers for Algernon* on the night stand, stopped for a second, then kept walking, then stopped again. He went back and picked up the book, sliding it into a zippered pouch on the outside of his suitcase.

Upstairs he shut the basement door behind him and locked both the deadbolts. He didn't want Theodore to get in trouble if the people he had gone to report to accused him of having left the door unlocked. Better that they thought Chester had just mysteriously disappeared, which would not be Theodore's fault. In the kitchen he set his suitcase down and opened the refrigerator door. He grabbed a bottled water and was about to close the door when he saw a deli packet with slices of corned beef in it, and next to it another deli packet, this one with slices of swiss cheese.

There's not enough time the rational part of his mind told him, while the non-rational part of his mind told him that there was always time for a deli-fresh corned beef and swiss cheese sandwich. He was wavering between the rational and the non-rational when he saw a loaf of rye bread on the counter which pretty much resolved the issue. A few minutes later he stood in the garage, a bottle of water in his left hand and a corned beef and swiss on rye sandwich, wrapped in a paper towel, in his right. In front of him was his Avis rental car. Chester put his suitcase in the trunk, slid into the front seat, took a bite of his sandwich, and put the key into the ignition.

And then Chester was gone like the wind.

Chapter Eleven

Tonorau opens his eyes.

His three older sisters, his two older brothers and his parents are still asleep in their hut overlooking the island's bay. He always wakes before them, eager to embrace the new day. The only other thing awake in the hut is Tonorau's dog, Crow. He can see the giant dog's dark eyes sparkling from under an old blanket near the fire pit. As Tonorau stands, Crow raises up on all fours, the blanket falling from his broad shoulders. Many of the people in the village call them the Twins. Some of the people call Crow the Shadow, but always in a cautious whisper.

The day that Tonorau was born, in this very hut, Tonorau's father had found a puppy sitting on the path that led from their hut to the ocean. The puppy was dark as night and so the father named him Crow. He had no idea where the puppy came from, or that within a year the dog would turn into one hundred and thirty pounds of solid muscle, with a massive head and iron jaws that could crush a grown man's arm.

He had placed the round ball of black fur next to his new pink baby, and despite the presence of seven other people in the hut, on that day Crow anchored himself forever to Tonorau. He never left the baby's side, sitting vigil until the boy took his first steps, and then walking shoulder to shoulder with the boy every one of their waking moments. You never saw Tonorau without Crow, or Crow without Tonorau. Although if Tonorau was standing behind Crow, then sometimes you couldn't see Tonorau at all. That's how big Crow was.

Tonorau had the run of the island. He had it from the day he turned five years old and the incident occurred.

On that day the child awoke in the middle of the night and wandered outside the hut, followed by Crow. No one knew he was up and about in the darkness. The elders of the village still hotly debate certain parts of what happened next, but what they all agree on is that as Tonorau and Crow walked away from the hut toward the ocean, a pack of four wild dogs came out of the brush toward the pair. Tonorau's father heard one high-pitched yelp, just one, followed by no other sounds whatsoever, only the stillness of the moonlit night. But for a father, that one cry was enough to jolt him from his sleep, and in a split second he surveyed the family members sleeping around him, saw who was missing and rushed outside and down the path to the ocean.

Where he found Tonorau.

And Crow.

And four dead dogs.

Tonorau was standing next to Crow, his small right hand stroking the dog's thick neck. Crow, his teeth bared and his jowls slick with blood, eyed Tonorau's father warily as the man approached. The father saw that there were no marks on his son or on his son's dog, and he saw that Crow was not panting or winded. When Tonorau's hand touched the wet blood on Crow's face, he leaned in for a closer look and then used the sleeve of his shirt to wipe the blood away. He smiled at his father, but Crow continued to stare at the man who knew to stand still as stone and wait until Crow was sure that any and all possible threats to Tonorau had vanished. When Crow's body finally relaxed and he laid down and put his giant head on his paws, the father slowly walked over and picked his son up and walked back to the hut, Crow padding quietly behind him.

In the morning the father and some of the elders gathered the bodies of the four wild dogs, two with their throats shredded and two with their skulls crushed, and buried them. The men were hunters and they knew the signs of a fight to the death, so they could not understand why there were no signs of a struggle. They could not understand why the father had only heard one yelp. They could not understand how Crow destroyed four dogs without suffering a single injury. But Tonorau's father knew then that no harm, either from earth below or heaven above, would ever befall his youngest child as long as Crow was by his side.

Tonorau steps outside the hut and into the grayness that comes at first light. He can see the sliver of the top round edge of the sun coming up over the ocean horizon. Crow licks his hand, and Tonorau would describe the feeling like that of sandpaper on a soft banana, except Tonorau has never seen sandpaper. In answer to the lick, he dips his hands into the bucket of cool stream water outside the entrance to the hut and holds his cupped hands for Crow whose large tongue sucks the water up in just a few slurps. Tonorau repeats the process four more times, three times for Crow and one time for himself.

Together, as they do every morning, they walk down the path to the ocean's edge. For some unknown reason, Tonorau cannot start his day until he steps into the water and feels the power of the ocean. He feels the wet sand between his toes and the waves against his legs. He raises his hands above his head and he thanks the sky for another beautiful day as the first strong rays of the sun warm his skin.

He thanks the sky in his head because Tonorau cannot speak.

Just as Crow cannot bark.

That's one of the things the elders can discuss for hours on end, how the Twins, who can't speak, can communicate so well, and how it came to be that a boy and a dog both born without voices would find each other. What they never discuss, what they all see happening but cannot find the courage to address, is the fact that a dozen years have gone by since the night of the incident.

And neither Tonorau or Crow have grown a single day older.

Chapter Twelve

Before Chester left Theodore's house, while he was in the kitchen making his sandwich, he put the two empty beer bottles and caps in the trash and wiped the condensation from the bottles off the counter with a dish rag. He also cleaned and put back the knife he used to put mustard on his sandwich.

He looked around the kitchen to make sure everything was clean and in order and was about to leave when he noticed Theodore's steno pad and pen on the kitchen nook table. He opened the pad and leafed through the pages that had shorthand scribbling on them until he got to a blank page. Using the pen, he wrote:

Dear Theodore,
It was time for me to leave. I'm sure you know why.
Thank you for the wonderful meals and the interesting discussions.
Yours Truly,
Chester
p.s. I took that book I was reading. I hope you don't mind.

Chester knew exactly where he was going as soon as he slipped behind the wheel of his Avis rental car in Theodore's garage.

He had to see Uncle Frank.

The sooner the better.

Chester had no idea where the Salt Lake City airport was, but he knew Santa Fe was in the next state over, so he turned on the car's navigation system and found the first interstate heading south. He stayed in the middle lane and put the cruise control on 55 mph. As Chester drove, he had a feeling of exhilaration. It felt good to be free and on the move. With his hands on the steering wheel and his foot on the gas pedal, he felt in charge for the first time in a long time.

The drone of the tires on the almost empty highway coupled with the comfort of the padded car seat and the haziness of the early evening sun disappearing into nighttime put Chester into a cozy mood of thought and reflection. He realized he had spent so much time discussing his revelation with Theodore over the past few days that he had not had time to discuss it with himself.

He knew that the day he had the revelation was not the day that he became the only real thing on the planet. It's not like the billions of other people on the planet were real and then, at the exact second that Chester had his revelation, they stopped being real. If the revelation came to Chester when he was fifty-two years old, then that meant for the past fifty-two years Chester had been going about his business not having a clue that the people he interacted with and the food he ate and the sunsets he saw were not real. They were always not real, from Day One.

The more he thought about it, the more Chester felt like he had been misled, even cheated, to have lived for more than five decades in a world that was a lie. Why didn't anybody tell me, he thought to himself, realizing even as he thought it that the only person who could have told him was him.

Which raised a lot of questions. Now that he knew, did everyone know that he knew, and knowing that he knew, was everyone going to treat him differently? Since he now would be observing people and things in a whole different light, would those people and things react to him in a different way? Would people still do what he expected them to do based on past experience, would the color red still be the red he was familiar with, would the same number of stars show up in the evening sky?

And why did it take fifty-two years before he realized it was just him on the planet? Was it his fault he didn't know earlier? Was he not smart enough? Was he too restricted by his highly organized and structured life to have looked outside the box and seen the signs? Could he have paid more attention or asked more questions and found out earlier?

And what if he had never had the revelation? Would his life have gone on with no changes or surprises, just more of the same mundaneness? How would that life compare to the life he was now going to be living knowing about the revelation? Would living the remainder of his life knowing that nothing was real be better for him than living the rest of his life being ignorant of that fact?

And what if he had gone to his deathbed never having had the revelation? What if he had been in a hospital bed with Harriette holding his hand as the beep-beeps on the heart monitor got fainter and fainter, and as he started to fade away, at that last moment before he was gone forever, one of the doctors leaned in and whispered, "Just thought you should know. Nothing is real, except you. When you're gone, we're all gone. Happy trails."

Time would tell if life pre-revelation was better or worse than life post-revelation. The scary part, Chester realized, was he was now trading the known for the unknown.

▼

Chester had a younger sister, Martha, but he had not spoken to her for many years. They weren't close when they were growing up, and once they both left the family home, it was almost like they had never been brother and sister. Chester tried initiating contact at the beginning, calling Martha on her birthday and on the big holidays every year, but she never reciprocated on his birthday or the holidays, even on the anniversaries of their parents' deaths, so eventually Chester just called her on her birthday and then after awhile he stopped calling her at all.

Their parents had died within one year of each other, both from cancer, just after Chester and Martha had both left for college, Chester on the East Coast and Martha on the West Coast. The one thing they did have in common was that when they finally left the nest, they both chose colleges as far away as possible from that nest. Neither of them had ever returned to the town where they grew up. Chester wasn't sure why he and his sister did not have the same warm and fuzzy feelings about their childhood and their parents that most other people had. Their parents had not been mean or abusive; they had merely been attentive, the way a cemetery caretaker is attentive. Favoritism was nonexistent for the most part, but Chester always felt that his parents disliked his sister a little less than they disliked him.

Their mother was an only child so there were no relatives on that side of the family, and his father had only one brother, Uncle Frank, who was in and out of their life in a sporadic way, depending on what adventure he was on and what country he was in. Once, after three years of nobody seeing or hearing from Uncle Frank, he had showed up at their house for a brief visit, which came just a few days after Chester heard his father say to his mother, "Frank's getting out."

As far as relatives went, Chester was left with a daughter he seldom saw, a sister he never spoke to, and a Black Sheep uncle who bounced around the planet like a steel ball in a defective pinball machine. Chester's parents, like Chester, had married late in life, so even his grandparents on both sides had passed away before Chester arrived.

Chester always looked at it that way, as in when he arrived, not when he was born. He felt like he had arrived at the house where he grew up like a stranger who had just shown up on the doorstep. He lived under the same roof as three other people and they shared meals and watched television together and talked about different things, but Chester imagined it was the same type of coexisting that would have happened if he and three strangers had shared a hostel for two decades.

In the car, after he had put a good thirty miles between himself and Theodore's basement, Chester made three phone calls. He knew Harriette would be worried sick about him, not having heard from him in days, but he was also someone who took his work responsibilities very seriously. So his first call was to Darlene.

"Darlene here."

"Hi Darlene, it's Chester."

"Yes."

"This is going to sound strange, but can you tell me what day it is?"

"Did you really just call me to ask what day it is?"

"I'm sorry. I've lost track of time. Today is Friday, right?"

Chester had quickly added up the days in his head before asking Darlene that question. He knew he had the revelation on Monday and flew to meet the Pringles on Tuesday. And he was fairly sure he had only been at Theodore's house for two nights based on the first night being cranberry-glazed, center-cut pork chops with Rosemary roasted red potatoes and fresh-cut green beans with almond slivers, and the second night being Parmesan-crusted chicken breast, scalloped potatoes and sauteed sugar snap peas. Eating, and enjoying what he ate, was one of the most important parts of Chester's daily life, and it was an internal calendar for him. When talking with Harriette and recalling a past event, Chester was more likely to say, wasn't that the night we had brown sugar meatloaf, baked macaroni and cheese, and broccoli salad, than he was to say, wasn't that the night we went to the movies?

"Yes, Chester, it's Friday," said Darlene.

"What time is it?"

"Really?"

"Yes, my watch stopped." Which it had. Chester made a mental note to re-set his watch after they spoke. He shook his wrist to get the interior mainspring turning again.

"It's nine o'clock."

"What are you doing at the office so late?"

"That's none of your business, Chester."

"You're right. I'm sorry."

"Chester, I'm very busy. What exactly do you want?"

"I need to use another week of my vacation time. I'm not going to make it back in time for work Monday."

"Okay."

"Okay? That's it?"

"Yes, I'll make a note of it. Now I have to go."

"Darlene?"

"What now?"

"Have I missed anything at the office?"

"Not really. Nothing important."

"Okay, I'll be back on ..."

"Oh, there was one thing."

"What?"

"Mr. Dundee died."

"What!"

"Your boss died yesterday."

"What happened?"

"Heart attack. On the ninth hole at Bardmoor Country Club."

"And you didn't think that was important?"

"I forgot."

"It happened yesterday."

"I've been busy."

"What's going to happen now?"

"My guess is either you or Phillip will get promoted."

"Really! Who do you think the president will choose?"

"I don't know. Do you play golf?"

"No."

"Oh well."

▼

When Chester was a child, Uncle Frank had made a big impression on him during one of his infrequent visits. That visit was one of the main reasons that Chester was an optimist. You might expect someone who felt like a loner all his life to be a pessimist, but Chester wasn't. On the contrary, he was quite positive and saw a silver lining behind every cloud. Whenever he saw a rainbow, even now in late middle age, Chester would daydream there was a pot of shiny gold at the end of it. Like when he and Harriette went snorkeling on their honeymoon in Hawaii.

Chester had booked the snorkeling excursion months before the honeymoon and had been very excited about it. Partly because, next to getting married, it was the most adventurous thing he had ever done. But mainly because he was one hundred percent certain that on the snorkeling excursion he was going to find buried treasure on the ocean floor, a chest filled with gold doubloons. Just about every day, even on their Wedding Day, Chester mentioned the snorkeling and finding the buried treasure to Harriette. The day they finally went snorkeling, Chester saw a lot of colorful fish, and even a small shark, but no gold doubloons.

"That's okay," said Chester to Harriette, "next time."

Chester was like that, being positive most of the time.

Because of the nuts.

The type you eat.

On a cold winter day, the nuts day, Uncle Frank had come by their house, unannounced as usual, with a bottle of Scotch whiskey under one arm and a woman who was a whole lot younger than him under the other arm. After an hour of uncomfortable chit chat and catching up—it always seemed uncomfortable for his parents but not for Uncle Frank— the four grown-ups ended up sitting around a folding card table in the living room playing bridge.

Uncle Frank, with half the bottle of Scotch gone next to him, sat across from the young woman, and his father sat across from his mother. Chester, who had turned eight years old the week before, sat on a tall bar stool next to Uncle Frank and watched them play. He could smell the pungent aroma of the Scotch, neat, no ice or water, wafting from the glass next to Uncle Frank's right hand.

Chester could not remember the name of the young woman who was with Uncle Frank, but he could remember, even forty-plus years later, what she looked like. She had blond hair piled high like a beehive on top of her head, big pouty lips covered in thick pink lipstick, horn-rimmed glasses with little rhinestones on the corners, and a tight black sweater cut so low that her two breasts, the size and color of softballs, were almost popping out. He noticed that whenever his mother wasn't watching, his father would steal a glance at the young woman. But he never looked at her face. He always looked at those two popping-out softballs, his eyes seeming to linger on the cavern between them. Chester did not know what his father's fascination was with those two things, but years later, when he was in his teens and he realized that the sight of a pretty girl made him feel all squiggly inside, he figured it out.

And it made him proud of his father.

Proud that a man who seemed so cold and disciplined would succumb to the lure of something so warm and permissive, and proud that a man who was so cautious and unadventurous would risk the wrath of his mother by taking a peek at another woman. Well, lots of peeks.

Next to Uncle Frank's glass of Scotch was a large bowl of peanuts in the shell. Uncle Frank would reach over and grab a peanut, crack the shell and then pop the peanuts into his mouth. He would do this with his right hand while holding his cards in his left hand, talking nonstop about his recent travels, and never once looking at the bowl of peanuts. For every five or six peanuts that Uncle Frank would pop open and eat, Chester would take one out and crack it open with both hands, pick the peanuts out, put them into his mouth and then, like Uncle Frank had been doing, put the empty shells back into the bowl. As they both ate more and more peanuts it took longer and longer to dig through the empty shells to find an unshelled nut.

Chester reached his hand into the bowl and with his fingers searched and searched for an unshelled nut. He went to the left and then to the right. He went up and then down. All he felt were empty shells. There were no more unshelled peanuts, so he gave up. With a sigh he pulled his hand out of the bowl and clasped his hands in his lap.

Uncle Frank, who during all the nut cracking and eating had not once looked at the bowl or at Chester, stopped talking and set his cards face down on the table. It was quiet in the living room all of a sudden.

Uncle Frank slowly turned to look at Chester. Chester's father and mother and the woman who was a whole lot younger than Uncle Frank all looked at Uncle Frank as he looked at Chester.

"Why'd you stop?" asked Uncle Frank.

"Because there aren't any more nuts."

"Are you sure?"

"Yes."

"I said, are you sure?"

"Uncle Frank, I'm positive. There is nothing left."

Uncle Frank looked at Chester, not like looking in his direction in a casual way, but right into Chester's eyes. They stared at each other to the point that the only thing Chester could see or feel in that living room were Uncle Frank's eyes. There was no question that Uncle Frank had Chester's complete and undivided attention.

"Chester, there's always another nut."

"But Uncle Frank, I checked. There aren't any."

"Chester, I'm going to say it one more time. There will always be another nut. Don't ever stop believing that."

Chester, not breaking eye contact with Uncle Frank, reached over and placed his hand in the bowl and started searching with his fingers. He went to the left and found nothing. He went to the right and found nothing. He went up and found nothing. He went down.

And found an unshelled nut.

A big one, one that when opened up would have three fat peanuts in it. He pulled the nut out and held it up to show Uncle Frank.

Uncle Frank nodded his head.

Chester nodded back.

The two couples resumed their bridge playing and a few minutes later Chester reached into the bowl again, his fingers searching. He soon pulled out another unshelled peanut, bigger than the last one.

Uncle Frank, who had not looked at the bowl or Chester again, smiled.

Chester's second call was also business-related.

"Avis Car Rental."

"Hello, this is Chester Fortunberry."

"Yes Mr. Fortunberry, how can I help you?"

"Is Darren Tucker in?"

"No, he's off today."

"What is your name?"

"My name is Reginald. How can I assist you?"

"Well, I can't bring the rental car back on Monday."

"Please hold while I look up your reservation."

Reginald put Chester on hold for a minute, then came back on the line.

"That won't do, Mr. Fortunberry. That car is reserved for another customer for pick up Monday afternoon."

"Can't you just rent them another car?"

"No. We are sold out all next week. So we must have your car back Monday morning."

"Not going to happen."

"Excuse me?"

"I'm in a bit of a situation here and I don't know when I will be able to return the car."

"Mr. Fortunberry, you signed a rental agreement to return the car on Monday. And that's what you are going to have to do."

"You're not listening, Reggie. It's not going to happen."

"The name is Reginald, not Reggie."

"What's wrong with Reggie?"

"Mr. Fortunberry, I do not have time to discuss my name with you. Just return the car on Monday please."

"No."

"No?"

"Yes, no."

"Sir, we will report the car as stolen."

"Well, Reggie, that's the least of my worries right now."

A few weeks after the peanut incident, Chester's father gave him a present. It wasn't his birthday and it wasn't Christmas, so receiving a present from his father was completely unexpected for Chester and completely out of character for his father.

Chester remembered even his mother was surprised at the dinner table that night when his father said, "Chester, I have a present for you," and reached into his pocket. He pulled out a tiny manila envelope, the type with the string that wraps around a metal circular tab to close the envelope, and handed it to Chester. Chester uncurled the string from the tab, held the envelope upside down over the palm of his hand, and watched as a coin rolled out. He held the coin up and saw it was a very shiny quarter. He looked at his father quizzically and his father said, "Look at the date."

Chester looked at the date and said, "1966. That's the year I was born."

"Yes it is," said his father. "I went to the bank special today and asked them to look in their vault to see if they had an uncirculated 1966 quarter and, believe it or not, they had one. I thought you would like having it."

Chester didn't know what to say. He wasn't used to getting surprises in the house he grew up in, especially surprises that showed consideration for him. Later, when he was a young adult, he would realize it wasn't a coincidence his father had made a gesture of fatherliness just weeks after Uncle Frank had showed him so much attention during the peanut incident.

The night he received the coin he was overcome with happiness, happiness because he had a shiny new quarter and happiness because his father had done something special just for him. In bed that night he rubbed the quarter between the thumb and index finger of his right hand again and again until he fell asleep. The next day he took the shiny new quarter to school, putting it into the change pocket of his dungarees. He didn't bring the coin to school to show his friends because he didn't really have any friends at school. He brought it so he could sneak it out during class and rub it between his thumb and index finger under his desk.

It made him feel good. That's why he brought it.

He took the coin out of the change pocket during all his classes that day, being sure to put the coin back before the end of each class. His last class of the day was arithmetic and he rubbed the coin between his thumb and index finger from the beginning to the end of that class, until the bell rang signaling the end of the school day. As the students jumped up to leave, Chester started to slip the coin into his change pocket but the coin snagged on the edge of the pocket and fell from his hand. Chester watched as the shiny new quarter hit the floor and rolled down past four desks before hitting the sneaker that was on Billy Barnett's right foot.

Billy Barnett looked down and saw the coin, then looked back and saw Chester looking at him. Chester raised his hand and gave it a tentative shake to let him know it was his coin that had dropped, but

Billy Barnett just sneered at him, picked up the shiny new quarter, put it into his pocket, and walked out of the classroom.

Chester didn't go to school the next day. He told his mother he was sick. He told her that he hurt inside.

Which was true.

▼

Chester's third call was to Harriette.

"Where in the world have you been, Chester? I've been worried sick."

"Harriette, you wouldn't believe me if I told you!"

"That sounds ominous. Are you all right?"

"I'm fine now."

"What do you mean 'fine now'?"

"Oh, I had one little problem, but it's all been fixed."

"What problem? What kind of business trip are you on? You gave me so little information before you left."

"Everything's fine. I'll tell you all about it when I get home."

"And when will that be?"

"In a few more days."

"What! You aren't coming home today?"

"I rented a car. I thought while I was up here I would drive down and see Uncle Frank."

"Uncle Frank? Why?"

"Well, he never visits us."

"He never visits anyone."

"Exactly. That's why I thought it would be nice to pop in and see him."

"Chester, you are not a popping-in type of person."

"Well Harriette, maybe you don't know me as well as you think you do," said Chester, but not in a mean way. He said it because Harriette said he might not be a particular type of person and it was a statement with which he did not agree. He also said it because he knew that at some point in the near future he would have to tell Harriette about his revelation, and this was a chance to plant the first small seed, to let her know there might be more to him than she realized.

"You don't have to be curt, Chester."

"I'm sorry. I didn't mean it that way."

"I'm just concerned. This is so not like you."

148

Chester cringed. There she goes again, he thought, telling him he was not acting in an expected manner. Why did everybody assume that all that he was, was restricted to what they assumed he was? He couldn't be too upset with Harriette, though, because, until he had the revelation, Chester had also assumed that all that he was, was what he assumed he was. That had all changed, but Harriette didn't know it. Not yet. But this was hardly the time to try to explain.

"I know you're concerned. I just had this strange feeling that while I was up here I should go by and see Uncle Frank. He's not getting any younger."

"Your Uncle Frank will outlive both of us. He's too ornery to die."

Chester laughed. "That he is."

"It's just that I miss you, Chester. It's lonely here when you're gone."

"I miss you too, Harriette. I'll be home before you know it."

"Chester, please be safe."

"I will."

"Promise?"

"I promise."

It sounded like an easy promise to make to Harriette.

But as Chester had discovered over the last few days, there was nothing easy about his life now.

Because later, after a ten-hour drive from Salt Lake City to Santa Fe, and after six hours of sitting and talking to Uncle Frank, Chester had gone to sleep. Or, at least, he had thought he was asleep when he heard a disturbing conversation. He wasn't sure if he was dreaming or if he was awake, but what he was sure of was that there were two voices and what those voices said scared him to death, dream or no dream.

"Tommy, break the fingers on his left hand."

"Okay, Dominic. What about his thumb?"

"His what?"

"His thumb. Want me to break his thumb too?"

"Do you want to break his thumb?"

"I don't know."

"Tommy, make up your mind. We don't got all day here."

"I can't decide."

"Do you like the man?"

"I don't even know him."

149

"But do you like him?"

"Not really."

"Then break his fucking thumb too."

"Dominic, why do we got to hurt him?"

"Theodore wants him back. And he wants him to know to never leave again."

"By breaking his fingers. And his thumb."

"That was my idea. Now, get to it."

But that came later. First Chester had to get to Uncle Frank's. And that part, the getting to Uncle Frank's part, turned out to be kind of disturbing as well. Not disturbing in a violent way like breaking fingers but disturbing because of what happened right before he arrived there.

At breakfast.

Chapter Thirteen

Chester had driven about two hours from Theodore's when he looked down at the Avis rental car's fuel gauge and saw that the needle was on the empty hash mark. He scanned the highway signs until he found an exit with several gas station options. He exited, pulled into the first service station he saw and filled up his tank. While he was pumping the gas, he noticed there was a liquor store next door. After paying for the gas, he walked over to the liquor store.

"Howdy, partner. Can I help you find anything?" asked the clerk, an older man with an unlit cigar in the corner of his mouth. He was wearing a short-sleeved white shirt with the faintest of yellow stains under the armpits.

"Yes. I'm looking for some Scotch," said Chester.

The man pointed to a rack against the left wall. Chester walked to the rack and stood in front of it for a full minute. There were so many different brands. He couldn't decide what to get. Starting from the left, he began to count the different bottles of Scotch on the top rack, moving sideways to the right as he counted. There were twenty-one bottles. He walked back to the start of the row and began counting the bottles of Scotch a second time. Halfway through, the old man sauntered over.

"Can't find your brand?"

"One second," said Chester, holding up his index finger, giving him time to finish counting the row of bottles a second time. Still twenty-one bottles. Chester turned and looked at the clerk. "I don't have a brand.

I'm not much of a drinker."

"You never drink?"

"A skosh."

"A what?"

"A skosh."

"What the heck is a skosh?"

"Skosh means a little bit."

"Then why didn't you just say a little bit?"

"Skosh sounds better."

The old man shrugged, rolling the unlit cigar from one side of his mouth to the other.

"You don't drink much, but you're looking for Scotch?"

"It's not for me. It's for my uncle."

"So, it's like a gift?"

"Yes."

"Is he your favorite uncle?"

"He's my only uncle."

"Well that settles it. You should get him the best of the best," said the old man, reaching up and taking a bottle from the top shelf. He took the unlit cigar from his mouth and pointed it at the label on the bottle. "Lagavulin, single malt, sixteen years old, very peaty, put hair on your chest."

"That sounds good. How much is it?"

"Eighty bucks."

"That seems a bit expensive."

"He's your only uncle, right?"

"Yes."

"Well, then ..."

"Okay. I'll take it. Can you wrap it?"

"We don't gift wrap here, but I have a very nice brown paper bag for it."

The old man walked to the register, rang up the purchase and handed Chester the bag with the Scotch. Chester took the bag but stayed standing in front of the counter looking at the old man.

"Anything else there, partner?"

"Do you ever light it?"

"Light what?"

"The cigar."

"Never. Quit smoking years ago."

"Oh, I see," said Chester. "Thank makes sense."

Chester left the liquor store and stopped at a traffic light at the frontage road that led back onto the interstate. Out of the corner of his eye he saw a young woman about a hundred yards away standing on the side of the frontage road with her thumb out. That's not very safe at this time of night in the middle of nowhere, thought Chester. But there was no way Chester would offer her a ride. He never picked up hitchhikers. It wasn't safe. The light turned green and Chester turned right, driving slowly so he could get a better look at the young woman. The closer he got to her, the more he thought about how dangerous it was for her to be out there all alone. No, just keep going, part of him said, while the other part of him said, what if that was his daughter?

Chester stopped his car next to the woman. He hit the power button and the passenger window slid down.

"Do you need some help?" asked Chester.

"Nope. Just need a ride," said the woman, bending over to peer into the car, looking Chester over from head to toe, and then leaning in a little farther to look into the car's back seat.

"Well, I never pick up hitchhikers. It's not safe."

"For me or for you?"

"For both of us, I guess."

"It's your decision, but I could really use a ride."

"Well ..."

"Where are you headed?"

"I'm going to Santa Fe. To see Uncle Frank." After he said it, Chester wondered why in the world he mentioned Uncle Frank. The woman had no idea who Uncle Frank was. Chester always gave out more information than the occasion called for. Thankfully, people usually ignored his non-pertinent information.

"Listen, I don't bite. Are you sure you can't help me out?"

Chester looked at the woman's face. She gave him a big smile, and above that smile were two startlingly beautiful powder blue eyes, partially hidden by long thick lashes.

"Okay, I guess it will be all right. Where are you going?"

"Looks like I'm going to Santa Fe," said the young woman, opening the car door.

The woman tossed a small backpack into the backseat and locked her door.

"Hi, I'm Storm."

"And your last name?"

"Just Storm."

"That's an unusual name."

"Maybe."

"My name is Chester. Chester Fortunberry."

"And you think my name is unusual?"

Storm reminded Chester of a porcelain doll with her thin frame, pale white skin, long black hair, pretty blue eyes and full lips. She looked soft but Chester knew, even after just a first brief visual inspection, that if he reached out and touched her, she would feel hard. He could see the muscle tone in her arms, the cords in her long neck, the strength in her hands, and the sharp edges of her cheekbones. She wore no watch or jewelry. On the inside of her right wrist was a small three-word tattoo that read, *So it goes.*

"All you have is that little backpack?"

"I travel light."

Chester drove onto the interstate and moved into the middle lane. He never picked up hitchhikers so he wasn't sure what the protocol was as far as who was supposed to talk first.

"Aren't you afraid someone might attack you?" asked Chester.

"Someone?"

"You know, whoever picks you up."

"Are you trying to frighten me?"

"No, I'm just posing a hypothetical question."

"I think you've seen too many movies."

"It could happen."

"Not to me."

"Why not?"

"Because if someone attacked me, I would kill them."

"Kill them?"

"In a heartbeat."

"But you're so tiny."

"It's not the size of the dog in the fight, it's the size of the fight in the dog. You can only be a victim if you allow yourself to be a victim."

"Yes, but ..."

"Chester, look into my eyes."

It wasn't what Storm said that surprised him, it was the way she said it, her voice as cold as steel on a freezing winter day. Chester kept both hands on the steering wheel and slowly turned to look at Storm. Her eyes, which had been a pretty powder blue when she got into the car, were now dark as coal and they were boring a hole into Chester.

"Stop that. Please," said Chester.

Storm smiled and in a flash the coal black turned to powder blue.

"Chester, I've been taking care of myself since I was a child. The kind of stuff you're asking me about doesn't happen to people like me. That kind of stuff happens to people like you."

"Why's that?"

"Look at me. Look at you."

Chester was quiet for a bit and then he said, "Yeah, I know."

"You have something in the corner of your mouth. Something yellow."

Chester looked in the rear view mirror. A dab of dried mustard was in the right corner of his mouth. He licked his finger and wiped the mustard off.

"Oh, sorry. I had a corned beef and swiss cheese sandwich a little while ago. I was kind of in a rush when I ate it."

"Why's that?"

Chester looked at Storm and hesitated.

"You wouldn't believe me if I told you."

"Try me. We've got a lot of time to kill between here and Santa Fe."

Chester looked at Storm again. He wasn't sure if he should tell her anything about the past few days, not because he thought she might be involved, but because he was scared she would think he was crazy and demand to be let out of the car. Chester didn't want to leave her all alone again on a remote highway in the middle of the night, and he also wanted to have someone to talk to over the next ten hours.

"Well ..."

"Go ahead. Stop being so mysterious."

Chester beamed when she said that. Chester had never been mysterious in his entire life. The fact that someone thought he was mysterious, or was being mysterious, made him feel special. Here he was, fleeing from bad guys in a car barreling down the interstate with a beautiful woman sitting next to him. When would that ever happen again? Besides that, what did he have to lose, he thought to himself. And then he marveled that it was the first time he could remember that he had ever done anything after first thinking, what do I have to lose?

155

So Chester told Storm the whole story, from the moment the revelation came to him up to the moment he picked her up hitchhiking. It took him almost a half hour to cover everything and during that time Storm only interrupted him twice.

The first time, very early in his story, was when he told her about his revelation.

"So you're saying that only you are real, and nobody else exists?"

"Yes."

"Well, I guess it sucks to be me," said Storm with a laugh.

The second time was when he mentioned seeing the two dark men for the first time. After he told her that part, Storm said, "Hold on." Then she turned in her seat to look at the empty highway behind them, and then turned back. "Okay, go on."

Chester stopped occasionally when recalling the events of the past week to give Storm a chance to ask other questions, but she kept quiet, staring straight ahead for the most part. When he finished, Storm still didn't say anything. Chester wasn't sure if she had tuned him out after the first few minutes or whether she was just shocked by everything he had told her. The longer the silence went on, the more uneasy Chester started to get.

"You're not saying anything," said Chester.

"I know," said Storm.

"Why not?"

"I'm letting it all sink in. Give me a minute."

"Certainly."

Storm eventually turned in her seat to look at Chester.

"Let me see if I have this straight. You are the only real person on this planet. Everybody else and everything else is a figment of your imagination. You were kidnapped by two dark men and held captive in a basement for several days. You escaped by using only your mind to open a locked door. During your escape you took time to make a corned beef and swiss cheese sandwich. You are probably being chased by a guy named Theodore, a God-voice and two thugs. And right now I am all alone with you in a car in the middle of the night on a barren highway with no other cars in sight. Have I summed it up correctly?"

"Yes, I would say so."

"Oh my," said Storm.

▼

"Is Storm your real name?"

"No."

"Who came up with that name?"

"One of my foster parents."

"One of them?"

"I had a lot of foster parents."

"Why Storm?"

"Apparently my behavior was somewhat akin to a hurricane and a tornado."

"Oh, so you were a problem child?"

"You could say that."

"What about now?"

"No longer a child. Still a problem."

"You don't seem like a problem to me. You seem quite pleasant."

"That's nice to hear. What about you?"

"What about me what?"

"Is Chester Fortunberry your real name?"

"Of course it is. Why would you ask that?"

"Sounds like the name of a character in a cartoon."

"But it's my real name."

"You have my condolences."

"I take back what I said about you not being a problem."

Chester and Storm looked at each other. Then they both laughed.

"Chester, why would you tell me all this? You don't know me at all."

"I feel like I do. Don't ask me why. I just do."

"Well, I must say, I do envy you."

"Why's that?"

"I would be overjoyed to find out other people aren't real."

"Why is that?"

"People suck."

"That's rather harsh."

Storm unlatched her seat belt and shoulder strap which set off the car seat belt alarm. She leaned forward and latched the seat belt and shoulder strap behind her and then leaned back against the restraints. The alarm stopped.

"What are you ..." Chester started to say.

"Listen, I know it's your car and you are in charge, but I don't like to be restrained."

"But ..."

"Chester, if you hit a deer and I go flying through the windshield, I promise I won't sue you."

"But ..."

"Chester, it's done. Don't worry about it. Okay?"

Chester nodded. After awhile Chester looked over at Storm and said, "Why do you say people suck."

Storm smiled, like she knew Chester would eventually ask that question.

"Have you heard about the children of Beslan?" asked Storm.

"No."

"Really? Kind of funny, isn't it? Considering your revelation and all."

"If you say so. What about those children?"

"It's a true story. They made a documentary about it, *Children of Beslan*. You should watch it. It will change your life."

"What's it about?"

"Terrorists attacked a grade school in the town of Beslan in Russia and took a thousand hostages. When Russian troops stormed the school, the terrorists massacred the hostages. They killed over four hundred people, half of them children. Those children went to school one day to learn about our marvelous world and on that day they were slaughtered by adults."

"That's horrible. When did it happen?"

"Ten years ago."

"That recently?"

"Yes. The same year Facebook was launched to bring people together in love and harmony and NASA put rovers on Mars to explore the wonders of the universe, terrorists were bashing in the heads of children with rifle butts. Right here. On our planet."

"That's horrible."

"The story of the attack is told only by the children who survived. One young girl tries so hard to give voice to the horror she saw. Her lower lip starts to tremble, slowly at first and then faster and faster, until her whole head is shaking. Chester, it will tear your heart out. Why are we the only species filled with so much hate that, in the name of government or religion, we can justify killing children?"

"I don't think I want to watch that documentary."

"Everybody should have to. It puts what we think our own insurmountable problems are into perspective. It's about living in a world where some children go to birthday parties and Little League games, while others are mowed down by machine guns."

"I understand. The world can be a very bad place. Buy why tell me that story?"

"Because you asked me why I don't like people. I could tell you about a lot more. Like concentration camps in World War II, or women and children hacked to death with machetes in Rwanda, or husbands who kill their ex-wives and their children before killing themselves. Trust me, of all the living things on this planet, there is only one that is evil. And it's man."

They were both quiet for awhile and then Storm spoke again.

"Have you ever heard of Bill Hicks?"

"Why even ask me? You know the answer."

"He was a comedian. He's dead now, unfortunately. Want to know what he had to say about people?"

"Sure, why not?"

"He said, 'I'm tired of this back-slapping, isn't-humanity-neat bullshit. We're just a virus with shoes.'"

"A virus with shoes. I like that."

"Let me try one more. Samuel Johnson?"

"Didn't he do the dictionary?"

"Very good, Chester. Samuel Johnson is known as the most distinguished man of letters in English history. Guess what he said about people?"

"I don't have a clue."

"He said, 'I hate mankind, for I think myself one of the best of them, and I know how bad I am.'"

"I like the one about the virus better."

"Me too."

Chester was ready to move the conversation in a new direction.

"If you were a virus, Storm, what virus would you be?"

"I guess the rabies virus."

"Why that one?"

"Because if I get my teeth into you, you're done for."

"I don't doubt that."

"What about you?"

"That's easy. The mumps."

"Is that really a virus?"

"Yes, indeed. It's part of the Rubulavirus family and it causes painful swelling of the parotid gland, sometimes even testicular swelling."

"Chester, you are an odd bird."

Chester saw a great opening based on Storm's comment. "Speaking of birds, Storm, have you ever heard of the Koro Bustard?"

"Yes, I have. It's the largest flying bird in the world."

"How in the world did you know that?"

"I'm just smart that way, Chester."

▼

"Storm, I agree with you. It's amazing how mean people can be to each other."

"So why do you allow it?"

"Me?"

"Didn't you create all the people, even the mean ones?"

"Let's not go down that road. I'm not up to it."

"Relax, Chester, I'm just pulling your string."

"Oh, okay. You know, you sure do have strong opinions about mankind."

"Not mankind, people. You don't deal with mankind, you deal with people. Mankind doesn't have an impact on your daily life, people do or, in most cases, a particular person does. That's the problem."

"Are you referring to anyone specifically?"

"Well, let's take you for example."

"What!" said Chester.

"Just kidding," said Storm.

Storm pushed her long black hair behind her ears. Chester saw that she was not wearing earrings. For some reason, he knew that she wouldn't be.

"Chester, did you see how when I went from speaking in general about mankind to speaking in particular about you, I really got your attention?"

"Yes, because it was personal."

"It's always personal. It's never about all the people. It's always about one person which is why you telling me your revelation does not surprise me at all because your revelation is all about you. It's your personal."

"Well, it is my revelation and not anybody else's."

"Exactly, because every person wants to be considered important by other people. Notice I didn't say they want to feel important. Those are two different things. A person who feels important but has no people around to acknowledge that they are important is an unhappy person. Self satisfaction does not exist for most of us. We perceive our value to be the value that other people place on us. The three things people crave most are safety, as in a roof over their heads and plenty to eat; belonging, as in being part of a family and a community; and mattering, as in being publicly appreciated.

"A friend of mine wrote a song called *Jasmine*. It was the most beautiful song I have ever heard. He would play it for me on an acoustic guitar in his apartment. I cried every time I heard it. He hung himself one day. I found his body. I actually cut him down. All he had in his apartment was a butter knife. Do you know how long it takes to cut a nylon rope with a butter knife?"

Storm paused. Chester kept his eyes on the road. He didn't want to look at her.

"I know why he killed himself. It was because he didn't think he mattered. He had only one person, me, to tell him that he was special. But one person was not enough. Now, John Lennon wrote a song called *Imagine* which is the second most beautiful song I have ever heard. But millions of people who heard that song told him that he was talented and that he mattered. That's the difference."

Chester looked over at Storm. She looked back at him with a look neither happy nor sad.

"If I ever wrote a great song or wrote a great book or discovered the answer to a great secret, I would never tell anybody. I would share it only with myself. And that would be more than enough for me," said Storm. "That's why I can't understand why you would tell anyone about your revelation. Why would you share something so beautiful with people who will want to destroy it?"

Chester didn't have an answer. Instead he said, "Why such deep thoughts from someone so young?"

"I've had a hard life. I have not had the luxury of learning things in a slow and leisurely way. I have had to ascertain truth and reality not out of convenience but out of survival."

"You mean you didn't go to school very much?"

"I'm not talking about textbooks. I'm talking about the school of life. Most people grow up in a structured environment. They have been domesticated by family and society. They are like pet dogs. I am a wolf. I had no choice. Here's the difference between you and me: You say of everything, it could be this or it could be that. I say of everything, it is what it is. I don't see gray areas. I only see black and white."

"That's kind of a pessimistic attitude, isn't it?"

"Chester, an optimist is just a pessimist who hasn't been raped yet."

Storm's remark startled Chester. He looked over at her, but her head was turned away. She stared out the passenger window for a long time as they drove through the pitch black night in silence.

▼

"I'm sorry," said Storm.

"For what?"

"Telling depressing stories."

"That's okay."

Storm bounced up and down in her seat excitedly. "Let's lighten the mood. Wanna hear my favorite joke?"

"Yes, please."

"Okay, there are these two cows standing in a field ..."

"Wait a minute ..."

Storm stopped. "Have you heard this one before?"

"I'm not sure, let me think. Two cows in a field?"

"Yes."

"No, I don't think so."

"Then why interrupt me?" said Storm, exasperated, no longer bouncing. "Timing is very important in telling jokes."

"I just wanted to make sure I hadn't heard it before. It's awkward for me if someone starts to tell a joke and I realize I've heard it before. I can't pretend I'm hearing it for the first time and laugh. It's awkward. I don't like awkward."

"So, if you haven't heard it before, can I proceed?"

"Yes."

"And you won't interrupt me again?"

"I promise."

"Okay," said Storm, starting the excited seat bouncing again. "There are these two cows standing in a field. One cow turns to the other cow and says, 'Hey, have you heard about that Mad Cow Disease that's going around?' And the other cow says, 'Good thing I'm a helicopter.'"

Chester was quiet a second or two and then he howled with laughter.

"Now that was funny," said Chester. "Tell it to me again."

Storm repeated the joke and Chester again howled.

"I like that joke for two reasons," said Chester.

"Which are?"

"First, because it's funny in an absurd way. And second, because right now I can comprehend and appreciate something absurd. A month ago if you had told me that joke, I would not have gotten it. It would not have been plausible to me, cows talking, one thinking it was a helicopter. My accountant's mind would have rejected the whole premise. But now, after my revelation, I seem to be more open minded. I like that."

Storm laughed. "It took you longer to explain why you liked my joke then it took me to tell you the joke. But good for you."

"Tell it to me again," said Chester.

"Maybe later. That was my favorite joke. Now, let me tell you my favorite story."

And so Storm told Chester the story about Pat Perry and the silver arrow.

"Believe it or not, I used to be a newspaper reporter. A long time ago. I was working at a paper on the East Coast when the city editor said 'Well, he sure pulled a Pat Perry' about a reporter's front-page article. I asked what he meant. He said Pat Perry had been a shy, wisp of a reporter with the smallest desk in the farthest corner of the newsroom. Pat quietly churned out run-of-the-mill articles that never made the front page. Every day the reporters went to the local coffee shop and never thought to invite Pat. He was just there, an anonymous fixture like one of the desks in the newsroom. He worked the worst shifts at the newspaper, so he was the only reporter in the newsroom one bone-cold winter night, which just happened to be Christmas Eve, when the phone call came in.

"And what a phone call it was. A state trooper had come upon a doe laying in the road. The trooper assumed the deer had been hit by a car, but when he checked, not only was the doe still alive, it had a thirty-inch silver arrow sticking through it's head. He placed the doe in the trunk of his cruiser and raced to a nearby veterinarian's office."

"Then what happened?" interrupted Chester in an anxious voice.

"Pat rushed to the vet's office and returned to the newsroom just minutes before deadline. He furiously typed away then handed his article to the city editor, saying, 'Get this in, please.'

"Not only did the editor get it in, he ran the story on the front page above the fold. And when the city awoke Christmas morning, they were greeted by a news story with Pat Perry's byline on it and a giant headline that read: *State Trooper Saves Rudolph the Red-Nosed Reindeer*.

"The newsroom phones rang all day on Christmas day with calls from both parents and children asking to talk to Pat. Letters, many of them with notes scrawled in crayon, arrived at the newsroom for Pat. Every reporter stopped by Pat's desk to congratulate him. Even the Publisher, an aloof man who seldom came into the newsroom, made the trek from his office down the hall to Pat's desk to shake his hand.

"After that Pat still got most of the boring news assignments, but the editors moved him to a bigger desk closer to the center of the newsroom. Everyone noticed a new bounce in Pat's step. A few of the reporters started inviting him to join them on coffee breaks. Pat retired in his early sixties and a few years later passed away in his sleep. The lead sentence in his obituary, which was personally written by none other than the Publisher, referenced the fact that Pat was the author of the Rudolph the Red-Nosed Reindeer news story. That's why whenever a reporter hits a homerun with a news story, they say he pulled a 'Pat Perry.'"

When Storm finished telling the story, Chester looked at her and said, "I like that story. I like it a lot. Pat Perry reminds me of me."

"Of course he does, Chester," said Storm. "Of course he does."

And as she said it, Storm reached over and patted Chester lightly on his right shoulder.

Just the way Harriette always did.

▼

"How long were you at the newspaper?"
"A year."
"Why did you leave?"
"I always leave."

Chapter Fourteen

Storm had told Chester a funny joke and an interesting story. Chester felt like he needed to contribute. He thought about a joke, a limerick really, he heard when he was a freshman in high school.

No one had told him the limerick. He had overheard one of the jocks tell his buddies while in the school cafeteria line. He heard it, thought it was funny in a deliciously naughty way, and he remembered it. He would tell it to himself every now and then, never telling it to anyone else, whenever he needed an inside-his-head laugh.

Storm would be the first person he ever told the limerick to.

Chester cleared his throat, which got Storm's attention, and then he said in a sing-song voice, "In days of old, when knights were bold, and rubbers weren't invented, you stuck a sock, right on your cock, and babies were prevented."

Storm jerked back, her eyes wide and her mouth open as if she was about to say the letter O. It was like she recoiled from him. Chester had never said anything in his life that made another person recoil. He was surprised and confused.

"What?" he said nervously.

"Chester, you said 'cock.'"

Chester looked embarrassed. His cheeks flushed red. "I had to. It's part of the joke," he stammered.

"You had to, or you wanted to?"

Chester thought for a moment, then said, "I wanted to."

"Say it again."

"The joke?"

"No, that word."

Chester hesitated, then said, "cock."

Storm laughed a deep and hearty laugh. "Chester, I don't know what's funnier, your limerick or hearing the word cock come out of your mouth."

"Why is that?"

"Because, coming from you it is so unexpected. I love it."

"You do?"

"Very much so. There is nothing more wonderful in this world than the unexpected."

Chester stopped being embarrassed. He liked doing something unexpected. He didn't think he had it in him.

"You didn't know you had that in you, did you?" said Storm.

"No, not really."

"Well, you do, Chester. Think about everything you've done, everything that has happened to you, over the past week. You have been living the unexpected. You are up to your neck in it. Isn't that marvelous?"

▼

"Storm, do you believe in God?"

"I want to. Desperately. But the proof eludes me."

"How about religion?"

"I can do without that snake oil, thank you."

"Why?"

"To paraphrase a quote I read somewhere, 'I don't have a problem with God; it's his representatives that I don't particularly like.'"

Chester looked out the side window of the Avis rental car at the coal black sky and the shiny bright stars. The sky looked like a piece of black paper mache that someone had pricked hundreds of times with a knitting needle, leaving tiny white holes in it.

"Look at all those stars. They're so bright tonight."

Storm leaned forward and looked through the windshield at the night sky.

"That's my salvation," said Storm.

"What do you mean?"

"That's my religion out there. All that space, all those planets. It's my escape from here."

"So, you want to be an astronaut?"

Storm laughed. "No, what I mean is the universe reminds me every day of how small and insignificant we all are in the grand scheme of things."

"Whose grand scheme?" asked Chester impishly.

"Why yours, of course, Chester. You made a beautiful universe."

"Thank you."

"From space, looking down, we look like so many tiny ants. Most people spend their days doing the same tasks over and over again, never traveling outside of a thirty-mile radius from their nest. People here have never seen the Golden Frog of Guyana and probably don't even know Guyana exists. People in Guyana have never seen the pronghorn antelope of Nebraska and probably don't even know Nebraska exists. Our view is so narrow because we are so self-absorbed. We barely know about all the unique things on our own planet, much less all the unique things in our universe. I find that strange, and also comforting. Knowing there is more to everything gives me hope."

"Hope for what?"

"Hope that we don't really matter."

"Why would that be comforting?"

Storm didn't answer him. She leaned forward again to look at the stars.

"Chester, do you know what our galaxy is called?"

"The Milky Way."

"And do you know how many stars and planets are in our Milky Way?"

"A thousand or so."

"No. There are billions, in fact hundreds of billions."

"Billions with a 'B'?"

"Yes, with a big ol' capital 'B.'"

"That's a lot."

"How many galaxies do you think there are in our universe?"

"Besides the Milky Way?"

"Yes."

Chester hesitated. If one galaxy, the Milky Way, had hundreds of billions of stars and planets taking up all that space in the universe, there couldn't be very much room left for too many more galaxies. You can only fit so much sand into a bucket.

"About a hundred."

"No, wrong again. There are hundreds of billions of galaxies in our universe."

"Again with a 'B'?"

"Yes."

"And do each of those galaxies have their own hundreds of billions of stars and planets?"

"Yes.

"That's amazing.

"I know. Mind boggling, isn't it?"

"It certainly is."

Chester leaned forward to look up at the stars, his chin resting on the top of the steering wheel.

"By the way, Chester, shouldn't you already know all this. You know, considering your revelation."

"I can't be expected to remember everything."

"This isn't like saying you can't remember where you left your car keys. It's a little bigger than that."

"I know. But ..."

"You don't have to explain anything, Chester. I'm just making conversation."

Chester nodded his head, leaned back in his seat.

"Chester, I presume you live in a house in a nice community."

"I do."

"Are you a good neighbor?"

"I like to think so."

"Are you an attentive neighbor?"

"Yes."

"Because being aware of your surroundings is important, right?"

"Absolutely."

"So, do you know the name of your next-door neighbor?"

"To the left or to the right."

"Either."

"The Carlins are on the left and the Tongs are on the right."

"Okay, you also live on planet Earth. Do you know the name of your next-door planet neighbor?

"You mean, what planet is closest to us?"

"Yes."

"I believe it's Venus."

"Very good."

"And do you know the name of your next-door galaxy neighbor?"

Chester didn't. He was stumped. "Uh, no."

"Well, do you know the names of any other galaxies in your neighborhood?"

"Uh, no."

"Chester there are hundreds of billions of other galaxies besides the Milky Way. They are all your neighbors, and you don't know any of their names?"

"Uh, no."

"Does that surprise you?"

"I never really thought about it before."

"Have you heard of the Andromeda Galaxy?"

"What's that?"

"That is our closest galaxy neighbor. It has over a trillion stars and planets in it. That's a trillion with a capital 'T.'"

"Wow."

"And if you are here five billion years from now, you will be able to meet the Andromeda Galaxy in person."

"Why's that?"

"That's when the Andromeda Galaxy will collide with the Milky Way."

"Oh my."

Chester was impressed. "I had no idea there was so much stuff in our universe."

"There is, and that's just our universe."

"There's more than one universe?"

"Everyone seems to think so."

"Who is everyone?"

"You know, the smart people."

"And what do they say?"

"Do you want the names of their theories or just the theories?"

"Let's keep it simple."

"Okay. These are a few of your choices. The universe is recurring, and will continue to repeat itself in the same way forever, expanding with a Big Bang and collapsing with a Big Crunch, again and again and again. Or, it's an infinite universe where every possible event will occur an infinite number of times. Or, it's infinite universes plural, where everything that could possibly have happened in our past, but did not, has occurred in the past of some other universe. Or, a new universe is created whenever a diversion in events occurs. Or, and this is my favorite theory, we are one of many universes that have been simulated on complex computer systems."

"Like we are part of a video game?"

"Yes, we are the game."

"But who's playing the game?"

"That's the million dollar question."

"That's a lot of theories," said Chester. "Seems like they all lean toward multiple universes that repeat themselves over and over again."

"Yes."

"Sounds like *Groundhog Day*."

"It does, doesn't it."

Chester had a confused look in his face.

"What's wrong?"

"I only remember making one universe," said Chester.

"Storm, why do you know so much about the universe?"

"I make it my business to know a little bit about every environment that I find myself in."

"You seem to be contemplating an expansive environment."

"It's still all one neighborhood."

"If you are telling me all this to make me feel small and insignificant, you don't have to do that. I've felt small and insignificant my whole life."

"What about now? Now that your revelation has revealed the truth? Don't you feel a little bigger, a little more significant."

"Well, yes, now that you mention it."

"Good, then enjoy it, Chester. You deserve it."

"I do, don't I?"

"Yes you do, my friend."

Chester liked that Storm called him her friend. Hearing her say that made him feel even better than feeling a little bigger and a little more significant did.

"Storm, do you think there is life on other planets?"

"Depends how you define life."

"You know, people like us."

"That would be my worst nightmare."

▼

"We aren't all that," said Storm.

"Excuse me?"

"I said, 'We aren't all that.'"

"I don't understand."

"People think they are all that and a bag of chips."

"I'm sorry. I still don't follow you."

"We think we are the center of the universe. At one point we even thought the universe rotated around us. Our narcissistic arrogance knows no bounds. Want to hear the stats?"

"Sure. I like numbers."

"Okay, here's how it went down. The Big Bang happened fourteen billion years ago. Earth came along four and a half billion years ago. And Modern Man, the version that was able to walk upright and make a fire, came along about two hundred thousand years ago. To put it into perspective, if you could walk around the Earth along the equator, the first mile you walked would be the length of time man has been on Earth and the rest of the miles you walked—to walk completely around the world at its widest point—would be the length of time that the Earth has existed without man on it. My guess is that man will be extinct within the next thousand years while Earth and the universe will continue on for many billions of year longer. So, when it's all said and done, our time on Earth will be of the same length and of the same relevance as a mosquito fart in the middle of a typhoon."

"Why will we be extinct a thousand years from now?"

"Take your pick. Nuclear annihilation. Worldwide plague. The computers kill us off."

Chester listened, but didn't say anything. They drove in silence for a bit.

"You forgot global warming," said Chester.

"Oh, yeah. That too."

Storm leaned forward again and looked up through the windshield at the night sky.

"Beautiful, isn't it?"

"Yes," said Chester.

"It looks like black paper mache that someone has pricked hundreds of times with a knitting needle, leaving tiny white holes in it," said Storm.

Chester felt the hairs on his arms stand up. That sounded like something Chester would say. In fact, it sounded like something he had thought just a few minutes ago.

"People spend all their lives looking down, or straight ahead, or to the side, or behind them, but they seldom look up. In their minds what is above them is just a ceiling. A ceiling that is blue and white during the day and black and white at night."

"A ceiling, like in a house?"

"Kind of. More like a box. We are box people. We feel more comfortable when there is a floor beneath our feet, walls on each side of us, and a ceiling above us. Whether it's a chilly cave or a luxury mansion. We work inside boxes, we drive around inside boxes, we shop inside boxes, we fly inside boxes, we make love and give birth inside boxes. The only time we leave a box, be it our home or office or car, is to travel to another box. So when we aren't in one of those little boxes, when we're outside, we think of what is above us as just another box ceiling. The proof of how small and insignificant we are is right there above us. We just have to look up at the stars and realize that, holy shit, we are only tiny specks. But we don't look up that much, and when we do, the enormity of what is above us escapes us."

Storm looked at Chester to make sure he was following her. Chester nodded his head so she would know that he was. And then the hairs on his arms stood up again, because Storm said, "It's like homeless people on the street. They are there, but we never really see them. We see something, but we don't see fellow human beings. We don't see what those bundles of rags represent. So we walk right by them."

The fact Storm had just described the black paper mache night sky the exact way he had thought about it a few minutes earlier and the fact Storm had just spoken about homeless people, more specifically about how non-homeless people don't see homeless people, unnerved Chester. It was like he was having a conversation with himself.

Storm sighed and leaned back in her seat. "You know, Chester, this really plays into your revelation."

"How so?"

"If you told the average person about your revelation, they would say you were crazy. They would say, 'Hey, what are you talking about? I'm standing right in front of you. I'm talking to you. You can see me and hear me. So how can you say that I don't exist?'"

Chester nodded. "I assume they would."

"Of course they would. But if you asked that same person about what is above them, about the billions of stars and planets, they would brush you off or plead ignorance. For them, none of what is above them really exists, even though they can see it. It's really no different than your revelation."

"That's an interesting point. And it reminds me," said Chester.

"Reminds you of what?"

"The intersection."

Storm waited. And waited some more.

"Chester?"

"Oh, sorry. It reminds me of an intersection I was at one day."

Storm looked at him, cocked an eyebrow.

"I can see it like it happened yesterday. I was in my car stopped at a light. It was usually a busy intersection, but that afternoon there were no cars in any direction. The sidewalks were empty. All of a sudden the clear afternoon sky turned black with dark clouds and roaring winds. It was blowing so hard the traffic lights were swinging back and forth. My window was down and I felt cold air engulf me. And for a moment, a moment that seemed to last forever, I felt like I was all alone in the world, like every living thing had just disappeared. I knew that wasn't possible. I knew that intersection was usually teeming with life. But I felt a loneliness and sadness that chilled me to the bone."

"That's interesting, Chester, but I'm having a hard time figuring out how it relates to what I was just talking about."

Chester thought for a bit, started to answer, stopped, thought for a bit again, and then said, "You're right. I don't know why I told you that story."

"No worries. When did the intersection thing happen?"

"Oh, a long time ago."

"Not at the same time as your revelation?"

"No, why?"

"Because that seemed like a perfect time for you to have your revelation. You know, feeling totally alone, the cold wind, the dark skies, all that stuff."

"No, I had the revelation in my bathroom. After my bowel movement."

Storm didn't respond. Chester was quiet for awhile, then he said, "That sounds a little strange, doesn't it?"

"Actually Chester, now that I've gotten to know you, it sounds appropriate."

▼

Talking about the intersection opened the door to another memory for Chester. Many years ago, before he met Harriette, Chester had sat on a big rock on a hill in the middle of a park forest. He couldn't remember why he was there. Maybe he was on a picnic with his family, or maybe on a class outing. He couldn't remember the details, but he could remember the rock and the trees and the glistening water in a small pond at the bottom of the hill.

Two things had surprised him that day.

The first was how quiet it was in the woods. Quiet for all his senses. Quiet on his ears because all he heard was the rustling of leaves and soft bird calls. He heard no loud voices or blaring car horns. Quiet on his eyes because all he saw was a pleasant green. There were no bright colors of garish billboards or sharp angles of buildings. Quiet on his nose because what he smelled was clean and natural. There was no cigarette smoke or car exhaust fumes. Quiet on his tongue because all he tasted was fresh air. There was no taste of fried food or bitter smog. And it was quiet on his skin because all he felt was the cool breeze tickling his face. There were no people brushing up against him or cars zipping past him.

It was quiet, Chester realized, because it was him alone. There were no other people and all of the sense-aggravating baggage they brought with them. He felt a calmness and peacefulness that he had never felt before. He liked it.

But in that calm and peaceful state of mind came the second thing that surprised him. And he wasn't sure if he liked it. It was the realization that he was there, in that forest, sitting on that rock, with just himself.

Chester was alone with Chester.

And just who was that person?

There were no other people or things around to influence or impact him. If he wanted to cross his legs, if he wanted to think about strawberry shortcake, if he wanted to yell, if he wanted to do anything, it was up to him. Up to the Chester sitting on the rock, and the Chester inside of him. For the first time it made the Chester on the outside, the one he knew best and who he saw in the mirror every day, wonder about the Chester inside of him. How well did he know that Chester, or did he even know that Chester at all? He felt like he, and everybody he came in contact with, knew the outside Chester. If the outside Chester fainted in public, people saw it. If the outside Chester sang a song,

174

people heard it. But if the inside Chester was jealous or heartbroken or added numbers in his head or thought about living on a deserted island, only the two Chesters knew about it.

Later, when Chester was in college and his professor talked about Rene Descartes and the whole I-think-therefore-I-am-thing, Chester immediately thought about his afternoon on the rock in the forest. The more the professor talked, the more amazed Chester was. Amazed that a realization he believed only he had ever had was given a voice centuries ago. Amazed that it was being taught in a classroom. He was so amazed that Chester, who never spoke in class, said out loud, to no one in particular, "Amazing!"

"Yes, Chester. Did you have a question?" the professor had asked.

The students, who had never heard Chester utter a single peep, turned to look at him.

"Oh, nothing," said Chester suddenly nervous and embarrassed.

"Chester, I heard you say something. Speak up. What do you think about Descartes' philosophical statement?"

Chester fidgeted, looked left to right. He felt like a trapped animal. "Well?"

"I think he had a very active imagination," Chester had blurted.

"Precisely," the professor had said in a loud booming voice. "Excellent answer, Chester."

Chester was as shocked that he had spoken in class as he was that whatever he said had pleased his professor. That would have opened the door for any other person to speak in class more often, but not Chester. He knew it was a fluke that he had been put on the spot and had pulled the right answer out of thin air. Once was enough. There would be no more "Amazing!" outbursts and no more answering questions in class for Chester.

Years later, when Chester and Harriette were having dinner, Chester had looked at the petite filet on his plate next to the unopened baked potato and two piles of green beans and broccoli. It was unusual for Harriette to serve two vegetables of the same color. That sure is a lot of green, thought Chester. All that green and the potato, which looked just like a rock, made Chester think of the afternoon he had sat on the rock in the forest.

Harriette noticed Chester staring at his food. "Anything wrong, dear?"

"No, I was just thinking," said Chester, who decided right then and there to do a test. He thought about something very unusual. He

175

thought about a yellow kangaroo wearing a summer dress.

"Harriette?"

"Yes, dear."

"I'm thinking about something. Can you tell me what it is?"

Harriette answered right away. "No."

"But you didn't even try," protested Chester. "I'm going to think of it again and see if you can tell me what it is."

Harriette set her fork down and stared at Chester. Chester thought about the yellow kangaroo in the summer dress again.

"Nope, no idea," said Harriette.

"Are you sure?"

"Chester, what's your point?"

"I guess you can't see into my mind."

"Of course I can't."

"But you know me better than anybody."

"Doesn't matter. Your mind is your own private world."

Chester realized Harriette had just summarized in one short sentence what he had spent hours sitting on a rock in the middle of a forest contemplating.

Harriette picked up her fork and took a bite of broccoli. She chewed the bite, swallowed and then looked at Chester, raising her right eyebrow.

"A yellow kangaroo wearing a summer dress," said Chester.

"What color was the dress?" asked Harriette.

Which was one of the many reasons Chester loved Harriette.

▼

"So Chester," asked Storm, "did you tell Harriette about your revelation?"

"No," said Chester, and he was about to explain why, but then he stopped.

Something wasn't right.

He thought about what wasn't right for a bit, and then he realized what wasn't right, and for the third time in less than five minutes the hair on his arms stood up. He looked at Storm.

"How do you know about Harriette?"

"Your wife?"

"Yes, that Harriette."

"You mentioned her earlier."

Chester thought about it, mentally recounting their conversations, and then said, "No, I don't think I did."

"Are you sure?"

"I'm positive."

"Maybe you didn't," said Storm.

Chapter Fifteen

"This is interesting," said Chester.

"What is?"

"Part of the reason I stopped to give you a ride, besides worrying about you being a young woman alone at night on the side of the road, was to have someone to talk to. And we've been talking about some very intriguing things. I've always been interested in space and the universe, more so now because of the revelation. What about time? Do you ever think about time?"

"All the time," said Storm.

"That's clever. The other day I was explaining the concept of time to Phillip."

"Who's Phillip?"

"Oh, I work with him."

"Do you like him?"

"I can't say that I like him, but I also can't say that I don't like him."

"Let me guess. He's younger than you and more outgoing than you and sometimes he picks on you in front of other people."

"How do you know that?"

"You told me."

"I did? When?"

"When you said his name. How you said it."

"That's interesting you could deduce that. If you were talking to Phillip about time, how would you explain it?"

"I wouldn't be talking to Phillip."

"Why not?"

"Because I don't like him."

"But you don't even know him."

"I know enough."

Chester laughed. "Okay, forget about Phillip. How would you explain time to someone you do like?"

"Aquariums," said Storm.

Chester waited. He was excited. He knew Storm was intelligent and succinct in what she had to say. He could not wait to see how she would go from aquarium to time. Picking Storm up hitchhiking, thought Chester, was one of the best things he had done since starting his journey.

"I'm listening," said Chester.

"Well," said Storm, rubbing her hands together, "think of space as a container and time as us moving through that container. Kind of like a goldfish swimming through an aquarium that stretches on forever. Using that analogy, when the goldfish swims forward, the water it swims through does not disappear. It's still there behind him. And the water it swims forward into doesn't just magically appear at that moment. It was already there in the aquarium in front of him. So, if the water behind the goldfish doesn't go away and if the water in front of the goldfish is always there before he swims into it, that can only mean one thing."

"Which is?"

"We aren't moving through time. All of time exists at once."

"Interesting. Are we still the goldfish?"

"Yes."

"Are we still swimming through the water in the aquarium?"

"Yes."

"Storm, believe it or not, this is kind of what I tried to explain to Phillip, but the example I used was the slap."

"Is that where you slap something to make a loud noise, wait a few seconds, and then ask the person you are talking to where the slap went?"

Chester just stared at Storm.

"Relax," said Storm with a grin. "It wasn't hard for me to guess how you would use the sound of a slap to explain time. Do you know why paintings have frames?"

"To hang them on the wall."

"Yes and no. Paintings have frames so we know where the painting ends."

Chester raised his eyebrows.

"We came up with inches and miles so we could describe the size of things and the distance between them. We came up with clocks to describe when things begin and end. The universe doesn't acknowledge hours or days or rulers or speedometers. Only we do. We have words we use to describe something when those words are just another form of measurement. When you hear the word *afternoon* you think of a specific segment of the day, but it's just a time measurement, as in that segment of the day that comes *after*-noon. It could just as easily have been called *before*-evening. We have this curious need to label everything around us, as if giving something a name, like space or time, will adequately explain it."

"So, what you are saying is ..."

"The past, the present and the future are just words we came up with. Those words are a defense mechanism to fool ourselves into believing everything is not happening at once. Without that white lie, we'd go crazy. We think as we are swimming through the aquarium, that the water, or time, we swim through just magically disappears and that the water, or the time, in front of us just magically appears. That's incorrect. There is no magic."

"So, we're all goldfish?" asked Chester.

"You're a goldfish. Me, I'm a piranha."

"Not a shark?"

"Too big. I prefer small and deadly. But let me continue."

"Please do."

"We are so sure there are only three aspects of time: past, present and future. Just like we believe there are only four dimensions: length, width, depth and time. Now scientists say there are ten dimensions and the fifth and the sixth have to do with the future and if we can master those two we will be able to travel back in time and into the future. Imagine that! But thinking there are multiple dimensions and multiple universes is really not absurd. My past is different than your past and my future will be different from your future. So right there, between the two of us, there are two different pasts and two different futures. Multiply that by the billions of people on the planet and you can see how many different pasts and futures there are."

Chester fidgeted. Everything Storm was saying was interesting, but she was getting off topic. He wanted to talk about time, not multiple dimensions.

180

"Sorry, I'm getting off topic aren't I?" said Storm.

Chester nodded, no longer surprised that she would say something he had just thought of in his head. He appreciated Storm's observations, but the more she talked the more left out of the discussion he felt.

"You know ..." said Chester to get Storm's attention. He was eager to participate.

"What?"

"... football."

Chester tossed that one word out there, just like Storm had thrown out the word "aquariums."

Storm smiled and said, "Go ahead."

"If I watch an old Superbowl on TV, I can see and hear the game, but I can't feel the stands, or smell the winter air, or taste the popcorn. But in the future I might be able to. Fifty years ago detectives had evidence with DNA on it that would eventually solve their cases. Something was at that crime scene they didn't even know existed. So, what is still around from that old Superbowl game that we don't know exists, but eventually we will? One day we may be able to feel and taste and smell that football game which could allow us to go back in time and be there while it happens. Because if matter is neither created or destroyed, then why not time?"

Storm nodded her head. "Your football example is good, but we already do travel through time. In our dreams."

"What do you mean?"

"I can dream about a barbecue I was at as a child and smell the smoke from the fire pit and taste the toasted marshmallows and see the colored balloons and hear the music playing and feel the grass under my bare feet. All five senses satisfied. I can also dream about being at a future event and see and hear and taste and feel and smell everything that will happen at that event."

"What kind of future event?"

"Say, riding a roller coaster at Coney Island on the Fourth of July in the year 2020."

"So, that could happen?"

"It's already happened."

"But it's in the future."

Storm waited patiently.

"There is no future, right?" said Chester. "Or past or present."

"Now you're starting to get it," said Storm.

"Are we done with time?" asked Chester.

"Almost," said Storm. "I have one more thing for you to consider. The moments we are aware of we describe as time. While the moments we aren't aware of we don't consider time. And that could be a mistake."

"Come again?"

"Follow me on this," said Storm. "Years ago if you took a Polaroid photo of a pecan tree, you would capture in that moment a single pecan tree. You could confidently describe that moment as being only one pecan tree. Today, though, if you took a photo of that same pecan tree with a high definition panoramic camera, you would capture in that moment dozens of other trees and houses and people on either side of the one pecan tree. Same tree, same moment, but two completely different descriptions of what that moment contained. So how do we know there is not much more to the moments we are aware of, on either side of them, than what we can see with our limited Polaroid eye?"

Storm stopped. "Wow, need to catch my breath."

"Yes, you've got my head reeling."

"Maybe because it is all in your head."

"Excuse me?"

"There are also some people who think time is simply the passage of memories from our short-term memory to our long-term memory. And since memories are only in our head, that would mean that time is only in our head."

"Sometimes Harriette tells me it's all in my head."

"There you go."

▼

Chester realized he and Storm were pretty much on the same page about time. She was even using some of the same arguments he had used with Phillip. He could have told her she was preaching to the choir, but it was comforting to hear someone else espouse the same beliefs. Plus, she was giving him some good analogies he could use the next time he discussed time with Phillip, or anyone else who expressed an interest in the topic.

"So do you believe time exists?" said Chester.

"Time may be the only thing that exists."

"How so?"

"Well," said Storm, "humans consider themselves unique, so they've based their theory of existence on their uniqueness. One is our unit of measure, and one plus one equals two. That's all we've learned. But one plus one has never equaled two. There are, in fact, no numbers and no letters. We've codified our existence to bring it down to human size to make it comprehensible, to forget its unfathomable scale. And if humans are not the unit of measure and the world isn't governed by mathematical laws, then what governs everything? Time is the only true unit of measure. It gives proof to the existence of matter. Without time, we don't exist."

"Wow, that sounded incredible."

"I stole it."

"Stole it?"

"From a movie, called *Lucy*."

"Who's Lucy?"

"Just see the movie, Chester. You'll enjoy it."

Chester made a mental note, saying the name of the movie several times in his head so he wouldn't forget it. Then he thought of a question.

"You said that without time we don't exist, but you also said you believe in time. So does that mean you think we exist?"

"Hard to say. We know an apple exists because we can bite into it. At the same time we talk about an idea but we have no proof from our senses that an idea exists at all since we can't see or touch it. Even known things like our physical bodies that are evidenced by our senses might not be real except in our minds. Things like shape, color, smell, texture, weight, temperature, and sound are all dependent on our minds. If there are no minds to apply those qualities to things, then those things would be unobservable and unimaginable. Since we can't make direct contact with reality outside of our own minds, we can't be sure reality exists."

Chester thought about what Storm had just said. It was a mighty long answer to a very short question.

"So, you're saying our minds exist, but our bodies might not?"

"I can go with that."

▼

"Chester, I hate to break it to you, but you're really not all that special."

"I never said I was special."

Storm, mimicking Chester's voice: "I'm the only real person. Nobody else is real. I know everything and I am everything. Look at me, look at me, look at me."

Storm gave Chester a playful shot in his arm. "And that's not saying your special?"

"I don't sound like that do I?"

"A little."

"But that sounded whiny."

"You do sound whiny sometimes."

"What I say, or how I say it?"

"Both."

"Thanks a lot."

"Hey, you asked."

"Why do you say I'm not that special."

"Because everybody thinks they're special."

"How so?"

"If you won millions of dollars in the lottery would you be surprised?"

"Absolutely."

"For how long?"

"Forever."

"No you wouldn't. You would be surprised initially. But eventually, as time went on, you would think that, of course, something marvelous happened to you. It was meant to be. It had to happen to you. Because in your world, you are the most important person in the world. Everybody thinks like that. Not just you. Even the most under appreciated person on the planet thinks eventually their ship will come in. Think about it. What if aliens landed on earth today? What if Jesus Christ did come back to gather everyone up for a trip to heaven? Initially, you would be surprised, but eventually you would think that this huge, momentous thing could only happen while you were alive to see it. It certainly couldn't happen after you were gone."

Chester thought about Storm's earlier comment that in a thousand years there would be no more people on the planet. He wondered if that was something he had already planned and just didn't know it yet. And if that was the case, how was it going to happen? He asked Storm about it.

"I'd have to put my money on a worldwide plague," said Storm, yawning. "Chester, it's been a long day for me. Do you mind if I take a quick cat nap?"

"No, go right ahead."

"Thanks."

"I'll wake you up if I see a car with two dark guys in the rear view mirror."

"Chester, you're a real card."

Chester liked that. It was like when she said he was being mysterious.

Storm took off the light jacket she was wearing, balled it up and used it as a pillow against the passenger door window. In seconds she was asleep.

Chester rolled his window down a crack to get some fresh air, and then rolled it back up when he realized the noise of the whistling air might disturb Storm. He was surprised that he himself was not tired or sleepy, but he knew he was operating on pure adrenaline.

Storm's breathing was low and throaty. He looked at her more closely, now that he could do so without appearing to stare. She looked older in repose, her fiery inner strength hidden by sleep. He noticed for the first time that the knuckles on both of her hands were covered with tiny white scars, and that the pinkie finger on her left hand was crooked, as if it had been broken and had not healed properly. He saw another scar on the side of her neck, a raised welt the size of a quarter. Her nose was dainty, but it was bent slightly to the side and Chester could tell that it had been broken at least once. Mixed into her long black hair were strands of snow white hair. Each thing he saw, each wound, made Chester's heart hurt.

Chester drove for another two hours and saw the sun slowly creep up over the horizon on his left as he crossed the border from Utah into New Mexico. He knew that Santa Fe, and Uncle Frank's house, was only a few hours away. He might not be tired but he sure was hungry. A roadside billboard listed places to eat at the next exit five miles ahead. He wondered what the best way was to wake Storm. He didn't think it would be appropriate to tap her leg or her shoulder, so he just said "Storm" in a quiet voice.

Storm snapped awake immediately. As she did, she looked quickly left and right and Chester saw that both her hands were balled into fists.

"Good morning! We're in New Mexico now. Are you hungry?"

"I'm always hungry."

"You and me both."

▼

185

Chester exited the interstate and pulled into a twenty-four hour diner. He and Storm got out of the car. They stretched at the same time, saw each other stretching, and both laughed.

"After you," said Chester holding the diner door open.

"Why thank you, kind sir," said Storm.

Chester walked through the diner to a table at the back. It was the first time he could remember intentionally taking a seat with his back against the farthest wall so he could see the front door.

"That's smart, Chester," said Storm. "You're learning."

She took the chair to his right, not the chair across from him, so that she too had a view of the front door.

Chester picked up the menu, looked at it for just a second, and then put it down with an exaggerated flourish.

"I know exactly what I want. I don't even have to look."

"And what's that?"

"I'm having two soft-boiled eggs and whole wheat toast. That's what I have at home all the time. I miss it. What about you?"

"I'll have the same."

When the waitress came over, Chester placed the order for both of them, and then spent the next minute explaining to the waitress in great detail how the cook should prepare a perfect soft-boiled egg. The waitress, to her credit, did not roll her eyes and instead listened patiently. She assured Chester that Castro the cook was an expert at making soft-boiled eggs.

"The cook's name is Castro?"

"Yes."

"Is he from Cuba?"

"No. He's from Iowa."

When the waitress brought their plates, Chester dug in while Storm, despite saying earlier that she was hungry, slowly picked at her food.

"Chester?"

"Yes?"

"Do you feel safer now? Now that you've put some distance between yourself and that basement?"

"Oh yes."

"And do you think your Uncle Frank will be able to help you?"

"I think so. Uncle Frank seems to know a little bit about everything."

Storm set her fork down, reached across the table and placed her hand on top of Chester's hand.

"Chester, you are a good person. You do matter. Don't ever question that. I don't know if your revelation is true or not, but I do know that there is only one of you."

Chester felt a little awkward, both because Storm's hand was on his and because of what she was saying.

Storm slowly moved her hand from his and stood up. "I'm going to the little girl's room."

She started to leave and then turned back.

"Chester?"

"Yes."

"You will find your answer. But be careful. Things are not always what they appear to be."

"Is that a good thing or a bad thing?'

"A little of both."

"Okay," said Chester, now feeling confused as well as awkward.

Chester finished his eggs and toast just as Storm came back and sat down.

"My turn" said Chester, standing up and walking toward the restroom. When he returned to the table, he saw that the dirty dishes had been cleared away and the check was on the corner of the table. He also saw that Storm's chair was empty.

Chester sat down, looked the check over to make sure the charges were correct, and then raised his hand to get the waitress's attention. She came over to his table.

"Is everything all right, sir? How were those eggs?"

"They were excellent."

"That's good to hear."

"Do you know where the young lady went?"

The waitress gave him an odd look.

"What young lady?"

Chapter Sixteen

It is midnight and the cool ocean breeze has strands of Tonorau's black hair, hair as dark and thick as Crow's black fur, dancing on his forehead. Tonorau sits cross legged outside his hut, Crow's head in his lap. Tonorau looks up at the night sky and marvels at the thousands of white pinpricks in its black canvas. He rubs behind Crow's ears and the dog closes his eyes and lets out a contented sigh, a sigh strong enough to compete with the ocean breeze.

Thousands of miles away a man is driving down a dark highway with a young woman and they are marveling at the same black canvas with white pinpricks.

Tonorau stops rubbing behind Crow's ears and the dog raises his head and looks into his eyes.

"Soon," says Tonorau.

Chapter Seventeen

"Well, look who's here. Catalina, come meet my favorite shitbird nephew, Chester."

Uncle Frank, holding the door open, looked back over his shoulder. "Where the hell is that little chili pepper?"

Chester stood waiting with his suitcase. It began to feel heavy. "Can I come in?"

Uncle Frank hesitated, still waiting for a chili pepper to show up, until Chester held out the bottle of Lagavulin Scotch.

Uncle Frank's eyes lit up. "Certainly, come in, come in, what the hell are you waiting for?"

Uncle Frank took the bottle with one hand, grabbed Chester's shoulder with his other and pulled him through the doorway, kicking the door shut with a back kick as he walked Chester into the living room.

"Take a load off," said Uncle Frank, pushing Chester down into one of the living room chairs. "I'll be right back. Gonna grab some glasses."

Chester set his suitcase beside the chair, leaned back and put his hands on his knees. Something about being around Uncle Frank always made him feel like a school kid again. A flash of color caught his eye. He looked through the sliding glass doors into the backyard. A lithe and attractive young Hispanic woman in a very tiny pink and white polka-dot bikini was using a long pole with a net to clean leaves out of the pool. Each time she bent over to reach into the pool with the pole,

Chester saw the muscles in her calves and thighs tighten like coiled springs. She was covered in shiny suntan oil which accentuated the strong lines of her body.

"That's Catalina. Not bad, huh?" said Uncle Frank, sitting in a chair across from Chester. He poured a healthy splash of the Scotch over the ice in the two glasses, handing one to Chester and taking a big gulp out of his.

"I don't drink, Uncle Frank," said Chester setting the glass on an end table next to his chair.

Uncle Frank ignored the comment. "I found her down in Colombia five years ago. Married her right away. Doesn't speak a lick of English. In fact she doesn't speak much at all, but she's a keeper."

"What happened to ..." Chester started to say.

"The last one. Long gone. Couldn't put up with me. Can you believe that," said Uncle Frank with a cackle.

Chester studied Uncle Frank. He had to be in his eighties, but he looked the same as when he made the occasional visit to the house where Chester grew up. Still thin as a rail, still with a full head of hair, snow white now, no longer black, still with tanned and leathery skin like rawhide, and still with those hard-flint eyes that looked like they cut could diamonds. He had a small gold hoop earring in his left ear. Tattooed above the knuckles of his right hand was the word *long* and above the knuckles on his left hand the word *gone*. That was new. Chester didn't remember those tattooed fingers. The ink was a washed-out green and the letters were ragged. Chester was no expert, but even he could tell it was not a professional tattoo.

"That's new," said Chester motioning at Uncle Frank's hands.

Uncle Frank held both hands up and looked at the back of his fingers.

"Got that in a very nasty prison in Honduras."

"Why *long gone*?"

"At the time, I didn't think I was ever getting out."

"What happened?"

"Got caught. That's a stupid question."

"No, I mean, how did you get out?"

"Escaped. How else would I have gotten out?."

Chester wanted to ask Uncle Frank how he had escaped from a very nasty prison in Honduras, but, despite his curiosity, he didn't. He knew it would end up being a long story about yet another predicament Uncle Frank had gotten himself into. And that's not why he had come to Uncle

Frank's. He was there to hopefully find answers to his own predicament.

"So, how long's it been, shitbird?" asked Uncle Frank, refilling his glass.

"Why do you call me that?"

"It's a term of endearment."

"Would you call Catalina that?"

"I wouldn't dare."

"Then why me?"

"Cause I'm not scared of you," said Uncle Frank with another maniacal cackle.

"Well, I wish you would stop calling me that."

"No problem."

Chester lifted his glass from the end table and held it to his nose, but didn't drink from it. The sales clerk had been right. The Scotch smelled very strong and peaty. He set the glass down again. It slid a bit in the pool of condensation on the end table glass.

"It's been about twenty years, Uncle Frank."

"That long, huh?"

"Yes. I thought we would have seen you at the funeral."

"Which one?"

"Either one, mother's or father's."

"I think I was tied up." Uncle Frank paused. "Or locked up."

Chester and Uncle Frank looked at each other and then they both laughed.

"Tied up or locked up. Now, you gotta admit, that was funny," said Uncle Frank.

After a bit Uncle Frank stopped laughing and attempted to put a serious look on his face. "I'm glad you're here, Chester. There's something I need to tell you."

Chester wondered what it might be. He hoped Uncle Frank, who was one of only two living links to his past, the other being his seldom-seen sister, could shed some light on his current situation. In the past week his whole world had been turned upside down. Things he thought were real were no longer real. His past, the history that he based everything in his life on as he moved through that life, was, he now realized, a lie. Add in the fact that even back when he believed his past was real, he had felt like a stranger in his house, and it made Chester wonder what else in his life was a lie.

The way things were going, Chester thought to himself, he wouldn't be surprised if Uncle Frank told him he had been adopted.

"You know you were adopted, don't you," said Uncle Frank.

"Did you just say I was adopted?" Chester's pinkie finger started tapping against his leg.

"Yes. Thought it was time you knew."

Chester was shocked. He didn't know what to do, what to say. Later, when he thought about it, he realized he was not quite as shocked as he might have been. Uncle Frank had verbalized something he had always had a sneaking suspicion about. It certainly explained the disconnect he felt growing up.

"I always wondered about that," said Chester.

"Well, you don't have to wonder any more. Mystery solved. You're an illegitimate bastard."

"That's harsh, and untrue. I might have been adopted but that doesn't mean I was illegitimate. Or a bastard."

Uncle Frank shrugged.

Chester started to speak and Uncle Frank put up his hand. "Don't bother asking me any other questions about it. I don't have any answers. I just know that we are related in name only and not by blood. But, if it's any consolation, I've always considered you to be my favorite nephew."

"Uncle Frank, I'm your only nephew."

"Ahhh, quit splitting hairs. Let's move on. So you got my letter?"

Chester was filled with questions. He wanted to ask Uncle Frank for more details about the news that, in the fifth decade of his life, he had just learned for sure he was adopted. Any person hearing those words would be desperate for more details. But when Uncle Frank said he was done talking about a particular subject, Chester knew it meant he was done talking. Uncle Frank was cut and dried like that. So, reluctantly, Chester moved on.

"Yes, I received your letter. That's why I'm here. Why did you send it to the Pringles?"

"To who?"

"Ed and Edna Pringle."

"Oh, yeah."

"Do you know them?"

"No, not really."

"So why did you send it to them, and not to me."

"Seemed safer that way. Wasn't sure who was watching your house."

"Watching my house!" said Chester, alarmed. "Why would anyone be watching my house?"

"You never know."

"But the Pringles? In Salt Lake City?"

"I knew you'd figure it out. You're a smart guy."

"Well, Ed Pringle wasn't too happy about the letter you sent to him."

"Why not?"

"You threatened to kick his ass."

"Got his attention, didn't it?"

"He said he was a Korean War vet and if you showed up there would be hell to pay."

Uncle Frank's face clouded over and his could-cut-diamonds eyes turned into slits. He jumped up, started waving his skinny arms around and stamping his feet.

"He said what? Why, I'd thump that son-of-a-bitch from here to kingdom come. Korea? That wasn't even a war, goddamnit. I was in the Big One, W-W-Two. That was a real war. Look at this."

Uncle Frank stalked over to the fireplace mantle, opened a polished cherry wood box and pulled out a gun and a knife.

"This here is my W-W-Two Colt. 45 and this here is my W-W-Two Ka-Bar knife. I killed my fair share of Krauts with these."

Chester, frightened, leaned back in his chair and put both hands up, palms out. "Uncle Frank, is that gun loaded?"

"Hell yes, it's loaded. What good is an unloaded gun?"

Uncle Frank slowly drew the blade of the knife across the hairs on his arm. "Lookee there, shaves those hairs right off. I keep this thing razor sharp."

"I see, I see," said Chester. "Can you please put both of those things away."

"Scares you, don't it?"

"Yes, very much so."

Uncle Frank smiled an evil smile and placed the gun and the knife back into the cherry wood box and closed the lid. Then he slowly walked back to his chair, sat down, took a sip of Scotch, and said, "Okay, shitbird, tell me why you're really here?"

Chester fidgeted in his chair.

"Come on boy, I don't got all day," said Uncle Frank.

Chester told Uncle Frank everything.

From the beginning to the end.

Then he stopped and waited for Uncle Frank to say something, but he didn't. So they both sat there for a bit. Then Uncle Frank asked a question.

"Was that Storm girl a hottie?"

"A hottie?"

"You know, a looker. Sexy."

Chester had just told his uncle he had been kidnapped and held hostage for a week and that he fervently believed everyone on the planet was a figment of his imagination. And the most important question Uncle Frank could think to ask him was how sexy a hitchhiker he had picked up was. Never mind that she disappeared into thin air at breakfast.

Chester ignored the hottie question and said, "It's just not fair."

"What's not fair? What are you whining about?"

"The revelation."

"What are you talking about, boy? You should be ecstatic. You're the Big Kahuna. You're bigger than any movie star or world leader. Nobody is bigger than you."

Chester shook his head, then stretched his arms out wide and looked up and down and all around. "You don't get it. I've just found out there is nobody here but me. Nobody else is real. I am now more alone than ever. I was alone the first half of my life. I had parents and people I went to school with and people I worked with, but I was still alone. Then I met Harriette and I was alone plus-one. I have only had a plus-one for the second half of my life. I always thought there was a possibility I could add to that plus-one, that I could connect with a few other people who might want to connect with me. Now, I find out that possibility no longer exists, that I will always be alone plus-one, and even my plus-one is not real."

Chester, who was not a demonstrative person and who did not particularly appreciate when other people used their hands when they talked, held both arms up again and shook his hands in exasperation.

"It doesn't make any sense! Wouldn't it be more fair if someone who had lots of friends and who had done lots of amazing things in their life found out that they were the only real thing after fifty-two years of living? That person wouldn't be as upset, because they could sit in a rocking chair on their front porch and think back on the wonderful life they had before the revelation. I don't mean to be bitter and I don't mean to be crass, but the best way to explain it is like this: I feel like a guy who has been shoveling shit his whole life and at some point he is given a treasure chest and when he opens up that treasure chest, he

194

discovers that it's just full of the same shit he's been shoveling all along."

Uncle Frank laughed. "Well, if you put it that way ..."

▼

Uncle Frank reached for the Scotch, then stopped and looked at Chester's full glass on the end table.

"Waste not, want not," he said, pointing at Chester's glass and snapping his fingers. Chester handed him the glass. Uncle Frank took a sip and smacked his lips. "Yummy."

Chester had many questions. And he wanted to get them all in before Uncle Frank was too far into the bottle of Lagavulin.

"Uncle Frank, why are we here?"

"That's a silly question. We're here because I live here and because I asked you to come see me."

"No, not here now. I mean why are we all here? Why do we exist?"

"I can't speak for you, but I'm here for medium-rare New York strip steak, imported single malt Scotch, and Catalina rubbing my back while I pretend like I'm screwing her."

"Pretend?"

"Chester, I'm fucking eighty-three years old. The teeth still work, but the dick doesn't."

"What about everyone else?"

"I don't care about other people's sex lives."

"No. Why are other people here?"

"Same answer. Don't know, don't care."

"But at one time or another haven't you wondered why you are here?"

"That's another silly question. I'm here because I'm here. If I'm hungry I don't wonder why I'm hungry. I'm just hungry. Don't make this more complicated than it has to be."

"But where did we come from? Where do we go after we die? Don't you ever wonder about that?"

"Chester, I thought about all that stuff once or twice when I was younger, but after you think about it once or twice, it's easy to figure out, so there's really no reason to think about it any more."

Chester's eyes lit up. Maybe Uncle Frank had found the answer.

"What did you figure out?"

"Okay, you ask why am I here? One of two things could have happened. I could be here, or I could not be here. But I'm here, and I like that option better. Then you ask where did I come from? If I'm not here, then it doesn't matter, and if I am here, it still doesn't matter. What matters is that I am here. You are trying to analyze what-is by asking what-if. Can't do it. There is only one what-is but there are a million what-ifs. You'll go crazy if you insist on asking about every possible what-if.

"This," said Uncle Frank, copying Chester by opening his arms wide and looking up, down and all around, "is what it is. Everything that is *is*, and everything that isn't *isn't*. Get it?"

Chester started to speak, but Uncle Frank cut him off.

"Chester, do you remember your Uncle Charlie?"

Chester looked puzzled. He thought a bit and said, "No."

"Take your time. Think back. Uncle Charlie?"

Chester thought some more, then said "no" again.

Uncle Frank pressed on, more earnestly. "You know, your father's older brother, the one with the limp from polio when he was a child, the one who worked for the railroad. You know, Uncle Charlie."

"Still no."

Uncle Frank looked at Chester for what seemed like forever, and then in a loud voice that startled Chester, he shouted, "Of course you don't remember Uncle Charlie, you dummy! There is no Uncle Charlie! There never was an Uncle Charlie! So do you want to ask your never-was Uncle Charlie why he isn't here and why he didn't come from somewhere? If it doesn't make sense to ask him those questions, why does it make sense to ask your always-has-been-here Uncle Frank those questions? You're gonna put yourself in a looney bin if you keep this up. A healthy curiosity is okay, but you're taking it to a new level."

"I don't think so."

"I do."

Chester and Uncle Frank stared at each other, neither one budging on the issue. Uncle Frank slowly cracked the knuckles on his left hand. Chester counted five pops. And then he cracked the knuckles on his right hand. Chester counted only four pops. He waited for a fifth knuckle pop, but it didn't come. That bothered him.

"I only heard four pops," said Chester.

"What are you talking about?"

"You cracked five knuckles on your left hand, but only four on your right hand."

"So what?"

"Well, you kind of left me hanging."

"But they're my knuckles."

"Yes, but I heard the pops. And there's one left."

"You mean this one," said Uncle Frank, holding up his right hand and bending his thumb up and down slowly.

"Yes, that one."

"And it bothers you that I didn't crack it?"

"A little."

"Too bad."

Chester frowned, then pressed on. "Who made you, Uncle Frank?"

"That's the easiest question you've asked so far."

"Why is that?"

"Because you and I both know who made me."

"And who was that?"

"You, apparently."

▼

"Chester, your whole woe-is-me thing is wearing me out. Have you ever considered you might have had more friends if you hadn't been so negative and had made the effort to make things happen for yourself? Look at me. I'm a scoundrel. I was born a scoundrel and I'll die a scoundrel. I'm not a people person. Not only do I rub most people the wrong way, I like rubbing most people the wrong way. Still, I have plenty of friends, I managed to get married a half dozen times, and I've had adventures that would make most men faint dead away. I made all that happen. I didn't sit around and mope.

"You're like a guy playing poker who's been dealt five cards and all you want to do is analyze them. Why are there fifty-two cards in the deck? Why not forty-two or sixty-two? Why are the suits black and red? Who made the cards? How many atoms are there in each card? Do the cards really exist or are they just in my head? You're analyzing life to death, Chester, and never getting to the point where you're living it. Everybody else is just looking at their cards and enjoying playing the game.

"On top of that, you're complaining about the poker hand life dealt you, but, according to you, you are the one who dealt the hand. That's like making yourself an apple pie and then complaining that you don't like apple pie."

Uncle Frank swallowed the last of the Scotch in Chester's glass and then refilled his own more than halfway. Chester could tell the liquor was fueling him up.

"Chester, this reminds me of a story a guy in Brazil once told me. His name was Pasquale and he was a poor man living a dull life. One night he was walking home and a Ferrari stopped next to him. The window rolled down and in the driver's seat was the sexiest, most beautiful woman he had ever seen. The woman asked if he needed a ride and when he said yes, she suggested he drive. Pasquale spent the next thirty minutes racing that sports car up and down the hills of Rio de Janeiro. Then the sexy lady rubbed his leg and suggested they go to her place for some naughty fun. She lived in a mansion overlooking Copacabana Beach. Pasquale walked through every room in the mansion, laying down on beds covered in silk sheets, washing up in a bathroom with gold-plated fixtures, shooting pool on an antique billiards table, watching a movie in the theater room. The woman had her chef prepare a gourmet dinner with caviar and lobster, which Pasquale washed down with a bottle of Dom Perignon champagne. After eating, he took off all his clothes and swam a few laps in the giant infinity pool. Then he slipped into the jacuzzi and smoked a fine Cuban cigar while his sexy hostess, who was also naked, sat in the hot tub and rubbed his shoulders."

Chester sat transfixed. "Then what happened?"

"That's what I asked Pasquale. He said, 'Frank, it was the most wonderful night of my life. A sexy young woman attracted to me, driving the race car, the mansion overlooking the ocean, the caviar and lobster, the champagne, the billiards table, the movie, the pool and jacuzzi, the Cuban cigar. It was a dream come true.'"

"And ..." said Chester.

"So I asked Pasquale what it was like to have sex with such a beautiful woman."

"What did he say?" asked Chester.

"He slapped his forehead and said, 'Ay caramba! Frank, I was so busy doing all that other stuff, I forgot to screw her!'"

Chester just stared at Uncle Frank.

"Don't you get it, Chester? Pasquale had a once-in-a-lifetime opportunity to have sex with the most beautiful woman in the world, but he was so distracted by all the little things that he forgot to enjoy the big thing. You are just like Pasquale. You are so distracted by questions about your life that you aren't enjoying your life."

Uncle Frank said something under his breath, something short like a single word.

"Excuse me?" said Chester.

"I wasn't talking to you," said Uncle Frank.

A small dog padded into the room and sat down next to Uncle Frank's chair. Without looking at the dog, Uncle Frank reached down and scratched behind his ears.

"What did you just say?" asked Chester.

"I said, *Cujo*."

"Who's Cujo?"

"Use your head, goofball. Who do you think Cujo is?"

"The dog?"

"Can't get anything past you, Chester."

"I didn't know you had a dog."

"Was I supposed to call and tell you?"

"No, I mean, I've been here for over an hour and I never saw the dog."

"Trust me, he saw you."

"But why didn't he come out earlier?"

"He knows better. He comes when I want him to come. But he is aware of every single thing that happens in this house."

Chester looked down at the tiny dog, a terrier of some sort, frizzy white with brown splotches, less than ten pounds of canine. Rather ugly with an underbite that left his two bottom incisors sticking out the sides of his mouth.

"And you named him Cujo?"

"Yes. Why does that surprise you?"

"Well, he's kind of small."

"Chester, it's not the size of the dog in the fight, it's the size of the fight in the dog."

"Storm said the same thing."

"The hottie?"

"Yes, the hottie."

Chester looked at the dog again. The dog looked at Chester.

"He's a nice looking dog," lied Chester.

Uncle Frank ignored Chester's comment and instead asked, "How many eyes does Cujo have?"

"That's a silly question, Uncle Frank."

"Humor me."

"Okay. Cujo has two eyes."

"Just like you. Does he have two ears and a nose and a mouth and teeth?"

"Yes."

"Just like you. Does he have a heart and a brain and a liver and two kidneys and two lungs?"

"Yes."

"Just like you. Can he see, hear, smell, taste and touch?"

"Yes."

"Just like you. Can he show emotion?"

"What do you mean?"

"Can he be sad or happy or angry?"

"I'm not sure. Maybe."

"Maybe? Are you serious?"

"Well ..."

Uncle Frank said another quiet word under his breath. In three quick bounds Cujo went from sitting next to Uncle Frank's chair to standing in Chester's lap with his front paws on Chester's shoulders, his snarling lips and bared teeth just inches from Chester's nose. The hair on Cujo's back stood straight up and a deep menacing growl came from his tiny chest.

"Don't move a muscle," warned Uncle Frank.

Chester, his eyes staring right into Cujo's eyes, didn't move a muscle.

"Still not sure about the angry thing?" asked Uncle Frank. He said another quiet word and Cujo returned to his spot next to Uncle Frank's chair. "So, does Cujo have intelligence? Can he learn from experience? Can he reason and make decisions?"

Chester almost said maybe but thought better of it and instead said yes.

"So Cujo has a face, just like you, and working parts in his body, just like you, and he can have emotions, just like you, and he can use his brain to make decisions, just like you. He even has a dick just like you. So my question to you is this, does Cujo have a soul?"

Chester raised an eyebrow. He knew Uncle Frank's questions were leading somewhere, but this was not the somewhere he had expected.

"Take your time," said Uncle Frank.

Chester looked at Cujo, then back at Uncle Frank.

"No, he doesn't have a soul."

"Why not?"

"Because he's just a dog."

"So physically he is like you in every single way, but when it comes to a soul, he is no different than a tree?"

"Yes."

"I think Cujo would disagree with you. Isn't a soul just self-awareness, the ability to consider things that affect only you. I guarantee you Cujo's life is as important to him as your life is to you. And if he feels that way—if he can demonstrate it by fighting an attacker to the death to stay alive—then how can you say he does not have a soul? Killer whales communicate with each other in their own special language. Parrots solve complex problems. Dolphins can recognize themselves in a mirror. A middle-aged pig is smarter than a three-year-old human. Are you saying they don't have souls just because they don't wear shoes or drive cars? That's a bit narrow-minded of you."

"How do you know all that stuff about animals?"

Uncle Frank tapped his head and said, "This isn't just a hat rack, buddy. Your Uncle Frank is a lot smarter than the average bear."

"My father used to say that."

"What?"

"Being smarter than the average bear."

"He got that line from me."

"Tell me about my father, your brother."

"What's to say? He was a drip."

"What do you mean?"

"Just what I said. He was a drip. He was my brother, but he was boring as a sheet of plywood. So were our parents. None of them had a spark. Maybe that's why I turned out the way I did, bat shit crazy. Somebody had to rise up."

"What about my mother?"

"Even more of a drip. Never liked her."

"Why not?"

"She seemed empty."

Chester thought for a moment. "I know what you mean. Growing up, I don't recall there ever being any excitement in our house. There was never any laughing, or even any yelling. I used to think we were all robots. Is that strange?"

"Not at all. I felt the same way when I was a kid. I did wild things just to see if I could get a reaction. Didn't work. So I did even crazier things. That still didn't work, even when the police got involved. Finally, I couldn't take it anymore and I just left."

"How old were you?"

"About sixteen."

"What did my father say when you left?"

"Didn't tell him. Didn't tell anyone. Just hit the road."

"Wasn't everybody worried?"

"I doubt it. To be worried you need emotions. None of them had them."

"Even my father."

"Particularly your father."

"Well, this is all highly depressing."

There was an uncomfortable silence, which was unusual because Uncle Frank was never uncomfortable and never quiet. Finally Uncle Frank spoke. "Chester, that's why I'm sure you were adopted. You aren't like your mother or your father. You have a spark. A small spark, but a spark nonetheless."

No one had ever told Chester he had a spark. But maybe in comparison to parents who were completely spark-less, he did have a spark. Even a small spark was better than no spark.

"Well, maybe spark's not the right word. Depth is a better word. There's depth to you Chester. Your parents had no depth."

Chester liked spark better, but he could live with depth.

"What about my sister? Was she adopted?"

"I don't think so."

"Why not?"

"Because she's a drip too."

Chester wasn't sure if being adopted and not being a drip was better than not being adopted and being a drip. He would think about that one a little more later on, but for now, it seemed like a wash.

Uncle Frank patted his thigh and Cujo jumped into his lap.

"Do you know what Cujo also has in common with you?"

"We both like you?"

"No, you like me. Cujo loves me."

"What then?"

"You both worry. Cujo doesn't worry a lot, but when he does, it's about things like, when is he going to get fed, when will I be back from running errands, is the cat from next door in our backyard? Things like that. You know what he doesn't worry about?"

"'What?"

"Where he came from, why he's here, and what will happen to him after he dies. Never enters his mind. You should think about that."

"Okay, Uncle Frank."

Uncle Frank drained his glass of Scotch, wiped his mouth with the back of his hand, and then told Chester a story.

"Back in the 1970s there was a politician named Earl Butz who got in trouble for saying there were only three things that mattered to a "colored" man—a tight pussy, loose shoes and a warm place to shit. Caused a big uproar. I'm not condoning the way he phrased it, but you know what, you'd be hard pressed to find three other things that are as important to any man, black or white. What I'm trying to say, Chester, is that it's more important to most people to know what's for dinner than it is to know who created the universe."

Chester nodded. Food analogies always got his attention.

Uncle Frank took a break from talking and stared at his nephew. The longer Uncle Frank stared, the more nervous Chester got. The pinkie finger on his left hand started twitching.

"What?" asked Chester to break the stare.

"Nothing. Just thinking."

"Thinking what?"

"That you are an odd bird."

"That's the second time in twenty-four hours someone has told me that. Storm said that too."

"I'm liking that girl more and more. By the way, you keep talking about this young woman. Aren't you married?"

"I am married. To Harriette."

"The chunky girl?"

"Uncle Frank, Harriette is not chunky."

"Well, she ain't thin. That's for sure."

Uncle Frank snapped his fingers and Cujo jumped out of his lap.

"Gotta take a whiz," said Uncle Frank, standing up. "You and Cujo get acquainted. At my age peeing can take some time."

Uncle Frank shuffled out of the room. Chester looked at Cujo and patted his thigh. Cujo looked at Chester, lifted his back leg and started licking his private parts.

Chapter Eighteen

"Wake up," said Uncle Frank.

Chester had dozed off in the comfortable living room chair. He opened his eyes and saw Uncle Frank standing in front of him, a trail of wet pee drops on the outside of his pants from his crotch down to his left knee. His zipper was halfway down.

"You hungry?"

"I'm always hungry."

Uncle Frank walked to the patio sliding glass door and opened it a crack. An incredible aroma of barbecuing beef wafted into the room. Chester was now wide awake.

"What is that wonderful smell?"

"Catalina is cooking our dinner on the grill."

Chester raised his eyebrows.

"It's marinated skirt steak with char-grilled onions, tomatoes and green peppers. She'll slice the steak thin and we'll put it on homemade flour tortillas with the vegetables. For dessert we'll have tres leche cake."

"Sounds marvelous," said Chester, smacking his lips.

"It will be. Trust me."

Chester licked his lips.

"What's tres leche cake?"

"It's a sponge cake soaked in evaporated milk, condensed milk, and heavy cream, and it's like a little bite of heaven."

"Oh my" said Chester.

Uncle Frank clapped his hands together excitedly.

"What do you say I whip us up a pitcher of margaritas before dinner? Would you like one?"

"I don't really drink."

"I didn't ask you if you drank or not. I asked if you wanted a margarita. Do you?"

"Okay," said Chester, not wanting to be rude.

"Frozen or on the rocks?"

"Frozen. With salt. And a Grand Marnier floater."

Uncle Frank looked surprised. "I thought you didn't drink."

"Right now I do," said Chester, still thinking about the skirt steak and the tres leche cake.

"Sit tight," said Uncle Frank, walking to the kitchen. Cujo jumped into Uncle Frank's vacated seat and laid down facing Chester, his head on his paws.

Chester patted his leg again and made a clucking sound with his tongue. Cujo ignored him. He did it again and was ignored again. Chester made a face at Cujo and, quietly so Uncle Frank wouldn't hear, said, "You sure are one ugly dog. You know that, don't you?"

Cujo licked his private parts a second time, still looking right at Chester. Chester knew he was doing it on purpose.

Uncle Frank returned with two frosty mugs filled to the brim with bright lime green margaritas. Chester took his mug in both hands, licked a half inch of the salt from the rim and then washed it down with a healthy sip of the slushy margarita.

"That's quite tasty, Uncle Frank."

Uncle Frank nodded in agreement. He moved Cujo into his lap, turned him over on his back and started rubbing his belly. Cujo's eyes closed and his tongue hung out the side of his mouth. Chester watched Uncle Frank briskly rubbing the dog's underbelly, from his neck down to his haunches.

"Jealous?" asked Uncle Frank with an evil grin.

"Not really. But it does make me uneasy when you rub his gonads."

"Gonads?"

"Testes."

"Testes?"

"Balls. His balls."

"Why didn't you say balls the first time?"

Chester shrugged.

"Low self esteem, that's why," said Uncle Frank.

"What do you mean?"

"You could have said balls to start. Everyone knows what balls are. And everybody else just calls them balls. No one says, 'Gee, my gonads itch.' But you use fancy words like gonads and testes to make yourself seem smart and special. That's a sign of low self esteem. And, for the record, I was not rubbing his balls. Because Cujo doesn't have any balls."

Uncle Frank held Cujo up from the back so his belly was facing Chester.

"See. Ball-less."

"You had him neutered?"

"There you go again. I had him clipped."

"Why?"

"Because he was a terror. He would screw anything in the neighborhood that squatted to pee. He'd be gone for days at a time. Reminded me of me in my younger days."

"So did you have yourself clipped?" asked Chester. He couldn't resist.

"That's a rather personal question."

"Well, while we're on the subject."

"Of course I did. Many moons ago. I didn't want any more little Uncle Franks running around."

"You have children?" asked Chester, surprised.

"I'm sure I do. Somewhere."

"You don't know?"

"Don't want to know."

"Why?"

"You're boring me. Let's go eat."

▼

Chester followed Uncle Frank into the kitchen. The kitchen table was covered with food, enough to feed a family of six. In the center of the table was a platter heaped with thin slices of strip steak mixed in with the char-grilled vegetables. Next to the platter was a large bowl of yellow rice, a large bowl of black beans and a plate piled high with steaming flour tortillas. There were a half dozen smaller bowls filled with whole jalapenos, avocado slices, sour cream, pico de gallo, guacamole, and habanero pepper sauce. Everything sat on a multi-colored mosaic tablecloth with matching cloth napkins.

Chester didn't know how or when Catalina had put all the items out.

He had not heard one sound from the kitchen the whole time he and Uncle Frank had sat in the living room.

Chester noticed there were only two dinner plates on the table.

"Catalina is not joining us?"

"No. She's a bit shy around strangers. Well, maybe shy isn't the right word. Leery. She's leery of strangers."

"But I'm not a stranger. I'm your nephew."

"I know. Maybe it's because you were adopted."

"Uncle Frank!"

Uncle Frank laughed. "Just teasing."

The enticing smell of all the food on the table was too much for Chester. He reached for one of the flour tortillas.

"Wait!" yelled Uncle Frank.

Chester, startled, looked at Uncle Frank, his hand hovering over the stack of tortillas.

Uncle Frank held up his right hand, wiggled his thumb, and then reached over with his left hand and cracked the thumb knuckle with a loud pop.

"Now," said Uncle Frank, smiling, "we can eat."

It was after he had eaten his second slice of the unbelievably moist tres leche cake and had slipped under the covers in the small guest cottage behind the main house that Chester heard the disturbing conversation, the one where the two voices talked about breaking his fingers and his thumb.

Chester opened his right eye just a crack and saw two very large and intimidating men in the bedroom, men who looked exactly like the two dark men he had seen at the Avis car rental place and at the Holiday Inn. He didn't know what to do. He could yell out for help or jump up in a defensive stance, but he didn't think that would stop the two men from doing whatever they had come to do. Or he could close his right eye and pretend like he had not heard the voices or seen the men and maybe the whole thing would just go away. So his options were yell out, jump up, or pretend. Chester went for pretend and closed his right eye.

And that's when he heard three noises, all of them loud.

The first noise was a crash.

The second noise was a gunshot.

And the third noise was a scream.

The crash, the gunshot and the scream put an end to the pretend option and Chester realized he would have to open both his right eye and his left eye to see what had caused the three loud noises. But just before he opened his eyes, he smelled three things.

The first smell was Scotch.

The second smell was suntan oil.

And the third smell was gunpowder.

Now Chester had six reasons to open his eyes, so he did. And what he saw looked like a scene out of a movie.

First, he saw one of the very large and intimidating men on the ground next to his bed, flat on his back. In the middle of his chest, right where Chester thought the man's heart probably was, there was a hole, about the size of a dime, and shooting straight up out of that hole was a stream of crimson blood.

Second, he saw Uncle Frank standing in the doorway of the room, a cigarette dangling from the side of his mouth and a glass of Lagavulin Scotch in his left hand. The door was hanging half off it's frame where it had been kicked in, and in Uncle Frank's right hand was his W-W-Two Colt 45 automatic pistol, a wisp of smoke floating up from the end of the barrel.

And the third thing Chester saw, the thing that shocked him even more than the first two things, was the second very large and intimidating man standing still as a statue halfway between the body on the floor and Uncle Frank in the doorway.

The reason the second man was not moving a muscle was that clinging to his back was Catalina, still in her pink and white polka-dot bikini, her strong, suntan-oiled legs locked around his waist. In her left hand she had a handful of the man's hair and she was pulling his head all the way back so that he appeared to be staring at the ceiling. In her right hand was Uncle Frank's W-W-Two Ka-Bar knife, the razor-sharp blade of the knife pressed into the soft white flesh of his exposed neck, right where Chester thought the man's jugular vein probably was. And if that sight was not startling enough on its own, Chester saw that hanging from the back of the second man was Cujo, his tiny teeth embedded in the man's thigh, his back paws swaying back and forth a good two feet off the ground.

When Chester saw those three things it was like a moment frozen in time, like he was looking at a printed storyboard from a movie and not the movie itself with motion in it. He felt like he could stand up and walk around the room and get a closer look at everybody and everything and nothing would move as he did. So he took that opportunity, while the moment was still frozen in time, to look at everyone involved and that's another reason that the third thing he saw made the biggest impression on him.

Because everyone in the room seemed to be demonstrably surprised, except for one person. The man on the floor, despite having obviously passed on to the great beyond, still had his eyes wide open and his eyes looked surprised about what just happened to him. The man standing up with a knife to his throat and a terrier biting his lower buttocks looked both surprised and scared to death. And Uncle Frank looked surprised and amused in equal measures.

But Catalina did not look surprised at all.

Not about the carnage in the room, or to be clinging to the back of a stranger, ready to slit his throat. She looked almost bored. And that surprised Chester more than anything else in the room.

Slowly, the moment frozen in time turned into real time. Uncle Frank stuck the Colt .45 into his waistband, took a drag off his cigarette and flicked it over his shoulder into the yard. He drained the glass of Scotch and stepped from the doorway into the room.

"Well, now you've gone and done it, Chester," said Uncle Frank.

"Me? What did I do?"

"I'm just kidding you, shitbird. Relax."

Catalina, still pulling the standing man's head back and still pressing the Ka-Bar knife against his throat, looked back over her shoulder at Uncle Frank, and asked in a very matter-of-fact voice, "Ahora?"

Uncle Frank shook his head and said, "Mas tarde."

"What's going on?" asked Chester.

"You're leaving. Right now. Grab your stuff and go," said Uncle Frank.

"But ..."

"I said go. Now."

Chester dressed quickly, stuffed loose items into his suitcase, grabbed the Avis rental car keys and his cell phone off the dresser and hurried to the door. He stopped in front of Uncle Frank.

"Thanks for dropping in. It's been a pleasure," said Uncle Frank with his all too familiar cackle. "Now hit the road."

"I want to say ..."

"Don't say nothing. I'll call you later. Get outta here."

Chester left, walking fast, his suitcase banging against his leg. He looked back over his shoulder and saw Uncle Frank nod his head at

Catalina.

And that's when Catalina smiled.

▼

Chester drove to the nearest Interstate, trying to stay calm and stick to the speed limit, even though his heart was racing and his hands were shaking. He didn't know where he was going. He just knew he had to get as far as possible from Uncle Frank's house. Ten minutes later his heartbeat was back to normal but his hands were still shaking, no matter how tightly he gripped the steering wheel. The pinkie finger on his left hand was having a fit. His cell phone rang and Chester looked at the number before answering. It was Uncle Frank.

"How you doing, boy?"

"I'm shaking like a leaf, Uncle Frank. What happened back there?"

"What happened? Me and Catalina and Cujo saved your ass, that's what happened."

"But how did you know those men were there?"

"Cujo saw them."

"Did you call the police?"

"Hell no."

"But what are you going to do with that body?"

"Two bodies."

"Two bodies?"

"No choice."

"This is horrible. I don't want you to get arrested."

"Don't worry about it. Catalina will disappear them."

"I don't understand."

"Chester, Catalina was raised by guerrillas."

"She was raised by apes?"

"No, you dummy. She was raised by the FARC in Colombia. She was paramilitary, a revolutionary. She's disappeared more people than Seal Team 6."

"And you married her?"

"Why not? She's beautiful and she watches over me like a hawk."

"But she's a killer."

"All women are."

"I never expected anything like this to happen."

"Hey, you gotta break a few eggs to make an omelette."

"This is a lot different."

"Not really. Listen, according to you, those two guys weren't even real. They only existed because you wanted them to. You said this is your big adventure. They were just part of the adventure."

"That sounds good. I like that. So they weren't real?"

"Of course not."

"Thank goodness."

"Oh, one other thing."

"Yes."

"I thought it would be nice if Catalina dropped in on your buddy Theodore."

"What! Why would she do that?"

"No loose ends, Chester."

"But isn't that dangerous?"

"Very much so. For Theodore."

"She's going there alone?"

"Of course not. Cujo's going with her."

"Uncle Frank, I don't think that's a very good idea."

"What else am I going to do with these two bodies?"

"I don't understand."

"Didn't you say Theodore has a basement?"

"Oh my."

Chapter Nineteen

Chester was driving aimlessly, with no particular destination in mind, which was disorganized.

His clothes and personal items were stuffed haphazardly into a suitcase in the backseat, articles hanging out where it was not fully zipped, which was disorganized.

His phone still had the wall charger attached to it, and was only twenty-seven percent charged, which was disorganized.

His shirt was untucked and his belt was latched loosely in the wrong belt hole, which was disorganized.

He looked in the mirror and saw that his face was shiny with perspiration and a few thin wisps of hair were sticking straight up into the air, which was disorganized.

Chester did not like being disorganized.

He knew that both his disheveled physical appearance and his disheveled mental state were due to what he had just seen in Uncle Frank's guest cottage and his hasty retreat from that disturbing tableau.

He saw a convenience store down the road and pulled into the parking lot. He looked in the front seat and then the back seat for a napkin or paper towel, but did not see one. So he cringed and used his shirt tail to wipe his face, then licked the palm of his right hand, cringed again, and used his moist palm to pat down the errant hairs on his head. He looked in the rear view mirror to give himself the once over, took a deep breath and opened the car door.

"Howdy, partner," said the clerk behind the counter. The man bore an uncanny resemblance to the old man who waited on Chester at the liquor store the day before. He too had an unlit cigar in his mouth and was wearing a short-sleeved white shirt with the faintest of yellow stains peering from under his armpits.

"Good evening," said Chester. He stopped and looked at the clerk. "You don't happen to have a twin, do you?"

The clerk looked surprised. "I do indeed. How in the world would you know that?"

"I think your brother waited on me yesterday."

"Really? What makes you think it was my brother?"

"He looked just like you."

"Really? And where was this at?"

"In Utah."

"Really? Well, I don't think that's possible."

"Why not?"

"I don't have a twin brother. I have a twin sister."

"Oh," said Chester, a little embarrassed.

Chester shrugged his shoulders and walked to the back of the store. He poured a cup of coffee into the largest Styrofoam cup he could find, added one packet of sugar and a dollop of milk from the dispenser, and put a lid on the coffee. He eyed a tray of pastries in a glass enclosed rack next to the coffee. The skirt steak and tres leche cake were only a few hours in the past, but nervous energy had made Chester hungry again.

"Are these fresh?" he asked the clerk over his shoulder.

"They were fresh this morning. Might be a little crunchy now."

Chester counted three blueberry muffins, two chocolate donuts, four glazed donuts and three cinnamon rolls. It took him just a few seconds to count all of the pastries two more times. He was so fast and proficient at counting that he didn't even realize he was counting as his eye settled on the cinnamon rolls. The sugar glaze on them looked the freshest and the shiniest. He studied the three cinnamon rolls, comparing the size and shininess of each, then opened the glass door and used a sheet of wax paper to pluck the middle roll from the rack. He walked to the clerk, set his coffee on the counter, put the roll on top of the coffee, and pulled out his wallet.

"What do I owe you?" asked Chester.

The clerk just stared at him, or, more specifically, at his feet.

"Hello?" said Chester.

The clerk looked up at Chester's face, then back down at Chester's feet, then back up to Chester's face.

"Are you alright there, partner?" asked the clerk.

"Excuse me?"

"I said, 'Are you alright?'"

"Why wouldn't I be."

"Blood."

"Blood?"

"Yes, blood. On your shoes and your pant legs. Looks fresh."

Chester looked down. His loafers, which were tan in color, and the bottom of his pants, which were also tan in color, were both peppered with drops of red blood. A few of the spots still glistened.

"Oh," said Chester.

Chester thought about the dark man laying on the floor of Uncle Frank's guest bedroom and the shower of blood that had pumped up from his chest. He must have walked through the spray of blood on his rush from the room.

Chester looked up at the clerk. The clerk looked at Chester. Neither of them said a word. Chester knew the clerk was waiting for an explanation.

"Oh, that's not my blood," said Chester.

"That's good," said the clerk. And then he cocked his head a little to signal he was waiting for more.

Chester fidgeted.

"Well?" said the clerk.

"Well, what?" said Chester.

"If it's not your blood, who's blood is it?"

Chester's mind raced. He said the first thing that came to him.

"I hit a dog ..."

The clerk stared again, waiting.

"With my car ..." said Chester.

Same stare, same waiting.

"By accident!" said Chester, adding a little exclamation at the end to let the clerk know it was his final answer and he could stop staring and he could stop waiting for more information.

The clerk nodded and pursed his lips. "Are you sure it was a dog?"

"Yes, I am."

"What kind of dog was it?"

"What do you mean?"

"Was it a German Shepherd or a poodle, or something like that?"

"I don't know."

"You know you hit a dog, but you don't know what type of dog you hit?"

"No. I'm not a dog breed expert."

"That's strange."

"Strange that I hit a dog, or strange that I'm not a dog breed expert?"

"It's strange on a lot of levels," said the clerk, who then, pointedly, so Chester could see, looked over at the store phone next to the cash register.

"Maybe you hit a person," said the clerk, one eyebrow raised.

"Maybe I didn't," said Chester, with a little force in his voice.

"Maybe you didn't? As in maybe you did?"

"No, I was using the word maybe for emphasis, just like you used it. Listen, are you going to ring up this coffee and sweet roll or not?"

"Sure. You don't have to get testy."

"Well, I'm not used to being interrogated when I buy a cinnamon roll."

"It's called a bear claw."

"What?"

"That's a bear claw, not a cinnamon roll."

The clerk took the unlit cigar from his mouth, a thin strand of spittle looping down from his bottom lip and arching back up to the soggy end of the cigar. He jabbed the cigar toward the roll, which snapped the strand of spittle in the middle, and said, "Yep, that's a bear claw you got there."

Chester felt his cheeks flush red with anger. After everything he had been through in the past hour, the last thing he needed was a know-it-all clerk intentionally trying to aggravate him.

"Does it have cinnamon in it?" asked Chester between gritted teeth.

"Yes."

"Is it a pastry?"

"Yes."

"Then it's a gosh-darned cinnamon roll!" said Chester in a loud voice, his outburst surprising him more than it did the clerk. Chester pulled a five dollar bill from his wallet, slammed it on the counter, grabbed the coffee and cinnamon roll, and rushed out of the store, hearing the clerk shout "wait a minute" as the door swung shut behind him.

Chester stuck the cinnamon roll in his mouth, moved the coffee to his left hand and used his right hand to open the car door in one fast and fluid motion. He inserted the car key, shifted into reverse, backed up, shifted into drive, and then sped out of the store parking lot, the cinnamon roll still clamped in his teeth. He had time for a quick glance in his rear view mirror where he saw the clerk's face mashed up against the store window, the store phone pressed to his ear, his lips moving rapid fire.

"Oh crap," said Chester.

▼

Chester pulled the cinnamon roll from his mouth, leaving behind the part that had been behind his clamped teeth. He chewed slowly. The roll was a little stale, but the more he chewed, the softer the bite of roll became and the better it tasted. He peeled back the plastic tab on the top of his coffee and took a big swig, the coffee soaking the bite of roll and giving it a whole new flavor. Chester was big on dunking. He dunked sweet rolls, doughnuts and even cookies into his coffee. He had watched his parents do it as a child and had followed suit. He hardly ever saw other people dunking, and on the few occasions when he did, it was always someone as old or older than him. Younger people just seemed to be in too much of a hurry to dunk. Their loss, he thought.

Chester took another bite of the sweet roll, and as he did a sliver of colored light bounced off the rear view mirror into his eyes. Before he even looked in the mirror, Chester knew where the colored light had come from. One look confirmed his guess and his pinkie finger started tapping away like a madman.

As the flashing red and blue lights of the police car came up fast behind him.

Chester knew the cruiser would catch up to him in a matter of seconds. He also knew he would have has hands full with the police officer, so he started wolfing down the cinnamon roll. As he frantically chewed, a flood of questions about the police car filled his head. That police car was not there a minute ago, and it was only there now because of Chester. Without Chester leaving a startled store clerk wondering about blood on his pants, that police car would not be in his life at this exact moment. Where was that cruiser before it got the radio call to check on a suspicious character? Did it even exist before then? And after the police officer pulled him over and they did their business and Chester drove off, what would happen to that officer and his patrol car? If they didn't exist for Chester less than a minute ago, would they exist a minute after he was gone?

Chester pulled to the side of the road and rolled down his window. The cruiser stopped behind him. In his side mirror Chester saw the officer get out and walk toward him. He could not see the officer's face because of how his side mirror was tilted. In fact, he could not see much of the officer at all with the red and blue flashing police lights bouncing off the side mirror. But Chester knew exactly what the officer would look like because he knew that the officer was only there in his life at that precise moment because of Chester. The officer would be a muscular white man in his mid twenties with a crew cut, non-smiling eyes and a curt manner. His uniform would be pressed to perfection.

The officer stopped at the back of Chester's car and Chester saw him place the palm of his hand flat against the rear side panel of the car, his fingers splayed out like he was about to catch a ball. The officer kept his hand on the car for a few seconds and then walked up to Chester's window, stopping just behind the window so that the door frame was between he and Chester.

Chester was not surprised.

He knew why the police officer put his hand on the car.

And he knew why he stood with the door frame between them.

Chester knew a lot about police procedure because Harriette liked the television show *Cops*. Actually, like was not a strong enough word. Chester felt Harriette was embarrassingly rabid in her enthusiasm for the show. She had seen every episode of the series since it began airing twenty years ago, and she had seen most of the episodes several times in reruns. It was the last television show anyone would expect mild-mannered Harriette to be a fan of, but she watched the show religiously. And since Harriette and Chester always watched television together, that meant Chester too had seen hundreds of episodes of the true crime show.

"I don't understand why you are so crazy about this show," Chester had whined those first few years whenever they watched an episode. Harriette's response was always the same. She would raise her arm up, point her open palm at Chester and, while never taking her eyes off the screen, say, "Shush, Chester. I'm trying to watch."

"But Harriette, it's the same thing every episode."

Harriette's hand would go back up, palm out.

Chester didn't mind the police officers. It was the other people on the show he didn't much care for. The police never seemed to deal with normal, rational people. It was always what other people would call the dregs of society. Chester would never call them that, and he did feel compassion for those less fortunate than him, but he also felt like he didn't need to see those people in his living room every day. But Harriette couldn't get enough of it.

In those first years, always against his better judgment, Chester would try again, saying, "Really Harriette, those people are not the nicest people to look at or listen to."

At those times, Harriette's left hand would stay in her lap. She would turn her head slowly to look at Chester, just like the young girl possessed by the devil did in that movie, and Chester could tell by the look she gave him that he had better just shush right up. And that's what he would do. In all the years they had been married, Harriette had never once raised her voice at Chester, and the few times he had been on the receiving end of an angry look, it seemed it was usually when he was criticizing Harriette's police show.

After watching an episode or two of *Cops*, Harriette, her thirst for true crime sated for awhile, will go to the laundry room to fold clothes or to the kitchen to put away dishes. Chester will stay in the living room and flip through the channels until he finds a show that he enjoys, like one of the cooking shows. Even though Harriette is no longer in the living room with him, Chester will still hear her. He will hear her because she will be singing to herself, just loud enough that Chester can make out the lyrics to what she is singing, which is always, "Bad boys, bad boys, whatcha gonna do when they come for you?" from the show's theme song.

Chester will just roll his eyes.

Then Harriette will poke her head into the living room and say, "Chester?"

"Yes, Harriette?"

"Did you know ...?"

"Know what, Harriette?"

"Cops is filmed on location with the men and women of law enforcement. All suspects are innocent until proven guilty in a court of law."

Before he can respond, Harriette will disappear, the sound of her chuckles trailing behind her.

Chester knew those show opening lines by heart, having heard them daily for more that twenty years. Hearing those lines always aggravated him, because it meant he was about to sit through another thirty minutes of watching and listening to not so nice people, and also because the lines made no sense to him. Shouldn't it be innocent unless proven guilty and not innocent until proven guilty. There was a big difference. It was a logical distinction, and whenever he pointed that out to Harriette all he got back in response was that open left palm.

▼

"Sir, turn off your car engine and place your hands on the steering wheel," said the officer.

Chester did as he was told and then leaned his head out the open car window and looked at the police officer.

"You're black," said Chester, confusion on his face.

"What?"

"You're black. I thought you would be white."

The officer frowned. Chester saw him move his right hand to the butt of the gun in his holster.

"Sir, please step out of the car slowly and keep your hands where I can see them."

Chester laughed.

"Something funny?" asked the officer.

"Oh, it's just that I have heard those exact words so many times before," said Chester.

The officer tensed, took two steps back, and pulled the gun from his holster. He held the gun down, flat against his thigh. With his other hand he keyed the radio microphone clipped to his left shoulder epaulet and said, "Unit 22A requesting back-up at Highway 80 and Montgomery."

As Chester stepped out of the car, the officer used his free hand to spin him around and press him up against the back passenger door. In a smooth practiced move, he holstered his gun, pulled out handcuffs and cuffed Chester's hands behind him. He pulled Chester's wallet out of his back pocket and then turned Chester around and leaned him back against the car.

"Just relax. You are not under arrest. This is for your protection and mine until I figure out what is happening here."

Chester laughed again.

"Why are you laughing again?" asked the officer, but not in an angry way, more in an amused way.

"Because ..."

"Let me guess. It's because you've heard those exact words many times before."

"Yes, that's why."

"You don't look like a felon."

"I've heard all those lines on *Cops*."

"The TV show?"

"Yes."

"You watch *Cops*?"

"Harriette does."

"Who's Harriette?"

"My wife."

"Your wife watches it?"

"All the time."

"What about you?"

"I watch it with her. But I don't like the show."

"Why not?"

"The people on it are not very nice. Not the police officers. The other people."

"I can't argue with you on that."

The officer looked down at the blood on Chester's shoes and on the bottom of his pants, then back up at Chester.

"You know why I stopped you?"

"Because of the store clerk."

"He thinks you might be a serial killer."

"Oh no, not me. I told him I hit a dog. It was an accident."

The officer pulled Chester's drivers license out of his wallet and looked at it.

"You're a long way from home."

"I know."

Another patrol car pulled up. The officer handed Chester's license to the new arrival who went back to his cruiser to call in the info.

"Listen," said the first officer, "if you hit a dog with your car, how did you get blood on your pants and shoes if you were driving the car?"

Chester hadn't thought about that. It was a very good question. He hesitated. The officer kept looking at him.

"I got out of the car to check on him."

"Him? You just said him. Are you sure it was a dog you hit?"

"Oh, I'm positive. It was a German Shepherd."

The officer looked hard at Chester, so hard that he squinted his eyes. "The clerk said he asked you what type of dog it was and you told him you didn't know."

This, thought Chester to himself, is why he usually never lied. One lie led to another and before you knew it you were tangled up in a web of lies.

"I just now remembered," said Chester.

"That's convenient," said the officer.

"But it's true," said Chester. "I thought I had killed the poor thing. But when I bent over to check on him, he jumped up, banged into my legs and then ran away. That must be where the blood came from."

The second officer walked over and handed the first officer Chester's license. "He's good. You got this?" The first officer nodded and the other officer got in his cruiser and drove away.

The officer turned back to Chester and started to say something when the headlights of an oncoming car came up over the rise in the road, coming from the same direction that Chester and the officer had been traveling. The car, a large, black, older model Lincoln Continental, got closer to them. The officer pumped his hand up and down and the big car slowed so that it glided past them as if in slow motion. Chester looked over the officer's shoulder and into the car as it rolled by.

In the driver's seat was a young woman wearing a pink and white polka-dot bikini.

It was Catalina.

The car seat was moved all the way up so she could reach the gas and brake pedals. Her small hands gripped the giant steering wheel and Chester could see she was sitting on a thick cushion. Even then, her head barely cleared the top of the dashboard. Catalina looked over at Chester for a split second, no sign of acknowledgment on her face, and then looked back at the road.

Chester also saw Cujo, his tiny paws propped on the top of the passenger side door, his tiny black nose pressed against the glass of the rolled-up window. Cujo smiled at Chester which was not that unusual because Chester had seen dogs smile before or at least make a facial expression like a smile.

But then Cujo winked at Chester. Only Uncle Frank would have a dog that could wink.

As the car passed them, Chester looked at the trunk. He wondered if there were two bodies in it. Chester was not a wagering man, but if he did have to bet, he would bet that the trunk was very full.

"Mr. Fortunberry?" said the officer.

Chester did not respond, so the officer said it again, "Mr. Fortunberry?"

"Yes," said Chester, refocusing on the officer.

"Where exactly did you hit this mystery dog?"

"In his back legs."

The officer gave Chester another hard, squinty look.

"Oh, sorry, I misunderstood you. It was a few miles from here. Near my Uncle Frank's house."

The officer looked at Chester's license again. His squinty eyes opened nice and wide.

"Is your uncle, Frank Fortunberry?"

"Yes. Do you know him?"

"Every cop in town knows Crazy Frank."

"Are you using the word crazy as an adjective or as part of his name?"

"Everyone knows him as Crazy Frank. No disrespect, but you probably have no idea what your uncle is capable of."

"Really? You don't say," said Chester, picturing Uncle Frank with the cigarette dangling from his mouth, a glass of Scotch in one hand and a smoking gun in the other.

Chester, who was still leaning back against the passenger door, looked down at the rear side panel of the car.

"You put your fingerprints right there, didn't you," said Chester.

"How do you know that?" said the officer.

"I told you. *Cops.*"

The officer offered up a half-smile. "You're right. That's evidence in case a stop goes bad for me."

The officer looked at Chester with what appeared to be a new found appreciation. "Also, you might have noticed I left my hand on the car for several seconds. You know why?"

"No, why?"

"I'm checking to see if there is any movement in the car, if somebody might be ducked down and hiding in the back seat."

"Oooh, that's good," said Chester. "I didn't know that one. I'll have to tell Harriette about that."

Chester was enjoying the conversation. He felt smart which didn't happen very often. "I also noticed that when you walked up, you stood so the metal door frame was between you and I."

"Right again," said the officer. "That frame can stop a bullet. Just how often do you and the wife watch *Cops*?"

"Every single day," said Chester with an exaggerated sigh.

"I can tell."

The officer uncuffed Chester and handed him back his license. Chester slipped it into his wallet. He knew the traffic stop was ending, which made him a bit sad.

"So, do you put your fingerprints on every car?" asked Chester.

"Only the ones I stop," said the officer, now with a full smile.

Chester stared at him for a second or two, confused, then he laughed.

"Okay Mr. Fortunberry, I'm going to say this and I know you've heard it many times before, but, 'You're free to go.'"

"Thank you officer," said Chester. He got back into his Avis rental car, and watched in the rear view mirror as the officer walked back to the cruiser. Halfway there the officer stopped, stood still for a second, and then turned around and walked back to Chester.

"Oh no," said Chester. He saw that the officer did not have his hand on his gun, which was a good sign. But he had a quizzical look on his face, which could be a bad sign.

"Mr. Fortunberry?" said the officer when he got to Chester's car. Chester noticed that the officer was standing facing his open window, not behind the metal door frame, which was another good sign.

"Yes, officer."

"Why did you think I was white?"

That question surprised Chester, but he also thought it was a good question for the officer to ask. It had slipped Chester's mind as well that the officer who he thought would be white had turned out to be black. But when he did think about it later, which he knew he would have eventually done, he would have wondered how good of a policeman the officer had been after all if he had just driven away and not asked Chester about it.

"Because of my revelation," said Chester.

"Your revelation?"

"Yes, my revelation. I had it just a week ago. It was quite profound."

"Do I even want to know?" asked the officer.

"Probably not," said Chester.

The officer looked at Chester, seeming to weigh his options. Chester wanted him to ask about the revelation as much as he wanted him to not ask about the revelation.

"You know what, Chester?" said the officer, which caught Chester's attention right away because the officer not only remembered his first name but was addressing him by his first name which took the situation from a formal traffic stop to an informal exchange between two people. Chester liked that.

"No, what?" said Chester.

"You may be a lot more like your Uncle Frank than I thought." The way he said it made Chester think the officer was impressed by that fact.

"You have a good night," said the officer, who turned and walked back to his cruiser, all the way this time.

Chester watched in his rear view mirror as the officer made a sharp U-turn and gunned his cruiser down the road. In just seconds he was gone. The road in Chester's rear view mirror was empty. The road ahead of him was empty. It was pitch black outside. And very quiet.

Chester sat in his car and did not start the engine. He felt the solitude and the darkness and the quietness.

And he wondered where the police car was now.

And if it had ever really existed at all.

Chapter Twenty

Chester knew he had to leave the Santa Fe area. He could not just drive around aimlessly. He needed a destination. He stayed on the deserted highway until he saw a sign announcing a north-south Interstate ahead. He took the exit going south and soon saw a sign indicating Albuquerque was just sixty miles away. He relaxed, knowing that a nice large city easy to hide in was just an hour away.

After awhile Chester saw a rest stop sign on the side of the highway, and as he looked at the big green sign with giant white letters something tickled inside his head but he wasn't sure what it was. A dozen miles down the interstate he saw another rest stop sign and he got that same tickling feeling inside his head. It wasn't until he had passed another of the signs that Chester realized the tickling in his head that came every time he saw a rest stop sign was his brain telling him he had not gone to the bathroom since the morning he had the revelation.

Not once.

Not Number One.

And not Number Two.

Chester wondered how that was possible. It had been almost a week since the morning of the revelation. That morning he had had a very satisfying bowel movement, but since then he had not relieved himself once.

Chester was no stranger to bathrooms. At his age it was not uncommon for him to get up in the middle of the night once, and sometimes twice, to urinate. He was sleepy when the need to relieve himself happened each night, so he would sit down on the toilet rather than stand on wobbly legs. In fact, the only time he stood up was when he was in a public restroom with urinals. And even that was a challenge if another person was standing at the next urinal. He had a shy bladder and would have to close his eyes and pretend he was all alone in the restroom to get the stream started.

Thinking back, Chester realized he did not use the lavatory on the plane when he flew to Casper, Wyoming to see the Pringles. That was particularly odd because Chester always used the lavatory on a plane, always right after the pilot came on the intercom to say they were about to land and everyone should stay in their seat with their seat belts buckled. Chester could sit through an entire flight without a single tingling feeling telling him he needed to go until the pilot came on to tell everybody to stay seated. At that precise moment, the tingling feeling would come on as strong as can be.

The first time it happened, Chester told himself they would be landing soon enough and he could just wait and use an airport restroom. But it seemed to take forever for the plane to descend that day. By the time the wheels finally hit the runway, Chester was twisted into a little ball with his legs crossed, his fists clenched, and beads of sweat rolling down his face. When the plane stopped taxiing, well before it got to the terminal, the pilot came on to say their arrival gate was occupied and they would have to wait ten more minutes. At that moment Chester's body relaxed and his legs uncrossed and his fists unclenched and he stopped sweating and he urinated in his pants.

It was one of the most embarrassing things to ever happen to Chester. When the plane finally pulled up to the arrival gate and everyone stood to deplane, Chester had covered the wet spot on his plane seat with the in-flight magazine and kept his briefcase in front of his wet pants crotch as he disembarked.

After that, Chester always stood up to use the lavatory just as the pilot advised everyone to stay seated, even though he knew it would spark the following exchange every time:

Stewardess (angry): "Sir, please return to your seat."

Chester (sheepish): "I really, really have to go."

Stewardess (incredulous): "Can't you wait?"

Chester (even more sheepish): "Trust me, I can't."

Stewardess (exasperated): "Make it quick."

On the flight to Casper Wyoming, when the pilot had come on the intercom to say they were about to land, Chester had felt no tingling. Which, in hindsight, was strange. Normally, every flight he took was fraught with worry from take-off to landing about his urinating situation, but on the flight to Casper, the first flight he had taken since the revelation, he had not thought about it once.

At the Pringles, despite a cup of very nice tea, he had not used their bathroom. Which was not quite as strange as not using the plane lavatory. Chester did not like using the bathroom at other people's houses, particularly older people's houses where everything was so neat and tidy. He knew without even going into the Pringle's guest bathroom there would be a fresh unused bar of scented soap in the soap dish and there would be two fancy and perfectly aligned hand towels hanging from the towel rack. If Chester used that soap he would leave a soapy film on it and if he used one of the dainty hand towels he would leave it wet and wrinkled. What a person does in a bathroom is supposed to be private, but if you used the bathroom at a neat and tidy person's house you couldn't help but leave lots of clues about what you did and what you didn't do in their bathroom.

When he was in Theodore's basement he had his own bathroom and Chester recalled taking showers in that bathroom and brushing his teeth and shaving in that bathroom, but he couldn't recall ever sitting on the toilet in that bathroom. And that was also strange considering how many big meals Theodore had prepared for him.

Chester saw another rest stop sign and squinted his eyes and clenched his stomach to see if anywhere in his body there was a sign that a stop at the rest stop's public restroom was necessary.

Nothing.

So he just kept driving.

▼

Chester's phone rang.

He answered it on the third ring.

Not before or after the third ring, but right in the middle of the third ring. Chester never answered the phone after the first or second ring because he didn't want the person calling to think he was just sitting there waiting for the phone to ring. And he never waited until after the third ring because he was afraid the caller, after three rings, would think he wasn't there and hang up. After years of practice Chester was quite the expert at answering a phone smack dab in the middle of the third ring.

"Hello, this is Chester."

"I know who you are. You don't have to tell me."

"Oh, hello Darlene," said Chester.

Darlene did not say hello back. What she said was, "Phillip wants to know, when are you coming back to work?"

The question, its bluntness as well as its content, took Chester aback.

"Why would *Phillip* want to know when I am coming back to work?" asked Chester, drawing out the word Phillip.

"Well, he's your boss, so he wants to know."

"Since when is he my boss?"

"Since this morning."

"Really?"

"Yes, really."

Chester was both stunned and speechless.

"Hello, are you there? Chester, I don't have time to chit-chat. When are you coming back from your vacation?"

"I don't understand."

"It's a simple question. What day will you be returning to work?"

"No, I meant I don't understand how Phillip is my new boss."

Chester heard Darlene sigh with exasperation.

"Chester, do you remember I told you Mr. Dundee died?"

"Yes."

"And do you remember I said the president was thinking of promoting either you or Phillip to Mr. Dundee's position?"

"Yes."

"And do you remember I asked if you golfed and you said no?"

"Yes."

"Well, there you have it."

"I still don't understand."

Darlene laughed, not a genuine laugh, more of an unanticipated, it-just-kind-of-slipped-out laugh.

"Chester, Phillip golfs!"

"Oh," said Chester.

"In fact, Phillip and the president left early today."

"To go golfing?" said Chester.

"Now you got it, Chester. So what do you want me to tell Phillip?"

Chester thought for a moment. He was unhappy to hear he was not being promoted. He was even more unhappy to hear he had just lost out on more money and responsibility because he was not proficient at a sport that had nothing to do with juggling and organizing and categorizing and polishing numbers for a ball-bearing-manufacturing company.

But Chester was still a company man. He figured he could find an airport and fly home by tomorrow and be at work the next day.

"Tell Phillip I'll be back in two days. And please give him my congratulations."

"Why would I do that? I don't particularly like the little prick."

Chester smiled when Darlene said that. He was sure what she was really saying was she thought Chester should have gotten the promotion. But he wasn't a hundred percent sure that's what she meant, so he didn't want to ask her if that's what she was saying between the lines. He didn't want to ruin it.

"Thank you, Darlene," was all Chester said.

"Why are you thanking me?" said Darlene, irritation in her voice.

"Well, because ..."

"Whatever, Chester," said Darlene, the irritation no longer in her voice. "You didn't ask me about the funeral."

"What funeral?"

"Jesus Christ, Chester, you can drive a body crazy. Mr. Dundee's funeral."

"Oh, how was the funeral?"

"Very unusual."

"Unusual how?"

"The pallbearers."

"What about them?"

"They were all wearing golf clothes."

"Golf clothes?"

"Yes, matching golf shorts, golf shirts, golf hats, even golf shoes with those spikes on the bottom."

"At a funeral? That is unusual."

"It gets better."

"How?"

"They brought the casket out to the cemetery on the back of a giant golf cart."

"You don't say. I had no idea Mr. Dundee was so big on golf."

"It all seemed a bit inappropriate to me," said Darlene, "although it was the most interesting funeral I have ever been to."

"Have you been to a lot of funerals?"

"No, that was my first."

"But if that was …" Chester started to say, then stopped. Better to let sleeping dogs lie.

"Okay Chester, you got me chit-chatting, even though I told you I didn't have time to chit-chat."

"I'm sorry."

"You should be. See you in two days."

"Okay, Darlene."

"Oh, one other thing."

"Yes?"

"When you get back the first thing you should do is buy a set of golf clubs."

"Really?"

"You want to get ahead in life, don't you?"

"Yes."

"Well then," said Darlene.

▼

Chester saw another rest stop sign and did the whole eye squinting and stomach clenching thing again.

And again nothing happened.

Thirty minutes later his phone rang. He looked at the number, didn't recognize it, but saw it was his home area code. He answered in the middle of the third ring.

"Hello, this is Chester."

"Hi Chester."

"Who is this?"

"It's me, Phillip."

"Oh, hello."

"That's two hellos, Chester," said Phillip.

"Oh, you're right. I'm just surprised. Why are you calling me, Phillip?"

"Well, it's time for you to get back to work." Phillip paused, then said, "Get it?"

"I don't think so."

"I said it's *time* to get back to work. You know, time, what we were talking about in the break room."

"Oh, I get it. That's clever."

"Thank you. I thought so. Well, how about it?"

"How about what?"

230

"When are you coming back from vacation? Now that I'm in charge, I've got my hands full and I've got a mountain of work waiting for you."

"Yes, I heard about your promotion. Congratulations are in order."

"Thank you. You're not upset they picked me over you are you?"

"No, I think you'll do a wonderful job. I told Darlene to let you know I will be back to work in two days."

"You did? She didn't say anything to me. I don't think she particularly likes me."

"Oh, I'm sure she does," said Chester.

"We'll see," said Phillip. "By the way what have you been doing on your vacation?"

"Trying to escape from some contract killers."

"Interesting," said Phillip. "Okay, see you the morning after next. Bright and early."

Then Phillip hung up.

▼

Chester was starting to get drowsy. He turned on the car radio and looked for a station with a signal. The only station he could find was playing Latin dance music. Not Chester's favorite, but it would help to keep him awake.

He was tapping his fingers on the steering wheel to the Latin beat when someone said, "Can you turn that music down please."

Chester reached for the volume and then stopped. On top of everything else, now he was hearing voices.

"I said, can you please turn that damn music down."

Chester looked in the rear view mirror into the back seat. Sitting behind him was a man who looked very familiar.

The man looked familiar because it was Chester's father.

Chester's heart started to race and the pinkie finger on his left hand began twitching. Chester looked back at the road in front of him, shook his head a few times to clear it, and then cautiously looked in the rear view mirror again.

"I'm still here," said his father.

Chester swallowed.

"Keep your eyes on the road, Chester. I don't want to die twice."

Chester disregarded the warning and kept looking in the rear view mirror.

"What are you doing here?"

His father laughed. "What am I doing here? Not, how am I here? I'm dead, you know."

"I know," said Chester. "I was at the funeral."

"So was I."

"But you were dead."

"Doesn't mean I wasn't there."

"I don't understand."

"You don't understand how I could be dead and be at my own funeral or you don't understand what I am doing in your back seat?"

"Both."

"Well, I don't have the time or the interest to answer the first question but I am happy to address the second question. I'm here because you've gotten yourself into quite the pickle."

"What do you mean?"

"Chester, we'll be here all day if you insist on playing dumb. I know everything that has happened to you, so let's cut to the chase."

Chester was impressed. He couldn't recall his father ever being so forthright and concise. Maybe it wasn't his father.

"How do I know you are my father?" asked Chester.

"Who else would be in your back seat right now?"

"Good point, but that's not adequate proof."

His father laughed. "Always the accountant. Everything needs to add up. It's got to be black and white. No room for gray."

"You're stalling," said Chester, surprised that he would challenge his father.

"Miss October," said his father.

"Miss who?"

"Miss October, Playmate of the Month."

"I don't understand," said Chester.

"That's the page the magazine was open to the day I came into your bedroom and caught you pleasuring yourself. I think you were about fifteen at the time."

Chester's face turned red. He remembered Miss October very well and he remembered equally well how embarrassed he had been that day when his father barged into his room.

Chester looked into the rear view mirror.

"Hello, father," said Chester.

"Hello, son," said his father.

Chapter Twenty-One

Chester realized he was angry. Surprised made sense. Angry didn't. But there it was.

"What are you doing here?" Chester demanded.

"What do you mean?"

"You're dead."

"So?"

"So, how can you be dead and be here at the same time?"

"Just because I'm dead doesn't mean that I'm gone."

"I don't understand."

"I didn't go away."

"Yes, you did. You died. I saw you in the casket."

"But I'm still here. Things that exist don't just stop existing. The magician's disappearing rabbit always comes back."

"How can your body be under six feet of dirt in a coffin and also be in the back seat of my car at the same time? Not to mention, your body looks pretty good considering years of decay."

"Thank you, Chester. I'll take that as a compliment."

"You're missing the point of my question."

"No, I'm not. I'm just confused that you are confused."

"Pardon me?"

"If I had showed up in your back seat before your revelation, then I would understand why you would be confused. But now, after your revelation, I would think you know everything is possible. That everything that is here has always been here and will always be here."

"Yes, but ...":

"No buts, Chester."

"If I can finish please."

"Go ahead."

Chester started to speak but his father cut him off again.

"Mind if I smoke?"

"I didn't know you smoked."

"I just started. I have a lot of free time on my hands."

"I'd prefer if you didn't."

"Too bad. I'm your father."

Chester's father pulled a cigar out of his top pocket.

"I thought you meant a cigarette. That cigar will smell up my car."

His father just smiled and said, "Do you know what Sigmund Freud said about cigars?"

Chester didn't answer. He wasn't happy that his dead father was sitting in his back seat talking to him and he wasn't happy that his dead father was about to light a foul-smelling cigar.

"Chester, quit pouting. Don't you want to hear an interesting story?"

Chester wondered why his father couldn't have told him some interesting stories when he was alive. That would have been nice, thought Chester.

"Go ahead," said Chester.

"I don't know if this is true, but supposedly Sigmund Freud was giving a lecture about phallic symbols to some college students. At the end of the lecture he pulled out a cigar, slowly unwrapped the cigar, stroked the cigar with his hand a few times, licked the cigar up and down each side to get it moist, then lit the cigar and lovingly took a long deep drag before blowing out a plume of smoke. Then he looked at his students and said, 'However, sometimes a cigar is only a cigar.'"

Chester didn't say anything.

"Get it? Sometimes a cigar is only a cigar. I love it."

Chester's father lit the cigar, took a deep drag, cracked the back window a few inches and blew the smoke out the window.

"You never did have a sense of humor," said Chester's father.

"Why are you here, Dad?"

"Dad? You never called me Dad before."

"I wanted to get your attention."

"That was clever. I've been watching you and I must say ..."

"Must say what?"

"You're a better man than I am, Gunga Din. You've turned out better than I ever thought you would. You've been both adventurous and industrious in recent days."

"Is that a compliment or a criticism?"

"Take it how you want. I know how I meant it."

Chester drove in silence for awhile, his father preoccupied with his cigar which quickly filled the car interior with thick smoke. Chester cracked his own window to suck more of the smoke out.

"Father?"

"Yes," said his father looking up.

"I know that while things do change, they also never really go away. So I understand that your soul or your essence, or whatever you want to call it, is still here after your body has turned to dust. My question is how can your physical body be in my back seat? That kind of messes up the time line doesn't it."

Chester's father took another deep drag off his cigar and said, "Chester, you know as well as I do that time does not go in a straight line."

▼

"I saw Uncle Frank earlier tonight."

"He's still alive?"

"Yes, didn't you know?"

"Of course, I know. I'm just voicing a wish."

"You wish he wasn't alive?"

"Well, I'm not happy that I went before him."

"Why not?"

"He always beat me in everything, even outliving me."

"You should see his new wife."

"I know, I know. Enough."

Chester's father puffed on his cigar, tapped the ash on the edge of the window.

"So what did Frankie have to say?"

"He told me I was adopted."

Chester's father smacked his open palm on his thigh. "That ... son ... of ... a ... bitch," he said, drawing each word out.

"Is it true?" asked Chester.

"I don't want to talk about it," said his father.

Chester was not going to let his father off the hook.

"Was I really adopted?"

"Your Uncle Frank never knew how to keep his mouth shut."

"Why didn't you ever tell me?"

"Because if we told you, you would ask the big question and we didn't have an answer to the big question."

"What big question?"

"The question you would have asked is, 'Where did I come from?'"

"What's so bad about that question?"

"We couldn't answer it."

"Why not? What else were you hiding?"

"We weren't hiding anything. We had no idea where you came from."

"An adoption agency?"

"No."

"A friend or family member?"

"No."

"An unwed mother?"

"No."

"A stork?"

"No, not even a basket on the front porch. One day you weren't there and the next day you were there. It was that simple."

"Well, who brought me?"

"You're not listening. No one brought you. Your mother and I woke up one morning and there you were."

"Where?"

"Standing at the foot of our bed."

"Standing? How can a baby stand?"

"You weren't a baby. You were about three years old."

"Oh my."

▼

"Chester, that's all in the past. Let's talk about the present. Do you think your revelation is true?"

"I'm not sure. What do you think?"

"I think what you think."

"I don't understand."

"Yes, you do."

"Don't talk in riddles. Do you think my revelation is true, yes or no?"

"A revelation is a personal thing, not a group consensus thing."

"You aren't going to answer my question, are you?"

"No."

"Why not?"

"Because it doesn't matter what I think. It only matters what you think."

"I'm getting a headache," said Chester.

They drove for a few miles without talking before his father said, "Chester, I'm curious."

"About what?"

"You don't seem to be as shocked as I thought you would be to have me in your back seat. Why is that?"

Chester had been waiting for that question and he was prepared with an answer. "I think it's because over the past week I have found out that anything is possible, while at the same time nothing is as it seems. The most important person in the world to me, Harriette, doesn't really exist. I was kidnapped by two dark men and held hostage in a basement. I was interrogated at length by a guy who looks like Clark Kent and is an incredible cook, with a fair amount of the interrogation devoted to a cat named Coco. I moved a pencil and opened a locked door using just my mind. I have had to arbitrate a dispute between a World War II veteran and a Korean Conflict veteran. I had the most incredible conversations with a young woman who vanished at breakfast. I met a sexy FARC guerrilla who disappears people. I saw one man shot to death and another man about to have his throat slit. I lost a big job promotion and pay raise because I don't golf. And a dog named Cujo winked at me."

"And ..." said Chester's father.

"And, at this point, having a discussion with my dead father is just not that unusual."

"You sound stressed. And you certainly have every right to be stressed considering everything that has happened to you in the last week. If you could turn back time and not have all those things happen to you, would you?"

Chester thought for a moment.

"I wouldn't change a thing," said Chester. Her looked in the rear view mirror and smiled at his father.

And his father smiled back.

"That's my boy."

▼

237

"Do you want to sit up front?" asked Chester.

"Thought you'd never ask."

"I'll pull over."

"No need," said his father.

Chester looked in the rear view mirror again. The back seat was empty.

"That's much better," said his father, cracking the front seat passenger window.

Chester looked at the cigar clamped in the corner of his father's mouth.

"Cuban?"

"No, Dominican."

"I thought Cubans were the best cigars."

"That's a myth. These are the best. Would you like one?"

"I don't smoke."

"I didn't ask if you smoked. I asked if you would like to smoke a fine Dominican cigar with your father."

Chester mulled it over, the said, "Sure, why not. I've done crazier things this week."

His father pulled a cigar from his shirt pocket and started to unwrap it.

"Dad?"

"Yes."

"Please don't do that whole lovingly unwrapping, stroking and licking thing with it."

Chester's father looked at Chester and then burst out laughing, slapping his thigh again with his open palm.

"Chester, I take it back. You do have a sense of humor."

He unwrapped the cigar, pulled a cigar cutter from his pants pocket, snipped off the end and handed it to Chester. He leaned over and snapped open a Zippo lighter under the end of the cigar.

"Draw deep and twirl the cigar around after each puff," said his father as he moved the flame back and forth under the cigar tip.

Chester took a puff, coughed, twirled, took a few more puffs, coughed and twirled again, and then blew out a healthy plume of smoke.

"There you go," said his father.

Chester felt proud he was smoking a cigar for the first time. Prouder still that it was with his father.

"Look how dark it is out there," said Chester. There were no other cars on the highway which disappeared into darkness past the headlights of the car. There was no moonlight and the stars were just tiny white pinprick dots. "It's like we are traveling through space."

"Chester, we are traveling through space, you silly goose. We are on a spinning rock that is hurtling through space."

They puffed contentedly on their cigars. Chester turned the Latin music up a notch to increase the energy in the car. The strong cigar, the casualness of the conversation with his father, and the droning of the car tires on the highway were making him drowsy and he wanted to be wide awake.

"Chester, was I a good father?"

"The truth?"

"Yes, the truth."

Chester paused, conflicted. Should an honest person always be honest?

"You were a great father."

"No, I wasn't. But I appreciate you lying."

There was an unwieldy silence in the car.

"Do you know why I was not a good father?"

"Not really."

"It was because I never felt complete. I always felt like some of the pieces that were needed to make me a complete person had been left out and the pieces that were there never came together properly. You know how when there is lightning outside, the picture on the television will be all broken up into little fragments. You can still see the action on the screen and still hear the voices, but the picture as a whole just doesn't come together?"

"Yes," said Chester.

"Well, that's how I felt about myself all the time. Maybe it was your fault."

"My fault? How could that have been my fault?"

"If your revelation is true, then you made me. And you didn't make me perfect."

"I'm sorry," said Chester.

"Don't apologize. Maybe your revelation isn't true and maybe I was how I was because of me and me alone."

His father breathed a deep sigh. Chester looked over and saw that his father was studying the backs of his hands.

"Chester, the reason I am here for you right now is because I was not there for you before. But I'm not here to solve any riddles for you or to tell you what to do next. I'm here for just one reason."

"What's that?"

Chester felt his father's hand on his shoulder.

"To tell you that you do matter."

Chester got chillbumps when his father said that. Part of him was happy to finally hear those words from his father, and part of him wished those words did not have the impact on him that they did.

Chester and his dead father rode in silence for what seemed like a very long.

Then his father asked, "Do you want to talk to your mother?"

"Is she here?"

"No, but she can be."

Chester thought for a moment, then said, "Not really."

"I don't blame you."

"I'm not trying to be mean."

"No explanations necessary, Chester."

They puffed some more on their cigars. His father leaned over and turned the Latin music up even more. "It's growing on me," he said.

"How is mother?" asked Chester

"Same as always, I guess."

"You guess?"

"I don't see her much."

"Aren't you in the same place?"

"It's a big place. She does her thing. I do mine."

"Is she happy?"

"Define happy?"

Chester didn't answer. He knew what his father was saying.

"You said it was a big place. What is it like on the other side?"

Chester's father took a deep drag on his cigar, then studied the red coal on the end, either stalling for time or trying to think of just the right answer. Chester wasn't sure which.

"I can't tell you."

"Why not? Is it a secret? Do you take some type of oath when you get there?"

"No. I can't tell you because there is no other side. There's just this side. There's only one side."

"There's always another side."

"That's where you're wrong. This side and the other side. Before and after. The beginning and the end. Everything is not two things. Everything is only one thing."

240

"You're wrong. What about a penny? On one side it's always heads and on the other side it's always tails."

"A penny analogy? You're really going with a penny analogy?"

"It works."

"You're wrong. If I give you a penny that is heads up. What's on the other side?"

"Tails."

"Are you sure?"

"Positive."

"Well, what if it's a special penny that is so big you can stand on it like you would a manhole cover. What would be on the other side then?"

"Still tails."

"Are you positive?"

"Still positive."

"Okay, now use your imagination. Let's say it's the granddaddy of special pennies and it's so gigantic that no matter what direction you look, you can't see the edge of the penny. In fact it's so big that if you jumped in a spaceship and traveled the speed of light in any direction you still would never get to the edge of that penny. Now, what would be on the other side of that penny?"

"Tails."

"Are you sure? Are you still positive?"

Chester hesitated. "I can never get to the edge of the penny?"

"No."

"So I don't even know if there is an edge?"

"Correct."

"Which means I can never turn the penny over?"

"Now you're getting it."

"Which means there's no proof that there is another side?"

"Yes."

"So, no tails? Only heads."

"Looks that way."

▼

"I have to say, of all the strange things that have happened to me recently, this is the strangest."

His father nodded in agreement. "Smoking a cigar with your dead father certainly qualifies as unusual."

"That's not the strange part," said Chester.

"It's not? Then what is?"

"Being with you and feeling like you want to be with me is."

"And you never felt like that when I was alive."

"No. Not really."

They drove in silence for a few miles, both puffing on their cigars, both staring straight ahead at the dark and empty highway.

"I'm sorry," said his father.

▼

"Chester, do you still have that quarter I gave you? You know, the one from the same year you were born."

Chester felt bad. He didn't want to tell his father he lost it. The fact his father remembered it reinforced how important the giving and the receiving of that coin had been five decades ago.

"It's somewhere," said Chester.

"That's good," said his father.

After a bit, Chester's father clapped his hands together and said, "Well, I best be moving on."

"What do you mean by moving on?"

"Just moving on. Leaving."

"Going to where?"

"To there."

"Where is that?"

"Don't you know?"

"No."

"Well, I can't tell you."

"Why not?"

"I don't want to ruin the surprise."

Chapter Twenty-Two

"Hello?"

Then louder. "Hello, you want my money or not?"

Chester opened his eyes. He saw a large, fleshy hand, two quarters pinched between the thumb and forefinger of the hand.

"Take it. I don't got all day."

Chester looked past the hand and saw an arm and beyond that the body of an overweight woman in a paisley dress, a lit cigarette in the corner of her mouth, one eye squinted shut against the smoke curling up from the cigarette. She was driving an old four-door Oldsmobile Delta 88 with a peeling blue vinyl roof.

"Were you asleep?"

"Yes," said Chester.

"You're allowed to do that?" asked the overweight woman.

"I'm not sure," said Chester.

The passenger side of the overweight woman's front seat was covered with empty Burger King wrappers, soft drink cups and french fries containers. The woman was holding both her cigarette and a giant, half-eaten hamburger in the same hand. She turned her wrist one way, took a bite of the burger, then turned her wrist the other way and took a drag off her cigarette while still chewing.

"Is that a Whopper?" said Chester.

"It sure is. And it's delicious."

Chester licked his lips.

The woman dropped the quarters she was holding into Chester's open palm, then pulled her arm into the car and put her hand on the top of the steering wheel. She stared straight ahead. After a moment she turned to look at Chester and said, "Well?"

"Well, what?"

"Are you going to open the gate or not?"

Chester looked around and saw that he was in a toll booth. He saw a big yellow button, so he pushed it. He heard a metallic grating sound and leaned out the toll booth window to see a mechanical pole raise up. The woman started to drive through. In the back seat Chester saw an infant boy under a cloud of cigarette smoke. Something about the child caught his attention.

"Excuse me, who is that ..." Chester started to ask the woman.

"No time. Gotta get rid of this rug rat."

He watched the woman drive off into the darkness down a single-lane road. He turned and looked in the direction her car had come and saw the same single-lane road disappearing into darkness. When he could no longer hear the engine of the woman's car it became very quiet and very still in the toll booth. There was only one toll booth and only one road, going in only one direction. There were no stars in the sky. The only light was a small pen light shining on the big yellow button. Next to the button was a Styrofoam cup of coffee. Chester picked it up and took a sip. The coffee was somewhere between warm and hot. He took another sip. It tasted good.

He wished he had a cinnamon roll to go with it.

Chester was sitting on a stool in the toll both, his feet on the ground. He swiveled his hips back and forth and the stool turned left then right. He lifted his feet off the ground and spun completely around on the stool. He did it several more times until he started to feel dizzy.

In the distance he saw headlights, then a car, then a huge body filling up the whole right side of the windshield. The huge body looked familiar. The car, a shiny black Cadillac, stopped and the driver's window slid down.

"Hi, Theodore," said Chester.

"Hello, Chester."

Theodore looked the same as he had the last time Chester had seen him. Same black chino pants and a crisp, white short-sleeved cotton shirt, the sleeves rolled up exactly one inch, showing his tanned and muscular arms. Same jet black hair, full and thick, combed straight back. Same glasses with thick black frames, like the glasses Buddy Holly wore. Same steel blue eyes.

The only thing different was the W-W-Two Ka-Bar knife sticking out the side of his head.

Chester looked at the knife. Theodore looked at Chester looking at the knife.

"Does that hurt?" asked Chester.

"A little," said Theodore.

"Not to pry, Theodore, but what happened?"

"A young lady in a polka-dot bikini."

"Oh."

Chester noticed Theodore's left hand was wrapped in a white dish towel spotted with blood. And his left thumb was missing.

"What happened to your hand?"

"She had a dog with her. A very mean dog."

"Oh," said Chester a second time.

"Where's your thumb?"

"The little bastard ate it."

Chester had to fight the urge to say "oh" again. Instead, he just nodded his head, shuffled his feet, and said, "Other than that, how have you been?"

Theodore gave Chester the look. The same look he had given Chester in the basement whenever he thought Chester was being ridiculous. He studied Chester, slowly looking him up and down. Chester remembered what it had been like to be under the Theodore microscope. His pinkie finger curled inward and started tapping the palm of his left hand. Chester put his hand behind his back so Theodore wouldn't see it.

"So, let me ask you a question," said Theodore.

"Okay."

"Are you still dealing with that revelation thing?"

"Can you define, dealing with it, please?"

Theodore raised an eyebrow. "You're doing it again."

Chester knew what he was doing again. He was answering a question with a question. He squeezed his left hand shut behind his back to stop the pinkie tapping.

Theodore sighed. "I'm asking you whether you still believe that cockamamie revelation."

Chester was impressed. He thought he was the only one to use that word. He had never heard another person say. "It's not cockamamie to me. It's real."

"Whatever," said Theodore, dismissively.

"Let me ask you a question," said Chester.

Theodore's face clouded over. "I'm the one asking the questions here," he barked.

Chester flinched.

Theodore grinned.

"I'm just kidding. Ask away."

Chester composed himself, took a few seconds to organize the question in his head, then said, "How can you be so calm and coherent, not to mention drive a motor vehicle, with a huge knife embedded in your head?"

Theodore answered right away. "Good genes."

"Good genes? That's it?"

"That's all it takes. A lesser man than me couldn't handle this."

"You mean a lesser man like me."

"You said it. I didn't."

Chester knew Theodore was going to say that.

And Theodore knew that Chester knew he was going to say that.

"Why do you set yourself up like that, Chester? You need to stop shortchanging yourself. There's more to you than you think. The more you think that there is, the more it will be true. You just don't get it."

"Get what?"

"You are everything I am. But much more. A whole lot more."

"That's not possible."

"Oh, yeah? Look at me. Look at you."

Chester looked at the knife in Theodore's head and at where his missing thumb should be and he realized that Theodore was making an excellent point. The time in the basement had been one-sided, with Theodore on top, but now, after the dust had settled, Chester seemed to be the winner.

"How does it feel to be in the driver's seat now?" asked Theodore.

"Technically, you are in the driver's seat and I am sitting on a stool."

Theodore sighed for the second time. "Chester, you are still a major pain in the ass. It's both endearing and aggravating."

"Is that a good thing?'

"Not especially."

Theodore reached up and grabbed the handle of the Kay-Bar knife and slowly tried to pull the blade out. He grimaced from the pain and stopped.

"You might not want to do that," said Chester, legitimately concerned.

"You're probably right."

Theodore adjusted his rear view mirror which was hard to do using a hand without a thumb. "Listen Chester, I really need to be going. How much is the toll?"

"It's usually fifty cents. But I won't charge you."

"I'll pay. I don't want you to get in trouble."

"No, really, it's on me," said Chester pushing the big yellow button. He looked back up and Theodore's car had already vanished into the night.

Chester started spinning again on the stool.

Even with the next vehicle still a hundred yards away, Chester could tell that it wasn't a car. Sure enough, it was a white shuttle van and, though he could not see the company lettering on the van, Chester knew it would have four big red letters on the side: A-V-I-S.

He quickly checked his pants pockets for his cell phone, pulled it out, put it to his ear and pretended to be having a conversation as the shuttle van pulled up and Darren Tucker rolled down the window.

"Mr. Fortunberry, where is ..."

Chester held his palm out toward Darren, and then with that same hand pointed at the cell phone against his ear. He gave Darren the nod that said he would be with him as soon as he was done with his phone call. Darren did not look happy, and the longer he waited while Chester pretended to be talking on the cell phone, the angrier it made Darren and the happier it made Chester. Chester even paced in a circle in the tollbooth, turning his back to Darren twice as he carried on his phantom phone call.

"Mr. Fortunberry." Louder this time.

Chester put his palm out again toward Darren and then held up one finger, signaling he would be done in just a minute. Finally, when he felt he could not carry on the charade a second longer, he snapped his cell phone shut, and said in the most pleasant voice possible, "Yes Darren, what can I do for you?"

"It's about time."

"Sorry to make you wait." He said it. But he didn't mean it. As Harriette liked to say, so-and-so just got a dose of their own medicine. In this case, the so-and-so was Darren.

"Mr. Fortunberry, where is the Avis car you rented?"

"Oh, I'm not done with it yet."

"I didn't ask if you were done with it yet. I asked you where it is." Darren looked left and right, then frontwards and backwards. "I don't see it anywhere. Is my car no longer in your possession?"

"*Your* car?"

"I mean Avis's car."

Chester had said *your car* to irritate Darren and buy a little time. Because as much as he was not a Darren Tucker fan, he had to admit Darren's question about where the Avis rental car was a legitimate question. Chester had no idea where the car was.

"You know, you didn't pay for the extra insurance. If that car has been stolen, you owe me for a new car."

"Owe you?"

"I mean Avis. And you know I mean Avis. Mr. Fortunberry, you are trying my patience."

"That's not my intent."

"I'm not so sure about that," said Darren, giving him a menacing look.

"How have you been?" said Chester in what he knew was a feeble attempt to change the tenor of the conversation. Surprisingly, it did.

"Oh, can't complain," said Darren.

"Who are those people?" The people Chester was referring to were the half dozen passengers sitting quietly in the back of the shuttle van.

Darren looked over his shoulder to make sure none of the passengers were listening. He leaned out the window, cupped his left hand to the side of his mouth, beckoned Chester closer with his other hand, and in a stage whisper said, "I'm making deliveries. Some of them are going to heaven, and some of them are going to hell."

"Heaven and hell? Do those places really exist?" asked Chester loudly.

Darren waved both hands excitedly at Chester and shushed him. "Keep it down. None of them know where they're going."

"They don't."

"No, of course not."

"But you know?"

"That's a silly question. I'm driving them there. I need to know who

248

to drop off where."

Chester peered through the van windows at the passengers. He cupped his hand to the side of his mouth and in his own stage whisper said, "Who's going where?"

Darren shook his head. "I can't tell you that. I'm sworn to secrecy."

"Oh," said Chester, disappointed.

Darren looked over his shoulder and then did the whole leaning out his window, cupping his hand and stage whispering thing again. "I will tell you this. See the sweet little old lady in the last row? The one with the blue hair? Well, she's in for a real surprise."

"No!" said Chester, shocked.

"Yes!" said Darren, a little too excited.

"But how? She looks so innocent."

"Nothing is as it seems," said Darren.

Chester wanted to tell Darren he was stating what was now obviously the obvious, but he didn't.

"So, which group do you drop off first?"

"The heaven group."

"Why them first?"

"Because, after that, the ones still in the van are a nervous wreck."

"That's an evil thing to do."

"Hey, gotta entertain myself somehow."

Darren looked at the tollbooth bar.

"How much?"

"Fifty cents."

"I'm a little short. Mind if I just deduct it from your car rental bill."

"Works for me," said Chester.

The next car looked longer than most cars. And it took longer to get to the tollbooth. It finally came to a stop and Chester waited as the driver manually rolled down the window. It seemed to take forever. It gave Chester time to study the car which was an emerald green Ford station wagon with fake wood paneling on the side. He remembered seeing a few of them in faded Polaroid photos from the 1970s.

"Nice car, Ed" said Chester.

Ed Pringle didn't answer. Instead, he just scowled at Chester.

"Where is he?"

"Who?"

"That sumbitch."

Ed actually said it like that. Like it was one word.

"What son of a bitch?"

"Your uncle."

"I haven't a clue."

"Don't lie to me."

"I'm not," said Chester, and he wasn't lying. The last time he had seen Uncle Frank he had been playing Wyatt Earp. Chester had no idea where his uncle was at that moment. Probably at his house, but maybe not.

Chester saw Edna in the passenger seat. In her lap was a plate of pecan sandie cookies. She leaned over and smiled at Chester. Chester smiled back. Edna held up one of the cookies and tilted her head slightly, an unspoken question asked. Chester nodded back. Right then, there was nothing he wanted more than one of Edna Pringle's homemade pecan sandie cookies. His mouth filled with saliva. He could already taste the first bite of that cookie, which he would chew and then wash down with a gulp of the lukewarm coffee in the Styrofoam cup. Edna reached across Ed, the cookie in her plump little hand. Ed, without looking at Edna and still scowling at Chester, took the cookie from Edna's hand and placed it back on the plate.

"He's not hungry."

"But ..." said Edna.

"But ..." said Chester.

"I said, he's not hungry. At least, not hungry enough to tell me where his uncle is."

So, that's how it's going to be, thought Chester. Give up Uncle Frank for a pecan sandies cookie. Chester thought about it. He realized the fact he was even thinking about it said a lot about his character, or lack thereof. But, hey, it was a pecan sandies cookie. And it was homemade. The cookies smelled like they had just come out of the oven.

Chester forced himself to swallow the saliva in his mouth and shook his head. "Like I said, I don't know where he is."

"Bullshit," barked Ed.

Chester was sure that was how Ed wanted to end their conversation, with a loud curse word and then speeding away in a cloud of dust, his tires squealing. Making a bold statement, being the tough guy. But before Ed could make that bold statement, he first had to roll his window back up and that took forever. Chester was a little embarrassed for Ed as he waited and waited while that window on the emerald green

Ford station wagon with the fake wood paneling on the slide slowly, agonizingly went up an eighth of an inch at a time. When the window was sealed tight, Ed put both hands on the steering wheel and looked straight ahead. He saw that the tollbooth bar was down so he turned and glared at Chester.

Chester hit the yellow button to raise the tollbooth bar.

But he took his time doing it.

▼

Chester heard the next car before he even saw the headlights.

The throaty growl of the engine told him it was some type of fancy sports car. He leaned out the toll booth window and after a few moments saw the headlights as the noise from the high performance engine increased. The driver hit the brakes and the car, a cherry red Lamborghini, screeched and skidded to a stop at the toll booth.

The dark-tinted window powered down and Chester saw a woman who looked a lot like Darlene, the Darlene from the ball-bearing-manufacturing company's personnel department. Except that this looked like the Playboy magazine version of Darlene. Instead of her mousy hair up in a bun, it was down and dyed platinum blonde. Her glasses were gone, replaced by blue eye shadow and inch-long eyelashes. Her lipstick was ruby red and her lips opened and closed seductively as she slowly chewed a piece of gum. She wore a black leather halter top that barely covered her huge breasts and a leopard-print miniskirt. It was the same full-figured woman he remembered from his office but what he once considered overweight was now undeniably voluptuous. The Lamborghini was in park but the racing engine had the car vibrating and Chester had to force himself to stop looking at the jiggling orbs under Darlene's halter top. In the passenger seat was a young, model-handsome, swarthy man in a sharkskin suit and a black silk shirt open at the collar. The man's tanned and manicured left hand rested on Darlene's plump exposed thigh, halfway between her knee and the hem of her miniskirt.

"How's it hanging, Chester?"

"Darlene?"

"The only and only."

"I didn't know you owned a Lamborghini."

"There are a lot of things you don't know about me."

"Who's your friend?"

"Nunya biz."

Chester felt a little embarrassed. He wasn't sure if it was because Darlene had caught him working when he was supposed to be on vacation, or whether it was because the way she was dressed, and the way she was chewing that gum, was getting him excited. Being stimulated by a sexy model or covergirl was understandable and nothing to be ashamed of, but being aroused by a woman who you had previously thought of as a frumpy spinster, well, that seemed naughty to Chester. And knowing that the woman in question knew she was having that effect on him made it embarrassing.

"Chill out, Chester."

"I'm just surprised."

"About the car?"

"No. About you. You look so ..."

"Hot?"

"Intriguing."

"I'll settle for that."

Darlene looked at Chester and then behind him at the toll booth.

"I thought you were on vacation?"

"I am."

"Looks like you're working to me."

"Darlene, I really have no idea what I am doing here."

"I'll tell you why you're here. You're here to raise that big steel bar so I can get to moving down the road. What's the toll?"

"Fifty cents."

Darlene snapped her fingers and the young, model-handsome, swarthy man reached inside his sharkskin jacket and pulled out a crisp $100 bill. Darlene slowly folded the bill in half, placed it between the exposed cleavage of her two bulging breasts, rubbed it around a bit, pulled it out and pressed it to her lips, leaving a perfectly formed lipstick kiss. Then she handed the bill to Chester.

"Keep the change."

"But ..."

"But, what?"

"What are you doing here?"

"Same thing as you, Chester. Just checking things out."

"But the car, your hair, that man. I had no idea ..."

Darlene stopped chewing her gum. She waved her hand at Chester and said, "Appearances can be deceiving. You of all people should know that. Am I right or am I right?"

Chester thought for a minute, then said, "Darlene, you are one hundred percent right."

"Damn right," said Darlene. She put her hand on top of the young man's hand and slid it up under her skirt, then grabbed the car's stick shift and revved the engine up to a roar. She looked at Chester, pouted her lips and said, "Now open the gate, sweet cheeks."

Chester hit the big yellow button and the suddenly sexy and voluptuous Darlene and the young, model-handsome, swarthy man and the cherry red Lamborghini shot through the toll booth like a rocket.

Chester looked at the folded $100 bill in his hand. He studied the ruby red lipstick kiss and then held the bill up to his nose and smelled an incredibly intoxicating perfume. As he did, he looked down and saw that little Chester had come to almost full attention, poking the crotch area of his pants up into a small tent.

"Oh my," said Chester.

The lights of the next vehicle looked unusual. The headlights were much closer together and much lower to the ground than the other cars. Plus, the vehicle seemed to be moving very slowly and Chester could not hear the engine. When it finally pulled up to the toll booth, Chester saw why it looked different.

"Nice golf cart."

"Thank you," said Mr. Dundee, who was dressed head to toe in blue golf attire: blue shirt, blue shorts and blue golf shoes. He even had a blue golf tee stuck behind his ear and there were two sets of golf clubs on the back of the cart, both in matching blue golf bags.

"I'm kind of surprised to see you here," said Chester.

"Don't get many golf carts through here?"

"Not the cart. You. I heard you passed."

"Yeah, surprised the hell out of me."

"I'm sorry to hear it. You were a very fair boss."

"Fair like average or fair like I treated you well?"

"Both."

"Fair enough," laughed Mr. Dundee.

"They replaced you with Phillip."

"I heard. I think you would have been the better choice."

"Did you ever mention that to the president?"

"Why would I? I assumed I would be around much longer than I ended up being around. Let me tell you, dying unexpectedly can be a real shocker."

Mr. Dundee looked at Chester and then, like Darlene had, at the toll booth he was standing in.

"Need I ask?"

"You can, but I'm not sure what I could tell you. I don't know how I got here or why I'm here, which, by the way, seems to be the two recurring mysteries I have been dealing with lately. What about you? After you passed so suddenly, did you ever think you'd be riding around in a golf cart again?"

"Nope. I don't know how everything that has happened to me recently has happened, or why it has happened."

"See, that's how I feel. If you had told me a week ago I would be in the middle of nowhere in a toll booth on a one-way highway, I wouldn't have believed it."

"Well Chester, strange things happen. If they didn't, we wouldn't have the word *strange*. I know that sounds silly, but the reason we have words like strange and unusual and unexpected is because strange and unusual and unexpected things happen."

Chester nodded in agreement.

"All of this is still a little new to me, Chester, so I have to ask. Are you dead too?"

"I don't think so."

"But you're talking to a dead person."

"Well, you're not my first this week."

"Ah-ha, see, that proves my point. Strange, unusual and unexpected."

"Mr. Dundee, do you know who I just saw? Darlene."

"The homely chubbette in personnel."

"When I saw her just a few minutes ago, she looked like a Playboy model."

"Darlene?"

"Yes."

"Chester, you may not be dead, but you must be dreaming. That goes way beyond strange, unusual and unexpected."

"On your way here did you happen to see a cherry red Lamborghini?"

"Yes. Ran me right off the road."

"That was Darlene and her man."

"Her man?"

"I think he was a gigolo."

"Darlene has a gigolo?"

"It appears so."

"Well, good for her."

Mr. Dundee took the blue golf tee from behind his ear and used the pointed end to probe at something in his teeth. He wiped the end of the tee on his blue golf shorts and put it back behind his ear.

"Chester, remember how those homeless people in New York upset you?"

"Yes. But they didn't upset me. The way other people ignored them upset me."

"I understand. But I just wanted to tell you that since I passed, I've seen a few things. And you don't have to worry about those homeless people."

"Why not?"

"It all works out."

"What do you mean?"

"I can't really explain it. Just trust me. It all works out for them."

Even though Mr. Dundee didn't give him an explanation about how it all works out for the homeless people, Chester believed him. And it made him feel better.

"Mr. Dundee, why are there two sets of golf clubs on your cart?"

"I'm expecting someone."

"Who?"

"Nunya biz," said Mr. Dundee. "If I tell you everything, then you won't have anything strange, unusual and unexpected to look forward to. Now, I need to get to the next tee box, so I have to go."

Chester didn't want Mr. Dundee to leave. It was lonely in that solitary toll booth on that solitary road. And Mr. Dundee seemed to have some answers.

"What's it like where you're at now?" asked Chester.

"Well, the golf courses are much better."

"They have golf courses?"

"They have everything. And everything is just a little bit better."

"How so?"

"There are no sand traps or water hazards and everybody shoots par. It never rains and you never lose your ball. And you know what the best part is?"

"No, what?"

"No greens fees."

"That's nice."

255

"Speaking of fees, what's the toll?"

"Fifty cents. But I won't charge you."

Mr. Dundee frowned. "Chester, that's not like you. You're an accountant. Money is your business. Now, do your job accordingly."

"Okay. That will be fifty cents, please."

Mr. Dundee reached into the well of the golf cart, pulled something out and dropped it into Chester's hand.

"That's a golf ball," said Chester.

"Nothing gets past you," said Mr. Dundee, who mashed down the accelerator pedal on the golf cart and slowly puttered down the road. The golf cart was almost completely out of Chester's sight when he heard Mr. Dundee yell, and Chester knew what he was going to yell even before he yelled it.

"Fore."

The next vehicle to pull up was big and loud. It was a jet black Dodge Ram 3500 pickup truck with a 5.7 Liter Hemi engine. Chester knew that because it said 5.7 Liter Hemi on the side of the truck. In the bed of the truck was a giant bale of hay. A Rebel flag bumper sticker was on the back of the truck window. Hanging from the rear view mirror was a leather strip with the bleached white jawbone of a small animal. Behind the wheel was a young man wearing a straw cowboy hat and denim overalls over a long-sleeved plaid workshirt. A toothpick was in the corner of his mouth. None of which seemed strange, except for the person under those clothes.

"Hello, Phillip."

"Howdy, Chester."

"Why are you driving that truck?"

"It's easier than walking."

"No, that's not what I meant. Why are you dressed like that?"

"Like what?"

"Like a farmer."

"I am a farmer."

"I thought you were the new head of accounting for our ball-bearing-manufacturing company?"

"I am. And I'm also a farmer when I'm not counting ball bearings."

"I didn't know that. You don't seem like the farmer type."

"What can I say? I like to grow things."

"What's your favorite?"

"Okra."

"The type you fry?"

"I like it better stewed, with tomatoes and onions."

"Oh, I've never tried it that way. Is it good?"

"It's an acquired taste."

Chester loved talking about food almost as much as he loved eating food. Which is why seeing his new boss, who usually dressed in snappy suits and drove a late model BMW, in a pickup truck with a bale of hay in it did not prick his curiosity as much as hearing about a new recipe for preparing okra.

"I'll bring some to the office next week," said Phillip.

"That would be nice," said Chester, excited.

Chester heard an oink. He leaned a little to the left to peer around Phillip into the passenger seat.

"Is that a baby pig?"

"Well, it's not a baby cow."

"Why is a baby pig riding in your truck?"

"Becaaaause ..." said Phillip dragging the word out.

"Because it's easier than walking," said Chester, answering his own question.

"Bingo," said Phillip.

"What's his name?"

"He's a she."

"Oh, sorry. What's her name?"

"How the hell would I know," laughed Phillip. "I'm just giving her a ride."

"Was she hitchhiking?"

"Chester, don't be silly. Baby pigs don't hitchhike. It's too dangerous."

Chester looked at the no-name baby pig again. She wasn't standing on all fours on the passenger seat. Instead, she was sitting down with her butt on the seat and her front legs up in the air. She had her shoulder seat belt on and a toothpick in the corner of her mouth. And she was wearing dark Ray-Ban sunglasses, like the type fighter pilots wear.

"Why is the baby pig wearing sunglasses at night?" asked Chester.

"Good question. I asked her the same thing."

"And ...."

"She didn't answer. Which I think is kind of rude."

Chester looked back at Phillip. "By the way, you'll never guess who just came through."

"Mr. Dundee," said Phillip.

"How did you know?" asked Chester, surprised.

"You told me to guess. I guessed."

"You guessed right."

Phillip nodded his head, a twinkle in his eye. It was the first time Chester had ever seen a twinkle in someone's eye. He had heard the phrase before, had read it more than once in a book, but had never seen it in real life. Until Phillip got the twinkle. And when Phillip got the twinkle, he honked his truck horn and it made a loud blast.

"Why did you do that?" asked Chester.

"Don't you know?"

"No."

"Wait ten seconds."

Chester waited patiently for ten seconds.

"Now do you know?" asked Phillip.

"Still no," said Chester.

"Where did it go?" asked Phillip, giving him a I-just-know-you're-going-to-get-this look.

"Where did what go?"

"The honk!" said Phillip. "That loud sound. You heard it ten seconds ago. It was there. It existed. Now where is it? Is it gone forever?"

Chester got it. He knew what Phillip was doing. It was the slap thing. He had paid attention to Chester when they had coffee that day in the break room. It made Chester feel good. It meant Phillip had listened to him.

"Very clever," said Chester. "And the answer is the honk is still there. It was always there and it will always be there."

"Damn straight," yelled Phillip, stomping on the gas pedal and driving right through the toll booth bar, snapping it in half like a brittle twig.

Chester leaned out and looked at the disappearing taillights of the Dodge Ram 3500 with the 5.7 Liter Hemi engine and at the tollbooth bar, half of it still sticking out from the tollbooth and the other half on the ground.

"Oh my," said Chester.

He just knew he would be blamed for the damage.

Chapter Twenty-Three

Chester was pretty sure he was asleep.

But he was equally sure he heard the words, "Oh my."

He had said those words after Phillip drove through the tollbooth bar, so he wondered if he was just re-hearing his voice again in his sleep. He thought about it and decided that, while they were the same two words, they had not been said in his voice. He opened one eye and looked out the tollbooth window.

"Chester, did you do that?" asked Harriette.

Chester opened his other eye. "Did I do what?"

Harriette, who was driving an orange Gremlin with a white stripe down the side, pointed through her windshield at the broken tollbooth bar.

"No, Phillip did it."

"Phillip from your work."

"Yes."

"Why?"

That was an honest question. An honest question that deserved an honest answer. Particularly if the person asking the question was your wife. But Chester couldn't resist.

"The baby pig told him to."

"Well, Phillip should not be so easily influenced," said Harriette, which was not really the response Chester thought he would get from Harriette. She never failed to amaze him.

"Harriette, I'm sure you are wondering what I am doing here. In this tollbooth. Let me explain ..."

"No need."

"No need?"

"You don't have to explain anything to me. I'm sure there is a perfectly good reason why you are here. So, don't stress out and get yourself all into a tizzy."

"Harriette, tizzy is not a substantial enough word to describe the state of mind I have been in since the day you dropped me off at the airport."

"Chester, did you look in the cockpit? That would explain you being in a tizzy."

"No, I did not look in the cockpit. And I am in much more than a tizzy. I wish you would stop using that word."

Harriette looked hurt. "No need to be snappy."

"But I'm in a bad situation and I don't feel like you are being sympathetic."

Harriette gave Chester a warm smile, the same smile she offered up whenever she wanted to calm him down. "Don't place too much emphasis on bad, Chester. The difference between a good haircut and a bad haircut is just three weeks."

"Meaning what?"

"What's bad now will soon be good."

"When?"

"In time."

"But you can't trust time."

"You can't explain it, but you can trust it."

"How so?"

"It's one of life's few constants."

"I'm confused."

"Don't be. You are on a journey. And journeys take time."

"But Harriette, I miss you. I miss our house. I even miss watching *Cops* with you."

"That's sweet, Chester."

"What's been happening back home? What have I missed?"

"Well, I got a cat. A kitten, actually."

"But you don't like cats."

"This one I do. She's special."

"What's her name?"

Harriette started to answer. Chester raised his hand to stop her.

"Wait, don't tell me. I think I know."

"Chester, how in the world would you know the name of a cat that you didn't even know I had until I just now told you?"

"Trust me, I know."

"No, you don't."

"Coco."

Harriette's eyes got big and round and she said, "Oh my. How on earth did you know that?"

"I'm just smart that way," said Chester.

"Of course you are, dear."

Seeing and talking to Harriette made Chester relax. For the first time in a long time he felt like everything was going to be okay. "Harriette, it is so good to see you. I have so much to tell you."

"I know you do. But now's not the time. When you're done, then we'll talk."

"But I need to tell you about my revelation."

"You had a revelation?"

"Yes," said Chester in a loud voice.

"The one where only you are real and nobody else is?"

"Yes!" said Chester in an even louder voice. Then in a much quieter voice, "How do you know about that?"

"I just do."

"But what about you, Harriette? Does than mean you aren't real?"

"I'm right here, Chester. I'll always be here. Don't you worry."

Chester looked concerned. Harriette smiled at him, nodding her head to emphasize what she had just said. Chester smiled back, a tentative smile. Chester could tell from Harriette's smile and her nodding that that part of their conversation was over.

"So, where are you going?" asked Chester.

Harriette did what Chester often did. She answered his question with a question. "Chester, did you happen to see a woman in a paisley dress with a three-year-old boy in her back seat come through here?"

"Was she smoking?"

"I don't know. How many women in paisley dresses with infant boys in the back seat have come through here tonight?"

"Just one."

"Well, that's the one I'm looking for."

"She drove through here an hour or so ago. But why are you looking for her?"

"I need to talk to her."

"About what?"

"I need to make sure she delivers that little boy to the right house."

"But why does that concern you?"

"Don't you know?"

"No."

"Oh my," said Harriette for the third time.

Then she blew him a kiss and slowly drove around the broken tollbooth bar.

▼

Chester saw another set of approaching headlights. Which made him think that, for a tollbooth in the middle of nowhere on a one-lane road, this place was like Grand Central Station.

The car that stopped at the tollbooth looked familiar. It looked just like the car Chester knew was parked in his garage at home. Same model, same color, even the same scratch on the right front bumper from the day Harriette clipped their brick mailbox at the curb.

Chester stared at the driver. The driver stared at Chester.

"You look just like me," Chester in the tollbooth said.

"You look just like me," Chester in the car said.

They continued to stare at each other.

"This is strange," said Chester in the tollbooth.

"This is strange," said Chester in the car.

Chester in the tollbooth frowned and said, "Are you going to repeat everything I say?"

"Are you going to ..." Chester in the car started to stay, then stopped, laughed and said, "Sorry, couldn't help myself."

The two Chesters continued to stare at each other.

In the lull Chester in the tollbooth noticed two things. One thing irritated him. The other thing alarmed him.

The thing that irritated him was the music coming from the car radio. It was loud and abrasive.

"Are you listening to heavy metal music?" asked Chester, his voice an equal mixture of astonishment and condemnation.

"Yes, I am," said Chester in the car.

"But I don't like heavy metal music."

"I do. And I'm not playing it for you. I'm playing it for me."

Chester in the tollbooth then thought about the thing that alarmed him, which was the car that the other Chester was driving. It was his personal car.

"Where is the Avis rental car?" Chester asked, his voice now an equal mixture of concern and accusation.

"What Avis rental car?"

"The one I rented."

"How would I know where a rental car you rented is?"

"But ..."

Chester in the car leaned over and turned up the car radio. "Wait a minute. This is one of my favorites." He started singing, "Generals gathered in their masses, just like witches at black masses .."

Chester in the tollbooth interrupted him. "I'm very confused."

Chester in the car stopped singing and looked up. "About why this is one of my favorite songs?"

"Among other things."

Chester just shook his head. He looked up and down the one-lane highway to see if another car was coming. Part of him wished one would. Chester talking to Chester made Chester in the tollbooth feel weird. He fidgeted on the stool and waited to see if the other Chester would ask him anything. He waited until he couldn't wait any longer.

"I have to ask," Chester in the tollbooth said to Chester in the car. "What in the world are you doing here?"

"I'm on an adventure."

"Excuse me?"

"I'm on an adventure. You know a journey with lots of ups and downs, lots of interesting surprises, some scary parts, some thrilling parts."

Chester felt like he was in a competition with Chester in the car. He felt like Chester in the car was trying to show him up.

Chester in the tollbooth puffed out his chest. "Well, you might want to know that I'm on an adventure as well."

"Doesn't look like it to me."

"What do you mean?"

"You're all alone in a tollbooth in the middle of nowhere."

"That's part of my adventure."

"I hope the other parts are a little more adventurous."

Chester's shoulders sagged.

Chester in the car pulled a pack of Marlboros from his shirt pocket and lit one of the cigarettes, blowing the smoke out of the side of his mouth.

"Okay, that's just too much."

"What's too much?"

"You're smoking a cigarette!"

"Settle down. What's the problem?"

"I don't smoke."

"Never?"

"No, never."

Chester in the car looked at Chester in the tollbooth and, with a sly wink, asked, "Not even an occasional cigar?"

"How do you know about that?"

Chester in the car raised his eyebrows.

"Oh, right. But that was a special occasion. I don't smoke cigarettes."

"And how was dear old Dad?"

"The same."

"Doesn't surprise me. Did you see mother?"

"No."

"Lucky you."

"I know," said Chester in the tollbooth. He smiled. And Chester in the car smiled back. They enjoyed the common ground, a pleasant momentary truce. Chester in the tollbooth savored the moment, and then said, "Still, smoking cigarettes? I would never do that."

"Good for you. I would. At least while I am on this adventure. In fact, I'm doing a whole bunch of things I've never done before."

"Like what?" said Chester, suddenly alarmed.

"Better you don't know."

"That frightens me."

"Again, not my problem."

Chester in the car took another drag of his cigarette then expertly flicked the butt out the window. He put both hands on the wheel, looked over and said, "Gotta jet. My adventure must continue. Raise the rest of that broken bar and I'm off."

Chester in the tollbooth reached for the big yellow button, then stopped.

"I should charge you the toll."

"You mean, charge you, don't you?"

"No, you."

"Why are you so hard on yourself? You've been like that your whole life. Give yourself a break."

"Don't you mean, give you a break, so you don't have to pay?"

"Six of one, half dozen of another."

Chester let that last statement sink in. And he realized Chester in the car was right. He was always too hard on himself. It wouldn't hurt to treat himself better.

"Okay, no charge for you."

"Thank you, squire," said Chester in the car.

He started to drive away, sticking his hand out the car window to get a high five from Chester in the tollbooth. Chester in the tollbooth hesitated, then leaned out and put his hand out to slap palms. But Chester in the car didn't slap his hand. Instead, he placed the palm of his hand flat against the palm of Chester's hand and as the car rolled forward the movement pulled his palm slowly across Chester's palm until only their fingertips were touching. And as Chester in the car's fingertips left Chester in the tollbooth's fingertips, there was the very briefest of moments when their fingertips were one billionth of an inch apart. And during that very briefest of moments, during that physical release between their hands, something intense happened.

Something so intense that no one could describe it or understand it.

No one except for Chester in the car.

And Chester in the tollbooth.

The next vehicle only had one headlight so Chester assumed it was a motorcycle. But he didn't hear an engine. And the light was very small. He heard a bell, like one of those bicycle bells where you move the lever back and forth and it makes a ringing sound. It sounded like a bicycle bell because it was a bicycle that rolled to a stop at the tollbooth. The only thing older than the bicycle, which looked like it was a prop from an old black and white silent movie, was the man riding the bicycle.

"Uncle Frank, why are you riding a bicycle?"

"Cause it's easier than walking, shitbird."

"I thought you weren't going to call me that anymore."

"My bad."

Uncle Frank was balanced perfectly upright on the bicycle. His feet were on the pedals, not on the ground.

"How do you do that?"

"You just push this little lever back and forth," said Uncle Frank, ringing the bicycle bell.

"No. I mean balance like that. Your feet aren't on the ground."

"You won't get very far on a bicycle if your feet are on the ground and not on the pedals, Chester. And notice I ended that sentence with your given name and not the other name I prefer."

"I appreciate that. Must have taken a lot of effort."

"Not really."

Uncle Frank was smoking a big fat cigar. Chester sniffed the air, smelling the cigar smoke. It smelled good.

"You are my first bicycle. I've had six cars, one shuttle van, one pickup truck and one golf cart come through here tonight."

"That's fascinating."

Chester didn't think it was fascinating at all to Uncle Frank. He decided to raise the stakes.

"In those nine vehicles that came through here, there were about twenty people," said Chester, pausing before adding, "and half of them were dead."

Uncle Frank cocked his head. "Now, that is interesting."

"Not fascinating?"

"No, sorry."

Chester shrugged. He had tried.

"Uncle Frank, am I dead?"

"I don't know, maybe. Let me see your hand."

Chester stuck his hand out the tollbooth window. Uncle Frank held Chester's hand, turning it over a few times and stopping when it was palm up.

"Wiggle your fingers."

Chester wiggled his fingers.

"Chester, did you just drop something?"

Chester looked down at his feet. When he did, Uncle Frank took the cigar out of his mouth and pushed the hot coal at the end of the cigar into Chester's palm."

"Holy cow," yelled Chester, snatching his hand back.

"Did that hurt?"

"Heck yes, it hurt."

"Good news then. You're still alive."

"Why did you do that?

"You asked a question. I investigated the situation. I came to a conclusion."

Chester put his palm up to his mouth and licked the burn spot.

"Why are you doing that?"

"You burned me!"

"I did? Where?"

Chester held his hand out, palm up. There was no burn spot. And his palm no longer hurt. Chester put his hands in his pants pockets. Better safe than sorry, he thought.

"I spoke to my father tonight."

"Oh yeah? How's he doing?"

"How's he doing? He's dead."

"I know, but besides that."

"I guess he's okay. We had a long talk."

"Did he mention me?"

"Once."

"What'd he say?"

"Called you a son of a bitch."

"That sounds like him."

"In fact, two people called you a son of a bitch. Father and Ed Pringle."

"Well, at least they're talking about me."

"He wasn't happy that you told me I was adopted."

"Ah, screw him. What can he do about it now? Did he fess up?"

"Kind of."

"Kind of? Either he admitted you were adopted or he didn't."

"I don't want to talk about it."

"Now you sound like him."

Chester took his hands out of his pockets and put them on his hips. He rocked back and forth on his heels. Being around Uncle Frank always made him nervous and on edge.

"Uncle Frank, if I'm not dead, does that mean I'm dreaming?"

Uncle Frank took two hard puffs of his cigar and the coal at the end glowed bright red. Chester took a cautious step back.

Uncle Frank didn't notice. "Have you ever worked at a tollbooth?"

"No."

"Have you recently applied for a tollbooth position?"

"No."

"Then my guess is you're dreaming."

"Uncle Frank, you make that assertion based on the fact that I have never worked at a tollbooth or applied for a tollbooth position and not on the fact that almost a dozen dead people have come through here in the past few hours?"

"Seems like a reasonable deduction to me."

Uncle Frank, still puffing away on his cigar, used his feet to spin the bicycle pedals backwards so the bike chain made a whirring sound. He did the cigar puffing and pedal spinning all while the bike remained stationary, perfectly upright. He held his arms out wide like he was balancing on the bike.

"Aren't you going to ask me how I can do this?" said Uncle Frank.

"No," said Chester.

Uncle Frank just shrugged. "I'll tell you what's funny. The guy who has lived his whole life in a box, doing everything society expects of him, the guy who never breaks the rules, is now the guy breaking the biggest rule of them all."

"Who is that?"

"You, Chester."

Chester felt tired all of a sudden. So many different people. So many different vehicles. So many different questions and observations and surprises. He wondered if this was what it was like for real tollbooth operators. The ones who weren't dead or dreaming.

"Uncle Frank, I'm getting tired. I'm ready to wrap this dream up. Do you have the toll?"

"Excuse me?"

"It's fifty cents to get through."

"You're going to charge me? After all I've done for you. You gotta be kidding."

"It's my dream" said Chester, "and I take my job very seriously."

"Well then, you're going to have to catch me," said Uncle Frank, tossing the cigar over his shoulder and shooting forward past the broken tollbooth pole.

Chester might have caught him, that's if he had even wanted to, but because Uncle Frank's feet were already on the pedals he was out of the tollbooth like a marathon sprinter. Chester knew Uncle Frank had planned his speedy getaway from the start.

"Son of a bitch," Chester said, under his breath.

But he laughed when he said it.

Chester watched the one-lane highway for another half hour but no more headlights appeared. He had finished off the coffee. He had spun around on the stool as much as he cared to. There was nothing else to do. He was bored. And sleepy. He leaned his head against the side of the toll booth and closed his eyes.

Chapter Twenty-Four

Chester awoke leaning against the front passenger seat door and window of the Avis rental car. He looked outside and saw it was sunny and that he was parked at a rest stop. His mouth was dry and what little saliva was in it tasted horrible. His head throbbed.

The driver's seat was empty. The car keys were in the middle of the seat on top of a folded piece of yellow-lined paper. Chester picked up the paper, unfolded it and read a handwritten note from his father:

You were starting to get drowsy, so I drove.

You needed the sleep.

It was good catching up.

We should do this again sometime.

—Your father

p.s. Sorry about the burn. I'm sure you paid extra for the insurance, though.

Chester looked on the driver's seat where the piece of paper had been and saw a burn in the middle of the seat the size of a nickel. It was a perfectly round hole in the imitation leather seat. He could see the seat stuffing through the hole. Oh no, thought Chester to himself. He could picture the smirking face of Darren Tucker. He thought oh no, and he pictured Darren Tucker's face, and then he forgot about the hole in the seat. That quick. Saw the hole, thought about the hole, forgot about the hole. The new Chester didn't have time to worry about errant cigar burns.

He got out of the car and stretched. Harriette told him that watching him stretch was like watching Elaine dance on that Seinfeld TV show. Because when Chester stretched, he threw his arms and legs out one limb at a time in rapid, jerky, almost spastic, movements like a windmill gone crazy. When he did it in public Harriette would hide her face and tell Chester that people watching him must surely think he was having a seizure.

Chester finished stretching and looked around. The rest stop parking lot was empty except for his rental car and an eighteen-wheeler semi-trailer truck. A young man with long stringy hair sat on a bench a short distance away. Chester nodded at the man. The man did not nod back. Chester saw the men's restroom, thought for a minute to see if he had that tingling feeling, realized he still didn't have to go. Which continued to be one of the strangest aspects of his journey. He stretched a few more times and then walked around the car to the driver's door. He opened the door and was about to slide in when he felt a hand grab his left shoulder in a vice-like grip and a sharp object poke into his lower back.

"Give me the keys."

Chester didn't know who was behind him squeezing his shoulder in a vice-like grip and he didn't know what the sharp object poking into his back was. But he wanted the person to stop squeezing and he wanted the sharp object to stop poking, so he put his right hand behind his back with the car keys in his open palm. As he felt the keys being taken from his hand, he heard a soft voice, a voice that sounded familiar.

"Let him go."

Chester looked back over his shoulder and the first thing he saw was the unfriendly man with the stringy hair who had been sitting on the bench and the second thing he saw was a tiny woman with jet black hair streaked with strands of snow white hair.

"Storm," said Chester, surprised.

Storm didn't acknowledge Chester. She looked at the man with the poking object.

"I said, 'Let him go. Now.'"

The man started to say something, but before the first word was out of his mouth Storm lunged forward and grabbed a fist full of the man's stringy hair in each of her hands, those small hands with the crisscross of tiny white scars and the crooked pinkie finger. She jumped into the hair and, as she came down, she jerked her two hands down hard and fast so that she landed on her knees and the man went face first into the asphalt of the parking lot with a sickening crunch. The man didn't move. Chester could only see the back of his head, now slowly being framed in a halo of crimson blood. He looked closer at the growing pool of blood.

"Is that a tooth?" asked Chester.

"Teeth," said Storm, grabbing an open folding knife on the ground next to the stringy-haired man before standing up.

Chester counted. "I see three teeth."

"So do I," said Storm, breathing heavily.

"Are you okay," asked Chester.

"I'm fine, Chester. How are you?" said Storm with a big smile. She looked at the knife admiringly for a moment, then folded it shut and put it into her back pocket.

"A friend of yours?" asked Storm.

"Uh, no. I think he was trying to carjack me."

"That he was. Another of your dark men perhaps?"

"No. I think I was just in the wrong place at the wrong time."

"I think you were in the right place at the right time," said Storm, laughing. She held up her arms, her hands balled into fists like a prize fighter, and flexed her biceps.

"Yes, but, but, but ... what are you doing here? Where did you come from? Where have you been? Do you need a ride?"

"Slow down, Chester. Take a breath. Thank you, but I have a ride," said Storm, pointing at a huge man walking out of the men's restroom. The man was gigantic, over six and a half feet tall and easily over three hundred pounds. And as black as midnight. He wore snakeskin cowboy boots, perfectly creased blue jeans, a western shirt with lots of snaps, a leather belt with a silver buckle the size of a cantaloupe, and a tall black cowboy hat with a white and black checkered head band. He ambled toward them, spitting out a long stream of brown chewing tobacco as he walked.

"What's the ruckus?" he asked in a thick Southern drawl.

"Chester this is Black Billy. Black Billy this is Chester, a friend of mine," said Storm.

"Howdy podner," said Black Billy, wiping his massive hand on the front of his jeans before offering it to Chester. "And who's the fella on the ground?"

"He just tried to rob Chester," said Storm.

"That didn't work out too well for him."

"No," said Storm. "His face has become intimately acquainted with the parking lot pavement."

Black Billy looked at Storm and said, "Honey, you sure got a funny way of saying things." He looked at the stringy-haired man on the ground and then at Chester and said, "Son, there's more to you than meets the eye."

Chester started to speak but Storm cut him off. "Don't let his size fool you. Chester can more than take care of himself."

Black Billy nodded his head approvingly. "It sure looks that way." Chester noticed when Black Billy said *sure* it sounded like he was saying *shore*.

The shock of almost being carjacked and the shock of seeing Storm again wasn't enough to quell Chester's curiosity.

"Are you a cowboy?" asked Chester.

"Not really."

"You sure look like one and you sure talk like once except that ..."

"Except what?" said Black Billy, narrowing his eyes a tinch.

"... you don't have a horse."

Black Billy grinned. "I got me a horse. A big one. Right over there." He pointed at the eighteen-wheeler.

"That sure is an impressive truck. I've always wanted to ride in one of those." And then, without missing a beat, Chester said, "So why is your name Black Billy?"

"Is he always this forward?" Black Billy asked Storm.

Storm just smiled.

Black Billy spit a stream of tobacco juice onto the back of the stringy-haired man's head. "Well, my best friend growing up was named Billy. And he was white."

"So he was White Billy and you were Black Billy?" asked Chester.

"Son, I grew up in South Texas. Billy was just Billy, and I was Black Billy."

"Well, that doesn't sound fair."

Black Billy laughed a big hearty laugh. It sounded like a clap of thunder. "Chester, you are a hoot."

Chester did not know what a hoot was, but since a big laugh accompanied his being called a hoot, he was confident being a hoot was a good thing.

Chester looked at Storm. "So what happened to you? You disappeared at breakfast."

"I didn't disappear. I just had somewhere else I needed to be. But don't worry. I'm never far away."

The three of them stood quietly for a few moments. Black Billy jerked his thumb over his shoulder at his truck. "Well, little lady are you still riding with me, or you going with the Karate Kid here?"

"I always dance with the cowboy who brought me," said Storm. "Besides I know exactly where you're headed. Chester, on the other hand, is a little unsure of what direction he is going."

Black Billy put his hand on Chester's shoulder. It felt like someone had placed a bag of cement on his shoulder. "I know these roads like the back of my hand. You need directions to anywhere in particular?"

"Well, I'm not really sure where I'm going."

"In general, or in life."

"Both."

"Can't help you with that. My advice is to just get behind the wheel and drive."

As they spoke, the man on the ground stirred. He put his hands out and started to push himself up from the asphalt. Black Billy, still looking at Chester as they talked, raised his right foot and booted the man in the back of the head with a swift kick of his heel. The man collapsed face first onto the asphalt again.

"I don't like road bandits," said Black Billy. He nudged the man with the toe of his boot. "Shit for brains is out like a light. I guess it's time we mosey on."

Black Billy reached out and shook Chester's hand again. "Good to meet you, little buddy."

Then he turned to Storm. "Well, little lady, if you're going with me, let's giddyup."

"Did you really just say giddyup?" asked Storm.

"Yeah, why?"

"And you think I talk funny."

Black Billy smiled and shrugged, started walking to his truck. Storm stepped up to Chester and gave him a hug.

"See you later, Mad Cow," said Storm.

"Not if I see you first, Helicopter," said Chester.

Chester watched Storm walk away. She looked so tiny compared to the hulking truck driver walking in front of her.

"Storm, be careful out there," Chester called after her.

Still walking, Storm looked back at him and winked. And, knowing he could see, she patted the knife in her back pocket.

▼

Chester drove for an hour until he saw the bright lights of downtown Albuquerque in the distance. He took the exit to the Albuquerque airport and looked for the car rental return signs. He pulled into the Avis lot and steered the car toward the attendant, a young man with a bald head and a tattoo of a leprechaun on his neck. The young man guided Chester into a parking slot with both hands up in the air, motioning him forward like the ground crew for an airplane approaching the jetway ramp.

"Keys, please," said the attendant. He walked around the car looking for damage, then opened the driver's side door to check the mileage. Chester had placed the seat belt buckle over the hole in the driver's seat. He chewed his lip nervously as the young man checked the interior of the car, then closed the car door.

"No damage, right?" said Chester hopefully.

"No, sir."

"Good thing I didn't pay all that money for extra insurance."

The attendant looked at Chester, then looked to the left and to the right to make sure no one else was around and said, "It's foolish to buy all that extra insurance."

"That's what I told Darren Tucker."

"Who?"

"Darren Tucker. You probably don't know him."

"Can't say that I do."

The attendant printed out the rental receipt from the credit card machine on his belt and handed it to Chester. Then he looked at Chester and said, "By the way ..." That's all he said before stopping. Chester knew no one ever said "By the way ..." and immediately finished the sentence. They always waited for the other person to say "Yes?" with a question mark.

So, naturally, Chester said, "Yes?"

"... I know about your secret."

Chester's eyes opened wide. How could the young man with the bald head and the leprechaun tattoo know about his revelation?

"How do you know about that? Chester stammered.

"No worries, my man. I got your back."

"Excuse me?"

"The burn in the front seat."

"Oh, that."

"Don't worry about it. I'll just say it was there when you rented the car. My good deed for the day. Plus, you seem like a nice guy."

"Thank you so much," said Chester. "Can I ask you one more question?"

"Shoot."

"What's the airport hotel here?"

"The Radisson. A shuttle comes by here every twenty minutes."

"Thank you, kind sir," said Chester.

A half hour later Chester was laying on his back on his hotel room bed staring at the ceiling. It reminded him of the first time he had laid on his back and looked up at Theodore's basement ceiling which, right now, seemed like such a long time ago.

Chester thought again about what he should do next. There were no more letters and no more clues and no more outside instigators, so it seemed like he had no other option but to return home. While the thought of going back to the comfort and familiarity of his own home after all he had been through should have made him feel good, it didn't. It felt more like he was ending a journey before the journey was over. As he thought those thoughts, he felt a rumble in his belly. Not an I'm-hungry rumble, but instead a find-a-bathroom-quick rumble. Chester thought it might be a false alarm so he waited. And the rumble came again, stronger this time.

"Finally!" Chester said, almost in a shout.

He swung his feet off the bed, jumped up and started for the bathroom, then stopped and went back and opened the side pocket of his suitcase and took out the *Flowers for Algernon* book. He went into the bathroom, sat on the toilet seat and started reading, waiting for the next big rumble.

And, of course, that's when his cell phone rang.

By the time Chester set the book down, after first folding over the top corner of the page he was reading, and rummaged through the pockets of the pants crumpled around his ankles, the cell phone was in the middle of its third ring. So Chester was frantic, but despite those obstacles he was still able to answer the call just as the third ring ended.

"Hello, this is Chester."

"It's Uncle Frank."

"Oh, hi Uncle Frank."

"Where are you? I hear an echo."

"I'm sitting on the toilet."

"That's wonderful.

"You don't know how wonderful, Uncle Frank. I haven't had a bowel movement in over a week."

"That's more information than I need to know. That said, are you finished or just starting?"

"Just starting."

"Okay, well I won't keep you. I just wanted to update you, buddy-boy. Catalina and Cujo just got back from Salt Lake City. Catalina said she had a wonderful visit with your friend."

"Uncle Frank, I don't want to know any more about that."

"That's fair. I'll spare you the details. What are you planning to do next?"

"I'm not sure what to do now. What do you think I should do?"

Uncle Frank didn't answer. Chester waited.

"Hello?"

"I'm thinking. Give me a second. All of this is above my pay grade."

Chester waited. He was confident Uncle Frank would have an answer. He would find that unshelled peanut.

"Okay, I got it," said Uncle Frank.

"What?"

"It's time you go to Bora Bora. I think you'll find what you're looking for there."

"But I don't have a plane ticket."

"Chester, don't you get it? You don't need a plane."

Chapter Twenty-Five

Chester's eyes were closed, but he was awake, so even with his eyes closed, he knew several things.

He knew it was daytime because he could feel the heat of the sun's rays on his cheeks and his eyelids.

He knew he was at a beach because he could smell the ocean and taste the salt on his lips and feel the surf crashing near him and hear the squawks of seagulls.

He knew he was laying on his back on top of sand because he could feel the itchy granules on the back of his neck and his arms and hands.

He knew he was not alone because he could hear the soft breathing of another person to his left and the heavy panting of some type of beast to his right.

Having no idea where he was and being nervous about the heavy beast panting, Chester, as he did the night in the guest cottage at Uncle Frank's when the two dark men came in, kept his eyes closed and hoped that everything around him that he could feel, smell, taste, and hear would just go away. He tried that for a few minutes but nothing changed, nothing went away.

"Chester?" said a voice to his left, a child's voice.

Chester opened one eye and then the other. He looked to his left and saw a young boy laying on his back on the sand next to him. The boy, shirtless and shoeless, wearing a cut-off pair of shorts, was looking up at the sky, his right hand over his eyes, a visor against the sun.

"Welcome," said the young boy.

"Where am I?" asked Chester.

"You know," said the young boy.

"I do?"

"Yes, you do."

Chester didn't think he knew at all, but he thought for a moment anyway, and said, "Bora Bora?"

"It could be."

"Could be?"

"Does it matter what beach you are on right now?"

"I guess not."

Chester looked at the young boy, studying his face.

"And who are you?" asked Chester.

"You know."

"I do?"

"Yes, you do."

Again Chester didn't think he knew at all, but for the second time he thought for a moment anyway, and said, "Tonorau?"

"Yes.

"How do I know that?"

Tonorau stopped looking at the sky and turned his face toward Chester and smiled.

"It doesn't matter, right?" said Chester, answering his own question.

"Right," said Tonorau.

Chester looked back up at the sky and then slowly turned his head to the right.

"Is that a wolf?"

"No, that's Crow."

"Excuse me, but that is not a crow."

"No, his name is Crow."

"You named a wolf, Crow?"

"He's not a wolf. He's a dog."

"He certainly looks like a wolf."

Tonorau didn't say anything.

"Does he bite?" asked Chester.

"Sometimes."

"Like when?"

"When he needs to."

"Will he bite me?"

"I don't think so. Pet his head."

"Are you crazy?"

"Trust me," said Tonorau. "Just reach out and pet his head."

Chester had no intention of trying to pet the head of something that was not a wolf but looked like a wolf, something that was incredibly large and unquestionably more aggressive than Chester. But the young boy, Tonorau, had been right twice already when he told Chester he knew things that he thought he didn't know, so Chester decided to trust him.

He slowly raised his right hand, the sun glistening on the tiny specks of sand that fell from his open palm as he reached toward Crow. Chester watched in slow motion as his arm straightened out and his hand got closer and closer to the dog's massive black head. Crow stared straight ahead at the ocean, his long pink tongue lolling from the side of his mouth, draped over a row of astonishingly large, bright white canine teeth. He seemed oblivious to the approaching hand, but when the longest finger on Chester's hand, the middle finger, was a fraction of an inch from Crow's head, the dog whipped his head to the left and clamped his jaws onto Chester's hand. The dog's mouth was so big that it engulfed Chester's entire hand. All Chester could see was his wrist disappearing into the side of Crow's mouth, like a white straw poked through a black sponge. It happened so quickly Chester did not have time to scream or faint.

"Don't move," said Tonorau in a soft voice.

Chester did not move.

"What do you feel?" asked Tonorau.

Chester thought speaking would go against the don't-move order, so he didn't say anything.

"What do you feel?" asked Tonorau again. "Go ahead. You can speak."

"I feel teeth on the bottom of my hand and teeth on the top of my hand. And it's hot in there and wet."

"Is he biting you?"

"No. He's kind of holding me."

"Are you scared?"

Chester started to say yes, but then he thought for a moment and realized he was not scared at all.

"No."

"You know, Crow could easily bite your hand off. It would be like snapping a tiny twig."

"Yes, I know that."

"And you're still not scared?"

"No, should I be?"

"No. Do you know why?"

"Not really."

"That power you feel from Crow. That power is you."

"I don't understand."

"Yes you do."

"What now?" asked Chester, since his hand was still in Crow's mouth.

"Crow," said Tonorau, again in the same soft voice.

Crow opened his jaws wide and Chester slowly pulled his hand back. It glistened with saliva. He wiped his hand on his pants leg and then held it up to his face and looked at it, both the front and the back. There were two perfect lines of pink dots on each side of his hand where Crow's teeth had lightly clamped his hand. Chester showed his hand, both the front and the back, to Tonorau.

Tonorau nodded. "How has your journey been, Chester?"

Chester started to answer, but then something dawned on him. He realized that while he thought he and Tonorau had been talking to each other, actually neither of them had spoken a single word. They were communicating quite well, but neither of them were moving their lips. Normally Chester would have been alarmed by such a realization and thrown into such a state that he could think of nothing else. But the way the past week had gone, the crazy experiences he had had that week, well, talking with someone when neither you or the other person actually talked just seemed natural.

"How do you know about my journey?"

"We've been with you every step of the way."

"We?"

"Crow and I."

"I don't remember seeing you."

"We were there."

"Okay, if you say so."

"But we're glad you're here now."

"I'm glad I'm here now, too. I think."

Chester paused, then said, "Why are you glad I'm here?"

"Because we're ready to go home."

"You and Crow?"

"Yes."

"This isn't your home?"

"No."

"Where is your home?"

"With you."

"I don't understand."

"Yes you do."

Chester, a bit confused, said, "But I don't think I've finished my journey yet."

"Are you sure?"

"Well, I haven't figured out yet if my revelation is true or not. That's what my journey is about."

"Your revelation?"

"Yes. Do you want to know what my revelation is?"

"I already know."

"Are you sure?"

"You exist. We don't."

"Well, that's a bit simplistic. But you pretty much nailed it."

Tonorau sat up and brushed the sand off his slender shoulders.

"Chester, do you think it is easier for you to believe only you exist than it is to wonder where everything came from, why everything is here, and what happens to everything when the end comes? Is it possible you have chosen the easy way out by coming up with an answer to what is not even the real question?"

"What do you mean?" asked Chester.

"To solve a riddle you must know what the riddle is. You have to clear away the clutter and determine what the real question is. Until you do that, you will never be able to come up with the true answer. I think your revelation is just a smokescreen. A very clever and intriguing smokescreen, but a smokescreen nonetheless."

"So I'm not the only one on the planet?"

"No."

"Are you sure?"

"I'm sure."

"But my revelation ..."

"Does not address the real question."

"So, I lied to myself?"

"No, it's more like you kidded yourself."

"That's possible, but ..." said Chester pausing, searching for the right words. "But my revelation was so ..."

"So what?"

"So special and unique."

"To who?"

"To me."

"So it made you feel special and unique?"

"Very much so."

"Don't you think everyone wants to feel special and unique?"

"I guess."

"Chester, you've never felt special or unique. What better way to finally feel special and unique than by convincing yourself that the only person in the world who can ever feel that way is you? If no one else except you exists, then you can be anything you want. You can be the king of special and unique."

Chester was quiet. He lifted up a handful of sand and watched the granules slip through his fingers. He could feel some of the fight going out of his argument, but he wasn't ready to give up on the revelation. He had been through too much to just fold his hand.

"But my revelation had to be about more than just making me feel special and unique. It struck a nerve somewhere. I was kidnapped for goodness sake. They were trying to stop me."

"Maybe it was you trying to stop you," said Tonorau.

"Why would I do that?"

"You were scared."

"Of what?"

"The revelation. What it really meant."

"I kidnapped myself?" asked Chester.

"I didn't say that."

Chester sat up. Tonorau reached over and brushed the sand from his back.

A giant crab came out of the surf and headed toward them. Crow started to raise up, his head pointed at the crab.

"Leave him alone, Crow. He's not bothering anybody," said Tonorau quietly.

Crow laid back down, looked over at Tonorau, then put his head on his paws and closed his eyes. The crab made a sharp left turn and zigzagged down the beach.

Chester was not convinced that his revelation was incorrect.

"If I die, my world dies with me, right?" said Chester.

"That part is true," said Tonorau.

"And if I die, then you and Harriette and Uncle Frank and everyone else no longer exists."

"That part is not true."

"Why not?"

"Because your world dies, not ours."

"But there's only one world, mine."

"Because you are so special and unique, right?"

"Well, yes, I guess."

"Chester, your world is yours and yours alone. And when it goes, it goes. But our worlds, which are also ours and ours alone, will still exist."

Chester mulled over Tonorau's words. "If you are right, then not only was my revelation wrong but it was also incredibly selfish."

Tonorau didn't respond.

"I said I was being selfish," said Chester.

"I heard you."

"But you didn't say anything."

"Everybody is selfish."

"Not everybody."

"Yes, everybody. They have to be," said Tonorau.

"Why?"

"Self preservation."

"I don't understand."

"Everybody wants to live, to survive. Every person, every plant, every tadpole, every moonbeam, every cell. Self preservation is selfishness. Don't feel bad about being selfish. That's like saying you feel bad about breathing."

Chester looked to his right at Crow. He had the urge to reach out and have the dog clamp down again on his hand. He wanted to see the whole process happen again. He wanted something he could see and understand and not have to question.

"Don't press your luck," said Tonorau.

Chester clasped his hands in his lap.

"Chester, what have you really been trying to figure out?"

"Am I real and is everybody else not real? At least that's what I thought the question was. Ever since that Monday morning. But now, after talking to you, I'm not so sure."

"Think about it. Isn't there a different question you have been trying to answer?"

Tonorau, who seemed to be right about everything, said to think about it, so Chester, in his analytical way, thought about it.

He laid on his back for a long time and thought about it.

Tonorau waited, not saying a word.

Chester took all his thoughts, the important ones, the ones that pertained to his present situation, and he juggled and organized and categorized and polished them, because he was very good at doing those four things, and he realized it made sense that a person who always felt alone would think no one else really existed except for himself. A person alone plus a person alone always equals a person alone. That was the easy answer, the obvious answer. But, and this is where Chester's ability to analyze things truly kicked in, it was an answer that did not address what Chester now realized was possibly the real question. An underlying question that had been there all along, hidden under Chester's misguided attempt to define everything from the perspective of aloneness. So Chester, after considerable thinking, per Tonorau's suggestion, and after doing those four things he was so good at, realized his revelation just might be a symptom, and not the cause.

"Ask me again," said Chester.

"Okay," said Tonorau. "What is the real question you have been trying to figure out?

"Why am I here?"

"I?"

"Okay, why are we here?"

"That's better," said Tonorau.

Chester looked over and saw Tonorau staring at him. He was smiling and he had a look in his eye, a look that was half wonder and half mischief.

"Chester, have you been trying to figure out the meaning of life?"

"Well, I prefer to call it the theory of everything," said Chester sheepishly.

"So you want to explain it all, put it into words?"

"If I can."

"Chester, trying to put that into words is like trying to take a picture of a whisper."

▼

Chester shrugged. When someone said in a conversation the words "is like" to make a point, they always used a comparison that overstated the issue. No, you couldn't take a picture of a whisper, but you could prove a theory. Chester thought it was the child in Tonorau showing his naivette.

"I am not naive," said Tonorau. "And I'm not a child. But that's neither here nor there. Tell me. What is this theory supposed to do?"

"Explain everything in one short answer."

"Preferably a single sentence. Or less. You know, like Einstein's E=mc2."

"A single sentence? That's a rather short answer for a big theory."

"I agree," said Chester. "It would take Harriette ten minutes to explain her corned beef and cabbage recipe to someone. If she can't explain how to cook a meal in a single sentence, how is anyone supposed to explain the theory of everything in a single sentence?"

"Or less."

"Right."

"Isn't the theory all about gravity?"

"Yes and no. The theories are all over the board. Some people look outward to galaxies and black holes and some people look inward to atoms and quarks."

"Nobody looks right here?" said Tonorau, patting the sand.

"That vantage point does not seem to be popular."

"But that's where we are. We're not out there and we're not in there. We're here."

Tonorau leaned over and lightly tapped the side of Chester's head with his index finger when he said that last sentence. "Yep," he said, lightly tapping Chester's head a second time. "Right there. It has to be there, because the quest to find the theory only exists in the human mind. It doesn't exist in elephants or petunias or french fries. Without the human mind, the question just never arises. If there is an answer, wouldn't it be found in the place where the question itself exists?"

"That sounds very logical. And I can relate to logical," said Chester. He tried to concentrate more on Tonorau's logic, but his stomach began to growl. He rubbed his belly and gave Tonorau a half-hearted smile.

"Don't worry. We'll eat soon. I told my mother you were coming. She makes a seafood chowder that is the envy of all the women in our village."

"Really. What does she put in it?"

"Everything."

"Everything? What is her theory on that?" Chester laughed.

▼

"Yesterday, today or tomorrow?" asked Tonorau.

"Is that a statement, or a question?"

"A question. Which of the three intrigues you the most?"

Now that, thought Chester to himself, is one of the most interesting questions he had heard since he started his journey.

"Give me a minute." Chester thought about the pluses and minuses of yesterday, today and tomorrow. Then he thought about which of the three made him the most excited.

"Tomorrow," said Chester.

"Why?"

"I know you think I am going to say because it is the unknown. Because I know what happened yesterday and I know what is happening today, and I have no idea what tomorrow will bring."

"Is that your reason?"

"No, that's not the main reason. It's part of the reason, but not the main part of the reason."

"And the main part is what?"

"Tomorrow means there is more."

"As in, more to come?"

"Exactly. Every today has a tomorrow promised."

"Sometimes what happens tomorrow is not good."

"That's just it," said Chester, excited. "When tomorrow becomes today and on that today something not good is happening, well, there's always the next tomorrow. If there was no tomorrow, then you would be stuck in that today forever. You see, it's all about time. Time is at the center of everything. At least that's what I think."

"What about right now, today, for you?"

Chester closed his eyes and felt the warm sun on his eyelids. "Right now, today, I'm good."

"So if today went on forever and there was no tomorrow, would you be okay with that?"

"No. No way."

"But you said you were good. Right now. Today."

"I like having a tomorrow waiting at the end of every day."

"But that won't go on forever."

"Why not?"

"What about when you die? There won't be any more tomorrows."

Chester knew Tonorau was going to say that. He had been patiently waiting. "When I die, there will be one more tomorrow. And I will live in that tomorrow forever."

Chester waited for Tonorau to speak. But he didn't, and a full minute went by. Chester waited. He knew Tonorau would say something eventually. Another full minute went by, and at the end of that minute, Tonorau said, "Out of the mouths of babes."

And Chester knew exactly what he meant.

▼

Chester thought about Tonorau's mother's seafood chowder and wondered if it would be in a white milk broth or a red tomato sauce broth.

"It's a coconut milk broth," said Tonorau. "So, who came up with that name, the theory of everything?"

"I'm not sure. It's called a lot of things. The Final Theory, the Ultimate Theory, the Master Theory, God's Plan."

"God?"

"Can't rule him out."

"So Chester, what you are telling me is you are trying to figure out the how-why-where thing, right?"

"The how-why-where thing?"

"Yes, how did we get here, why are we here, and where are we going after this?"

"I like that. The how-why-where thing. That makes more sense than the theory of everything. More to the point. So, yes, that's what I guess has been at the root of my revelation. Finding the answer to that question."

"Why is it so important to you to find that answer?"

"Because I need to know."

"Because ... you ... need ... to ... know," said Tonorau slowly, spacing out the words. "Do you see that palm tree?"

Tonorau pointed down the beach to where a palm tree arched up from the soil, it's trunk curved into a half moon, it's top covered in wide, brilliantly green palm fronds and dotted with fat coconuts.

"Yes."

"Do you think that tree wonders what ten divided by two equals?"

"That's a silly question. Trees don't think."

"How do you know?"

"I just do."

"So, it also doesn't wonder how it got here, why it is here and where it will go after it dies?"

"Of course not."

"And not knowing the answer to those questions does not affect it's existence one single bit?"

"Again, of course not, because trees don't think."

"Trees must do something similar to thinking to live longer than all other things on this planet. That palm tree is healthy and vibrant and will live for more than a hundred years, longer than any human being. There are trees on this planet that are over four thousand years old. They were here long before Jesus Christ was born. Trees live and grow just like you and I. And they eventually die just like you and I. And they do that entire process without wondering about the whys and hows and wheres of their existence. Not knowing the answer to the question, much less knowing there even is a question, does not change the life of a palm tree or a giraffe or a moth one tiny bit. So why are you different?"

"I've always been different. We both know that."

"That's not a very good answer."

Chester frowned.

Tonorau pointed at the sun. "Chester, do you think the sun contemplates its existence?"

"No."

"Why not?"

"The sun doesn't contemplate at all."

"But we do, don't we? We are busy little bees, full of questions, not realizing our questions are merely our inability to not be able to accept the obvious."

"You're losing me."

"Chester, do you have any idea what conditions had to exist, had to be fine tuned, for us to be here on this planet?"

"Conditions?"

"Yes, billions of things had to align in just the right way at just the right time for us to exist. For you and I to be sitting on this beach. We are the result of a quantity of variables our minds can't even fathom. An extra atom here or there, a few degrees hotter or colder, and we would not exist. We marvel at the wonder of it only because we are here to wonder at the marvel of it."

"So, I did a good job?"

"Chester, you didn't make us. You didn't make everything. I thought we had that settled."

"But if I had ..."

"Then, yes, you would have done a good job."

"Thank you," said Chester.

"You're missing the point. The odds of winning the lottery are astronomical, but eventually someone picks the winning lottery ticket. There is always a winner. We accept that and don't question it. But when the same thing happens in the cosmic lottery, when everything is lined up perfectly and we win the big prize which is this planet and our lives, we can't accept it. We desperately want to know why and how it could happen. But someone was always going to eventually win that cosmic lottery. Why not us?"

"So, we're a fluke?" said Chester.

"Kind of. We are that one black rose in a field of red roses."

"An aberration?"

"Some would say that."

"Just a virus with shoes?"

"And some would say that too," said Tonorau.

"So, if we weren't here to be conscious of the universe, it wouldn't exist?" asked Chester.

"Basically."

"Kind of hard to prove one way or another, isn't it?"

Tonorau laughed. Then, in a quiet voice he asked, "Chester, are you afraid you don't matter right now, and that when you die everyone will forget about you and you will continue to not matter as everyone else's life goes on? Do you think that's why you had the revelation that only you are real? As a way to protect yourself?"

Chester thought about that, and as he did, Tonorau added, "But you do matter now, Chester. And you will matter long after you are gone. I know I can't convince you of that, but it's true."

Chester appreciated Tonorau's kind words, but he kept thinking about what Tonorau had said about him being afraid. It made sense, but the more he thought about it, the more he realized it was not why he had the revelation.

"No Tonorau, my revelation was not about me trying to make myself feel special and unique right now. It really is all about the how-why-where thing. Maybe it's because now that I'm fifty-two years old and now that I am closer to my death than to my birth, I just want and need to know what this has all been about."

"All?" said Tonorau.

"Life," said Chester.

"But it's still all about you, about your life, isn't it, Chester? It's about you finding an answer. You haven't said you want to find the answer so you can share it with the world. And there's nothing wrong with that. You came into this world alone and you will leave this world alone. Wanting to know why you were here at all is just natural. You've heard my thoughts on what the answer might be. What do you think the answer is?"

"You mean the theory of how-why-where?"

"Yes."

"I don't know."

"Are you sure."

"You sure do ask me whether I'm sure a lot," said Chester.

"Well then, what do other people think?"

"It's always something new. Every year someone comes up with a new theory and when they do, they all say the same thing about their theory."

"Which is?"

"This is it!"

"Maybe they're close."

"I don't understand."

"Are you sure?"

"You're doing it again," said Chester.

Chester and Tonorau both lay back on the warm sand. Crow's panting continued. Chester thought about how heavy the sun must be on such a large dog with thick fur.

"Crow's okay," said Tonorau. "He knows how to cool off."

As if he had heard, Crow stood up on all fours. A shower of sand fell from his thick coat. In three bounds he splashed into the ocean surf and disappeared. Chester watched, waiting for Crow to come back up. But he didn't.

"Where did he go?"

"He's exploring."

"Underwater?"

"Yes."

"I didn't know dogs could do that."

"Most dogs can't."

"What if he runs into a shark?"

"Bad for the shark."

Chester didn't doubt it. A few minutes later Crow came back, emerging from the ocean like a giant sea monster, his black hair matted and slick with water, his eyes dark coals. He shook himself vigorously, spraying Tonorau and Chester with cool water. It felt refreshing. Crow padded back and laid down on the right side of Chester, using his massive tongue to lick the salt water off his paws.

"Chester, give me your hand," said Tonorau.

"Not again," said Chester, exaggerated fear in his voice,

"Relax. Just give me your hand."

Chester stretched his arm out and held his hand, balled up in a fist, over Tonorau's chest.

"I have a present for you. Close your eyes and open your fingers."

Chester closed his eyes and opened his fingers. He felt something smooth and heavy drop into the palm of his hand. He pulled his arm back and tilted his hand up toward his face. Nestled in the creases of his palm was a shiny quarter. He held it closer and looked at the date. The date was 1966.

"Is this ...?"

"Yes."

"Oh my," said Chester. He rubbed the quarter between his thumb and index finger and smiled. As he rubbed the quarter, he stared up at the sky, moving his head slowly from left to right and then right to left.

"Chester?"

"Yes."

"Stop counting the seagulls."

"I'm not," lied Chester.

"Yes you are."

"You're right."

"How many are there?"

"Including the gray one?"

"There's a gray seagull?"

"Yes. The white ones won't let him get close."

"Why not?"

"I guess because he's different."

"Like you?"

Chester didn't answer. But he smiled. Then he said, "There are nine."

"Including the gray one?"

"Yes."

"Maybe the gray one isn't different."

"What do you mean?"

"Maybe he's special and unique."

Chester didn't answer. But he smiled again. Then he said, "I never thought of it like that."

Chester closed his eyes.

But he was still awake.

He laid there for a long time with his arms crossed over his chest, rubbing the shiny quarter between the thumb and forefinger of his right hand.

He laid there for what could have been minutes or hours or even days. He wasn't sure and it didn't really matter.

He laid there until he no longer felt the heat of the sun's rays on his cheeks and his eyelids.

He laid there until he could no longer taste the salt on his lips or smell the pungent aroma of the ocean or hear the surf crashing or the seagulls squawking.

He laid there until he could no longer feel the itchy granules of sand on the back of his neck and his arms.

He laid there until he could no longer hear the soft breathing of Tonorau to his left or the heavy panting of Crow to his right.

He laid there, very still and very calm, until he could see nothing and hear nothing and taste nothing and smell nothing and feel nothing.

And it was then, when all that was and all that is and all that will be was inside the cocoon that was Chester, did it finally come to him.

Three short words.

This just is.